THE
TWO LIVES
OF SARA

Center Point
Large Print

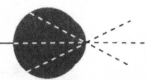

**This Large Print Book carries the
Seal of Approval of N.A.V.H.**

THE TWO LIVES OF SARA

CATHERINE ADEL WEST

CENTER POINT LARGE PRINT
THORNDIKE, MAINE

This Center Point Large Print edition
is published in the year 2022 by arrangement with
Harlequin Enterprises ULC.

The text of this Large Print edition is unabridged.
In other aspects, this book may vary
from the original edition.
Printed in the United States of America
on permanent paper sourced using
environmentally responsible foresting methods.
Set in 16-point Times New Roman type.

ISBN: 978-1-63808-508-9

The Library of Congress has cataloged this record
under Library of Congress Control Number: 2022942276

For Uncle Cookie and Uncle Rudy.
I couldn't have asked for more.

ONE

It's the heat you never get used to. The way it bullies you at night. I wait for the creak of the bedroom door, the dull thud of footsteps, the pulling back of covers and the heavy sink of his body next to mine on a mattress, but none of it comes. It'll never come again. A friend saw to that. And I got on a bus, and I came to Memphis. I birthed you.

Mama Sugar and I tell people your father died in a car accident. But that's not true is it, child? People tell me they're sorry for my loss, but I'm not sorry.

You squirm when you suckle. You can never be still. You're always hungry or crying or cooing or laughing. Never sleeping or giving me peace. And everyone says you're handsome. They talk about those pretty green eyes of yours. Everyone says you're a blessing, but they don't know, do they? I know. Everything. You still suckle and lightly pull on the meat of my nipple though I'm almost dry and have barely anything left to give, but you don't care.

Mama Sugar knocks on my door, like she does every morning before the sun is up, when little strips of gold lay themselves below the deep blue of night. "Look at 'em. Growing like a weed."

7

She scratches her left palm. Her green apron with yellow daisies is covered in patches of flour. "Bring Lebanon downstairs. He gone fall asleep in a little bit anyway. You need to get him on a steady schedule soon though. He's almost five months now."

"You know him better than I do."

"Naw Sara-girl, you his momma. You know him." She scratches her left palm again. "Damn. I must got some money comin' in." Mama Sugar and her superstitions. Her good fortune somehow lurking beneath her wrinkled skin.

I stare at your face. You stop suckling and smile, as big as Mama Sugar. And all I want, all I yearn to do, is disappear. Instead, I will take you downstairs with me into a kitchen even hotter than this small room with its bed and the dresser and the turquoise suitcase with a doll inside. I'll lose myself in flour and sugar and eggs and extracts of vanilla and lemon and almond. I'll try to find a piece of me still lush and thriving in smells from the stove baking biscuits Mama Sugar made or in the skillet frying bacon and eggs.

I'll try to forget though I have you to remind me. Little bastard.

"Be down in a few minutes," I say.

There's a crash from the hallway. "Dammit, Amos! Where's my grandbaby? You leave Will alone again? I told you don't come up in here drunk! Should be at home with yo son and leave that nonsense on out in them streets!" Mama Sugar slams my door. Voices, muffled and not so muffled, bicker then apologize. There is again stillness and suffocation. And your eyes, like his, flutter open and shut, fighting against rest, but finally you fall asleep. I tie a clean scarf, light pink, on my head. It will catch the sweat on my brow as I work in the kitchen. It won't catch tears though, but I lie and say they're sweat. I wrap you in a blue blanket and have the same thought I always do: How long would it take for you to die if I place a pillow over that nose like mine but those eyes like his?

I won't though. I'm not a monster and I have enough to answer for, my friends have enough to answer for on my behalf, and so I'll take you downstairs and let people fuss over you and treat you like a little king. I'll try to ignore you and this constant rolling in my stomach and dampness on my flesh I can never seem to keep cool and dry.

The hallway is dim. Amos' door is closed as he snores and sleeps off whatever mischief he discovered during the night.

"Sara! Sara-girl! Come on down here and go get me four green tomatoes from the garden!"

The stairs are steep and winding. There are seventeen of them, which I count in my head. I watch them and your face because any jostle will

9

wake you and I'll have to try and get you back to sleep. Please don't wake up. And you don't.

Maybe there is a God.

Mama Sugar's husband sits quietly, patiently at the table. "Hey little man!" Mr. Vanellys whispers as his tall, slender, dark frame lumbers up from the too-small chair at the kitchen table next to Mama Sugar. "Can I hold him for a little while, Sara? He seems to wake up when you put him in that crib."

"Sure. Thank you." Me not having you in my arms is fine. I can use them for better things like picking perfectly ripe green tomatoes from the garden.

"Stick to the vines nearest to the shed," Mama Sugar orders. "Those ready to be picked. The other ones gonna need another week. Probably more."

"Jesus, Lennie Mae! She smart. She know how you like things. You worse than a drill sergeant ever was. Let the poor girl be," Mr. Vanellys whispers, but his voice is still deep and commanding. He rocks you gently to and fro as he sits down again, the bottom of his pants briefly revealing a flash of steel covered by a black sock and a shoe beneath that on his right leg.

I turn away and go into the garden. It is quiet there. The air doesn't cling so much to me. My fingers squeeze the tomatoes, making sure they don't sink too far into the skin.

The alabaster three-story house with the bright red trim stands clustered together on Hubert Avenue with smaller houses on its right and left. A black hand-painted sign with THE SCARLET POPLAR lazily swings in a slight eastern breeze. Creaky wood stairs serenade my ears as I make my way back into the house.

Mama Sugar nods in approval when I bring back the four tomatoes. I take the biscuits from the oven. Soft thuds on the floor above knock some dust from the ceiling, but I've already covered the food and Mr. Vanellys is satisfied you're sleeping deeply enough to place you in the crib with the faded flowers and peeling paint, the one that held Mama Sugar's daughter before she died of pneumonia at four years old. Her name was Bonnie Lee.

"Well, Memphis ain't gone wait for me to get these cars back on the road, least my customers ain't," Mr. Vanellys declares.

"Least you could do is grab your son. Make sure he get an honest day's work. Amos like bein' with you and only he get those engines runnin' the way they need to be."

"Lennie Mae, he your son too and *that boy* ain't gone be no good at the shop in that shape. He can come by when he ready. I might have somethin' for him to do, keep him busy, out of trouble, least for a little bit."

"Mmm-hmm."

"Best get ready 'fore the rest of them boarders come down lookin' for some of your good cookin'."

"You tryin' to flatter me, Vanellys?"

"Nah, you been too smart for that since I married you."

Mr. Vanellys wraps his long arms around her ample waist and kisses Mama Sugar on the cheek.

"Sara-girl, now I'm leavin' you with the understanding—" Mr. Vanellys begins.

"—that my wife is a difficult woman to deal with but master of this humble domain. And I must do whatever I can to help her maintain order over her realm," I finish his sentence, the one he's repeatedly recited to me since I stepped through the doors of this place a year ago.

Mr. Vanellys laughs. "And I ain't gone trust no one else but you to do it."

He rests his hand on my shoulder. He knows for some reason affection, a hug or a kiss, no matter how innocent, wouldn't be welcomed, so he lightly pats my shoulder, a gesture kind and warm, but I still don't want him to touch me.

"Y'all have a good day." He turns back to Lennie Mae. "Send Amos over when he ready."

The door behind me squeaks closed, and Mama Sugar and I are alone again before the other boarders come down for breakfast and shovel food in their mouths without thought for the care it took to make it.

· · ·

"You comin' to church tonight? Supposed to have a travelin' minister all the way from Philadelphia."

I open the refrigerator, placing the unused eggs back on the second shelf. "No. I've said before church isn't . . . it isn't something I do. Not anymore."

"I know what you said. Don't mean I'ma stop askin'."

"We need more grits." The box in my hands is barely half full. "I'll grab some this afternoon."

"Oh! Make sure you get some more bacon and sausage. You know my brand. I want—"

"King Cotton. I know." I hate saying that name as it rolls from my lips. But that's the only bacon and sausage Mama Sugar says is quality enough for the boarders and fits her budget. I'm not arguing with Mama Sugar about the merits of a name or its likely hooks in rusted chains and once fertile soil across the north and south.

"And please get me some apples. I'm fixin' to make me a couple pies for dessert. Them men upstairs lackin' manners and cut out big ole pieces."

"Mmm-hmm." A shiver runs down my spine. Apples. My father loved to eat them. Gingerly flaying the skin with a small sharp knife.

William walks through the back door. Without greeting or manners. With a hole in his blue shirt

13

and two holes in his black pants. He slumps in the chair like half-kneaded dough and mumbles, "He here?"

"Amos came in a little bit ago. Sleepin' upstairs," Mama Sugar answers.

"Figured he was gonna come to you since you're closer."

Mama Sugar walks over to the table with a plate loaded with bacon, eggs and two biscuits.

"I can't eat all this."

"William Larkin Blanchette, I didn't ask what you could eat. You too skinny 'cause your daddy would rather gamble and drink than take care of you. You need somethin' in your belly and I wanna see my face on that plate by the time you done."

William stares at the food.

"You think I'm gonna repeat myself, Grandson?"

He grabs the fork. Mama Sugar bends down and kisses his bush of nappy brown-black hair. "Good boy. Got some fresh clothes you can wear 'fore school starts." William eats slowly at first and then faster and faster until the plate has little but crumbs and small spots of grease.

"I need you to take him to school, Sara-girl."

"Where is his school?"

"It's uh . . . . Hyde Park Elementary. Up on Tunica Street."

My fingers are soggy. Caked in flour and

14

cornmeal and buttermilk, salt and pepper. Mama Sugar takes each battered tomato slice from me, placing them in the hot grease. "The Scarlet's gonna be busy without me."

"And I been doin' this longer than you been on this earth. I can handle the people under my roof. He been skippin' and think I don't know. But I know all. I see all."

William slumps farther in his chair. Mama Sugar looks at his face. William won't meet her eyes. "You too smart to be doing that," she scolds.

At the stove, Mama Sugar finishes the last of the fried green tomatoes, laying them on napkins to collect the remaining oil. "Your clothes are on my bed."

William shuffles up the stairs and without turning around mumbles, "Thank you."

I wash my hands, picking the batter from underneath my fingernails. "We got six guests. William can get himself to school and I—"

Mama Sugar turns off the faucet, my hands only half-washed. "Do what I ask and take him." There's no give in Mama Sugar's voice.

Turning the water back on, I finish rinsing my hands and then dry them. I walk past the crib up the stairs to Mama Sugar's room. Small sounds of rising bodies, groans and squeaks from beds echo in the halls. There are four small rooms and a bathroom on the second floor. Three larger rooms and a bathroom on the third floor. One large room and a bathroom in the attic that Mr. Vanellys finished converting a month ago for him and Mama Sugar.

It's there William is hunched over on the edge of the bed, wrinkling the sheets and reading a book, *Georges*, by Alexandre Dumas. "School starts soon. You haven't washed up or changed yet."

"Won't take me that long. I'm getting to a good part, and I'll get a lecture from Mr. Coulter if I can't tell him what chapters five and six are about."

"It has a happy ending from what I remember." The truth is I know every line of that book. My momma read it to me when I was a little younger than William, before I could see the bones in her wrists and circles under her eyes. "It's for a test?"

"Nah. Mr. Coulter gives me extra reading assignments and we talk about 'em after school."

"He must think you're somebody. That you're special."

"He thinks *everybody* is somebody special," William replies.

"I'm going downstairs. Be ready in ten minutes. Mama Sugar isn't gonna get on me because you got lost in daydreaming."

His eyes don't move from the book's pages. "Mmm-hmm."

• • •

I dodge the small, puckered cracks in the concrete of the sidewalk. Maple trees and oak, large houses and small, a corner church and rumbling cars; kids running and moms yelling; neighbors greeting each other and horns blaring. Happiness is here in this heat-embedded city on a bluff near a mighty river. There is a glimmer of joy as I take in these sights, and I don't know why. There are bad things here and bad people who don't want us to rise, to be. But on we move from our homes to our jobs like nothing malevolent hovers, like there aren't two water fountains or two entrances to a theater or two worlds in this city, in this nation, split between black and white skin.

William's head is still bowed, his nose so close to the pages of the book, it's a wonder he hasn't fallen on his face. But he takes this path every day to school. He's aware of everything around him, but tunes it out, words on a page the only reason to keep moving and breathing. I remember feeling like that, like a book was salvation.

"How much farther? I need to get back to The Scarlet."

"You can go. I'll be fine making it by myself," he answers.

"I gave my word I'd see you to school so that's what I'm doing. You'll be rid of me soon enough, but I tell you what, if you skip class today and

Mama Sugar hears about it, finishing that book will be the least of your worries."

William's eyes never leave the pages of his book. "Take the next right on Hunter Avenue."

"I know."

Looking up, William smirks. "Okay, Sara."

"So do you go to school with . . . other kinds of kids?"

Will stops, again looking up from the book at me. "It's school. I'm not the only one there."

"I mean—"

"Oh. Nah. White kids go where they go. We go where we go for the most part. But Mr. Coulter said that's why we gotta study hard. He said it won't be like that forever."

"You believe him?"

William shrugs. "Don't know why grown folk think it means that much. Like we're not studying for a test. It's like we're studying for a war or something."

The boy isn't that far off. I know he already sees it. The edges of what other people think his humanity to be, how he's to be treated because of his race, something over which he has no control but somehow has to fight to find some kind of control over. But at least he's got a few people in his corner like Mama Sugar and this Mr. Coulter. Some part of me is relieved he doesn't have to be the first child or adult to walk through the doors of somewhere he's not welcome. To hear shouts or curses; feel the blast of a water cannon or the heat of a fire or the teeth of a dog. To be the first doesn't mean glory or applause or fame. Most times, it means fear and sacrifice. Sometimes being first means death.

"You study for Mr. Andersen's arithmetic test?" asks a young girl in an emerald dress three steps behind us. Matching bows adorn two thick black braids touching her shoulders and a third one down to her midback. She strolls up on my other side looking at William, waiting for his answer. "So?"

Rolling his eyes, William drops his arms down to his sides, the book dangling to his right. "Yeah Diane, I studied enough. Why do you care anyway?"

She coughs, hard and phlegmy. Sweat dots her forehead. "Well . . . it might be nice to have *some* competition."

I pat Diane's back. "Are you okay?"

"Yes ma'am. It's the heat. That's what Daddy says. Memphis heat can heal you or kill you."

Diane laughs or wheezes. The sounds are the same in my ears. She looks at William. "I've had the highest grade in arithmetic class three weeks . . . in a row."

"Won't be four," counters Will.

"We'll see." The girl in the emerald dress walks ahead of us. Slowly. Grabbing on to each fence post as she makes her way down the street.

William puts the book back up to his face. "Diane thinks she's so smart. She doesn't know everything."

Children run to a red brick building almost a block wide with four snow-white pillars, two flanking each side of the main entrance. The American flag and a small bell tower are perched atop the roof. Sunlight illuminates large open spaces, distilling the air with the smell of grass and wilting flowers.

"Okay, you can tell Granny you saw me here."

"I'll be back around when school's over."

"I got studies with Mr. Coulter, remember? Can you let Granny know it was tutoring?"

A simple explanation like tutoring is good enough for Mama Sugar to trust someone else with William? But I'm the cynical type. The mean type. The unforgiving type. My left hand dully throbs as my nails dig into my palm.

"Sara!" William waves his hand in front of my face. "You okay?"

"I'm fine." I scan past William to the doors of the school. "I should probably meet this Mr. Coulter."

William shakes his head. "School is barely three blocks away from the house. I'm practically grown. Can't have you *and* Granny fussin' over me."

I flex my hand, my nails leaving a light imprint in my flesh. "Three blocks you're not making lately. Besides, I don't like you enough to fuss over you, but Mama Sugar said to make sure you're good so that's what I'm doing."

"I'm expecting you to have some thoughts for me on *Georges*, William," a voice says from behind.

It's his smile that strikes me first, seemingly genuine and ear to ear, a subtle charm behind it. In that upward bright arc, there's an invitation beckoning me to return it. I don't.

He extends his hand to me. "Jonas Coulter. Pleased to meet you."

I turn to William. "When are you gonna be done? I wanna let Mama Sugar know when to expect you back."

"An hour or two before dinner. Mr. Coulter doesn't keep me too long after class."

Jonas clears his throat and lowers his hand. He fidgets with his black tie. His indigo suit mirrors a dusky sky before the moon emerges from the clouds.

"This is Sara," William answers for me. "She works with my granny as a cook."

"Ah, The Scarlet Poplar. Nice place. Ms. Lennie has always taken good care of our people. And Sara, do you have a last name?" He smiles again.

"King," I reply.

"I see."

A boy William's age shouts, "Hey Willie Boy,

21

that yo momma with Mr. Coulter? You tryin' to be teacher's pet already?" He laughs.

"Caleb! Principal's office," booms Jonas Coulter. The boy's face scrunches up, and he plods inside.

Jonas turns back to William. "Head over to my room. Door's open. Finish up those chapters in peace."

William trudges to the door of the school. His shoulders lowered. The book he so earnestly read on the way to school now hangs loosely in his hand.

"William is thirsty for knowledge, a bright boy," says Mr. Coulter.

"How do you know?"

Jonas Coulter cocks his head to the left as if he's shaking water out of his ear to make sure he heard what I said, to make sure he didn't mistake what I asked; that ready smile fades from his dark brown face. "I've been a teacher for a while. I know students like William. *I was him.* Smart but restless. Easily distracted because he needs more stimulation than a classroom can sometimes provide."

There's a measured way in which he uses his words that I don't like. He savors the three-syllable ones. Like he's so smart, so above any and every person he encounters. Maybe he'd like to give me a book to read. Maybe he thinks I'm ignorant. I could talk to Jonas Coulter about *Georges*. How he had to leave because of a terrible fight. How, in the end, his brother helped save him. But Mr. Coulter wouldn't want to hear from someone the likes of me because he believes himself superior.

"You think you make a difference with William if you give him some books? Tell him he's special like you wanted someone to do for you?"

"He *is* special, Ms. King." His emphasis on "Ms." no doubt a dig at someone with a child and no husband. Does he even know that about me? Maybe he's stressing the fact I'm alone.

"William has a brilliant mind. There's a reason I give him extra reading assignments. Hungry minds need food. William's mind is especially ravenous."

"So, you're his savior, then?" I ask.

Mr. Coulter steps back. "No. I'm only a teacher. William can save himself if he has the tools to do so, if he sees what I see."

"Which is?"

"His potential. We all have it Ms. King. You do too."

"Why thank you for telling me how special *I am,*" I say, rolling my eyes.

"I meant no disrespect. I merely meant—"

"Save the speeches for those kids in there who don't know any better."

Jonas Coulter scoffs. "Good day, Ms. King." His tall frame quickly strides back into the building. Whatever it is, whoever he is, I don't like this man. Some people think they know everything. But as aggravating as he is, Jonas Coulter doesn't seem to mean William harm. Truly wants to teach him, help him. Which is more than what Amos does.

Three girls rush past me, laughing big and bright. "I won," the one in front yells. "Naw you didn't," the middle girl argues. "Come on, we gonna be late," the third one says, and pulls the first one by her arm. And there's a pain deep in my belly, a heat in my chest because I remember some version of those three girls. A time long ago and in a city far north of Memphis.

TWO

———≋———

"Naomi said you'd likely be arrivin' today. Come on in, sweetheart," she says. The night's so ungodly dark, I wonder if I'm still dreaming on a bus southbound for Memphis. But the warmth of her hands on mine signals I'm awake. "Most folks 'round here call me Mama Sugar. Don't ask me where that name came from."

The Scarlet Poplar smells of melted butter, bread, saffron and the bodies of hardworking men. On each side of the large white wooden door, Mama Sugar opens three windows to channel whatever meager coolness the now-falling rain creates.

"So, you're Sara, am I right? You like to be called by anything other than that?"

"No ma'am." I remain near the threshold, to my left a living room and in front of me are stairs and to my right a small hallway leading to a large kitchen at the back of the house. There's a weak rumble of thunder.

"Well, what my niece, Naomi, call you back home? Or your momma? Your daddy?"

"Sara. Everyone calls me Sara."

"Suppose people'll call you what makes them feel good and right in themselves. So, you just

Sara. In and out. I like that. Means there's no pretense to you."

I squeeze the handle of my suitcase and move toward the stairs. "Should I find an empty room, or do you have a preference where I stay?"

Mama Sugar turns off two matching, amber-colored lamps in the living room, then takes my turquoise suitcase and heads up the stairs. "I reckon people see me as a sweet soul, that's why they call me Sugar. But people don't be knowin' you as well as they think they do. And I don't see myself that way. Truth 'tween us, I ain't all that accommodatin' 'cept when I gotta be for these boarders. Can't always be nice an' friendly when you runnin' business in Memphis. Sometimes you gotta make them calls, be sour as a lemon." She laughs. "Anyway, my husband, Vanellys, you gonna meet him tomorrow likely, he call me Lennie Mae, my God-given name. Well, him and a few others call me that," she rambles.

Mama Sugar pauses on a step, raising her arm and wiping her brow. She picks up my suitcase again. "Said all that to say, makes no nevermind to me which name is used. I answer to both."

With every step, the fabric of my long red-and-black skirt presses against my swollen belly. The thread holding the skirt's top button seems to loosen with my every movement.

"You must be hungry. That long of a bus ride. Still got some leftovers I can heat up for you."

"No ma'am. I'd rather sleep."

"Fine, fine. Well, we serve breakfast at seven in the mornin'. Sharp. You rest and get yourself settled tomorrow. You start work the next day. Friday. Sound good?"

"I can work tomorrow."

"The only one you need to impress is me, and I'm tellin' you to start Friday. I'm gonna put you to work believe that. Get some time to yourself like I said."

The steps seem to go up forever. I try and grab my suitcase, but she swats my hand away.

This woman holds my luggage like it's a welcomed treasure. She talks to me like she knows me. Like we share history and secrets and are bonded by blood. To her, I'm no more a guest than her own child. And I feel at home. But it's stupid to trust her so quickly, to be at ease in a stranger's home so freely.

The thunder grows louder. Rain pelts, an uneven drumbeat, against the windows. "Mmm. That's God givin' back to us. That's what rain is. Grace and mercy," she says.

We arrive on the top floor. Finally. Mama Sugar turns around. "Naomi one of my few nieces I can trust, one of the few in my family matter of fact." Mama Sugar glances at my stomach. "We can figure out the rest. Ain't no use worryin' 'bout things over which we don't got control. I ain't gettin' in your business like that. Least not right now."

"Well, he—the father, I mean, I—"

"I ain't judgin', chile. Had my share of troubles too. Tell people he's dead if it comes down to it. Best way to bury your problems or keep people from questioning you 'bout 'em is to talk about death. Makes people feel uneasy and they drop it."

"Do you want to know?"

"You wanna tell me?"

I grab my suitcase, looking down the pale white hallway. "Which room is mine?"

"Second one on the left."

As I open the door, an oak tree branch taps the window, its skeletal wooden finger shaped by a quick flash of lightning.

This is home. For now.

———≈———

"Hey Ms. King!" Short and balding, Malone Blue totters up to me in front of a home with yellow shutters.

"Oh . . . You remember me?"

"This big ole head remembers a lot of things." Malone laughs. "You been in my shop with Vanellys enough. He always braggin' on how you and Lennie Mae keeping them boarders happy."

"Well, that's nice of you to say."

"Saw you comin' over from that school there. You settlin' in alright? This city bein' good to you?"

I unbutton the top button of my sky blue blouse. "It is. It is."

Malone still stands in front of me. "Can you let Vanellys know I found that fuel pump for the Chevy Bel Air?"

"I suspect he's at his garage already so you can probably catch him there."

He reaches in his pocket, takes out an orange handkerchief and pats his head. "Suppose I can. But it's always good talkin' to folk, even 'bout small things."

No clouds have floated in the direction of the sun, its brightness burning my skin. "Apologies, Mr. Blue. Guess I've never been one for small talk."

"Well, I'm probably keepin' you from somethin'. I'ma head to my shop. Mind the business that pays me. You have yourself a good day, Ms. Sara."

"You too, Mr. Blue."

Sinclair's Grocery sits on Eldridge Avenue, two blocks away. I might as well grab the flour, grits and apples while I'm out now.

Momma points out Ashland Avenue on our way home from church. She tells me it always runs north and south; that if I ever get lost, I can find my way home by finding and following that street. "Always know where you're going. Pay attention to street names, Sara. You never know if you gotta be the one to make your way home on your own."

At first, I turn left on Hunter Avenue and then remember I gotta go right or else I'll eventually pass by Mama Sugar's church, and I'd rather not pass by one or go in one again. Ever.

"Sara! Sara! Come over here," orders Ms. Mavis from the front porch step of her green-and-white home. Her ivory apron is lightly streaked with cinnamon and dotted with tiny tears of vanilla extract. "I'm tweaking that caramel cake recipe a little more. Need you to taste this real quick before I head over to the bakery."

"I'm running behind—"

"Won't take long. Plus Lennie Mae says you got good sense when it comes to how things ought to taste."

Ms. Mavis shoves a small plate with painted roses in my hand, a sliver of still-warm cake waiting for my judgment. Fawn-like eyes wait for my verdict. The cake is moist and buttery. The icing is soft, not grainy, melts on my tongue. But . . . there's too much . . .

"Your face is tuned up all the wrong way. I'ma have to start from scratch 'cause—"

"Sugar. All you need is a little less sugar. The cake is fine. The icing was a little too sweet."

"See! I knew it! I shouldn't have added so much, but Nathaniel kept telling me it's fine." Ms. Mavis looks back at her husband. "Thanks Sara. Give that little baby of yours a big ole kiss from me."

"I will." I hand Ms. Mavis back her plate with the little roses and walk toward Sinclair's Grocery.

A bright white awning covers the fresh straw-berries, oranges, watermelon, their colors vibrant. The blond-colored brick front boasts two wide wood-encased windows and on them the words *Fresh Produce* in flat gold paint. It wouldn't surprise me if Mr. Sinclair picks the fruit himself. He's meticulous like that. Meticulous. I know multisyllable words too, Mr. Coulter.

"Hey Ms. Sara." A voice from behind startles me. Mr. Sinclair struts out to the fruit stand. "You want some of dem apples? Got some good 'uns today," he brags.

I swallow hard, but agree, "They look mighty appetizing, Mr. Sinclair."

"Aww, you call me Paul. Done told you that plenty." His weathered hands set out the last of the fruit. A basket of tomatoes sits next to him.

I nod, running my hands over the light fuzz of the peaches, some as big as fists. The back of my mouth waters. "Actually, I'm gonna take these." I hold up a peach in my hand.

I'll tell Mama Sugar Mr. Sinclair was out of apples and only had peaches. She can make her cobbler instead. I *love* her peach cobbler. Buttery crust latticed, crisscrossed, the perfect amount of cinnamon complementing the flavor, not overpowering it. Perfection. Besides, her cobbler is bigger than her pie, so she won't have to make two of them. I'm helping Mama Sugar. Isn't that what I'm supposed to do?

"I'm gonna go grab bacon, some grits and vanilla too."

"Vanilla in the third aisle in the back. Grits up front with the bacon. The King Cotton brand she like. Let me know if you need some help."

The floor is so clean I'd eat my next meal off it. All the shelves have not a box or bottle out of place.

"You puttin' the items on credit, Ms. Sara?" Mr. Sinclair yells from outside.

"Yes sir."

I take three large boxes of grits, two packages of bacon and two rolls of sausage, placing them in the handcart. Toward the back of the third aisle, I grab vanilla and cinnamon, the McCormick brand. Mama Sugar isn't gonna use anything else. The corner of my eye catches a man in a jacket with a dark and light brown checkered top. He removes his tan fedora with a chocolate-dyed band above the brim. His hair is straightened, wavy and slicked back in a conk.

The man stands next to me smelling of congolene and cheap aftershave. Too close. I scoot over a few inches.

"Hello miss. I was hoping you could help me." He sniffles and pulls out an amber-colored handkerchief and dabs at his nose. The man flashes a smile but there's nothing behind it. Nothing genuine, no joy or kindness. Jonas Coulter, annoying and uppity as he was, had something behind his smile.

Grabbing a box of cake mix, I turn my back to the stranger. "I'm afraid I can't help you."

His grin widens. "Aww hell gurl, Memphis is friendly. Friendly enough."

The man with the vacant smile steps closer behind me. I take another step away and pretend to read the ingredients on a box of cake mix as if they are the most interesting words in the world.

"Well I'm not looking for friends so if you'll excuse me . . ." I try to walk past, but he blocks my way. I glance at the picture window. Mr. Sinclair is outside carefully stacking a new display of fresh vegetables.

A thin strip of space separates our bodies. There is a door past the third aisle to the right. If I turn and run, I can make it. I don't think he can catch me.

"We all need friends, Sara," says the stranger as he puts his hat back on.

I search for something sharp. Something I can

hurt him with if he tries anything and I mean *anything*. But there are only packaged bottles of cloves and lemon extract and sacks of flour. Nothing to cause this man the kind of possible harm he means for me.

"Oh, forgive me. I know you but you don't know me, do you? Lennox, Lennox Black, but folks 'round here call me Lucky. And I know you, Sara. Yes. I. Do." He sucks his teeth and continues, "Memphis is a busy place but a small place. Everybody get to know everybody real quick 'round here. I hear you help Lennie Mae at The Scarlet Poplar in Hyde Park. Hear you got a son too."

I drop the bottle of vanilla. It breaks.

"You good here, Ms. Sara?" Mr. Sinclair calls out from the front of the store, casually making his way back to me.

Lucky's eyes burn a hole through me. I plaster a smile on my face. My bottom lip wavers. "Clumsy. Dropped the vanilla. Everything's good. Thank you."

"We catchin' up, Paul. Go on outside. Fetch me some oranges. My little Diane loves her some oranges."

Mr. Sinclair looks past Lucky to me. He doesn't question Lucky. He takes in my wavering smile and shaky words as affirmation things are fine and goes back outside and begins bagging oranges.

"Now I was mindin' my business when I saw you walk in here buying these nice spices and things and wanted to know when I could get my money."

"What money?"

"Amos. He owes me 'bout $200."

"How is Amos owing you my problem?"

Mr. Sinclair glances back at me and he stares. Lucky follows my gaze and Mr. Sinclair looks back to his produce, examining the fruit and vegetables with far more concentration than I've ever witnessed.

"If I don't get my money from him, I'm gettin' it from Lennie Mae. I know his momma got it." He casually places his left hand in his pocket, his jacket pulling back slightly, the handle of his gun visible to my eye as he intends it to be. He smiles like my father smiled when he skinned apples. Nausea roils my stomach.

"Tell Amos to get me my money. Today. I ain't waitin' no longer." He leans in and whispers, "I can be real mean an' nasty. Don't make me do that. I don't wanna if I don't have to."

THREE

They are up when I return to The Scarlet. The Boarders.

Elvin Sanders clomps downstairs. A stampeding herd of cattle are more delicate.

"What Mama Sugar cooking this morning? Sure hope it's grits. Is it grits, Sara?" Elvin strokes the thinning gray-black hair on top of his head. "Maybe pancakes. I could go for pancakes too."

I shrug. Lennox Black's eyes haunted me the four blocks home from Sinclair's Grocery. I rush past Elvin to the kitchen.

Tell Amos to get me my money.

Mama Sugar hunches over the stove. She wipes her forehead as her other arm stirs the large pot of grits. The baby, my son, is awake in the crib. He's enjoying the movement, the rising bodies and clamoring footfall.

"Mama Sugar . . ." I begin.

"Sara-girl, go grab me the big red bowl. You know where it is."

Without much thought I turn and grab the big red bowl from the middle cabinet on the second shelf behind the huge yellow bowl and the green plastic cups. I hand it to her, and Mama Sugar washes the bowl though she washed it last night.

She harbors a weird fear the bowl somehow collected fast-growing germs in the still moments of the night, and those new germs could make the boarders sick. It wasn't true though. Mama Sugar takes so much care and pride in everything she does. All she has is her name, and every wipe of that bowl, every plate of delicious food, every clean, comfortable room solidifies she's a hard worker, good at taking care of her business, good at keeping honor behind her name since Amos seems hell-bent on destroying it.

"I gotta tell you what happened at the grocery store," I plead.

"Yeah Sara-girl. Okay. Okay in a minute. You got my flour and my apples?"

I reach into the paper bag and hand her the flour. I set down the vanilla. "Sinclair's only had peaches."

"Do I look like I got Boo Boo Da Fool written on my forehead, Sara-girl? Paul *always* got apples and everything else."

I don't meet Mama Sugar's eyes, continuing to set out the peaches in a white bowl I pull from underneath the kitchen cabinet. It's big enough to fit the ones I picked, juicy and ripe.

"Hey Ms. Lennie! You got them grits for me?" Elvin comes through the kitchen and sits down in the chair closest to Lebanon. The paunch in his stomach slightly straining against his jean coveralls and touching the edge of the table.

Lebanon reaches for Elvin, who starts to pick him up but looks at me hesitantly. "It's okay," I say. He gently lifts the boy onto his garbage worker's uniform, at this point clean, but come the end of the day, I dread to think about the stench that will follow him through the door.

He bounces Lebanon on his knee. The baby with his toothless grin, his happy babbling causes no warmth in me; nothing moves me to return his innocent affection, nothing urges me to hold him—something made from me but made from someone else too.

Elvin looks up from playing with Lebanon. "Anybody come by and ask for me?"

"Nah honey. Not yet, but you go on and make sure you fill your plate," encourages Mama Sugar.

Booming from the door. "Lennie Pie! Lennie Pie! Gimme some of dat food or else I'ma sho' nuff die!" spouts Buster Fairbanks, his wide body barely clearing the door. He winks as he passes me and sits next to Elvin. The chair squeaks as he does.

"Yo old lady take you back, Elvin?"

Elvin's faced reddens. "She will. This—" he gestures around the kitchen "—this here be temporary. Not like I was sleepin' with her sister."

"You right, you right," says Buster. "Her cousin is this much better." He holds his index finger and thumb together. Buster laughs, the sound filling the house and ringing outside of it.

"Y'all can talk that unsavory nonsense in them streets. Not in here. Am I understood?"

They both sheepishly nod. "Yes ma'am."

Lebanon now reaches for Buster, who takes him and gently lifts him above his head. His tiny arms and legs flail about and high squeals escape his mouth.

"Aww you gone leave me, huh?" Elvin pretends to pout, crossing his arms but chuckles. Why are people so drawn to the child? The boarders. People in the neighborhood. Strangers on the street. What do they see that I can't? He's only a baby. One I don't want. One I never wanted, but so many others seem to. Grabbing the biscuits and sizzling bacon, I place them in the middle of the table. Mama Sugar returns to the stove and turns it off. Steam rolls off the grits. I place the bacon and sausage in the refrigerator.

Buster tucks a napkin in his shirt. "Vanellys leave for the garage yet, Lennie?"

"Yeah and if you got up early enough, you could've left with him."

"Too busy making sure the numbers are right. You know Vanellys is great with a car. Horrible with them books."

"Horrible with the books, huh? And you good with arithmetic?" Elvin adjusts his overalls. "What's 456 times 37?"

"Sixteen thousand eight hundred and seventy-two," Buster confidently answers.

Elvin blinks, tilting his head. "I . . . uh. Man, you playin'."

"Use all ten fingers and ten toes. I'm right. I know numbers."

Returning to the stove, I whisper to Mama Sugar, "I need to talk to you now! It's important. It's about Amos."

Mama Sugar smiles, but it's a phony action of her mouth. "Look I know you got something to tell me, but it can wait. Specially when it comes to Amos. These men with hungry bellies can't. Let's do what we supposed to do and then you can tell me all what happened at the grocery and what's going on with Amos. I can tell you it ain't all that bad. I seen it all with my son. Trust me," she whispers. Mama Sugar doesn't want the boarders to know about Amos' problems, especially if it means they don't come back to her. Amos is her son, but The Scarlet is her baby, her business. Nothing gets in the way of that.

Three more people come downstairs, and there's six bodies in the kitchen sitting at the table. Buster sits Lebanon on his lap and starts piling his food into his mouth, somehow keeping the baby perfectly still, and soon Lebanon begins dozing and falls asleep. Elvin takes him from Buster and puts him back in the crib behind him so . . . gently, with such care and I wonder how he can feel that for the boy. How do *I* feel that for the boy?

Mama Sugar's right. I can't blurt out what's going on with Amos, and it's best to get breakfast out of the way. We'll get the place quiet again, wait until most of the bodies from this house are gone to jobs or devilment or aimless roaming of the streets.

"Ms. Lennie, thank you so much for your hospitality," says one of the men at the table. He's clad in an olive green suit. "I don't think my own mama cooks a better breakfast, but don't tell her I said it." He chuckles and rises from the table. He takes out ten dollars from his pocket and puts it in Mama Sugar's hand. "Oh! This is more than my rate, Professor Thomson."

"I know, but this is one of the nicest boarding-houses I've ever set foot in. You deserve every penny, and you have my undying gratitude, Ms. Lennie."

"Hey Professor, where you stayin' tonight?" asks Buster.

"I should be back in Tuskegee by this evening," Professor Thomson replies.

"Yeah you goin' back to Alabama. Should take you five, maybe six hours. But if you still wanna rest, there's another real nice place that serves us. In Birmingham, I think."

The professor pulls out a green book from his brown satchel and thumbs through a few pages. "Ah, yes, the A. G. Gaston Motel, owned and operated by us. Yes, yes. But I doubt I'll need it.

41

I'm aiming to return home by nightfall so I can prepare for my classes. These new scholars have no appreciation for Humanities."

"Oh *Humanities* . . ." Buster draws his face down in exaggerated matter. "Fancy Professor. Fancy." He then takes a sip of his orange juice and keeps his pinkie finger in the air.

The professor places the green book back in his bag. Mama Sugar shakes his hand and tells him, "Be careful on them roads. Get home safe." A lone country road, a black man and his car, any one of these things dangerous on their own, but combined can become lethal. We don't always make it home. Less now, but years prior, there were abandoned cars and then desecrated trees where these vanished people were found. There was a boy named Emmett who came from my city, Chicago, and went to Mississippi and never came home to his mother, Mamie.

Sometimes we leave and never come back. And as Professor Thomson departs The Scarlet Poplar for Alabama, to a black university of higher learning, where I could've only hoped to go, we all inside of ourselves pray a silent prayer or think a good thought that he never finds himself among that mournful fellowship.

"After you finish up your plate, go on and wash the rest of them dishes. I'ma start on tidying up," says Mama Sugar.

"Aren't you gonna eat? Aren't we gonna talk? Everyone else is gone."

"In a little bit." She grabs the broom and dustpan and goes to the living room.

Amos saunters into the kitchen from the back staircase. His glossy black mane puffed up to a pompadour, a mountain of hair at the front gently rolling its way to the nape of his neck. A folded green scarf is tied around his edges, keeping them laid and smooth. He snatches the last of the bacon and biscuits from the serving plates by the sink. Whiskey from the night before seeps from his skin.

"That was your momma's breakfast."

"She wasn't gonna eat it no way," he says.

He puts a strip of bacon on one of the biscuits and shovels it into his greedy mouth, smirking at me.

"I know one thing that will wipe that look off your face."

Amos leans against the sink chewing on the last of Mama Sugar's breakfast. A dollop of bacon grease misses his lips and drips down his angular chin. "And what's that?"

"Lennox Black's been looking for you."

He coughs hard, his eyes grow wide. Glancing back at Mama Sugar in the front room, he tries to erase the fear creasing his forehead. "It's a bad streak. I done won more from him than I lost," he whispers.

"Don't know why you're telling me. You best make it over to that man and tell him."

Amos tosses his plate in the sink, bits of bacon and biscuit crumbs still clinging to it. "I'll take care of it." He folds his arms across his chest. "Don't know why Lucky stalkin' 'round town puttin' my business out in the street."

"Tell your momma about Lennox Black so I don't have to."

"You don't have to now," counters Amos.

"That man doesn't seem the type to take late payments, and if he comes around here looking for you, he may try to get the money from Mama Sugar or your daddy at his garage."

Amos stands up straight, his height dwarfing mine by at least four inches. "Keep quiet about this, Sara."

"Or what?" The knives are in the drawer to my right. The one Mama Sugar uses to skin chicken she keeps on top of the smaller ones.

"I'm not gonna tell you the world is a terrible place," Momma says. She stands at the stove, her graceful fingers picking out bones from canned salmon. "Too many people say that and it's not true. Well, not entirely. The world is good. And we have the chance to be the same, but you can't choose for people who they will be, like people can't choose that for you. Be vigilant in this world but be open." Momma grabs a knife and starts chopping onions. "But if you run into

44

someone who chose poorly, who doesn't choose to be good, do what you must do, my love. Run. Fight. Most important . . . survive."

"Amos! Come here, stop talkin' to Sara-girl," Mama Sugar yells from the living room.

Amos turns around and follows the sound of her voice. "Okay Ma. Got some errands to run then I'll swing by the garage."

My hand is on the drawer where Mama Sugar keeps the knives. My fingers grip the knob so tight my knuckles throb. I don't remember reaching for it.

Mama Sugar stops sweeping in front of the door. "Nuh-uh! You go on down to the garage now! It's almost ten o' clock and your daddy's up to his eyeballs in work!"

"I'ma go do what I need to, then go help him. Promise."

Unfastening my apron, I drape it across the back of the closest chair. I glance at the baby in the crib. His arms reach for me. I walk to the front room.

"You promise things all the time, son. I don't want no more promises. I want you to do right for once!"

Amos' eyes narrow. "Doin' the best I can, Ma. Always putting me down. I'm runnin' an errand. I'll help Daddy after." He brushes past Mama Sugar and walks out the door, slamming it behind him.

Her shoulders sloped, Mama Sugar removes the pictures from the mantel. A story of her life in black and white, in small, genuine moments. There are photos of her younger self. One in front of a wood shack, two unruly pigtails jutting from her head. Next to this picture is another one of Mama Sugar and Mr. Vanellys in their twenties probably, her hair in stylish pin curls under a fedora; Mr. Vanellys in an army uniform next to her with a bright smile looking like he won a million dollars. Slightly behind that photo is one of a small toddler in a bonnet and too-frilly dress, Bonnie Lee. There's a picture of Amos standing in front of Mr. Vanellys and Mama Sugar, his small, fat hand tugging at her striped dress. Behind all of those pictures stands another frame; it carves out its own space. It shows a boy in blue jean overalls in front of a tree, alone, unsmiling, staring to his right.

She places all of these pictures on the mustard yellow sofa, using a dust rag on the chunky pine mantel above the fireplace. Her hands press down on the wood with such force I fear it might fall to the ground.

I pick up the picture of she and Mr. Vanellys. "Y'all look nice in this one."

She continues to wipe down the mantel.

I put down that picture and pick up another one. "Amos doesn't look like he's in too much trouble in this one."

Mama Sugar selects another rag, dabs a small amount of oil and begins to polish. I pick up the picture of the unsmiling boy.

"This isn't Amos."

Mama Sugar snatches the picture from my hands and puts it back on the sofa. "No, it isn't."

"Who is—"

"Sara, most times I can't get you to say two words. Now you suddenly a chatterbox?"

Her sharpness, her shortness. This is a bad time to mention Sinclair's Grocery and Lucky and Amos owing money, but Amos isn't gonna say anything. Mama Sugar needs to know what's coming. There's never a good time to deliver bad news.

"Listen, I know you got a lotta things on your mind right now and I hate adding to it but—"

Mama Sugar wipes her brow. "You wasn't adding to it, darlin'. And I'm sorry for getting . . . riled up. Got a lot on my mind right now."

She picks up each photograph and sets it back in its place as it was before. Mama Sugar takes the picture of the unsmiling boy, tracing it with her finger. "This was my oldest. Oliver. Lost him too."

"I didn't mean . . . I didn't know you had . . . I'm sorry."

Mama Sugar returns the picture to the mantel. She pats my arm.

I take her hand. "Earlier, when I was at the grocery store—"

A knock on the door interrupts us. What the hell? See, this is why God doesn't exist. I'm trying to tell a good woman about something that could harm her or her husband or her selfish-ass son, and someone is at the door.

The knock has to come now? Why not in five minutes?

"Hello, hellooo!" says Cora Morgan in a sing-songy voice as she enters the living room. Her sleeveless blue flower-pattern sheath dress rests at her calves.

Her perfectly coiffed reverse bob à la Diana Ross sits atop her high cheekbones and softly curved nose. "Sorry to intrude Ms. Lennie Mae. We are sorely in need of your counsel. The church board is having a hard time deciding on the Revival's venue. Some of them want it on the north side of the property. Others are bellyaching the north side won't fit enough people and the tent and . . . ugh if I have to hear Deacon Bunche talk one more time about what they did in the '20s, I'm pulling out the left side of this bob." Cora points to her head.

"Oh and you're here too, Sara. God is in Heaven and working. Lawrence told me to tell you to bring Lebbie to him soon. Time for his checkup."

"Dr. Morgan is good with Lebanon, he is," Mama Sugar offers.

Cora is too familiar. Speaks to me like we're old friends. She has a nickname for *my* child. She's married to a doctor. If I had a glass, I'd drink from it and raise my pinkie like Buster. So many siddity people in Memphis. Jonas Coulter. Cora Morgan. They'd be fine up North in Chicago or New York, but they're down here and flaunt their affluence and education in my face.

I untie the pink scarf on my head and smile tightly. "I'll bring him by. Probably next week if the doctor is available."

"Oh, I can tell you it won't be a problem. But what is a problem right now is this Revival planning. I need Ms. Lennie's help for a little bit. She's the only one who can calm everyone down. Find an answer everyone can live with. Can you manage things here, Sara?" She takes Mama Sugar's hand, guiding her to the door.

Cora is not in charge of this place or me. Why does she act like she's the Queen of England? She possesses some assumed authority, and it crawls underneath my skin. I gently take Mama Sugar's wrist and squeeze it.

"I still need to talk to you. It's important, remember?"

"So is the Lord, chile. I'ma be back. We'll talk then."

She pats my hand. "Take care of the house and make sure you here when William gets home. You hear me, Sara-girl?"

Defeated. Deflated. I let Mama Sugar go. "Yes ma'am."

Mama Sugar leaves and closes the door.

God. Can I ever be rid of Him? People put God before everything, and He'll be the main reason for their sorrow and hurt. If they'd listen to a person on earth telling them about something important instead of some imaginary man in the sky, we'd probably be better off.

Me. Mama Sugar. All of us.

FOUR

I strip the bedding. It's been three days since it was last washed. I sweep the hallways. The baby cries. It's more a shriek than a cry. The baby reaches for me, and I don't want to pick him up, but I do. And I clean him and change him and put him back in his crib.

The house sings. It creaks and groans. But there's another kind of music I crave. Living. Pulsing. Throbbing. The white RCA tube radio on the second shelf waits for me. I turn it on. I turn the volume up.

Relief. The notes through the static are still enough for me to enjoy. The Mar-Keys play "Last Night." Trumpets and saxophones, bold and saucy Agile organ notes weave themselves through the melody until the repeated blues riff fades.

She comes on. Nina. Heard her on the radio more when I was in Chicago, but there are little miracles every day, that's what momma said. Voice deep, abiding and flawless. She sings of a plain gold ring. Drums and the flourish of a piano as I caramelize sugar. Music keeps me company as I make Ms. Mavis' caramel cake. She didn't give me her recipe, but I know how to make a cake. I watched my momma. I watch Mama

Sugar. The rest is common sense and correct measurement. But it is also creation under your control. It's freedom. It is peace.

It is what I do.

I place three cake pans in the oven and lightly step away, turning off the radio. Fallen cakes after hard work is a tragedy. It's shameful.

There's a light tapping on the window in the front room.

Lebanon's small broken cries follow me as I open the door to see the mailman wave and walk to the next house. The mailbox is crammed full of letters and other envelopes. The boy's cries grow louder. Echoing, filling every space of the house, every particle coddling his impatient shriek. I pick him up and he quiets some. I check on the cakes and set him down on the rug near the fireplace. He looks up with those eyes. His face soaked in tears. But his crying doesn't stop. He shrieks, tires some, then whimpers, then works his way back to crying. It's a cycle of more noise and less noise. There is a door that I can open. There is a door I can walk out of. Twist a knob and go. I can't give him what he needs. I have nothing of myself. And all I can do now besides picking up a log or twisting a knob is sort mail for strangers sharing a home. So, I will do that.

There are fifteen pieces of mail so far. I take what I've separated and place it on the small oak stand next to the door. Three envelopes are left.

Two of them are for Mama Sugar. The last piece of mail is for me.

It's from Violet. Violet Potter. Her married name. It smells lightly of magnolias. I miss that smell. A low whine from below and I pick the boy back up, go outside and sit on the swing porch. A hot breeze gusts, slightly more merciful than an open oven.

Dear Sara,

None of the things I want to say in this letter are things that I can write anyway, but I wanted to talk to you and, even though me and Naomi haven't heard from you, we think about you all the time. We talk about you. We miss you. And I figured you'd want to know how we're doing.

Naomi is engaged! It's Gialan White from First Baptist on the West Side. I didn't see that coming. They're so sweet together though. And Naomi is happy like she was before. We're trying to find our way again.

Some more news to share, though I didn't want to tell you this in a letter, but I'm expecting! It must've happened right after me and Thomas' wedding. I'm due in November. They had a party for me. And I wanted you there. Naomi did her best to fill your space, but you aren't replaceable. I hope you know that.

Thomas wants a little girl! Can you believe that? My personality. Another Violet Morrison? Jesus help us all! I'm hoping for a boy. I dream about what if I have a boy and our boys are friends. We could raise them together. They'd be friends like we were. But they'd be better and free and the world we have we'd make it better because we're better or we can try to be.

I hope you write back soon or call. I hope this letter finds you well. I hope Memphis is growing into a beautiful place for you because you deserve that. You deserve everything even when you tell yourself you don't.

Forever and to the end.
Violet

Forever and to the end.

It is what we said to each other. Violet, Naomi and me. In a church named Calvary. In Chicago. Those few words, reading them, comfort me; create such a longing to return to my friends, *my sisters,* to a life that was ugly, but they made the ugly parts of living pretty enough to bear. Bear my father. Bear my shame. Bear my place in a world longing to force me into a dark tiny space though my very soul knows there's something more for me. But here I sit on this porch in my dark tiny space, this letter bringing me a bitter fragment of light.

It's hard to see Hubert Avenue and the park on the next block. It's a wavy mirage behind my tears. I command them to stop. They come harder and harder. I wipe them away with one arm and hold the baby with the other, but salty water still leaks from my eyes. He's sleeping again. Mama Sugar is right. I need to get him on a schedule. While he slumbers in my lap, I imagine I'm waiting for my husband to get home. A tall broad man who's as smart as a doctor and loves me and wants to find me waiting for him. I am happy for my friends. I am. I imagine things are normal. That my life is . . . normal. My past is not my past. This child is not my child. But this isn't possible. Not with the boy. Not with me as I am.

But what is normal anyway? A word for people to ignore their problems, something to swaddle themselves in, something to give them the ability to dream of more than what they have and who they are. Maybe I'm lucky. I don't have to lie to myself that normal exists, that dreams exist, so I'm far ahead of people who think they can change things, change people. Like Jonas Coulter, the one who's going to save William and all the other black children at school from something more dangerous than dreams or normal—the belief the world will treat them fairly.

So I am as I am with all my scars and living.

I best get on with life as it is and as it always will be. I need to peel the potatoes and boil them. I need to season the flour for the chicken and be light on the onion powder because Mama Sugar will sneeze if there's too much in there. I need to get the house ready for the influx of bodies coming back to their temporary home. I need to take the cakes out of the oven. Let them cool. Make the caramel icing. Stop daydreaming.

Let me continue as I am. Wishing is for children, and I haven't been a child in a long time.

There's a parade of men and women who just got off work marching down the block and up the stairs of homes in the early evening light. Some tired. Some not. Some smiling. Some frowning. But each with another set of chores and family obligation on top of whatever else was endured the hours before.

Will sulks on the porch, his arms folded in front of him. There are about four books piled on his right. I stay perched at the screen door, listening for Lebanon, who I hope is still asleep in his crib. "Come in and get cleaned up for dinner," I tell Will. He doesn't move. There's an enthusiastic squeak and the hollow thud of the door as it closes behind me. If Mama Sugar gets in and Will's not where he needs to be, she'll scold me—not Amos—about Will. He's not my child, but now I have to walk him to school and see after him when I didn't ask for the responsibility. Once again, something is thrust upon me, something I did not ask for, something I do not want.

"I know you heard me. Smart as you are, you think making me mad is how you wanna end your day?"

He looks up at me and he sighs. His pile of books has six, not four, stacked together, the top one *The Weary Blues* by Langston Hughes.

"Is you sighing supposed to move me, William?"

"It's a lot of work. Mr. Coulter gave me this book and this one—" he holds up *The Dream Keeper and Other Poems* "—and I gotta write a theme on top of the one he assigned the rest of the class." Will folds his arms. "I read one book. He gives me two. I read two, he gives me three."

"S-so you want me to be sorry for you because the man's trying to educate you? Make you better?"

"It's a lot—"

I roll my eyes, but not at Will, at the fact I'm agreeing with that siddity teacher from this morning. "Are you gonna complain or are you gonna work? Those are your choices, boy. Save Mama Sugar, no one wants to hear a black kid cry about having to read too much. Especially when you know some of us wasn't even allowed to not so long ago." I bend down, my eyes level with Will's. "You best get on with being whatever you can, however you can." I look off the porch toward Gooch Park. "A lot of us don't get that chance."

Will wipes his face with his arm and grabs his books, shuffling to the front door.

"Will." He turns and looks at me. "That teacher isn't doing this for nothing. He said he sees potential in you. *Potential.*"

He nods and walks through the door.

Elvin's smell wafts up the stairs before he does. I don't know how much more my nose can take. "Dinner ready yet?"

"Does my ass on this porch signal your dinner is ready? Mama Sugar had to run to the church so dinner might be late. I'm gonna start in the kitchen in a bit though."

"It's been a helluva day," he says.

"Yeah. It has." Violet's letter is folded in my pocket.

In front of us, a woman bister-hued and straight-backed briskly walks past the house. Her yellow, knee-length dress glorifying her luscious, deep brown skin.

"Simone! Simone! Baby!" shouts Elvin. He runs down the stairs after the lady, whose long legs carry her farther from the house and almost half a block away before he catches her. Elvin says something I can't make out. Simone's full lips turning downward, she shakes her head and walks away from Elvin, leaving him on Hubert Avenue where I am one of the few witnesses to his defeat. He marches back to The Scarlet Poplar, a scowl fixed on his face. Elvin stops in front of me; garbage and sweat and fear and whatever other mixture embedded his skin hovers in the air around him.

"Why can't y'all cut us a break? Women gotta make us suffer when we make a mistake," he complains, certain his transgression isn't *that* bad. Elvin makes his sins small so he can bear them. His words should be enough. And Simone should forget. Gloss over her pain and act like it's no more than a paper cut when it's an open infected wound, an exposed heart, a piece of her shattered. But she's expected to somehow rebuild herself, and again welcome the one who did the breaking. Why must Simone show mercy? Rein in her pain? Swallow everything. Hide *everything*.

"She shouldn't have to help you make amends for *your* wrongdoing," I say. The blood rushing to my face has nothing to do with the season or the sun. "That's your problem." My finger points in his chest and digs in. "Have you thought about what you did to her? How you hurt *her?* Or did you only want a warm bed to be in?

59

Was *something else*—" I glance below his waist "— doing the thinking for you? Do you even care?"

Elvin walks toward the door. "I need to wash up."

"Yeah, you go do that."

Elvin slams the screen door and I breathe deep. I need a minute before I go wake up the baby sleeping in my room. He's gonna cry hard and loud. Waking him up when he doesn't want to or giving him a bath or feeding him mashed peas, making that boy do anything before he's ready is a goddamn fight.

Oil pops and crackles in the black cast-iron skillet. Mama Sugar dredges chicken pieces in flour with pepper, seasoning salt, garlic powder and a hint of onion powder. Also, a dash of cayenne. If someone asked me, I couldn't tell them how many teaspoons or tablespoons are needed for these spices. We measure with our minds, knowing by eye or taste when there is too little of an ingredient or too much and can find the proper herb or seasoning to moderate. We are magical like that. But it's a process that we watched our mothers (if we were lucky) and our grandmothers perform. Each generation instructing the other how to put their love in mixing bowls or pots or skillets and then on a plate for their family and before that, for their masters' families.

"Thought you wanted me to make a cobbler? Why you go ahead and make a cake then?" Mama Sugar asks.

"I wanted to give you one less thing to do, I guess. Plus the peaches will be fully ripe tomorrow or the day after."

"Okay. Tomorrow then." Mama Sugar carefully places the chicken wings, legs, thighs and breasts in the skillet so each piece has space but as many can fit in as possible, a scrumptious meaty puzzle of crispy goodness.

My caramel cake sits on the countertop to my left. Three-layered. Perfect. Its taste, I hope, is perfect too. I needed to do something perfect. Music and flour and measurements. Every good and perfect thing I've made comes from a recipe and skilled hands. Every calming moment, even when things around me rage.

For the third time, Mama Sugar glances at the back door. William writes in his notebook, the scratches from his pen filling the silence. Soon Elvin, Buster and the rest will herd themselves into the kitchen all grabbing hands and full mouths.

Thin lines of cloud stretch past cobalt skies, overwhelming the Memphis night. In a yellow housecoat, Mama Sugar winds her neck from side to side and removes the pieces of chicken, placing them on a collection of napkins from different restaurants or businesses she frequented.

Grease drains from each piece of fried chicken and, when satisfied, Mama Sugar places four pieces on a large oval-shaped dish with painted pink flowers.

Mr. Vanellys slams the door and walks through the kitchen. Mama Sugar exhales long and slow. She smiles at Mr. Vanellys, who remains stone-faced. "Dinner's almost ready. You best run up them stairs and wash up."

His eyes never leaving Mama Sugar's. His voice is low and deep. "That boy almost cost me business not coming in. All that gettin' up and crawlin' underneath them cars with this." Mr. Vanellys raps his walnut-sized knuckles against his right leg, a hollow metal sound lightly echoing in the kitchen.

She sucks her teeth and looks back at her chicken. "Got-ta be mo' careful!" She pulls out two pieces slightly browner than the rest of the chicken but no doubt as good as what was already on the flowered plate. "He don't ever learn. It's like doing right for him is some kinda weakness."

William stops writing and stares at his grandparents, his essay all but forgotten. I keep mashing the potatoes. I tried. I tried to tell Mama Sugar about Amos, but she was too busy with Revival and boarders and whatever else. Or maybe she's so used to being disappointed in him her sadness blurred together with all the other sorrows she had, a collage of buried emotions and lived-with regrets.

Amos is probably off gambling somewhere, getting himself further in debt and Mama Sugar further in trouble. Mr. Vanellys rubs his right leg for a few moments. "I'ma go upstairs. Clean up real quick 'fore them people come and pick them bones dry."

Mama Sugar grabs Mr. Vanellys' hand. "You know I'ma always save you the big piece of chicken." She winks and Mr. Vanellys chuckles, but it's sad and his sadness touches a part of my heart I wish it didn't.

There's a banging on the door. Impolite and incessant. Mr. Vanellys looks at Mama Sugar. He straightens up, his walk stronger and not the shuffle he entered the kitchen with. "Comin'! Comin'! No need for all that noise!"

The person knocks again, harder, the frame rattling. Mr. Vanellys ambles to the front room and swings open the door, "Now how can I help—"

It's him. Jonas Coulter. His nice indigo suit wrinkled, his bright white shirt streaked with dirt and blood.

His?

No.

Jonas drags in Amos, barely able to hold his weight, and then collapses to the floor heaving out of breath with Amos, bloody and not moving.

FIVE

Mama Sugar drops the big fork she's using for the fried chicken and rushes to the door. William runs past me, but I grab the back of his shirt.

"Stay here."

"Sara, I want—"

"It's not about what you want!" He shrinks from me the tiniest bit. I breathe deep. "Look, seeing him like this might . . . I don't know, give you a bad dream or something. Stay here. Watch Lebanon. Make sure he stays safe. I can trust you to do that, right?"

William looks past me at Jonas, Mr. Vanellys and Mama Sugar trying to tend to Amos and get him up, away from the door. I slide my body or as much of it as I can to block his view.

"Can I trust you, Will?"

He walks to the crib and picks up Lebanon and sits back in his chair. He opens his book and reads. He bounces Lebanon on his knee, and the baby reaches up, his fat fingers clawing at Will's shirt collar.

I leave them and walk to the living room. Even with Mr. Vanellys' help Jonas struggles to lift the mostly limp Amos. Mr. Vanellys' right leg begins to shake. I nudge him out of the way and take his place.

"Sara-girl, you don't gotta do that."

"I don't want to, but it's gonna be hard enough to get him situated. And . . ." My gaze drifts down to Mr. Vanellys' right leg. He swallows, relinquishing his place. Jonas' stance steadies.

Elvin and Buster run down the stairs, stopping dead in their tracks when they see us. There are at least two other able-bodied men who could help drag Amos up these stairs, but they stand there. Frozen.

"Can y'all stop standing there like pillars of salt? Get the hell outta the way!" I order.

"Gentlemen, if you don't mind . . ." Jonas chimes in as if I needed him to make what I said sound nicer. This isn't the time for niceties or pleasantries or good manners.

"Take him up to our bedroom. More space," Mama Sugar says. She looks at Buster and Elvin. "Y'all fetch Dr. Morgan 'fore he make it back up to Orange Mound. I think he's still around the church."

"We'll go get him," volunteers Buster. He and Elvin rush past me and out the door.

Amos moans; his breath is rancid and uneven. His dirty and musty body stains my dress. Jonas and I begin our trek upstairs.

"Are you okay? Your hand is shaking," says Jonas.

My body has memories. There are things that take me back to a place, and even when my mind doesn't want to travel there, some part of me will. My right hand takes me back to Chicago, to a church and hands around my neck. "It's fine. I'm fine. Worry about Amos." I quickly flex my hands twice and steady myself on the banister and climb.

Amos wriggles around in pain on the bed, moaning low and pitifully.

Grabbing his shoulder and arm, I steady him. "The more you move, the more you hurt." And I pray he moves a little more.

Jonas places a pillow behind his head. His long fingers gingerly poke and prod around Amos' chest and stomach and his left leg. He puts his hand on Amos' forehead. "Okay, brother, looks like a few ribs might be broken. Your leg too, but that's probably the worst of it."

He's gentle with Amos, far gentler than he deserves. Gentler than I'd be. "How do you know that's what's wrong? We're not at a hospital."

"Dealing with children, I've seen it all. Bruises, broken bones, scrapes. He'll be okay once Lawrence gets here. Besides, they're not gonna take him to Collins Chapel Hospital unless they're sure he's gonna die. I don't think that's the case."

Amos howls in pain, and Jonas gently puts his hand on Amos' bloodied forehead. "You're good, man. You're gonna be okay. We'll get you fixed up." Amos quiets some. His howls turn to whimpers.

Floorboards creak behind me. Will stands there with Lebanon staring at Amos on the bed. A tear falling from Will's cheek.

"Can't you follow one damn instruction? Why the hell did you bring the baby up here too?"

"You told me to watch him, but I still wanted—"

Leaving the bed, I walk to William. "I told you it's not about what you want. The world doesn't work that way. Now if I tell you to stay downstairs—" I lower my body to meet his eyes "—I mean stay downstairs."

Lebanon begins to cry. William's eyes widen with fear and if I was burdened with some deep love for him, his look might hurt, cause me to change the tone of my voice or even apologize. But there isn't time for love or kindness. Fear works better than those things most often anyway. That's what I know. But then tears leak from his eyes, and if Mama Sugar sees her only grandson crying, my ass might wind up next to Amos in this bed.

I bend down and look at William. "Look, look. Come on with the crying. I'm sorry. Go back downstairs. The doctor will be here soon."

"William—" Jonas' voice is soft but firm "—I promise you it'll be okay. And I know we're not supposed to promise things like that, but

I'm going to promise you he'll be okay. Go downstairs."

He leaves the doorway with Lebanon.

"You were harsh with him," says Jonas, his voice hitting my ears with a bit of edge, some assumed moral authority he believes he holds over me. And he does not. No one has authority over what I do or what I say. Not anymore.

"Life is harsh and doesn't coddle us. Better he knows it now." I turn to Amos' broken body on Mr. Vanellys and Mama Sugar's bed. Life hasn't treated him kind, but he probably did his own damage and this is his repayment.

My legs are weary from walking and carrying a body up three flights of stairs. From my mind I push William's sad eyes and Lebanon's cries.

Tangerine-tinted light shyly splays itself on the nicked bureau to my left. A vase of fresh wildflowers shows the first signs of wilt. Jonas swiftly takes off his jacket, his movement fluid and sure. He gingerly lays it across the chair in the corner of the room, as if the jacket is still as pristine as it was this morning. The morning, a part of the day that now seems like a year ago from this moment, in this room, with this man and Amos.

Jonas places his hands on the wall near the door. His back to me, he blindly grasps and gropes.

"What in God's name are you doing?"

"Looking for the light switch."

"To your left."

An electric glow brightens the room. Squinting, the carnage of the dirt and blood over the bedsheets and comforter slowly come into focus. I witness the consummation of crimson and white, the deeper of the two hues spreading its tendril-like arms, resting in a set pattern holding their distinct colors. It is beautiful and sickening. Amos' eyes are blackened, the right one almost swollen shut.

"Me and Cora were *this* close to home," a bass voice comes from the doorway. Dr. Lawrence Morgan strides in, his brown suit expertly tailored to his tall and thin frame. Probably Cora's doing as nothing can be out of place, everything orchestrated to be practically perfect. Even Lebanon takes to her more than he does me. My annoyance of her pops up out of nowhere despite everything; despite a man hovering between life and death, I still think about how I wouldn't mind tripping her or maybe giving her a quick slap.

"Well Ms. Sara, it's nice to see you're in good spirits despite present circumstances," says Lawrence. His soothing voice fills the room; my muscles even relax the slightest bit.

"Didn't realize I was smiling."

Lawrence removes his suit jacket and lays it on the same chair as Jonas'.

"Far as I can tell, he's got some broken ribs.

His leg too, probably," offers Jonas. "Think we need to get him to Collins Chapel, Dr. Morgan?"

"Well let me see, Mr. Coulter," he responds with the lightest sound of amusement at Jonas using his title.

Jonas rolls his eyes. "Yeah, I know we're not in front of a bunch of people, but I'ma still give proper respect."

Jonas' pitch-perfect dialect and grammar relaxes around Dr. Morgan, and I'm tempted to ask why, but Amos is the priority and he's still squiggling around like a bloody worm. "Can we give him something for the pain?"

"Eh, let me assess then I can determine what needs to be done," replies Lawrence.

His hands examine Amos' body, much like Jonas' did minutes earlier but in a learned way. Jonas' previous efforts are hopelessly clumsy when compared to Dr. Morgan, who expertly maneuvers around the damaged parts of Amos. He's a conductor directing a delicate symphony. His eyes closed, he angles his fingers in particular ways, applying pressure on certain areas and then nodding as if they gave him the answer of what ailed them. Then he moves on to another part. It's fascinating.

When I was younger, I played doctor. Bandaged up my dolls and gave them stale candy as prescriptions for their pain. Momma smiled at me. She let me fix her too, put bandages on her legs and arms, but not her hair. She didn't want me to mess up her hair. Momma said I could be a doctor. That she wanted me to be one. That it wouldn't be easy, but I was strong and smart. And she hugged me, clutched me to her. Then let me fix another part of her. Until I couldn't. Until nothing could and she died. And I was left behind and my dreams no longer seemed possible.

I hold Amos still as best as I can so Dr. Morgan can finish his work and so Amos doesn't hurt himself further. But he deserves pain for what he does to Mama Sugar and Mr. Vanellys, the worry and pain, the regret and sacrifice; the agony of the smallest hope he can still be a good father to Will; be the man they raised him to be. That is what it means to love for them. That kind of love is dense and desperate. I do not want any part of this, but I still try and force him to not move.

"Baby, all you gotta do is be still and breathe," Momma says. *"Pain is gonna do what it does. Sing a song in your head. Think about the park where you swing so high you might turn into a bird right there and fly away. Think about flying, my love. Think about flying."*

"Breathe. Think about something nice. Stay still," I hotly whisper. "It's a few broken bones. I've been through worse."

Jonas cuts his eyes toward me, but I ignore him and focus on Amos. There could be good in Amos buried, so deeply buried, he himself may not seek it out, not notice it. And I know this stillness.

"You were pretty much in the ballpark Jonas. Ribs are fractured. Not broken. Leg is broken. I'd prefer to take him to Collins, but questions will be asked about . . . what happened."

"No! Can't say nothing 'bout that, Doc," mumbles Amos from the bed. He grabs Dr. Morgan's arm. Tears spring from his hooded brown eyes. "Please man. *Please!*"

"I can't tend to you as properly as needed here. It's better to head over to Collins."

Amos groans. "Come on, Doc. I know you can treat me right. You can . . . do a fine job. Here. Whatever happens, happens. I can't go to Collins."

His gaze travels up and down Jonas' body. "You want to tell the story, Jonas?"

Jonas avoids Dr. Morgan's eyes. "Things are . . . complicated, Larry. You know this."

"Okay, okay. We'll keep it between us, but I'm going need to set that leg and it will hurt. Badly. I got some medicine. I could get you better at the hospital but since you want to stay here, there's only so much I can do. Me setting this leg is going to be anything but pleasant. You understand?"

Amos shrinks back in his bed. He looks like a child, and part of me wants to comfort him. I grab his hand. "You want me to bring Mama Sugar up here? Sit with you?"

"Nah Sara, but ummm . . . Can you get my dad?"

"Yes. I need fresh hands to help me hold him down. Get Mr. Vanellys and those two gentlemen who came to fetch me," orders Dr. Morgan.

"Buster and Elvin?" I ask.

"Yes, thank you, Sara."

Jonas takes his jacket from the corner in the room and puts it back on. "You're a good man, Larry."

"I'm gonna miss *Tales of Wells Fargo*. You know I love that show!" Dr. Morgan loosens his tie, then chuckles. "Well, I know we all gotta sacrifice, right? Bring those men up here. Thank you both for getting Amos this far."

I let go of Amos' hand. I must be getting soft. This place with its lazy sunsets and honey drawls and cool breeze sometimes allows me to forget for a moment how I got here.

The hallway from Mama Sugar and Mr. Vanellys' room seems to stretch farther than I remember it doing before, and the floors creak louder.

"You handled yourself well in there," says Jonas. "Done that before? You appeared quite adept, capable of that. Most people would've frozen."

"Yeah, well, I'm not most women."

"I said most people, Ms. King. Not most women."

Though we're two floors above the living room, voices and the smell of chicken and butter reach us. Mama Sugar probably salvaged the mashed potatoes. Jonas remains a step or two behind me. I move faster to create more distance, but as I increase my pace, he increases his, like we're playing a game.

In the living room with the fireplace and logs stacked in neat little rows, Mr. Vanellys smokes with Buster and they're mumbling on about something my ears can't catch. Their rolled cigarettes grudgingly dissolving between their fingers and turning into small piles of ash on the floor that I'll have to sweep again tomorrow.

William still reads his book or at least stares at its pages until he sees Jonas and me. He runs for the stairs, but Jonas blocks Will with his body. "Give Dr. Morgan time to work."

"Dr. Morgan needs Buster and Elvin to help set Amos' leg," he says.

I put my hand on Mr. Vanellys' shoulder. "Amos asked for you."

Mr. Vanellys puts out the cigarette in his calloused hand, placing it in his left pocket. He and Buster head toward the stairs and climb. Will plods back to the couch and sits down. In the corner closest to the fireplace, Elvin groans slightly. "Man, I left one job come back to another one."

"I can go back upstairs," volunteers Jonas.

74

I turn to Jonas. "No. Elvin can go. That's what Dr. Morgan said, and you've done enough." Elvin's muddy eyes narrow. My jaw is tight. I clinch my hands. I will fight a man. I have no problem because I know I can kill a man, and if he kills me along the way, then I'm still in a better position than I was this morning.

"Elvin," says Mama Sugar, "go on up there. It shouldn't take long, and I can always put this toward room and board, take a little bit off for helping out like you did tonight."

Elvin's face softens, the gentle plea in Mama Sugar's eyes would've probably persuaded me to move a mountain for her. "I—I'm sorry Ms. Lennie. I'm tired is all. You don't have to do all that. I was raised better."

He trudges from the fireplace, passes Jonas but cuts his eyes toward me. At least he smells better than he did when he first came home. I don't look away. He'll need Dr. Morgan if he lays one hand on me. But Elvin makes his way up the stairs, his feet moving as if they were bogged down in molasses. Jonas' face is set in this placidly mean way as he stares at Elvin, who disappears from our sight. The set of his jaw slowly relaxes, and a warmness returns, the one I saw early in the morning at the school. Perhaps I imagined the look. Why would he care what Elvin says to me or how he looks at me? I must've imagined it.

"Dinner is probably gonna be another half

hour or so," says Mama Sugar. "Hopefully this all calms down and we can get some food in our bellies. Late but the good Lord says we need to eat. He didn't say what time in the Bible."

And she laughs. Despite everything the day has put upon Mama Sugar, she laughs. And I envy that, to look past the bad and grab some crumb of happiness or hope or whatever it is that causes a genuine sound of joy to leave her lips.

We are immortal; our struggle and unwavering ability to fight on is immortal.

Lebanon coos on Cora's lap. He grabs for her pretty gold necklace. He grabs for her earrings. He grabs for everything. "What do you want, little one?" She presses her still perfectly made-up face to his and he giggles on her unwrinkled dress. He cries with me and giggles with her. His light fat fingers cupping her face and brightly smiling in it.

Above the living room ceiling, there is a wail, a sharp cry and cursing, muffled thumps of haphazardly placed footsteps and a hurried mumbling of orders to calm down or to shut up. I can't make out which. Will looks up at the ceiling, then returns his gaze back to his book, never turning a page. Cora turns Lebanon around and bounces him on her knees. And he reaches for me. With that smile, the one I coveted a moment ago. There's a sharp pain. In my belly. When my baby smiles at me.

When I open the front door, a rush of air slightly cooler dries some of the sweat from my arms, cleans a bit of Amos' sour smell from my skin. The door creaks closed behind me and again Jonas is at my side on the porch. I move another few feet to my right and he stays put, reaches inside his jacket pocket and retrieves a pack of Lucky Strikes.

"Want one?" His deep umber fingers place the offering on the wooden railing.

"I'm fine."

"I normally don't smoke but tonight, you know." He takes the cigarette, lights it. Holding the smoke in his mouth for a minute, he then slowly pushes it out, making a circle. "Took me three months to figure that out," he says. "Among all the fine education I've acquired in my short time on this earth, learning how to blow smoke rings might be one of my finest accomplishments."

"Not a fancy degree?"

"There's something to be said for a worldly education." He flicks some of the ash from his cigarette. "Tried to teach Larry how to do it. He damn near burned down his house!"

And before I stop myself, before my brain can tell my mouth to quiet, I laugh.

". . . never seen Cora so mad. She was ready to spit nails. I swear he slept on the couch for at least a week!"

I laugh harder and there are tears but not from anger or fear but a wholly warm space I didn't think I possessed. Jonas covers his mouth, laughing too. His knuckles are scraped, bloodied. He takes another drag from his cigarette, this time holding the smoke in his lungs and slowly exhaling it through his nostrils.

"You found Amos and brought him back?"

"Not exactly."

Playing coy is for the birds and I'm not going to pull it out of him. If he doesn't want to tell me, fine. Mama Sugar no doubt needs some help in that kitchen. I head to the door.

"I heard shouting and yelling by May St. near Chelsea Avenue, up the block," begins Jonas. "I saw a man taking on three to one. I didn't know it was Mr. Blanchette until I was closer. He and Will look so much alike, but I only met him once or twice before. Anyway, those men had him on the ground, but he managed to get in a few good licks here and there before he went down."

Jonas chuckles sadly. "I helped Mr. Blanchette . . . I fought those men with everything I had. And I won. I'm not proud, using violence like that, but . . . I hate a bully."

"Me too."

Jonas grasps the ending of each word as if he's trying to give them the respect and weight he believes they deserve. The ripped left pocket of his white shirt is stained with dirt and blood.

"Anyway, can't say I could identify the guys. They ran off. I'd make a report, but those officers don't give a damn about something like this. They'd rather we kill each other. Save them the man-hours," muses Jonas. "We gotta do better than this. There's got to be better for us than this." His arms gesture around the porch.

"Well, we can't save everyone."

"Doesn't mean we shouldn't try."

"Lofty ideas, Mr. Coulter. Those can kill you."

"Well Ms. King, I can't think of a worse death than to live a life and do nothing with it."

I can think of worse. I've lived through worse. So, I'll leave Jonas to his high-minded ways. I can't say it'll do him any good, but he seems to be a decent man, and to tear him down with no reason is as evil a thing as I can think of.

Mama Sugar opens the door and walks out onto the porch. "I done calmed my nerves down some so we need to feed these people. Get yourself clean and come help me finish up in the kitchen." She looks Jonas up and down. "Go on and wash up as best you can Mr. Coulter. I'ma set a place for you."

"Thank you, Ms. Lennie, but it's late. I should be heading back—"

"I'm setting you a place," says Mama Sugar, each word out of her mouth its own sentence.

Jonas pinches the dwindling cigarette between his fingers, then buttons his jacket, covering his stained shirt as best as he can. "Yes ma'am. Thank you."

"Very well then. Sara-girl, come on."

Fingers of cerulean light graze the porch railing. Dusty moonglow lays itself against the arm of his rumpled indigo suit, which was pressed and crisp when I first met him.

"Guess you'll have to oblige my company a little while longer, Ms. King."

"I've dealt with worse, Mr. Coulter."

I follow Mama Sugar through the door and leave Jonas alone on the porch.

SIX

"All I know is I'll walk my black ass somewhere now 'stead of taking the bus. White people done lost they minds 'cause we wanna sit next to 'em," says Elvin. He opens the three windows spanning the wall next to the back door. Next to the door are three open shelves holding flowers, herbs and the radio. Elvin rotates his right arm in wide circles, then takes two chairs from the corner of the kitchen and places them around the long pine-knotted table.

"Gonna need to put some heat on this shoulder. Amos daggone near broke it doing all that jerkin' around when Doc was settin' his leg."

I glance to my right, but the hallway is empty. I listen for any kind of movement. Cries from Amos, the shuffling of Dr. Morgan's feet down the stairs, but there's nothing. It's barely an hour since Jonas dragged Amos through the door, but it feels like days. Trouble always stretches time out much longer than it need be.

"Happy to be done with it," says Buster. He slithers up to my left side, reaching past me to the mashed potatoes, a spoon clutched in his hand. I swat it away. His large, bourbon-colored eyes drop in defeat, and he slinks back to the table, sitting next to Elvin. Cora strolls into the kitchen and sits down with Lebanon on her lap. He yawns. She leaves an empty chair between her and Buster.

"Well, I can tell you them people are trying to make things better for us. We in the last half of the century. Got a Catholic president. Got some people standing up for what's right. Even trickling down here in Memphis. Them college kids from LeMoyne Owen did them sit-ins downtown at McClellan's Variety and then the libraries. I mean why not be able to sit next to anyone black or white and eat a meal or read a book or ride a bus outta state? I pay taxes, and my hard-earned money spends no worse or better than white people. God bless 'em. Freedom people," says Buster.

"Freedom Riders," corrects Jonas.

"Whatever you call 'em. Like I said, God bless 'em. 'Cause my ass—"

Mama Sugar slams her hand on the countertop, whips around and stares down Buster, then glances at Elvin. "This a boardinghouse, but it's God's house all the same!"

"Apologies, Lennie. What I meant to say was, I am happy these Freedom *Riders,*" Buster says, looking over at Jonas, "are fighting 'cause I'm too old for that. Done all the fighting I want to do in a lifetime." Buster looks over at Mama Sugar, her face softening the slightest bit, returns her gaze to the chicken, patting off the excess grease.

"All I know is we deserve every bit of what we work for. Shouldn't be a need for all this turmoil. It's like the world can't spin unless there's chaos afoot," she muses and glances at the stairwell.

"Dr. Morgan'll be down shortly. He said Amos is gonna be good. What? My word don't mean nothing?" Mr. Vanellys puts his arm around her, and she turns her body away from him.

"You're not a doctor. Sometimes you say things gonna be okay and they're not. So, let me hear Dr. Morgan's words for myself."

Mr. Vanellys walks over to the table, his right leg slightly dragging, a light scraping sound filling the room. He sits next to the empty crib with the faded paint flower, touching it for a moment. "I'm going outside on the porch for a minute. I'll be back," he says.

Jonas looks up for a brief second and returns his attention back to Will and his book. "Okay so how does *The Weary Blues* start off?"

"With an alliteration," answers Will.

"Why do you think Hughes did that?"

Will looks at the ceiling again. Jonas closes the book and Will's eyes drift to his. "Read beyond the words, Will. Why do you think he did that?" repeats Jonas.

"Get our attention. Make an impression, I suppose. Let us know what's coming."

"Okay so what else? That can't be all you think when you read it."

Will sits up. His eyes dart back and forth for a moment. I place the corn in the middle of the table, and I wait for his answer.

"I mean the man in the poem loves the blues, but he's sad too," answers Will. "When the blues *are* playing, when the man hears it, he's happy. And I guess he feels like someone else for a little bit, but then it's over. So, he's happy when the music is playing but then it stops . . . and it's only him again. The him before the blues started playing. That's why it's sad. I mean that's why it's sad to me, Mr. Coulter."

"Okay. Enough. We need some kinda lively talk," says Buster. "Lennie Pie, can I turn on this here radio?"

"Go on ahead."

Buster walks to the wall closest to the back door, reaches to the second shelf and turns on the radio. He fusses with the dials until we hear the unmistakable croon of Elvis Presley blare through the room.

"Turn the station, please. I'm finally getting Lebbie settled," says Cora.

"Just as well," Buster says. "Ain't got much against him, but all he doin' is singing our music. But he get paid for it. We don't."

"You ain't lied," agrees Elvin. "First time I heard that man, he was singing 'Hound Dog,' but the first person made me feel some kind of way 'bout the song was Big Mama Thornton."

84

"Bet you she ain't seen a dime from him singing it."

"A dime. Shoooooot! You mean a penny," says Elvin.

"That's how it is with our art," agrees Jonas. "With our science. Our inventions. Our breakthroughs. Our lives. We create. White people take it and then say it's theirs. We don't exist. They do. But we'll change that. Step by step."

Mr. Vanellys returns from the porch, cigarette smoke lingering in the air behind him. He closes the door. Mama Sugar removes the aluminum foil from the plate holding the rest of the chicken, placing it on the table with the rolls and food. "Now everyone this chicken is still warm. I wanna see some clean plates when dinner is over."

Mama Sugar looks at Mr. Vanellys. "Wash your hands," she says to him. He walks over to Mama Sugar and kisses her on the cheek and does as she orders, scrubbing his hands in the sink. She smiles weakly. He then sits down at the head of the table.

Buster turns the dials again. Raspy and bold, Tina Turner, guitars and a steady drumbeat pulse through the small speaker. Over and over, she sings, " 'I think it's gonna work out fine.' " He turns the volume down when he sees Lebanon dozing on Cora's shoulder, then walks back to the table. "Guess Ike and Tina know better than anybody how this day's gonna end."

Jonas looks at me, but I break his gaze and take Lebanon from Cora's arms. He whimpers and starts to cry, but I place him in the crib with the faded paint next to Buster. And he settles again, his eyelids fluttering open, then shut, then open again.

He fights everything!

"Such a little blessing. I can make a bottle," offers Cora. She smiles.

I don't return Cora's smile. Would she talk about blessings if she knew how the baby she covets came to be? "He's fine. I know what he needs," I say, mustering all the confidence I'm able to in this cramped kitchen. But I don't know what he needs. I silently beg him to fall asleep and not make a fool of me in front of her.

Open. Shut. Open. And I stand above him, watching his chubby little arms and legs and thick brown hair. He has my nose and maybe my lips. He opens his eyes again, those eyes, and my stomach churns.

Sleep. Come on child! I rock the crib to the beat of Tina's voice and I hum the song. His eyes stay closed, and his breathing slightly deepens.

"Aww, see, you good with him, Ms. Sara," Buster says.

I stand up straight and smooth my dress. "Of course, I am his momma after all." Cora shifts in her chair. She lays her napkin on her lap and reorganizes the order of the silverware.

"Now, we're supposed to get two new boarders this week. One of 'em is another professor but not from the black college in Alabama. This one is from the college in Atlanta," says Mama Sugar.

"Morehouse?" asks Jonas.

"Yes. Morehouse, and Mr. Coulter, if you would've given me two seconds, I'd have said the name. You a teacher but you gotta remember other people know things 'sides you, am I right about it?"

Jonas adjusts his tie, looking up at Mama Sugar. "Ah, Ms. Lennie, I meant no disrespect. I was excited at the news. I'm sorry." And he smiles and it's easy and simple. Like he wasn't smiling to stop a fight but meant the apology. Or I'm damn tired. This has been a helluva day and I'm tired. That's all. The last thing I need to focus on is a smile.

Scratchy static from the tube radio plays parts of "One Mint Julep." Horns roar. Will taps his foot to the beat of the song. I glance at Lebanon, who remains fast asleep in the crib, a little smile crosses his face. I guess he's a Ray Charles fan.

Mama Sugar sits on the right-hand side of Mr. Vanellys. I sit down across from Will. And, all together, we hold the hands of the persons to our sides and bow our heads. Mr. Vanellys' deep solemn baritone makes his plea: "I'm not a

87

worthy man but you saw fit to still bless me with a home and a family. And God, I thank you. In rough times and good times. We're askin' you Lord to have mercy on every person here . . . whether or not they want your mercy. They need it the same as us all. In Jesus' name . . ."

"Amen," replies all 'round the pine table. Including me.

Dr. Morgan walks into the kitchen and washes his hands at the sink near the stove. Mama Sugar rises from the table, hands him a fresh towel, and as he dries them, she sits back down. Dr. Morgan begins, "Two of his ribs are fractured. As for the rest, it was a bad break. The leg I mean. We set it—" his eyes travel to Elvin, Buster and Mr. Vanellys "—and it's looking better."

Mama Sugar's hand clutches Mr. Vanellys' arm.

Dr. Morgan continues, "Now, if that leg gets discolored or starts to smell, I don't care how much he protests, you get him over to Collins. The rest are scrapes, bruises and contusions. All of those should heal in a week or so. I gave him some medicine for the pain." He hands Mama Sugar a pill bottle. "If he asks, one every four to six hours. No more." Mama Sugar puts it in her apron, patting it twice. Dr. Morgan slides out the empty chair next to Cora, who touches his hand and smiles that perfect little smile of hers. He returns it. Tiredly but genuinely.

Mama Sugar then serves Dr. Morgan. Somehow managing to fit three pieces of chicken with rolls, mashed potatoes and corn on one plate.

"Ah, Ms. Lennie, I greatly appreciate the hospitality, but I don't need all of that—"

Mama Sugar gives him the look, the same one on the porch with Jonas, and like Jonas, Dr. Morgan stops protesting.

"This is some of the best bird I've ever eaten. We were probably friends in another life," says Jonas. He finishes chewing and turns to Dr. Morgan. "Ms. Lennie said one of the boarders coming this week is someone from our alma mater."

"Morehouse! Ah, good times," reflects Lawrence.

"Well, you did meet me prowling around Spelman like all Morehouse men do, so you're absolutely right, it was a very fine time," Cora says and laughs, freely. I grip my fork and eat the mashed potatoes I helped make, trying to push her laugh from my mind.

Will wipes his mouth. "You went to doctor school at Morehouse?"

"No, they don't have a medical school. I went to Howard University in Washington, DC—"

Mr. Vanellys puts his elbow on the table, pointing at Mama Sugar. "Lennie Mae, we got family in DC, don't we? Uh . . . it's uh—"

Mama Sugar narrows her eyes, looking down at Mr. Vanellys' elbow. "My great-auntie Shinettra."

Mr. Vanellys sits up straight, his elbow sliding off the table. "Yep. Sure do!"

Dr. Morgan finishes eating a roll and continues, "Well, I became a doctor, married this one, who was finishing her English degree at Spelman, and came back to Memphis. Help our people. There aren't enough of us. Not nearly enough. There was a need up North to be sure, but Lord knows down South our need always seems exponentially greater. Can't say I know how else I can assist in our survival besides doing what I'm doing now."

Dr. Morgan loosens his tie. "But Morehouse was a great school. Besides, I met this riffraff—" he gestures to Jonas "—my first year there."

"Second," corrects Jonas. "I . . . uh . . . had to come a year or so later than you. It was my freshman year. Not yours. We all can't be lucky like Lawrence over here and get in at eighteen." Jonas smiles again, but it is a tight movement of his mouth.

The Marvelettes plead on the radio for the postman to wait. The drums and piano and guitar infusing the stifling air with the coolness of black voices. Cora bops her head side to side and mouths along a few of the words.

"Now you know I don't normally let this radio go on during dinnertime," Mama Sugar says, "but this tune is a little catchy. Who is this?"

"Uh, the Marvelettes," answers Jonas.

"The Marbelettes? That's an unusual name for a group, isn't it?""

"No ma'am. The *Mar-velettes,*" repeats Jonas. He takes another bite of his chicken.

"Still seems strange name, but like I said, this song does got a rhythm."

"Don't worry, Ms. Lennie, I won't tell the church board you like some of the devil's music," says Cora.

Mama Sugar chuckles. Buster wipes his hands and stands up from the table. "I'll do you one better, Ms. Cora," he says, offering his hand. Cora looks over at Dr. Morgan, who shrugs. She takes it.

"See, none of you youngins know about how we danced back then."

"And none of them's gonna know now. You was the worst dancer ever walked the face of this here earth," says Mr. Vanellys.

Pretending to frown, Buster looks at Cora. "You see how they do me, Ms. Cora?"

"Oh, he's kidding. Aren't you, Mr. Vanellys?"

"No. I ain't," he replies with a straight face, and takes another bite of corn.

Buster slides to his left and his right. He's behind the beat. His legs bend about strangely and he steps on Cora's nice shoes, but she laughs. Buster and Cora dancing is a welcome distraction from what's upstairs, from what's beyond the ivory-tinged walls of this house. For now, there is music and a fraction of peace we call our own.

The front door creaks as I open it. Jonas stands on the porch. Tucked away in the shadows of an oak tree across the street is someone else. He prowls around like one of the monsters Momma used to read about in my fairy-tale books. He never crosses the street but gazes at the top window. The ember bloom of a cigarette lighting his face.

"Ms. King, are you okay?"

"Y-yes. Sorry, Mr. Coulter. Mama Sugar wants you to have a plate to take home. There are two slices of the caramel cake I made. You look too skinny and need some meat on your bones."

"Well, Ms. Lennie has always been very direct."

"Oh, she didn't say that last part. That was me."

Jonas laughs out loud, too loud for this time of night at a respectable boardinghouse. That laugh again manages to take me with him and I laugh. The second time today. For me, it could be a record. But I stop quicker than I want to because of the monster across the street, with a lit cigarette and bad intentions. But I know what to do with monsters.

Jonas follows my gaze across the street. "What the hell—"

"Lennox Black. Has to be," I say.

He puts the plate down on the porch chair behind him. "Lucky?"

I look back at Jonas. "You know him . . . personally?"

"In passing, mostly. From what I hear he runs numbers, a little bit of loan-sharking. A little bit of gambling. A little bit of everything." Jonas pinches the bridge of his nose. "His daughter Diane. She's in my English class with Will. Smart. Lucky picks up Diane from school. Every day now. Sometimes in the middle of the day. Doctors appointments or something. So he says."

A black Chevy screeches down the street, pulling up to the curb. The dark figure enters the car, and it drives away. Low uneven squeaks from the sign above the door provide an unwelcome tune. Again, the Memphis heat bares down, suffocating as it did earlier, near dawn, when Lebanon wouldn't sleep.

Turning back to Jonas, I look him up and down again. Rumpled dark blue suit, rigid stance. Fists clenched. "He's probably making sure Amos got the message. Give him his money or it's gonna be worse next time. Probably a lot worse."

The shriek of the tires still echoes down Hubert Avenue. As I grab the railing, a small, jagged piece of wood tears the skin of my left palm. Small crimson drops dot the wood stairs. Tiny things cause such damage. Opening his jacket pocket, Jonas takes out a handkerchief, somehow still pristine and white, and presses it on my hand.

"So, I guess you get to play savior again. This makes three times today?" I smile to let him know I mean no harm, that I feel a bit different about him than I did this morning.

Jonas looks up at me. "Does it hurt?"

"No," I answer. A tuft of wind lifts the bottom of my yellow dress. "You look . . . what's the word? Pensive. You still thinking about what happened? The fight?"

Jonas' full lips are in a straight line, concentrating a lot harder than he should be on a small scrape. "I suppose I am," he says.

"Well from where I stand, it's a good thing you got there when you did," I say. "Sometimes kicking someone's ass is necessary. You know, for the greater good."

Jonas smiles. "And here I thought earlier today you wanted the ass kicked to be mine."

"Well . . . maybe a little, but you came off siddity, Mr. Coulter."

"Apologies, Ms. King. Apparently, you are not the only one who thinks that's something I need to work on. Shall we start over? Hello, my name is Jonas Alexander Coulter."

Does this man mean me harm? Don't things always start off this way? A man at first doesn't appear to be mean or cruel. Jonas is a teacher, but my father was a pastor, allegedly a man of God.

Titles, though there is nobility in them, make no difference if the man with the title holds no goodness within himself. Is Jonas good? Would I even recognize good if I saw it?

"I'm Sara Michelle King."

He offers his hand, with bloodied knuckles, and I shake it, with drying blood on my hands too.

SEVEN

"Mama! Ma!" screeches Amos. His high-pitched whines disrupt the tenuous calm of the kitchen. Lebanon starts crying, and I cut my knuckles on the box grater.

"Come on now little king. Look, look I'm gonna tell you a story," consoles Buster. He takes Lebanon from the crib. "I got a fine one for you this Saturday mornin'."

Buster sets Lebanon on his knee facing him and starts bouncing him up and down. "Okay so once upon a time there was a princess named—" he looks over at me "—Lennie Mae. The princess' name was Lennie Mae."

I stick my tongue out at Buster, who laughs. Lebanon babbles and smiles. His fingers grab for Buster's left cheek.

Mama Sugar chuckles. "You ain't no good, Buster. Name that princess Sara. You best name the hero of the story after his mama."

"Who says I'm the hero?"

"Oh gurl, hush up and let Buster tell his story!"

"I'm hurtin', Ma! Please!" Amos shouts again. Mama Sugar's shoulders sag.

I put down the box grater. "I'll go."

"Like lambs to the slaughter," says Buster.

"I'll be fine," I say.

"I'm talking 'bout Amos. He keep this up, and I'm pretty sure I'll see his bed on the sidewalk in front of The Scarlet 'fore long."

"Thanks Sara-girl. That boy was never good when it came to pain, but you men never are." She looks over her shoulder to Buster.

"I'll be good with anything you want so long as I get first dibs on them hash browns," he says.

Mama Sugar reaches into her apron and holds the pill bottle in her hands. A piteous rattle as she shakes out five and gives me one.

"Don't say it, Sara. This past week with him hurt done felt more like a year, and the time moves easier if he got something more to calm him. He's calm. I'm calm. 'Sides I don't give him that much more than what Dr. Morgan prescribed."

Mama Sugar doesn't meet my eyes. She takes a plate and puts on three crispy strips of bacon, two biscuits and the grits. She pours a cup of tea, cuts a wedge of lemon and places it on a small saucer. She takes the pill and puts it on the saucer too. She places the items on a red-and-white metal TV tray and hands it to me. "I'ma finish gratin' these potatoes and make you a plate. You been such a help this week."

"It's fine. This is what I'm here for."

Mama Sugar doesn't realize the sanctuary she provided a girl with a child and no husband. With her smiles and hugs when I let her hug me. I'd deal with a thousand Amoses for her. But I won't

97

say this. I'll take the food and tea and pill to her ungrateful son. I'll let her serve me breakfast in a hot kitchen.

The farther I tread upstairs, the more unrepentant and sour the heat. With each step, my feet fight the swampy moisture of the early September morning. Amos, shrunken, in the covers, rolls his neck. He sits up as I enter with his food and his medicine. Will sits close to Amos on Mr. Vanellys and Mama Sugar's bed, his shadow reaching across the floor to my feet, lanky arms moving about with a book attached to his right hand.

"And they're taking Georges to die. And it looks like it's over. Then Dad, guess what?"

Amos rolls his neck again. "What Will?" His voice is flat and distant.

"His older brother Jacques saves him! I thought for sure it was gonna be one of those books with a sad ending 'cause Mr. Coulter has me read books with sad stuff in them too, but this wasn't a sad ending at all."

"Boy, I had enough of these books and Mr. Coulter this and Mr. Coulter that." He grabs *Georges* from Will. "This don't do you good anyhow. They don't care if black men are learned. They make you shine they shoes or a garbageman or a mechanic like your granddaddy. Them books don't make you nothing big." Amos throws the book, missing me by a few inches.

"Least he cares enough to teach me anything," mutters Will.

Amos reaches for Will, who bolts from the bed to my side.

"Mornin' Sara," mumbles Amos. He eyes Will, who retrieves *Georges* from the floor and sniffles, leaving the room. His head bowed so low I can't see his eyes or face. I lay the tray on the dresser and place the slices of bacon next to the biscuits, so they won't fall though maybe I should let them. "You know that boy loves you and wants you to love him back. You don't have to be so . . . cruel to him, Amos."

"Who the hell you think you talkin' to? You don't even wanna hold your own child. My momma's practically raisin' him. You best look at yourself first 'fore you come in this room all high and mighty telling me what to do with my son!"

I retrieve Amos' food from the dresser. The plate with three slices of bacon, two biscuits, steaming grits and tea.

"Give me my meal and keep on doin' what you doin'—keepin' house and cookin'. That's all you good for and you can barely do that."

My grip on the tray tightens.

"You ain't nothin' but another hanger-on, an unwed momma expecting people to help you, but you can't even keep your legs closed."

"My . . . husband died in a car accident."

Amos sits up in his bed. His angular, hollowed

99

face sneers in a hypocritical rebuke. "Yeah sure he's dead. You had a husband like I had a million dollars."

And he laughs, this gravelly hideous sound coming from his mouth. I put the red-and-white tray back on the dresser. I take the pill on the saucer and hand him the tea with the lemon wedge, and as he reaches for it, I pour the tea on his lap. The hot cinnamon-colored liquid spreads, and as Amos goes to scream, I cover his mouth with my hand and whisper, "You're a weak little man who treats the people who love him like shit. So, what you're going to do is be nice to Will and thank Mama Sugar for all she's been doing for you these past few days or so help me, I'll let Lucky and his boys in this house at night so they can haul you off and teach you another lesson. Am I understood?"

Amos slowly nods. I take my hand from his mouth, poking my finger between his ribs, digging into his skin, the color of wilted leaves. "I didn't hear you."

"Yes Sara! Yes!" he hisses. A tear escapes his sunken eyes.

"Good." I saunter back to the dresser and hand him his food. "I'll be back to change your sheets in a couple of hours."

———≋———

"Give it back!" I yell. I reach for Louisa as Charlie Green laughs, holding my doll up, out of my grasp. Leaves of crimson with gold and leaves orange with dots so dark they look like burn marks flutter down onto the damp concrete.

"Boo-hoo! Little Sara want her dolly?"

Charlie lurches back, stumbling, almost dropping Louisa into a muddy puddle of water. Stick arms hold power as a girl in a blue dress pushes Charlie again. "She said give it back! Do it or I'ma beat you so bad, you gonna run back to your momma!"

"You ain't doin' nothin'. Best stay outta this 'fore I whip your ass! I'm bigger than y'all."

"And you stupid! That's why you in fifth grade instead of seventh," taunts a small girl in a red dress with a white collar.

Charlie's face drops for a moment, then creases in anger. Ugly and deep. He swings at me and the girl in the blue dress. The girl in the red dress with the white collar stands in front of us, taking the brunt of his hit. She stumbles but doesn't fall. The other girl kicks him. Charlie yells. I grab my doll. And we run. Fast. Down 63rd Street. Our dresses flitting against our knees. My legs feel like rubber bands. We stop, bracing ourselves in front of a black iron fence, letting a breeze cool us, slow the sweat trickling down our necks.

I clutch Louisa. "Y'all didn't have to help me."

"That's a nice way to say 'Thank you,' " retorts the girl in the blue dress.

"Well, we saw Charlie messin' with you and I don't like a bully," says the girl in the red dress with the white collar. "You don't need thanks for doin' the right thing. That's what my daddy says."

Red dress girl smiles. Blue dress girl doesn't. Charlie would've had Louisa if not for them. Momma would tell me to say thank you. If she was at home. In the bed with flower sheets that is gone, like she is gone. Momma would've told me to be polite. Introduce yourself. You were raised better.

I look at the girl in the red dress. "Did Charlie hurt you?"

"No. My cheek only stings a little. I get a whuppin', it hurts a lot more than that," she says.

"Thank you." I look at them. "I'm Sara."

The girl in the blue dress walks over to me. "I'm Violet. I seen you at church," she says. "My daddy's gonna be the pastor there someday."

The girl in the red dress nods in agreement. She looks down at my doll. "What's her name?"

"Louisa."

"That's a pretty name. I'm Naomi," she says.

I let Naomi hold Louisa. She cradles her like a baby.

We have air now. We can speak. We are free for a time in falling leaves and misting rain.

———≈———

As I close the door, my cheeks are arched upward. I'm smiling so hard it almost hurts. I don't know when the last time my face did that.

"Thank you, Sara," a voice to my left says.

"Jee-zus! You scared the mess outta me, Will!"

"I'm sorry." And then, he wraps his long, scrawny arms around my waist. I freeze. His hug is a kind thing, wanting to burrow its way to pieces of my broken and scattered heart. This boy can't learn to love me. He doesn't know me. And I can't love him. I don't have enough room. I'm not built for it. I carefully unwrap his arms from around me.

"Enough of this. Go downstairs and get something to eat."

Will grins, an almost cocky motion of his lips. "You like me, don't you, Sara?"

"Boy! Leave me be!"

He laughs and gallops down the stairs. In my hand is the pill. The one I didn't give to Amos. It's a small thing. The color of fresh milk. Its imprint embedded within my palm. If this pill is supposed to relieve pain, why not my pain? Why not *my* pain be relieved even for a moment?

It doesn't taste good or bad when I swallow it. There's only a chalky residue on my tongue. Shouldn't there be something? A floating away?

A freedom? A sense of being untethered to the regrets and the nightmares and the grief weighing me down, a thousand-pound invisible stone around my neck.

No. A chalky aftertaste and nothing. For now. Maybe there'll be something later. Something I can grab, savor.

"You sick, Sara-girl?" questions Mr. Vanellys from behind me, a hammer in his right hand, a box of nails in his left. "Didn't mean to scare you."

"You didn't."

"Okay 'cause I saw you jump a bit."

My nails dig further into the palm of my hand. "Oh, didn't notice. Strange . . ."

"So, you sick then?"

"Yes. I'm sick I suppose."

"A headache?"

A heartache really, this deep twisting from within, a spreading infection groping and clawing through muscle and bone and memory. "It's an all over pain, Mr. Vanellys."

"Yeah, well, when they invent something other than a pill for that, let me know." He chuckles low and sad. Dust particles float among the sunbeams from the only window in the long hallway.

"I'ma finish shoring up these floorboards since everybody's up," he says.

There's a slight shift of weight from my left to my right, but the floorboards are straight. And the dust is crystallizing, dazzling and sparkling. I should lay down for a bit.

"Sara-girl, I'ma need you to do something for me if you can."

"Yes sir?"

"I know Amos ain't easy." He rubs his head, his brow creasing deeply. "Lord Jesus, as his daddy I know my son ain't easy, but he ain't always been understood by me well as he could. Old age makes you see your time as a young man clearer. I was hard on him. And anyway, I wanted to make him tough, but Lennie coddled him and . . . well, what's done is done but I found out when people go through hard places, they don't need tough an' they don't need coddling. They need mercy."

I wonder if my face looks different. I flex my fingers again and check for any differences. My skin is still my skin. Mr. Vanellys' face is still his face, but the ceiling is lower than I remember.

"Mercy?" The word slowly tumbles from my lips. "Hard times don't seem to have made you mean or weak. Mama Sugar either. I mean she's kind." I see Mama Sugar in the kitchen rolling dough for biscuits as the sapphire horizon bleeds into crimson-apricot skies. "We all got hard times. Some of the things we go through are down-right, well, hellish, but you both are good."

Mr. Vanellys closes his eyes and lets out a deep breath. "You didn't always know us, Sara-girl, and good, well, good takes time for most people,

I reckon. And kindness that can damn near take a lifetime."

"Doesn't mean I need to feel sorry for Amos."

"I ain't saying feel sorry for Amos, Sara-girl," implores Mr. Vanellys. "I'm saying . . . mercy is in short supply. Giving a little of it, surely means you can find some yourself when you're in need of it."

I place my hand on the wall, something solid, so the world tilts less, so Mr. Vanellys' words can take root. "I'll try."

"All I ask." He touches my shoulder for a moment. "You sure you alright?"

"Mmm-hmm. Gotta help Mama Sugar finish in the kitchen."

Momma said, "Focus on what you can count. Collect the numbers of things. It gives your mind somewhere else to go."

Counting helps ground me. There are twenty-five steps from the third floor to the first, that's eight more steps than the back stairway in the kitchen. We have five boarders. Two of them are new. Breathe deep. Look down. There are only ten stairs left. Then seven. Then three.

The kitchen is much the same as I left it. Mama Sugar is finished grating the potatoes and places them in a towel she folds twice. I reach for the potato-filled towel, and she swats my hand away. "I'm good on help for now. Like I said, I'm fixin' you a plate."

A finger taps my shoulder and I turn around. Will lays a flower next to me on the counter then goes to the table. The flower is long-stemmed with small violet buds on both sides. Will sits back down at the table. He opens *The Weary Blues* and starts to read. *Georges* lies on his right.

"False blue indigo flower," Mama Sugar says. "Or blue false indigo or something like that. He used to give his momma, Constance, them flowers. She told me what they was. Kept them in a book."

There's a small empty cobalt-colored bottle on the open shelf on the back wall.

"Can I use this one?"

"Go on ahead."

I fill the blue bottle halfway with water and place the flower in it. I can't reject the boy or hurt his feelings. But I'm not Constance. I don't want to be a momma to my child, but I don't have a choice there. Will needs to learn because someone is decent to you, it isn't an invitation to love them. It's a chance to witness decency and move on with your life. I loved too easily. Especially when I was a child.

". . . and the princess who was oh so pretty and *smaarrrt,* told the mean ole king get back," says Buster, who bounces a squealing and giggling Lebanon on his knee. "And when he wouldn't leave, she bopped him on his big ole head, and it hurt so bad he ran away. And no one ever heard from that mean ole king ever again. And the princess . . . named Sara—" Buster looks over at me and grins "—took her son and they lived in their house on top of a gigantic mountain. And she made him pancakes anytime he wanted. The end."

Mama Sugar chuckles and applauds. "Good story, but your behind ain't gettin' pancakes this morning. You eatin' what I make."

Buster laughs. "Well, a man can dream and that's all my stories is anyway."

Mama Sugar turns around and pats the middle at the table and I sit. Buster takes Lebanon and puts him in the high chair next to my seat. Mama Sugar places a small bowl of grits in front of Lebanon. In front of me are grits and hash browns and bacon and biscuits.

I feed Lebanon first. He likes grits. Way more than mashed peas, but anything tastes better with enough butter and sugar. His little bowl almost empty, he keeps turning his head when I put the spoon to his mouth.

"Come on. You only have a bite or two left."

"Chile, he's done with them grits. Stop being so impatient with him. He can't say he full yet. He feed off you. You angry. He's angry. You happy. He's happy," counsels Mama Sugar.

I put his spoon down and wipe his mouth and grit-covered cheeks with a napkin as I nibble on my now-lukewarm bacon. Still crispy and salty. Still so damn good. Lebanon's arms reach for me. I lean back. And he whimpers. It's too early on a Saturday for this.

You don't even wanna hold your own child. I hear Amos' words.

Whimpers turn to short bursts of mewling cries, and I scoop Lebanon up from the high chair and set him on my lap and the crying stops. He reaches and tugs at the clean moss green collar of my dress. He tries to stand with his wobbly, chubby legs. He has teeth coming in. Two at the top. One at the bottom.

"See, when you patient and happy. He's patient and happy. Keep being happy like that, Sara-girl," says Mama Sugar.

It's odd to feel something resembling happiness looking at him. And he lays his head on my shoulder. Yes. He has my nose and lips. He dozes. Curly hair tickles my neck. He doesn't seem so heavy, at least not as heavy as he does other mornings.

"Yeee-p." Buster rears back in the wood chair, which dully creaks. "My stories make all the youngins calm and peaceful."

"Why don't you put some more food in your mouth, so I don't have to hear anything else coming out of it for a while," retorts Mama Sugar.

"Hmmphf." Buster shovels more hash browns

in his mouth and follows it up with a healthy bite of a biscuit. "Lennie Pie, you got any honey for these biscuits?"

Mama Sugar opens the cabinet above the stove and grabs the jar of honey, placing it in front of Buster. Friendships are strange evolving collections of laughter and fights and secrets, this rarified brew of humanity you choose to share with another person. And I want that again. To feel close to someone. To share with someone. The way I did in Chicago.

Lulled voices from the living room grow louder. A tall lanky man in a gray suit walks through the door of the kitchen, one of the new boarders. The professor from Atlanta. David-Something.

"Good morning, ladies," says David-Something as he unbuttons his jacket. "I'm telling you Howard University's first black president was a Morehouse graduate," he says over his shoulder. "Ask Larry. He'll tell you. It was Mordecai Wyatt Johnson."

"Fine, I'll ask Larry," says the voice from behind. "He can settle that bet, but you're wrong about the other thing. Morehouse was founded on a Tuesday."

"It was a Thursday," rebuts David.

"Tuesday. I'd bet two dozen of Ms. Lennie Mae's fluffy biscuits," the voice from the living room says. And this voice I know, a bright clear tenor. There's confidence in the answer. Jonas appears a few seconds after David-Something.

"Good morning." He smiles wide at me, Mama Sugar and Buster. "I'm schooling young Mr. Rainier here on Morehouse history."

Ah, that was it! David Rainier.

David pulls out a chair and sits next to Will. Jonas sits a chair away from me. Mama Sugar puts the last of the bacon, grits, hash browns and two biscuits on David's plate. He starts with the biscuits and takes a bite. In three bites it's gone. "Ms. Lennie, I might have to extend my trip a whole year for these," says David as he holds up the last biscuit on his plate and begins to devour it and the rest of the food.

Mama Sugar begins cleaning the dishes, scratching and scraping grease and crumbs and pieces of meat from the cast-iron skillet with care.

"You want me to grab the steel wool?"

"No Sara-girl. I don't want steel wool. That's the last thing you wanna use on cast iron," she says. "Remember, that'll take off all the seasonin' from other meals. What makes the food good is all the other meals you made before. Why don't you start on them plates and cups in a little bit?"

"He looks like you," says Jonas. "Handsome little man."

"Thanks," I say and stare, waiting. Waiting for him to break my gaze, for those twinkling eyes of his to lose their luster and dull. For his face to pucker and his full lips to turn downward in reproach.

Lebanon squirms in my lap. A little of his drool drips down my shoulder. I rise, laying him in the crib. A quick smile flashes across his sleeping face. Dr. Morgan told me once this was only a reflex, something babies do. It didn't mean they were happy or peaceful . . . or anything really. But maybe the boy is having a good dream. Maybe he's in the place Buster told him of. A pretty house high in the mountains, far from here. Maybe in his dream I am there with him. Maybe in his dreams I want to be.

I walk toward the sink. "Should start now with the dishes so people will have something to eat off of."

I run the water until it almost scalds me. That's how Mama Sugar likes it. The symphony of clanging silverware and plates from Buster and David, the gentle turning of pages by Will, fill my ears. The purple flower in the cobalt glass has perked up with water and the sunlight from the kitchen window.

Mama Sugar takes out a large ham hock from the refrigerator, then a large silver pot from the bottom cabinet. She grabs a two-pound bag of pinto beans from the pantry.

"Sara-girl, I meant to ask if you going to Revival. Week from today. Gonna be a good time in Jesus. We gonna have preachin' and food. Even some games for the children."

I close my eyes and breathe deep. "You asked me last week and the month prior and the month before that. You asked when I got here a little after last year's Revival. I'm . . . Church isn't . . . No ma'am. I'm not going."

"I know when and how much I asked you." Mama Sugar gingerly cleans her cast-iron skillet in the hot water with a little coarse salt and a clean tattered rag.

"Lebanon is too small to play games, and I don't have anyone to watch him." I gesture to the crib. "Revivals can run all night, especially with some of them preachers and however many offerings they wanna take up. Besides, you're the one who keeps telling me to get Lebanon on a schedule."

Mama Sugar takes the big silver pot and a spoon and bangs on it. Will, Jonas and David jump in their chairs. Then she walks over to the crib. I do too. Lebanon hasn't moved. His eyes still closed. His breathing still steady.

"Lebanon can sleep through Christ's Second Coming when he finally goes down. He needs to be under the good Lord's word. Train up a child."

"Proverbs 22:6. Heard that all my life," I say.

Jonas turns around in his chair and stares at me, his left eyebrow raised.

"Well, I didn't know you knew the scripture like that," says Mama Sugar.

Will huffs. "Granny, can I go out on the porch and read?"

"Go on," she says.

Will leaves the kitchen. I walk back to the sink, scrubbing the silverware harder, waiting to see my face on each spoon, fork and sharp knife.

"It ain't about Jesus. You spend all your time here at The Scarlet. Barely say 'Hi' to anyone. It'll do you and Lebbie good to get out. Come to church. It'll be good to meet the people you live 'round." Mama Sugar puts her hand on my shoulder. "And for them to meet you, Sara-girl."

Why do people believe you go to church to be around good people? I've rarely met good people in a place with tattered Bibles and unanswered prayers. Church is where you learn about the world in its worse forms. The pretty clothes and false smiles. The lingering fingers in the collection plates that bought my father's tailored suits and fine jewelry. Gossiping old ladies, their looks, making sure my dresses are below my knees enough for me to be saved or at least look the part. A place that was built for release and confession turned into a place for repression and secrets. And all the while our true lives remain hidden. We talk of God's goodness, of salvation, none of us really knowing or seeing either of them. Good people rarely are behind the walls of a church.

"I'm going to Revival," says Jonas. "Some mighty good food is going to be on those church grounds. I can promise you that much. Maybe go and stay for a little while."

"So, your charm and potato salad are supposed to convince me?"

Jonas clears his throat. "Obviously not . . . and I didn't say anything about potato salad. Though um . . . yeah I'm pretty sure that'll be there too."

"Besides your job, do I ask you to do much else for me, Sara-girl?"

"No ma'am."

Mama Sugar is pulling her card, the one all black women over a certain number of years seem to possess. This implicit understanding that the weight of them in your lives and all the sacrifices they made, not only on your behalf but on the behalf of others, outweigh *your* wants and desires. And you are not to refuse them when they ask you to do something *without* them verbally asking you to do anything. It's a deep abyssic stare. Maybe I'll get to use this card in another thirty years or so.

I shrug. "I'll think about it."

"Think about it?" Mama Sugar dries the now-clean cast-iron skillet with vigor.

"I like keeping to myself. It's less trouble that way." My mind races back to that night, in

Chicago, watching Saul as his blood slowly seeps from him and onto the floor.

"Sara-girl, ain't nobody or nothin' perfect, but nobody mean you harm there, baby. 'Sides, what's the worst that could happen at a church?"

"You'd be surprised. You'd be *very* surprised," I answer.

EIGHT

We're preparing for war, to feed an army. God's Army as Mama Sugar calls it. Birds fly outside the kitchen window, perching themselves on the empty clothesline, brightly singing their morning song. I lift my left leg, rotating my ankle. Sweat collects at my brow, my blue scarf catching most of it. I wipe the rest away with the back of my hand. Grabbing the two cake pans from the dish rack, I wonder if I heard Mama Sugar correctly. "Cream the butter and the sugar by hand for both cakes? Don't you have a standing mixer. It's faster."

"Gurl, it's broken. Tastes better anyway when you cook and bake by hand. You get that extra lovin'."

"Doesn't your church thing start in a few hours?"

"Yes, *Revival* is in a few hours, but as long as we there before noon, then we'll be fine."

"I'm still not set on coming. Who's going to mind The Scarlet if we're all gone today? Saturdays are busy."

Mama Sugar wipes her forehead and starts humming a song low and reverently. "Thank you, Laww-d." Her last note arches upward. Stirring the collards in three timed circles, she puts the lid back on top of the big silver pot. Lebanon pulls himself up in the crib, smiling and babbling some undiscernible language.

Poking my finger into the still-wrapped butter, it forms a small crater. I drop it in the bowl, then measure the sugar and stir. Mama Sugar's eyes watch, stalk, calculate to see if my technique measures to her standards.

"Why you so stiff? You seen me do this enough."

"You're staring at me so—"

"Chile, I ain't worried about you."

A protesting squeak from the back door and the uneven thump of foot and scrape of wood, Amos comes into the kitchen on crutches. "Good morning, Mama. Perfect day for the picnic. You workin' hard. Lookin' regal doing it too. Oooh! Yes ma'am, this kitchen smells like heaven right here!"

Amos totters over to my side. "Oh, uh, why don't I throw this out for you, Sara? That flower's lookin' mighty sad."

I lightly push his arm away. "It's fine. Thank you." The water in the blue glass is a cloudy amber, and some of the petals have fallen around it.

"Okay, okay. We'll, if y'all need me I'm gonna be around, you know." His gaze falls to the crutches. Amos kisses Mama Sugar on her cheek.

"You look good, son."

Amos hobbles to the front room. Amos looks good in her eyes because she needs him to. Because if he's anything else, if he's back to gambling and drinking, then how would she explain to herself that despite doing all she could, her son is still . . . broken? Something that came from you can't be made whole and despite doing everything you know to do; you may be the very reason he faltered in the first place. Who wants to live with that? So, you don't think about your faults. You don't think about his. You live in a space where everything can be fine if you convince yourself it is. And if anyone tries to show you otherwise, they are the enemy of the counterfeit peace you've built for yourself. And there is the adversary of progress, the inability to fix yourself or someone else.

"Perfect, Sara-girl. Couldn't have done a better job with that butter and sugar. You was a woman on a mission."

Mama Sugar bends down to the lower cabinet and reaches toward the back and brings out a clear bottle full of something with the label missing. She opens it and hands it to me.

Unscrewing the top, I put my nose to the bottle's opening. "Rum!"

"Shhhh! You announcin' it to the whole house!" Mama Sugar chuckles. "A special ingredient. Put that in last."

"How would church members feel if they knew

they were eating something with rum in it?"

"Gurl, the good Lord isn't sendin' no one to Hell for a little rum in a cake. But I don't wanna hear no one else's mouth so this here is our secret."

"Yes ma'am."

"Ahhh . . . seeing you smiling makes things even better. You and Amos making this old girl happy."

My cheek twitches. "Is anyone else helping with the food today?"

"We got six of the deacons barbecuing, and they always put they foot in that 'cue, except Deacon Bernard. He burns the meat sometimes. If it's him, we gotta keep an eye out. I'm bringin' my greens and the pineapple upside down cakes. Mavis bringin' her caramel cake and potato salad. And I know Dorothy Ann's gonna bring her pound cake, which don't nobody eat 'cause it's dry."

"What do you do with it?"

"Cora wraps it up and throws it away at her and Dr. Morgan's house. Everybody from the church bringin' somethin'. People need to feel they contributin'."

"So, we really don't have to make the cakes and the greens?"

"It was asked of me. I do what they ask of me at church."

"At church only?"

Mama Sugar opens the pot of greens again. "Well . . . I believe in what the Lord says about obedience—most of the time."

"There's a lot about obedience in the Bible and half the time people use it to keep you down. Make you do what they want, and it has nothing to do with God. That much I know."

"Well, I know I'd love to see you and Lebbie this afternoon. Tell people you the one made these cakes. Take some credit for all the hard work you do 'round here."

"You can take credit. You do more around The Scarlet than I do."

She hums a low brooding tune for a few moments and then sings, "Help me Lawd. Mmmm. Laww-d Jesus." With the dip of her tone on the last note, she places the lid back on the pot and looks at the stove. "This right burner done gone out. Shoot!" She lifts the pot but her left arm doesn't bear the weight. Some of the pot liquor spills onto the floor. I grab the pot and place it on the left burner and turn it on.

"An hour. Can you promise me we'll only be there an hour?"

Mama Sugar puts her hands on her hips. "I can promise that you gonna want to stay after you meet everyone."

"Well burnt meat and dry pound cake doesn't seem much of a reason to stay, but miracles happen."

"Including God deliverin' you from that smart mouth of yours."

The boy laughs. "What you laughin' at Lebbie? You laughin' at your momma and how she can't resist me?" Mama Sugar kisses Lebanon on his forehead. "We'll leave in about three hours. Be ready."

I turn my attention back to the cakes. "For church folk? Always."

"All God's children got one thing in common, my lovely girl, they ain't perfect." Momma smiles at me in the living room. "God's children can still make mistakes. Be thoughtless or lie. Do the wrong things. But God's children, flawed as we are, the true ones, we always try and do better. So if you struggle or you see someone struggling, seek understanding. You don't know the wars people fight on the inside. No one save the Lord knows about those inside battles." Then Momma grimaces for a moment, grabbing the back of the brown chair where Daddy sits and sometimes sleeps. She counts backward and breathes, then starts sweeping the wood floors of the apartment. Dust looks like sparkling stars falling to the ground.

Lebanon squirms on my lap. His arms reach for the front seat where Mama Sugar sits. His arms then reach for Cora, who I'm sure would hold him and play with him if she wasn't driving. Her smiling eyes search the back seat. Lebanon focuses on Gooch Park, a few minutes from The Scarlet. He's drawn to it like I was when I first came to Memphis. I'd walk the paths, heavy with him, to the east side of the long green field where the trees are tall and the breeze was best. It was there when he forced himself into this world; when all I wanted was a walk, to forget for a moment he existed. I struggled back to the house where I felt my body shift in the most painful ways I could imagine, where Mama Sugar put a cool rag on my forehead. And Dr. Morgan delivered Lebanon, placing him on my chest. And I wished to disappear. I wished to feel nothing for the baby in my arms, but my heart still grew in a way I didn't believe possible. And I hated myself, for loving him despite how he came to be in this world, and how I had, for better or worse, came to be a mother in it.

Cora carries us in the foam green Chevy Bel Air, cruising from Hubert Avenue to McLean Boulevard, then to Jackson Avenue. She stops near Hernando Street and Pontotoc Avenue, half a block from the sand-colored limestone of a church. The bell tower's height seems as big as a building in Chicago. The middle structure is almost swallowed by a white framed, stained-glass window with ethereal shades of crimson, cerulean and emerald. There is a girth to the building, a heavy expanse of mortar and stone and lumber. And it is . . . magnificent and abiding and timeless, almost as if nothing could destroy it. I believed when I was young, when I walked past my church's doors, nothing could hurt me, but that was a silly, childish notion, to let a building, a church, make me feel safe. This place dredges up memories from my deep parts, my dark parts.

And all I see is Calvary Hope Christian Church, a place that saw the best and worst of who I was, the best and worst of everyone that walked through its doors. If I close my eyes, I hear me and Violet and Naomi. Our laughter. Our fights. Our secrets. If I ponder too long, I see my father behind the pulpit. In my room at night. On the office floor. His blood flowing. A piece of glass. A yellow blanket.

Cora takes Lebanon from my arms with no protest from him. Little traitor. Mama Sugar grabs the pineapple upside down cakes. I lift the still-warm pot of collards nestled between blankets on the car floor.

"Sara-girl, you okay? You want me to take them greens?"

"I'm fine. This church . . . it reminds me of home."

Mama Sugar smiles. "That's nice."

"You said an hour, right? I only need to be here for an hour?"

Her eyes narrow, and the bright arc of her mouth slowly turns down. "Sweetheart, if you feelin' that bad about being here, I'll ask Cora to drive you back. We less than fifteen minutes from home."

I straighten my back and steady my hands as best as I can. "I'm okay. I'll help."

The large field across the street hosts swarms of strangers with folding tables laden with Southern cooking. Children laugh and zip through the loose crowds of people.

"Sister Lennie! Come on over here! We got your place ready," shouts a woman from across the street.

We cross to the field. I set the greens down on the table where the woman stands. Children run past us, squealing laughter trailing them.

"I win!" yells one of them, a girl I recognize in a sunflower yellow dress. She bends down, wheezing, but a triumphant smile adorns her face.

"Diii-ane. Those not even the rules," whines a boy next to her.

"Girl! You betta not get that dress dirty! Your daddy would lose his mind. Come over here now!" orders a tall curvy woman in a periwinkle skirt and blazing white blouse. "You gotta stay nice 'fore we go over to your appointment."

"My game Abraham. My rules." Diane saunters off in her yellow dress, her face less full and more angular. Her once long hair now bundled in only a simple braid at the top of her head. Abraham crosses his arms and kicks the ground and walks in the opposite direction.

Mama Sugar turns away from the children playing. Ms. Mavis brings her two caramel cakes and sets them down next to Mama Sugar's and touches her shoulder. Mama Sugar tenses for a moment, then places the pineapple upside down cakes with the other cakes, pies and cookies. Ms. Mavis playfully shoves her aside.

"We'll see whose cakes are gone first, Lennie Mae. I had your girl help me with that frosting." They laugh.

"Yeah, Sara-girl. That's my secret weapon there."

"You Lennie Mae's girl over at The Scarlet Poplar?" asks the woman who yelled at us across the street.

I nod and smile.

She looks me up and down in a flowered dress that goes past her knees. "I'm Sister Ella. So you from around here? What school did you go to? 'Cause you look familiar. Didn't you go to school with my son Thaddeus over at Douglass? What year did you graduate? Actually, you look younger than Thaddeus. Come to think of it, you probably was with my baby girl Bernice. She graduated in '59."

Sister Ella narrows her eyes and folds her arms, trying to place me, my face, into some imaginary world where we met or where I'd have wanted to meet her. "You know what? You probably know my little cousin Jerome in Binghampton. Or it could be I seen you with my older sister Rita in

Whitehaven. I swore I saw you with her this past Wednesday. Or maybe . . . Ooop!"

Mama Sugar pokes Sister Ella in her side. "You over here givin' Sara-girl a hard time?"

"No, Lennie Mae. Getting to know her." Sister Ella stares, expecting me to answer her questions as if she hadn't asked me five different things in the span of five seconds, and simultaneously offered up half of her family tree. "So, what about it?"

"No ma'am, I don't think I know the people you mentioned."

"Oh no, she's not from around here with that diction. Up North, am I right?" says a woman to my left.

"Yes ma'am."

"From where? Detroit?"

"Chicago."

"I'm Sister Henrietta," she introduces herself. She links her arm in mine and walks. And though I'm not eager to follow, I do so anyway. What choice do I have? She's an elder.

"You met Ella. You live with Lennie Mae," she chuckles and points to her left. "Then that's Brother Orlando."

Brother Orlando gives a polite nod but concentrates on the meat slowly browning on the black grill in front of him.

"Next to Brother Orlando is Minister Blue."

I play with the top button of my sleeveless

127

green dress that falls at my knees. "Mr. Malone. He owns the hardware store on Hollywood Street. I go there with Mr. Vanellys sometimes."

Sister Henrietta points clockwise. "Then next to them is Deacon Bernard."

The one Mama Sugar says burns the meat.

"Then we got Sister Nanette and Sister Carolyn, and sitting in the blue chair is Elder Dorothy Ann."

She bakes the dry pound cake Cora throws away.

These introductions aren't overwhelming. Memorizing and categorizing people in church isn't hard when you've had to do it all your life. The polite faces and curious eyes. The listening ears and ready mouths are as much the foundation of us, of black churches, as the brick and concrete holding together the temples in which they worship. In some way I'm comforted by this lack of change; that north or south, east or west, older nosy people are always going to be around.

No matter what.

"So, you're from Chicago?" asks Sister Carolyn. Amber-hued skin and curly brown hair frame her angular cheeks.

I look down at her and nod.

"Yeah lotta people moved up there. Detroit and Harlem, too," says Sister Henrietta.

"Not everyone wanna stay here. Plus that yellow fever's what really started us goin' up North," offers Sister Ella.

"Well, Henrietta not only that. Disease a reason to go. But people be a disease all they own," says Sister Carolyn.

"You right about it," agrees Sister Henrietta.

Mama Sugar mentioned it once. In passing. Yellow fever. An epidemic. Mama Sugar said there were mass graves around the city where the dead are buried, but no one can remember where all of them are. The people that could afford to leave fled, and those who couldn't, the black and the poor, stayed. And black people did what we always did, what we're built to do, survive. We helped others survive, too. Because in the very fabric of who we are, we can't shed this destructive need to put others before ourselves. Yet somehow despite our reckless and kind humanity, we still pull ourselves up and over whatever seeks to destroy us.

"Oh! I got family in Chicago," says Sister Nanette. "My big brother Harris moved up there fifteen years ago, but we don't see him hardly. You know Harris? Harris Johnson? He lives up in . . . I wanna say Bronzetown? Bronze City? Bronze—"

"Ville. Bronzeville."

"That's it! So, you live in Bronzeville?"

"No ma'am."

Sister Nanette's deep brown eyes probe, almost trying to will an answer from me.

"I appreciate Mama Sugar inviting me to

Second Presbyterian. You have a lovely church."

"Second . . . No, no, no. This is Clayborn Temple."

"Oh. Because the front said—"

"It hasn't been Second Presbyterian in many years. Since '48 or '49," says Sister Carolyn.

"Oh." Biting my bottom lip, I scan for Lebanon. Cora has him, angled on her hip as if he's hers. She talks to Lawrence, who smiles down at her, and, for a second, they are picture perfect. For a moment, my child is not my child and I get to admire a cute family at a church function. Cora meets my gaze and glides my way with Dr. Morgan and *my* Lebanon.

"Getting acquainted I see," Cora says. Lebanon's whole fist goes into his mouth, drool slowly flowing down his arm.

"Mmm-hmm." I reach over and take Lebanon. I wait for a whimper but nothing. He takes his fist from his mouth and looks up and smiles. There's another tooth coming in.

A firm polite line crosses Cora's mouth. "We're preparing for grace in a bit so if you're not finished setting up, this might be the perfect time to tie up those odds and ends."

"Oh, we're about done here," says Mama Sugar. "I know 'cause look who showed up just in time to *not* help."

On the east side of the lot, Buster, Elvin and Mr. Vanellys walk past the tables. Eyes coveting every morsel of smothered chicken, peach cobbler and corn bread. Amos straggles behind with Will at his side. Maybe I should get Will. Have him with me. But he's smiling. Has a book in his hand. He'll be fine. Why do I even care?

Elvin rubs his hands together. "Been waiting for this all week!" He reaches for a plate, and Sister Henrietta slaps his hand away.

"Elvin Enoch Woodrow Sanders, you know we ain't said grace yet and I raised you better!"

"She invoked every single one of your names. You best listen. They can have your homegoing right here, *Woodrow*. We got at least six deacons, a pastor and enough food for your repast," says Buster. He laughs, wiping tears from the edges of his eyes.

Elvin sheepishly looks over at Sister Henrietta. "I was only looking at the food. Wasn't gonna do nothin' yet." There's a small whine to his voice, one I imagine everyone has talking to their mom and one that doesn't go away no matter how old you are because you are their child. Maybe it comes from a longing, a knowledge you will never be able to outgrow a parent's authority. Or maybe I'm assuming because that's what I want to think since Momma left me so soon. My longing for her, my anger at her leaving me alone in this desolate world, visits me at unexpected times. But grief and loss don't go by a calendar, and they really don't give a damn about your sanity or your schedule.

"I'm starvin'. They got us runnin' detours with the trucks 'cause of that hospital up the road they're building," complains Elvin.

"St. Jude?" asks Dr. Morgan. "It's a children's hospital. One specifically for treating cancer. Supposedly they're to treat everyone regardless of race."

"I'll believe that when I see it," says Sister Carolyn. "If I had a dollar for every time a white person broke a promise, I'd be 'bout as rich as Robert Church ever was."

"St. Jude, yeah, that's the name," says Elvin. "Supposed to be built by next year, but we'll see. I can't keep doing all these routes though. And you know everything breaks down all the time. Spent at least an hour fixing my truck and still had to finish my shift. Ask me if they gave me overtime so I can tell you no."

Sister Henrietta rearranges the dessert table, placing the two- and three-layer cakes behind the pies and cobblers. "Well, we gonna thank the good Lord for what we have. And He'll provide whatever else we need. And I betta not catch you around this food again until it's time. Understood? I don't want no excuses from you. Do right like I taught you."

"Yes ma'am," replies Elvin.

Mama Sugar leans over. "If you wanna still go home you can, but it's gonna be plenty empty."

"You say that like it's a bad thing." Lebanon squirms in my arms. "Besides, he needs a nap."

"No, he needs to let some of that energy loose."

"He can do that back at the house. Looks like you have everything set up fine. See, it didn't even take an hour."

"Aww come on Sara," coaxes Buster. "You stay 'round long enough you'll see Elvin get scolded by Sister Henrietta again. I can daggone near guarantee that."

"You mean Woodrow," says Mr. Vanellys. He chuckles.

Elvin folds his arms. "Woodrow is a respectable name and this heathen—" he points to Buster "—can't talk about nobody's name. None of us even know what his real name is."

"I know," says Mama Sugar.

"So do I," agrees Mr. Vanellys.

There was a piece of mail three months ago from the Veteran's Office. One for Mr. Vanellys and the other envelope Buster said was his. It had his full name on it.

I laugh and so does the boy. It's some wonderful game to him too. "Even I know Buster's name."

Elvin frowns, the lines on his forehead creasing ever deeper. "To Hell with all of y'all!" he says, storming off to the north side of the field.

Sister Henrietta, only a few feet behind him, whips her head around and yells, "Elvin!"

The roar of laughter is immediate. And it is

hearty and free of any real worry or fear. Another precious piece of time where I consider there might be something in this life called joy; there might be a world in which I don't wait for disaster.

"You snort when you laugh," a voice says from behind.

Jonas stands near a tree, the trunk of it swallowing his shadow.

"Your tie is crooked and your pants are too short. I can see your socks."

Jonas playfully clutches his chest. "You're vicious, Ms. King. Absolutely vicious."

"I may be vicious, but I don't snort when I laugh. My laugh is . . . regal."

"Like your last name."

"Huh, now you want to compliment me?" Lebanon begins squirming again. There is a small bench near the tree where Jonas stands and I don't want to sit next to him, but I have to entertain the boy or else he'll start crying. It's a lesser evil to sit by Jonas than have Lebanon cry. Jonas can make of it what he wants. I can't control what he gleans from my actions.

A silver-and-black 35 mm camera hangs around his neck, something like Thomas had back home. He'd take pictures of me and Violet and Naomi. The last picture Thomas ever took of us was in front of Calvary Hope. My father was still alive. I was pregnant with Lebanon in that picture.

"You're a teacher *and* a photographer?"

"I am a man of many talents." Jonas turns toward me, flashing a cocky grin. He fidgets with a dial on the left side of his camera. "I need to get back on your good side or whatever side of you that won't cut my throat with your words."

He angles the camera in my direction. "I wanna take your picture."

"Why?"

"Posterity. Nice sunny day. Don't you want a picture of you and Little Man?"

"It's Lebanon. And I guess I can't stop you."

He places the camera to his eye, the lens focusing on me, on Lebanon. What does he see on the other side of the lens? Why does he want to do this at all? Why does he want to remember me?

Whir-click.

A tall older man, around Mr. Vanellys' and Mama Sugar's age, stands about twenty feet away. He fans himself with his straw hat. "All heads down and eyes closed . . ." A hush falls over the crowd of chattering bodies. Heads bow one by one. Jonas lowers his head. I stare at Lebanon. Hold him as his small, unsteady feet plant themselves on my knees.

"Dear Lord, we come to you. Humbly as we know how . . ."

Daddy would begin prayers like this. We come to God humbly. Bended knee and body bowed. And people closed their eyes. Some clasped their hands together, skin stretching, tented knuckles. Beads of salty water on their brows. I did this too. Prayed when I believed it was a thing that produced results. When I believed the act translated into some unseen protection, resulted in some intangible love from a man in the sky; from someone who was supposed to love me but broke me in a way no one told me existed. And when I found out this kind of brokenness was real, what kind of prayer or sacrifice, what tears or loathing, what of myself could I offer?

". . . in the matchless name of Jesus, we pray. Everybody say . . ."

"Amen!" rings out from the crowd of bodies in the lot across the street from the church that reminds me of my church in Chicago. I don't want to call it home, but I have no other name. Although "home" belies an innocence and peace Chicago no longer holds for me. It is where I come from. I call it what I call it.

It is what it is.

"Where's your friend? The Morehouse man."

Jonas aims the camera on Brother Orlando near the barbecue grill. He takes a picture. "David left this morning. He was right about the day Morehouse was founded though. It was a Thursday."

He focuses the camera on Mama Sugar and Sister Ella and exhales long and slow.

Whir-click.

I stretch my eyes. "Be still my little heart! The great Jonas Coulter *doesn't* know everything?"

Jonas turns his camera toward the church. *Whir-click.* "Okay, okay. I was wrong, but that doesn't happen often." He puts the camera down and sits on the bench next to me.

"Seriously doubt it."

Lebanon's body twists from me to Jonas. Both of their faces plastered with big smiles, though Lebanon's has a considerable amount of more drool.

"May I?"

I hold on to Lebanon. I like Jonas and I'm loath to admit this, but liking someone doesn't mean you trust them.

"Little Man, I believe your momma wants to hold on to you for a little bit so why don't I sing a little song?

"Standing at a table is a cute young lady
And in her pretty arms is a chubby little
  baby
I might make her laugh but she say she
  don't snort
She'll say my tie's too crooked and my
  pants too short
But I'ma move on and let Ms. King have
  her say
'Cause Lord knows that's better than
  getting in her way."

Jonas leans back, allowing the tree to brace him. "See, you're laughing."

"It's a chuckle. Not a laugh. There's an important difference." I sit the baby back down on my lap and turn to Jonas. "Your tie *is* crooked. I wasn't saying that to be mean."

"Yes, you were." Jonas places his camera next to him and straightens his tie. "You got bite, Sara. You got a lot of bite, but there's some soft there."

There isn't any soft anywhere, but if it helps Jonas to think better of me, I can't control that either. My eyes scan to the left. Will is talking to Amos, who stuffs food in his mouth, teetering on his crutches. "I hope you're not teaching William *your* poetry."

"Ha! No. Only the writers that have actual talent. Dumas. Hughes. Hurston. Baldwin. Brooks. Wright. As many black writers as I can get the children to read." Jonas flexes his neck from side to side. "I need them to see we're masters of the written word too. I need them to be well-rounded. Ready for a world that will challenge their intellect, body and spirit at every turn because of the skin they were born into. And I need to, in my way, prepare them for that. Shaping a mind is as revolutionary as you can get."

"They're not soldiers, Jonas. They're children."

"Didn't you tell me life doesn't coddle kids like Will? That he better get used to how hard life is now?"

I wince. "I did, but I . . . Well, is that why you spend time with Will? To prepare him?"

"With Will it's more than that. He has a yearning, a passion for knowledge. He's got the mind for it, the energy, but it needs to be directed in a positive way. Like me when I was younger. If some of my teachers didn't take the time with me then, I wouldn't be the person next to you now."

"The teacher, the photographer or the bad poet?"

Jonas' smile crinkles the skin around his midnight-colored eyes. "All of them."

"So, you think he has a good mind?"

"There's a book I love, and the author says by truly educating you inspire people to live better lives, to start with life as it comes to them and make it better."

Cocking my head, I reply, "Carter G. Woodson. *The Mis-Education of the Negro.*"

Jonas again fidgets with the dials of his camera but doesn't take a picture.

"My mom read it. After she died, I took the book and read it myself. My mom's writing was in the margins of some of the pages." There's a lump in my throat. I swallow it, stuffing the memories of my life back into a dark space, a space where if I don't look often, I won't long for.

"Reading that book made me want to become

a teacher." He gazes out into the field. A line of children runs past. Laughing. "To quote someone more contemporary though, Medgar Evers said education was created to keep us down, or uh . . . subservient I think is the term he used. And I can't be part of that system. I won't. I'm gonna do my best to teach them. Give them what I didn't always get in a classroom."

"And what's that, Mr. Coulter?"

"Hope, Ms. King. Hope."

Lebanon begins to whimper. Jonas looks down at Lebanon and reaches out his hand, and the baby takes his finger, calming down the slightest bit.

"I should probably get him home."

"I can drive you back to The Scarlet if you want," offers Jonas, his eyes never leaving Lebanon's face.

"No!" a voice shouts. I shield my eyes from the sun, and in the distance Will grabs for his book as Amos rips the pages out of it, yelling something, something I can't hear. Something cruel, no doubt, that he can't take back. Amos throws the book to the ground. Will picks it back up, running from his father. Ripped pages land on the grass and scatter across the field.

I don't remember how I make it to him, but I know Mama Sugar is holding Lebanon when I push Amos to the ground. People are staring at me. I don't care. If he wants to be mean to someone, he can be mean to me. And I'll give him every damn thing I got. I'll give him every bit of mean and cruel right back!

"Someone go get my grandbaby!" yells Mama Sugar.

"We'll find him, Lennie Mae. Will couldn't have gone far," consoles Mr. Vanellys. He, Buster and Elvin fan out across Hernando Street. Jonas passes me and helps Amos off the ground. He's lucky I only pushed him. I wanted to punch him, but we are on church grounds.

"Look, my temper got the best of me. I—I didn't mean it," says Amos.

"You never mean it until somethin' goes wrong," says Mama Sugar. "All you do is mess up and say you sorry. And it don't never set things right! I'm so . . . tired of you."

"I'll go down Pontotoc Avenue. Maybe Will went that way," says Jonas.

I put my arms around Mama Sugar. "Will didn't get that far. He'll be back soon." Lebanon reaches for me, though I let him stay in Mama Sugar's arms. I stroke his hair. "Sons always return to their mothers. It's the natural order of things."

Mama Sugar turns her head, staring at Amos' slumped figure sulking off, finally bracing himself against a maple tree. She breathes deeply. "And God help us, we're gonna love 'em. No matter what."

The church bell tolls six times, clanging an unwanted hymn—about three hours have passed, with no sign of Will. Sister Henrietta holds Mama Sugar's hand.

Sister Ella sits on Mama Sugar's other side. "Thaddeus called himself running away once. Chile, he was under the porch the whole time. I was so mad I wanted to whup his behind, but all I did was hug him. That's what you gonna be doing by night's end with Will. Certain of that."

Sister Carolyn stands at the west end of the lot. She turns her head up and down the street every few minutes. Arms folded. Buster, Elvin and Mr. Vanellys return at last. Jonas approaches from the east. All of them with grim-set mouths and no William. Mama Sugar clutches Lebanon closer to her as he dozes.

Amos still rests against the maple tree. His eyes do not search for his son. He does not tell Mama Sugar it's going to be okay. He doesn't hobble on his crutches to look for Will. My feet sink deep into the grass as I make my way to Amos. I lean over him, my left hand digging into the bark. "You better pray to God we find him or there's gonna be no one to keep me from you. No one."

NINE

My fingers grip the inside car handle. They are numb. The bright cherry-hued leather seat sticks to my skin. Jonas and I roam down Eldridge Avenue in his car. Jonas makes a quick right on North Trezevant Street. We head back up toward Hunter Avenue and we're back on North Hollywood Street. No skinny boy holding a torn book walks these blocks.

Whitaker's Grocery, a two-story, wine-colored brick building, sits on the corner less than a block from the lone traffic light swinging above us. Red. No other cars on the road but Jonas still sits. Above the store, the glow from apartment windows casts anemic shadows below.

"There's no one here. We can go," I say.

"I'd rather wait."

"You're that worried about a ticket?"

The light turns green. Jonas' car doesn't move.

My thighs again stick to the leather. I shift in the seat. "Jee-zus! Can we go?"

"Does it look like I give a damn about a light, Sara?" Jonas doesn't raise his voice. He turns toward me, his eyes looking past me out toward the gas station on Chelsea Avenue. "It's a four-way intersection. It's a better vantage point to see Will from far away."

The light turns yellow and then red again. Jonas finally eases off the brake and slowly drives past the empty buildings. Wide panes of glass and hearty brick temporarily abandoned to the night. Barren lanes where black commerce thrives during daylight hours.

I should've kept Will with me or had him stick close to Mama Sugar. Made an excuse to Amos I needed his help with the food. Said the pot of greens was too heavy for me to carry. Said I needed someone to watch the baby. Anything, *anything*. But I left him with his father. That was a mistake. My mistake. Will isn't my child, but don't all children need some kind of protection? Another set of eyes to watch for them; or love them or defend them? If only there were these things for me, where would I be? If I tried harder to watch out for Will, he'd likely be back at The Scarlet. But Will is somewhere in the night. And it could swallow him, disappear him like it disappears so many of us. Would we find him safe? Or hurt?

Or dead? We could find Will dead.

Tell Amos to get me my money . . . I can be real mean an' nasty. Don't make me do that. I don't wanna if I don't have to.

Lennox could have Will. Could've scooped him up. Taken him somewhere. Would it even matter to him Will is the same age as his daughter Diane, learns in the same school, shares the same teachers? Money brings out the worst. The need for it, for the power it commands, creates a hole deep enough nothing can fill it and there's nothing you wouldn't do to keep what you have. Hurt a man. Kill a boy. That's a pittance to some. All for dyed green paper with pictures of dead white men.

Or maybe Will's greatest threat isn't Lennox Black. Maybe it is what exists beyond Lennox. Something Lucky's money and nice suits and sly grin and brutal thugs can't even protect him from.

We are clustered in these blocks, but we don't freely stroll even within these boundaries because we know others are not bound by blocks or laws or decency. And they can come and take what they see fit, for sport, for destruction. Will isn't much younger than Emmett.

What is a whistle? What is a walk down a lonely road? By our very existence we are guilty of everything and nothing. By our strength, we are incapable of living in peace though we seek any means to obtain it. What is a black boy's life? What is a black girl's life? What value does it have in Memphis or Chicago or New York or anywhere else? What value did Will's life have to me until his absence forced me to measure any kind of grudging affection I held back. And now here I am, without Will and his blue-purple flowers and big smile.

"We'll find him," says Jonas as if reading my mind. His gaze never leaves the borders of his windshield.

"I shouldn't have been talking to you or let you take pictures of us."

"Sara—" Jonas lets out a long breath "—talking to me or posing for a picture didn't do you any harm. And what happened isn't your fault. It isn't mine either." He reaches for my hand. I cross my arms.

"Being angry at me isn't gonna bring Will back any sooner. So, work with me."

I keep my arms folded across my chest and stare out the window.

"Will was angry. He ran. I did that too," says Jonas. "Sometimes you don't have another weapon in your arsenal. Sometimes running is the only way to keep you safe, keep you . . . sane."

"What in God's name would you have to run from?"

"There are lots of reasons to run, Sara."

North Hollywood Street gives way to Golden Avenue. The tires of Jonas' car form small cyclones of cinnamon-colored dust swirling and lightly coating the windows and hood. "My reasons for running aren't different from others. My dad died when I was young. Momma married again. And me and him . . . we didn't get along."

"My father didn't remarry when my momma

died. I wish he did," I offer. I wish a lot of things but wishing does nothing. A shard of glass and a friend, however, can work wonders.

Jonas flexes his neck from side to side. Deep and inky black, the sky offers no solace. No moon. No stars. Only the milky glow of dual headlights provides a dull beacon of what lies ahead.

"We'd fight and my mom . . . she didn't step in. Ever. He'd probably beat her too if she'd tried. But after a fight, she'd see to me. Cook my favorite meal or give me a penny she could barely afford. Then clean me up and send me off to school. And soon as I could, I left. Haven't been back. I sent letters though. To Momma. She passed a couple of years ago. Her name was Lillian. She always meant well, tried to do right by me as best as she could."

He chokes out the words like he's trying to expel a poison; one I've tasted. "My point being I guess sometimes kids are pushed to a limit and they leave, but Will won't go too far. He has Ms. Lennie Mae and Mr. Vanellys and me and you."

Jonas glances over at me. His smile the only brightness in the car. I return it for the briefest moment and then return my gaze outside.

Amos tore the pages out of Will's book and Will ran away. I didn't run after him right away. I should've but I sat there. Frozen for a moment. And when I ran, though I moved as quickly as I could, it was to hurt Amos. And that decision, my temper, could cost Will dearly.

To care for someone means when I fail them, it devours me. Infects every memory. Leaves a deep, pulsing longing I cannot sever myself from. This. *This.* This is why I loathe love. The return of love. Or the withholding of it. Love in any shape leaves me hollowed out. Desolate. Love is better left to the undamaged. Love means someone else can control, manipulate the very fabric of who I am, and then render me powerless.

And I need my power.

"Would Will hide at the school?"

"Possibly," Jonas replies. "Actually, very likely." He accelerates the Impala. Pebbles ping off the low-riding car's wide chrome fender.

Hyde Park Elementary School sits dismal and dark, deplete of childish energy. Crisp and bleak the American flag flaps above us, a reflection of our futile efforts and the dwindling hours.

"One of the back windows is always loose. He could've opened it. Shimmied in." Jonas digs in his pocket, retrieving a set of keys, and opens the door. He looks back.

"I'll stay here in case he comes from the front."

Jonas nods, entering the unlit building.

A black canvas of sky enshrines my view and I walk. No clear direction. No purpose other than to find Will. Get him back to Mama Sugar. Banish this constant unwanted ache inside me.

God, you're likely not there, but I'm covering my bases. If you cared about a little black boy, which I don't think you do, but if you're feeling merciful, bring Will back. You haven't done much for me. I don't know what you do for any of us, but let me find him.

"He's not here." Jonas returns a few minutes later and locks the door behind him. He jogs back to the car and turns it on.

Yep, that's what I thought, God.

Alabaster light bathes the lawn. Small wild-flowers poke up from emerald green grass. Near my feet, a blue-violet flower bends in the soft breeze.

False blue indigo flower . . . Or blue false indigo or something like that. He used to give his momma . . . them flowers . . . Kept them in a book.

"You didn't need to slam the car door." Jonas' brow furrows. Lines creasing his normally smooth skin.

"I don't care about the damn car door. Get me back to The Scarlet. I have to ask Mama Sugar something."

Pulling up to the white house with crimson trim, I pass people walking in and out of the door. Flashlights are clutched in hands. Buster comes outside on the porch, an uncharacteristic grimace on his face.

Inside Amos sits on the dull yellow couch, picking at his nails, never raising his head to acknowledge us. Lebanon sleeps in Mama Sugar's arms. Mr. Vanellys walks through the back door and also stands in front of Mama Sugar. She looks up, eyes wide, and then her lip trembles when she sees Will is not with us. She rocks Lebanon back and forth. Breathes deep. "He's gonna be somewhere. He didn't vanish off this earth. My Will is somewhere."

I bend down. "I got an idea, and it's thin but it keeps running through my head. Where was Will's momma buried?"

Mama Sugar leans forward. "We buried Constance at Mount Carmel up on Ellison and Bellvue. Her grave's under a tree. A crepe myrtle."

Leaving behind the oppressive warmth of The Scarlet Poplar, Jonas and I again race to another place, hoping this time, *this time,* we'll find Will. He can ask me as many questions as he wants. He can tell me about all the books he reads. He can even hug me. I need Will to be okay.

"How far is it? The cemetery."

"Not far. Not in this car," answers Jonas as he turns on the radio.

"For the second day in a row, the Soviet Union has conducted nuclear tests . . . President Kennedy is still hopeful a diplomatic resolution can be reached—"

150

Jonas turns to another station. A song about raindrops, of longing and love and loss, fills the car. Strings of violins and guitars elevate Dee Clark's gossamer falsetto as it pierces the silence. Jonas mouths the words.

Another song comes on the radio, and another one after that as the car winds down a dirt path past the gates of Mount Carmel Cemetery. Light reaches only a few feet in front of us and the lower halves of oak and maple trees.

"You go east. I'll head west. If one of us finds Will, come back to the car and wait for the other."

Jonas nods. "Meet back here after a half an hour."

I walk westward, over my shoulder I shout, "Look for a crepe myrtle tree. There can't be too many of them here."

Dove gray headstones jut from the earth, some freshly etched, some weathered, some crumbling, some straight, others crooked. Rows of our lives, the joys and sorrows, the victories and failures, all condensed to a few words on a monument that says mother or father, son or daughter, sister or brother.

How can we fit all we are onto something so small?

Winding branches bow and creak against soft winds. Past a grove of maple trees is a crepe myrtle beckoning me. Graves flank my sides as I inch closer, and there is a sculpture near the middle headstone, crumpled and small, sleeping. Without moonlight or stars, it's difficult to make out much and cemeteries are funny places, places where your imagination is more likely to tease you.

A trunk with mottled bark supports the arching tree, and the sculpture fixed next to the middle headstone is wearing gym shoes.

He's warm and breathing, dirt on his cheek, and he's snoring. Loudly. A tattered book next to his body. I shake him so hard he bolts up and scoots away from me.

I grab Will's shoulders. "Do you know . . . Why didn't you . . . We've been . . ." I try to choke out words or sentences. His eyes grow wide as he shrinks from me. And I want to hit him. Hard. I want him to feel what he's made me feel these past few hours, but all I can do is look at his face; the face that smiles bright, the eyes always reading, the arms that embrace me when I defend him. I don't hit Will. I hug him.

"Sara . . . Sara . . . can't breathe."

"Do you have any idea what we all went through? How the hell did you even get here? You walked all those miles?"

Will takes a deep breath. "After I ran, I started making my way here. I needed to talk to her. Sometimes I come here if it gets bad. Mr. Blue saw me walking and gave me a ride. He was heading out of town to visit his sister in New

York. It's her birthday. I told him Granddad was gonna come get me."

"You lied."

"I didn't know what else to do. I'm tired of trying with him, Sara. If she was here, he'd be better." Will looks over at his mother's gravestone. "I don't even remember how she looked, but I remember how her skin was the same color as mine. We had the same nose too. And when she hugged me, it'd be so hard like she wasn't ever trying to let me go. Like you just did."

Will's bottom lip quakes and a tear runs down his cheek. He quickly wipes it away. Taking his face in my hands, I say, "Sometimes we want people to be able to love us a certain way and they can't. But it doesn't mean something's wrong with you, okay? You're still a good boy, and you're smart and you had so many people worried about you."

"Even you?" asks Will, a quivering grin on his lips.

Patchy green grass scratches my skin. Pebbles of rock-hard dirt dig into my knees, but I could be standing in hellfire right now and still be relieved I have Will in my arms. "I haven't been that scared in a long, long time. You can't do that again. If it gets bad, you can come to me. I'll protect you, okay?"

The soft crunch of grass under shoes greets our

ears. "You owe me some gas money, William. But I'll settle for some extra book reports."

Will picks up the torn book and hands it to Jonas. "I'm sorry."

"It's okay. It's only a book. Replaceable. You, however, are not." Jonas walks to my side and bends down and ruffles Will's hair.

Tears cascade down Will's face, and he hugs me again and doesn't let go. I don't let him go either. Will's sobs grow harder and louder, but there's so much he held in. So many things.

Pulling away, Will meets my eyes. "You love me though, right? Did I mess that up?"

"No. No you didn't mess that up, Will." I swallow hard. "I . . . love you too."

Will made me say it. Worse, he made me feel it.

What will that do to me, to him, to all of us?

How dangerous is my love?

TEN

"You walked into the cemetery to get him?" Buster's eyes stretch. "You brave girl. You real brave." He eats a slice of bacon. "I don't care if Jesus himself tell me He got a thousand dollars waiting past them gates, I ain't going into no cemetery for nobody."

"Nothing was gonna stop Sara," brags Mr. Vanellys.

I take an apple from a white bowl on my left, wiping it off with the bottom of my apron. I cut out the core and peel the first one, twisting the knife in a spiral, slow, methodical, like my father. I place the apple in a blue bowl on my right after I'm done.

My father, Saul, wasn't a good man. Not one piece of him, but a parent's role is to teach. Even if it's how to never become like them. And I guess if he couldn't teach me good things, I'd learn from him the bad. And then decide if I'd follow in his footsteps or Momma's. Even now I try to choose her over him as much as I can. But, every once in a while, I don't. Every once in a while, I find something worthy in the bad my father taught me. Like how to be deliberate in action, whether taking money from a collection plate or skinning an apple, everything you do deserves your strict attention—good or bad. Otherwise, you can get caught stealing or wind up dead on the floor of a church.

Mama Sugar clears her throat. "Yes, yes it got mighty exciting 'round here for a bit, but that was two weeks ago. Y'all talkin' about it like it happened yesterday."

Whistling from the hall, Elvin walks through the kitchen doorway smiling ear to ear. "Morning everybody! Hasn't God made such a glorious day?"

"Finally got religion?" asks Mr. Vanellys.

"Naw he startin' to get back in good with Simone, I reckon," whispers Buster. Mama Sugar slides up behind him and whacks the fleshy bottom part of his neck. Buster rubs his stinging skin. "Still said what I said."

Mama Sugar taps me on the shoulder. "Sara-girl get the door please. Maybe Amos came to take Will to school."

I return her smile. "It's possible." Walking toward the living room, I stop at the stairs. "Will, get the lead out. School's in half an hour!"

As I put my hand on the doorknob, I hope the other side doesn't hold Amos. And it doesn't, but someone far worse greets my eyes.

"Nice to see you again. Don't you look pretty in your cute, little red apron." Lucky tips his tan fedora at me as he brushes past the threshold, without invitation. His checkered blue-and-beige

156

polo shirt and khaki pants reek of English Leather cologne. "Came by for a friendly visit."

"Does this visit include a beating like the one you gave Amos?"

Looking over his shoulder, his gaze grows colder. "Maybe."

He strolls into the living room, standing in front of the fireplace. "Lennie Mae keeps her home spotless." He stops at the mantel and stares at the pictures. He picks up the one of Mr. Vanellys, Mama Sugar and Amos, shaking his head.

My left jaw throbs. My teeth clench like I bit down on an apple or a pear or a peach, something where I'd need to tear thin skin. "Amos hasn't stayed here in weeks. He barely comes around since he's gotten better."

Lucky picks up the picture of the unsmiling boy in the blue jean overalls and sets it down quickly as if it was a piece of hot coal. "Somethin' sure smells good."

Clamoring from the kitchen invades the front room. "Food is for the boarders. Not criminals."

Lucky turns from the kitchen and walks back to me. "Ohhh chile you sure is spicy. I like that in my—"

A paring knife stops him. The one I used to skin apples minutes ago, the one I pulled from the pocket of my *cute, little red apron,* casually digs into his stomach. "You need to leave *now.*"

Lucky inches forward. "Ain't going nowhere

'til I speak with Amos. He traipsing all 'round Memphis drinking and gambling but can't pay me my money? I got plans for it."

A smirk tugs at the edges of my mouth. "He's got one good leg and you can't catch him? Doesn't seem like you're much of a *'businessman.'*"

Lucky cranes his neck, his gaze traveling upstairs. "I gave him enough warnings and I been plenty patient. Now tell him to get his ass down here—" he turns back toward me, his eyes narrowing "—or else."

"Are you hard of hearing? He's not here!"

If I knew where Amos was, I might tell Lucky. If Lucky killed him, would that be so bad? Mama Sugar and Mr. Vanellys would mourn, yes, but they'd have Will, a piece of Amos, apparently the only good piece of him. And being without a parent, one hardened and suffocating all the good that might yet blossom within you, what damage would it *actually* cause Will?

Sometimes a dead father is better than a live one. Sometimes death isn't a burden, sometimes it's a blessing.

Ungracefully plodding down the stairs, Will's scrunched face concentrates on the notebook paper in front of him. "Sara, can you please take another look at my essay before I hand it in? I want—"

I stuff the knife back into my pocket. Lucky

smiles, wide and taunting, turning around. "Don't I know you boy? You in the same class as my Diane. She say you and her go toe-to-toe in math. She good at arithmetic though like her daddy."

Will's eyes search out mine. "Y-yes. I'm partial to English class though."

Lucky strides toward the kitchen. "That's nice, real nice. Now if you'll excuse me, I got some business with your grandma."

"Go upstairs, Will. I'll get you when it's time to go to school."

"But Sara, you just told me to hurry up."

Whatever my eyes tell Will, whatever scowl creeps over my face, gets across what I need him to understand—do what I say and by God, do it now!

"I'll be in Granny's room."

Abundant and easy laughter rising moments ago from the kitchen stops as Lucky enters. I'm right on his heels and stand in front of Mama Sugar. She pulls me back a few steps to her side and hunkers both hands on her hips. "Look, I don't know why you coming to me. Amos is grown. Any debts he got are his. His alone. You can see yourself out 'cause ain't nothin' for you here."

Bacon sizzles and pops in the cast-iron skillet. I turn down the fire and remain on Mama Sugar's left.

Lucky's grin disappears. "From what I see you

raised him. And if something happens to him, his debts become yours. Only right. Now I don't wanna do anything else to poor ole Amos. And I don't want nothin' unfortunate to befall your little family or your little business, but if I don't get my $200, a broken leg and some cuts and bruises gonna be the least of Amos' worries—and yours."

Placing his right arm back on his hip, Lucky proudly reveals the handle of a revolver. I search out Lebanon, who remains asleep in the crib with the faded painted flowers. I want him close, to pick him up and put him in my arms and flee, but I stay by Mama Sugar.

She steps closer to Lucky. "That's supposed to scare me, boy? Fear is the tool of a weak man. You ain't scarier than them men in white that came and took my daddy and oldest brother 'way and hung 'em from trees when I was nine. You ain't scarier than bare cupboards or an empty belly. And Lord knows you ain't scarier than your daddy. That man knew how to bring down holy hell when he didn't get his way, so I dare you to do your worst, son. I promise you I'll do mine if you try something here."

Lucky sucks his teeth and flexes his right hand. "I. Want. My. Money!"

"Leave, Oliver. Told you there's nothing here for you," answers Mama Sugar.

"Don't call me that."

"I'm your momma. That's what I named you. Oliver. I don't care you goin' by a street name."

"You wasn't *any* kind of mother to me," he fumes.

"Boy, you want your money from Amos, you get it from Amos. If you wanna learn to do right and get a respectable job, I'll welcome you back with all the love in my heart. But if you step foot in my house again with this foolishness, you won't be steppin' out."

I brace myself on the countertop next to the stove. I close my gaping mouth. Mr. Vanellys, Buster and Elvin rise from their chairs. Mr. Vanellys stands behind Mama Sugar. The other boarders remain seated. Shoveling pancakes into their mouths. Heads whipping back and forth, the scene more entertaining than an episode of *As the World Turns*.

"Your old man with one leg gonna protect you?" Lucky chuckles. "Or them?" He points behind him to Buster and Elvin. "The other shriveled war vet and a garbage man?"

Mama Sugar walks up to Lucky or Oliver or whatever his name is. She stands in front of her son. Her enemy. Amos' brother. A criminal. A father, too. All these labels at once. All the conflict and chaos that comes from being too many things.

Lucky's right index finger lightly grazes the handle of the gun. Buster raises both his hands in front of him. "Now listen, Lucky, I don't know you well." His eyes dart from Lucky's waist to his eyes. "Don't pretend to know or understand your grievances. But I do know you got good sense enough to act better than this. And . . . well frankly speaking. You plain outnumbered. Not enough bullets in that gun for all of us. Now . . . please, I wanna eat my food in peace and so do the rest of these men. There ain't a need for any of this."

"We can talk in the front room instead of you embarrassing me and yourself like this," says Mama Sugar.

"Time for talk is over, Lennie Mae. Don't care if it comes from you or Amos." Lucky points his finger at me. "Like I told her, I can do this the nice way or the nasty way."

"Do what you gotta do, son. I said what I said."

He drops his arms from his waist, the handle of the gun disappearing behind his jacket, a boldly vicious grin disfiguring his face. "Y'all have a real pleasant day." He grabs an apple from the white bowl and takes a bite.

"Fresh and crisp," he says, walking out of the kitchen. Lucky closes the door, gently, a light thud announcing his exit. I shudder.

Mama Sugar turns to the boarders. "Deduct a dollar from today's room and board. Apologies for that rude interruption. Excuse me for a moment."

Mr. Vanellys starts to follow Mama Sugar but thinks better of it and sits back down at the table with Buster, Elvin and the rest of the boarders. The men pile more food onto their plates. There is no more talk, only smacking, chewing and the slurping of juice.

"In Sinclair's Grocery, Lucky told me Amos owed him money. I tried to tell you but . . . You were already going through a lot. Then Amos came back hurt. I felt bad for not telling you."

In her room, I walk to the dresser, next to Mama Sugar. "But I wasn't the only one holding something in."

"We always holding on to somethin', Sara."

"You said your oldest son was dead."

Mama Sugar looks at her reflection in the mirror. "I said I lost him. Lost means a lot of things to a lot of people. To you it means dead. To me it means my son took a path he don't know how to get back from yet."

"You never told me about any of this."

"Did I ask you 'bout your past when you came here? I left you to it. Still do even when I wanna shake you sometimes."

"Maybe talking will help you in a way it doesn't help me." I smooth my apron, the small lump of the paring knife teasing my fingers. "We all need different things to help get us through the bad stuff that comes our way."

Mama Sugar smiles. It is lonely, one of those smiles you make so you don't cry. "I was married before to Oliver's daddy, Matthias Black. Matthias used to call him Lucky. I called him Oliver. Named him after my daddy. Oliver Lennox Black."

She sits down on the bed, rubbing her palms up and down her thighs. "Matthias, my first husband, wasn't a good person. But there's always hope when you first meet someone, y'know, that by you bein' you, you can help someone else be better. Foolish to think that 'cause a person need to want to be better and Matthias didn't *ever* want that. He was fine with who he was and what he did."

I sit down on the bed next to Mama Sugar as she continues. "One day, I left with Oliver. Told Matthias I was goin' to the grocery store. But I hid a suitcase under the porch the night before. Almost got away, but he found me on the train platform right 'fore it came in. Told me I could go but had to leave Oliver. He was about six years old. And . . . I couldn't go back to that, to Matthias. Told Oliver to go back to his daddy." She wipes away tears with the back of her hand. "I decided to save myself. Told myself what I needed to leave—that I was only going a few cities away, that I'd come and see Oliver, that he probably wouldn't remember me anyway."

Her left hand is damp as I take it. "Came here. Met Vanellys. Had Bonnie Lee. Then Amos. And eventually we built The Scarlet Poplar. Sent Oliver letters. Don't know if he read 'em. But after Matthias died a couple years ago, Oliver started comin' around. And I thought it was a gift, a way to start over. Thought I could meet Diane, that she and Will could know one another since they're cousins. All these bright ideas in my head and heart. But Oliver wanted me to use The Scarlet Poplar for something else, a place where he and his buddies could come in and do . . . I don't know, God knows what. He thought I owed him. And in some ways I do, but not like that." Mama Sugar looks out of her window to the tree in front. "Thought I could love him past the pain, his and mine. Past all my mistakes. But he'd have none of it. Oliver is hard the way his daddy was. And, after a while, I left him to that. Became hard in my way too."

Mama Sugar tightens her grip of my hand. "I'm proud of a lot of things I did here, but there's going to be a part of what I did, leaving Oliver . . . a part of me that won't ever be . . . I don't know . . . not torn up, some part of me that always feels like I'm being battered from the inside out."

This part of Mama Sugar's story echoes inside me. That knowing; that state of constant inner decay, rings truer than any warm smile or full hug from her. Her tragedy, her anguish, her regrets, I feel in me some kind of bereft kinship.

Her brokenness means I'm not alone in my brokenness.

"I gotta go now, Sara," pleads Will from the doorway. His eyes travel to Mama Sugar, and he takes a couple of steps toward us. "I can go to school by myself. I won't—"

"I'll be downstairs in a minute."

Will sighs. "Okay." His footsteps fading, and stopping, likely by the front door.

"Whatever the inside of you says about you, doesn't mean you gotta believe it. We're crueler to ourselves than others." I lay my head on Mama Sugar's shoulder. "My momma said save for God, no one else gets to judge what you do in this life. So, try to be kinder to yourself. I don't know if it'll work, if we can forgive ourselves for everything we've done, but maybe we can start."

Mama Sugar puts her arms around me. "I'll try if you do."

We embrace for a moment. Sometimes healing, giving yourself a measure of peace, doesn't last as long as the chaos preceding it.

But we take what we can get.

The boarders are gone. Will waits by the door. I go to the kitchen. Greasy plates with scraps and drained drinking glasses clutter the table. Mr. Vanellys places Lebanon on the floor and lets him walk while gripping both of his fingers. The boy's steps are steadier than a couple of weeks ago, than a couple of days ago.

"You should head to the garage."

Mr. Vanellys glances up at me. Lebanon totters toward the stove, but he steers Lebanon toward me. "Buster'll make sure things are fine until I get there."

Lebanon laughs, then wobbles and finally falls, braced by Mr. Vanellys. I pick him up. "I'm taking the baby with me and dropping off Will at school. Go to work. I'll clean all of this up."

"I should go and check on Lennie and—"

"She's gonna be fine. You should go to work. I've got this."

"Yeah, I can see you do, Sara-girl." Mr. Vanellys kisses me on the forehead. I don't pull back.

"Thank you." He winks and walks out of the back door.

Will's hand is on the doorknob. I settle Lebanon into the stroller. "We got about fifteen minutes, but we'll make it. Now let me read that essay," I say.

We walk down Hunter Avenue. My eyes scan Will's jagged cursive writing. Lebanon amuses himself in the stroller reaching for wafting dandelion fluff.

"Best keep your eyes on the path in front of you before you trip over your own feet."

Will bites his middle fingernail. "Your face is puckered up like I didn't do a good job. I promise I read that essay over and over."

"Unless you're a mind reader, you don't know what's going through mine. And *How It Feels to Be Colored Me* isn't an easy read. It's got layers. Hurston made sure of that. Let me finish and I'll give you my thoughts."

I don't smile, not yet. I don't want Will to get a big head, but from the first sentence that boy has me.

Zora Neale Hurston didn't think about the fact she was black, but people can change how you see things and how you see who you are.

Springdale Street rushes toward us. The roar of young voices, the impatience of morning and all the possibilities of the looming day press down.

When Zora is younger, she doesn't know being black can be hard because she's around her people all the time and family can protect you from ugly things, but it can never stay like that forever. One day, you pick up on how being black makes you different . . .

Eldridge Avenue is just ahead. The school on the block, a crimson-bricked receptacle for black bodies and education.

You can hear something or see something or something happens to you. Then your world isn't the same. Nothing can protect you. Learning this can hurt, but only if you let it . . . You have the power to figure out if who you are is good or bad. It's no one's choice but yours.

Children are in perfect lines, each teacher at the head, leading them up three steps and into Hyde Park Elementary School's three-arch entrance. I return his essay. "It's good."

"Good? That's all?"

"Yes, Will. Don't expect people to praise you. Have enough confidence in what you do so you never need anyone else to make you feel like a whole person."

He cocks his head. "Okay. If you say it's good then Mr. Coulter will probably like it. You're tougher than he is."

"Boy, get out of here."

Will laughs. He bends down to the stroller and tickles Lebanon, who lets out a shrill giggle, and jogs toward his classmates supervised by Jonas. He lines up by his height. He's now almost at the back. Will was closer to the middle of the line around September.

Jonas waves to me and comes over. "You were cutting it close, Ms. King." He grins, soft and charming.

"When you read his essay, you'll see why. You should give him that A+ right now."

"You're confident in William's abilities, huh?"

"Aren't you?"

His grin blooms into a smile. "I'll bring Will back after school. Only got a few more days until the end of the school year and then you're rid of me."

"Well as Cora says, 'God is in heaven and working.' "

Lebanon reaches for Jonas. "Aww. Can't right now Little Man, but I'll see you soon."

The school bell rings. Jonas leaves me and leads the children into the building. His smile, his energy out of my reach and sight.

"You ain't gotta turn off that radio on my account," says Mama Sugar as she winds her way around the table, a rag damp with soap and vinegar. Her palm pressing firmly down on the wood, cleaning it of crumbs and grease and dirt.

I turn up the radio. Nina again. "He Needs Me." Suave, dexterous piano notes, soft rhythmic cymbals. Longing and heartache. Mama Sugar stops wiping the table, closing her eyes and exhales long and slow. "She a good singer. Swore for a second I was back at the party when I first saw Vanellys. Mmmph. Sounds a little like Billie."

"Yeah, yeah she does."

Mama Sugar makes her way to the head of the table with her rag. "Who's that again?"

"Nina Simone."

"Tina?"

"Nee-na. Nina Simone."

I rest my hand on Mama Sugar's shoulder, gently pulling her from the sink. "You go rest. I'll finish cleaning."

Mama Sugar takes Lebanon out of the stroller. "I can take Lebbie at least so you don't gotta worry about that too."

"Put him in the crib. I'll take him out on the porch and play with him in a little while."

Mama Sugar still holds on to my son. "It's not a bother—"

"No, he isn't a bother, least of all to me. Please put my son in the crib and go upstairs and get some rest."

"Well, excuse me. I could've sworn I was the owner and operator of this here fine establishment, but someone's trying to take over sooner rather than later." Mama Sugar chuckles.

"Stop it." A small smile bending my lips. "See, this is why I can't be nice. Go on."

"Alright chile." Mama Sugar slowly walks toward the back stairway. "I'll be back down in an hour or two."

The sink full of dishes is light work. I wash and rinse. I dry and stack. Lebanon speaks his own language. A mix of syllables not yet forming complete words. I try to decipher if anything resembles English. He whimpers and reaches for me. There are no more dishes in the sink.

I pick him up. "Why are you crying, my son? Hmm?" He lays his head on my shoulder. He wanted me. Only me. And there is a little world I've made for us, like Buster's story where I'm a princess. Lebanon and I live in a house high in the mountains. And we are safe from monsters. From the past. From what I thought I was and what this boy was to me. It's easier to hold him. To see me in him. Only me.

There is a soft mint green blanket with pale yellow trim on Mr. Vanellys' chair. I lay it on the floor and sit with Lebanon in the living room. Above us hovers the mantel with the black-and-white photographs and complicated stories. Mama Sugar bought small little wooden blocks for him. They are near the firewood.

I grab the blocks and Lebanon begins to stack them, and they teeter and fall. He laughs and tries again. There's a knock on the door and a dull thud in the mailbox.

So many letters. I sort them. I listen for Mama Sugar, but there is no creak from the floors above. The last letter is from Violet. I hold it in my hands. Let the magnolia perfume fill my nose. Lebanon builds the blocks. They teeter and fall. He laughs.

Violet will talk about her life. Her child. Her husband Thomas. About Naomi. The church. I look back at Lebanon. If I am to be what I need to be for him, there are things I can't have tether me back to that place. I can't partake in her life anymore. Violet and Naomi are the past. Lebanon is my future. He must be, if I hope to have one.

You angry. He's angry. You happy. He's happy.

And I am looking for more than happy. I am looking for joy. Maybe it's here. In Memphis.

The mail is in neat piles. The unopened letter is in my hand. I tear it in two, then in three. Every act of destruction is freedom. I'm glad you're happy Violet. But I can't be with you anymore or I will die, not all at once, but in parts until I have nothing left to offer my son.

―――――≈―――――

"You think Hell is hot as a Chicago summer?" asks Violet. She leans back on the wooden bench, then hisses, "Damn splinter." The smallest drop of blood buds at the tip of her index finger. She digs in her green purse and pulls out a Band-Aid.

"I don't think it's the fire that's scary," says Naomi. She bares her body to the sun, her sky blue shorts lightly flapping against a meager breeze. "I think it's the people there. Or maybe it's knowing that whatever you did on this earth got you in Hell." She sighs. "Why you talkin' about this kind of stuff anyway? We're at the park to relax. Got only a few more days until we give up our freedom to school."

"Yeah, but we'll be in high school. We're

pretty much grown," says Violet. A small grin plays on her lips. "All I want is a little freedom, but I gotta figure out how much freedom I need to be wanting. Too much you go to Hell. Too little freedom that's a little bit of hell too."

"Hell isn't about the fire or what you did wrong," I say. "It's about what the other souls can do to you."

Violet lifts her emerald cat-eye sunglasses, flashing me the brown of her eyes. Her glasses match her purse. I love those glasses. "Oh do tell, Sara. King Saul's daughter wanna grace us with her wisdom?"

"My daddy being the new pastor of Calvary Hope has nothing to do with my thoughts. I mean at least yours is assistant pastor."

"Stop being so sensitive. I was joking." Violet sets her glasses back over her face. She crosses her legs and bobs her knee up and down. "Well, kinda. This heat is making me cranky is all."

"Ladies. Forever and to the end. Our pact. Stop the bickering," orders Naomi.

"Forever and to the end," Violet and I respond.

I stay silent on the bench for a while. Violet's jab cuts a little deeper than she probably meant. But sometimes our friendship, hers and mine, it's a competition. It's an unbalanced love. But no one else can come at me like

Violet or else she'll have their hide. And if anyone hurt her or Naomi, I'd hurt them too. Kill them if I had to. Sometimes feels like I got enough anger for the whole city.

"Hell is scary, but it's not 'cause of fire or your sins. Hell's scary 'cause of the other souls. Because someone hurting that much will do anything to visit that pain on another even for a moment's relief," I say, finishing my thought.

Naomi shudders. "Y'all keep talking about Hell if you want. I'm getting some ice cream." She stands up and crosses the street to Mr. Arrington's grocery store. My white cotton shirt sticks to my skin.

"I was gonna give you these earlier, but I forgot," says Violet. She digs in her green bag and pulls out a pair of sunglasses like hers, but red. Ruby red. "I got 'em yesterday. Knew they'd look nice on you. Most everything does." Her lips form a crooked smile. "Put 'em on!"

I do. And everything is different shades of black.

"Whew chile, you hot! You stylin'." Violet laughs, clapping her hands.

He'll take these from me. King Saul. My father. He'll tell me red is the color of sin. Call me a Jezebel or a whore or both. Look at me hard and something evil will cross his eyes. And tonight, I'll pay for it. With a beating. With something else worse than that. But I want my friend's gift. To cherish it. No matter the cost. Because I deserve a reprieve from the Hell I live. I deserve ice cream and ruby red cat-eye sunglasses and to be with my friends whose love is my small, uneven piece of heaven sitting on an old wooden bench during the Chicago summer.

———❦———

"I'm thinking meat loaf tonight. I'll make two big ones," says Mama Sugar. "Easy. Simple. And can feed at least eight men." She opens the kitchen cabinets. "Hmmm. Peas."

Please don't say mashed potatoes. Please don't say mashed potatoes.

"And . . . mashed potatoes." Mama Sugar pulls a five-pound bag of potatoes from the pantry. Ushering her out of the way, I grab the bag and heave it on the counter.

She looks at the shelves on the back wall. The small pots of rosemary and thyme are bare. "First let me go grab some herbs from the garden."

Mama Sugar leaves me in the kitchen. The front door opens. Muffled voices grow clearer and clearer still. Jonas walks into the kitchen. Will strolls in behind him, a bold grin ornamenting his face. He has a dimple in his left cheek. Never noticed that before. He digs into his bag, retrieving a paper with a large red A+ and an arithmetic test boasting a 98%.

"So you're neck and neck with that girl Diane, huh?"

Will shrugs. "She hasn't been at school all week. She normally messes with me on the playground, but Mr. Lennox picks her up at lunch now and she leaves for the day. She's lucky she doesn't have to stay in school."

"Being in my class is torture for you, is that it?" teases Jonas.

"Didn't mean it like that. Happy I got a good grade, is all," says Will.

I remove potatoes from the sack. "Oh, so I'm to be impressed?"

Will catches a potato rolling toward the edge of the counter, placing it next to me. "Like you said this morning, I don't need someone to make me feel good about what I already did."

"Eh, I didn't quite say it like that, but, yeah, that was the gist."

Will hugs me and I hug him back. Squeeze him. "Proud of you boy. Now get started on your homework."

He runs upstairs. Jonas stays. "School's ending next week."

"You keep saying that."

Jonas grins. "Sara, do you have to make every-thing so damn difficult?"

Opening the middle drawer next to the stove, I grab the paring knife. "Keep cursing and see if

Mama Sugar don't come in here and knock your eyes in the back of your head."

He takes my hand. I pull it back. "I'm trying to ask you out. I want to show you a good time. Don't close yourself off to something you want to open the door to."

I glance at the back door. "You're too poetic for your own good, and pretty words don't work on me, Mr. Coulter."

Leaning against the counter, his skin is slick with a light sheen of sweat. "Well tell me what works on you and for you, Ms. King." An ivory shirt showcases his well-defined chest, and I don't want to pay attention to this, to him. I don't want to feel these things. I'll blame the weather. Memphis has a different kind of heat.

"Mama Sugar is gonna have your hide for leaning on her counter. Are you trying to meet your Maker sooner rather than later?"

He quickly stands up straight, a soldier at attention doesn't have better posture.

"I ain't havin' no one's hide," Mama Sugar announces from behind me, and I whip around. "Now tell this nice boy 'Yes' Sara-girl."

"Mama Sugar—"

"Say yes," she urges; her voice is so soft. Lebanon stands up in the crib and coos and claps his hands, and Jonas picks him up without asking me and I want to say something, but they look so natural together.

"Come on Little Man," says Jonas. "Your momma smiling is the only 'Yes' I need. See you tonight."

Jonas used Mama Sugar, my son and those eyes of his. That body of his. That mouth of his.

I didn't stand a chance.

ELEVEN

Mr. Vanellys leans on the back door in the kitchen. "You know it ain't too late to take me up on my offer, Sara-girl."

"I'll be fine—"

"What kind of sense you makin'?" interrupts Mama Sugar. Lebanon totters over to her. He grabs the end of her flowered housecoat. Mama Sugar picks him up.

"You're going to spoil him if you keep doing that," I say.

"What I spoil, I can unspoil," says Mama Sugar, her gaze never leaving mine.

I look at the table. Will grins ear to ear.

"Stop listening to grown folks' business. Go in the living room and read your book." He plods off past Mr. Vanellys to the living room and sits on the yellow couch, closest to the kitchen door. "She a grown woman. She don't need a chaperone, Vanellys."

"Respectable young ladies like Sara-girl need to make sure they protected. Ain't I right about it, Buster?"

"Man, don't bring me into this." Buster sucks his index finger, a small drop of blood budding at the tip. "Daggone it! I ain't had to skin taters since we was stationed in Naples in '44."

"Doing a little bit of kitchen work won't kill you," says Mama Sugar.

She turns back to Mr. Vanellys. "And who you gettin' ready to protect? Jonas is a good boy. Sara is a good girl. And I feel sorry for Jonas if he'd try something."

"I know that's right," chimes in Buster. He chuckles.

"Thought you was stayin' out of it," says Mr. Vanellys. He folds his arms and mumbles, "I know what I'm talkin' 'bout."

They talk around me about me. "I'll be back in a couple of hours if that. I'm not your child. I can handle myself."

Mr. Vanellys' face drops. "Didn't mean nothin' by it. Wasn't trying to overstep my authority."

"I didn't mean—I appreciate you."

"I know, Sara-girl. I know." Mr. Vanellys waves his hand in dismissal of my harsh wording.

"I'm gonna go change."

Buster's hand clumsily grips the potato, slicing it with the paring knife, taking more potato than skin. Mama Sugar sucks her teeth. "Man, you're gonna be the death of me. Watch Lebbie."

Buster puts the knife on the table. Mama Sugar hands my son to Buster, who sits him on his knee. She snatches the knife next to him. Her fingers expertly grip and flay the vegetable. "I swear men wouldn't know what to do on this earth if women weren't on it with 'em. Helpless. All of you. Helpless."

Mr. Vanellys still leans against the kitchen door. I kiss him on the cheek. I don't look at his face before I go upstairs.

"A lady can be pretty and not exposed," Momma says to me as she looks at herself in a full-length mirror. She puts on white gloves up to the bottom of her elbow. They cover light purple bruises on the bottoms of her arms.

I have two nice dresses. Sunday dresses. One I brought in my turquoise suitcase when I left Chicago. One I bought myself as a birthday gift three months ago. I didn't tell anyone it was my birthday.

Gold and white. Calf-length. Sleeveless. No gloves.

Am I going somewhere fancy? Should I even bother bringing out this dress? Is this what dating someone is like?

Violet told me her first date with Thomas was bad. We were barely in our second year of high school, and she wasn't allowed to go out, but we told her parents we were studying for a big history test. Naomi and I helped her get ready. Violet wore a pink dress. Thomas spilt cocktail sauce on her lap before the first course. She stood up and twisted her ankle when she slipped in it. Thomas broke his glasses catching her, and he needed them to see practically anything. At the end of the night, Thomas carried her back to Naomi's home in his arms. *A disaster* is what she called it, but Violet smiled when she said it. She laughed about the whole godforsaken event like it was the best thing in the world. "What kind of man will carry you a mile and a half when he can barely see? A good one. A real good one. Thomas is for me. I know that the way I know a pair of shoes are the perfect fit when I slip my feet inside them." Then, she grinned, a sloppy exercise of her mouth.

I hated Violet for her happiness, the hopefulness of it, and the belief I'd never be able to possess anything close to it.

There is a bareness when I look in the mirror, something vulnerable in my reflection, taking in the measure of who I am. It's not about beauty or the absence of it. It's about what lies beneath my skin. It's what my reflection testifies to, the things not washing away with water or covered with a dress or a smile.

Who can love the person I see in the mirror? Can I love myself? Because if I can't, how can I ask someone else to love me?

It's mystifying and aggravating for someone to see all the possibilities of good in you. For Jonas to see good in me means there's some part where it shows. If I opened myself up, truly let Jonas see me, not whatever fiction he's created in his head, would he stay? Would he still fight as hard for me as he does now?

And this is the terrifying part. Not the possibility for Jonas to know all I am, and leave, but the fact I want him to know me at all.

Mama Sugar cracks open the door and peeks her head in. "Sara-girl, you seen my blue mixin' bowl—Why you cryin'? Jonas not comin'?"

"I wasn't crying."

She walks to me and cradles my face in her hands. My tears flow. I taste them, witness them create a small creek of water in Mama Sugar's palms, a tributary of tempered longing.

"If you knew . . . if Jonas did, of who I was . . . before here. You wouldn't want me. He wouldn't either." I wipe some of the tears away. "Mr. Vanellys talks about mercy but there are limits to it. I've seen those limits." I sniffle.

Mama Sugar lifts the bottom of her apron and wipes my face. "Calm all this down. You makin' 'bout as much sense as Vanellys downstairs right now."

"But—"

"Nuh-uh. You don't get to destroy the good things you got blessed with. God gave 'em to you. You can't take them away. Even you aren't *that* powerful." Mama Sugar sits down on my bed. She pats the spot next to her, and I sit down too.

"We all done things Sara-girl. I got my own stuff as you seen this mornin'." Mama Sugar takes a deep breath. "Remember, you told me only God got room to judge. I reckon that rule holds true for you like it does for me. It don't matter 'bout me. It don't matter 'bout Jonas. It don't matter 'bout whatever you did before you came here. *You* get to write your story now. *You* get to run your race. And if I learned anything over my time on this here earth is don't give no one the power to do those things for you."

Mama Sugar hugs me, fiercely, like I imagine Momma would if she were still here. There is a warmth and a protection, like nothing in the world can tear us apart from one another in this moment. My body lies peaceful in her arms as she rocks me back and forth. I close my eyes and breathe deep and I . . . just *am*. Oak tree branches divide the sunlight into bold peach-hued fingers, clawing their way down the wall of my room.

"You start cryin' again, you gonna mess up your pretty dress and I'll have to give you one of my old flower dusters to wear."

Vibrations course through me, the outward thumping of her chest as she laughs at her own joke, a sweet force of movement.

"I could wear a burlap sack and Jonas would say I look pretty."

"You probably right but wipin' snot off your face will go a long way too. I can tell you that much," says Mama Sugar. She laughs again.

My lips quivering, I smile, a tenuous movement of my mouth.

"Okay Sara-girl. Go on. Clean your face. Finish gettin' ready. I gotta get back." She stands up. "Can't leave Buster or Vanellys alone for too long or they get ideas."

"Come downstairs when you ready." Mama Sugar squeezes my shoulder, then leaves the room and closes the door.

I open my turquoise suitcase. Splayed in a lonely corner is my rag doll, Louisa. Embedded in the stringy black yarn of her hair are the remnants of Momma's smell, what I remember it to be. Inhaling deep, I try to find it again, that comfort, those memories, the golden pure ones. I try to find courage to do something new, create my own story, find a happy ending that's *mine*. I put Louisa back in the suitcase and grab a hand towel from the top of my dresser.

I walk to the bathroom. In the mirror, splotchy patches cover my forehead and cheeks. Cool water rushes over my hands, refreshing me, as I splash it on my face, quelling the once rising warmth under my skin, the redness silently fading. A jarring din of voices rise from the back staircase: Mama Sugar, Mr. Vanellys and Buster. I'd rather leave without an audience.

Softly I walk down the front staircase. Will remains on the couch eavesdropping on the conversations behind him, the book in his hand slack, resting on his lap, his eyes narrowed in concentration. I clear my throat. He tightens his

186

grip on the book, almost shoving his nose in the pages.

"Hmm. Book's that interesting?"

"Yeah, yeah." Will turns the page, the faux concentration tickles me.

I sit down next to him on the couch. "What're you reading?"

Will flips the book to the cover. "*The . . . Ru-bai-yat of Omar Khay-yam*?"

"Are you asking me a question about what you're reading or are you telling me?"

I shake my head. "Here's a question you *can* answer: What are Mama Sugar and Mr. Vanellys talking about?"

"Granddad still wants to chaperone you. Said he was gonna follow Mr. Coulter's car and Granny said if he did, she'd lock him out of the house."

Will giggles. He looks at me up and down and whispers, "Where *are* you and Mr. Coulter going?"

"To a cute little place called None of Your Business."

Will frowns and again opens his book.

I tussle Will's hair. He huffs, puts his unread book down beside him and fixes it. As I stand, Will grabs my wrist, his mouth open, wanting to say something, but nothing leaves his lips. I bend down and kiss him on the forehead. "I'll be home soon. Watch Lebanon for me."

He solemnly nods. "Okay."

Gently I close the door behind me. With the screen door I take even more care. The porch creaks as I lightly step on it. The stairs loudly squeak as my sunflower-colored, low-slung heels announce each movement. Turning around, only Will's curious brown face peeks from behind the gauzy white curtains.

Jonas fidgets with two silver dials near the radio. "You sure you're not cold?"

"This is the third time you asked about the temperature. I swear I'll let you know if I'm cold."

Jonas drives down Chelsea Avenue, past the streets and shops I now know; past the few familiar blocks I allow myself to roam before I retreat to The Scarlet Poplar. Small ranch and tract homes, bigger bungalows give way to vaguely familiar roads. We glide past Clayborn Temple. Goose bumps dot my skin. My eyes travel up the church bell tower. Down it. Stained glass that offers no color, no blazing array of hues. They're muted by the dusky navy-painted sky.

Will runs off and we can't find him. Amos leans against a tree with a shriveled heart and dead eyes. My father preaches at a church. He's in his office. His hands are around my neck.

"Knew it was too cold." Jonas fiddles again with the dials.

"It's not cold."

"But you're—"

"It's not that, Jonas."

"What do you mean—" He glances at the church. "I got you." He accelerates. Clayborn Temple and Hernando Street blur past, and he makes a right on Main Street. Jonas slows down in front of a furniture store and a building offering loans for those tight on money. Across the street sits a place, wider and taller than most of the businesses on the block. Tan- and sienna-tinted bricks appear almost ivory underneath the awning ringed in blinding electric light. The name MALCO is fixed to the front sign above the entrance in gold lettering against a candy-apple-red background. Emblazoned in big squared black letters on the marquee is the featured movie: *West Side Story*. Below that, two wide glass doors with brass handles. This dazzling, shimmering part of the theatre is flanked by smaller, two-storied brick appendages on each side. The back of the building, a large force of mortar and manpower, rises, eclipsing the front in size.

"This is the Malco Theatre," says Jonas. "First movie I ever saw was here with my momma. *Alice in Wonderland.* We went in around the back." Jonas clears his throat. "Got our tickets in a different lobby. Sat in the upper left gallery, far and away."

I swallow hard. My palms are damp. "I saw

Alice in Wonderland too. At the Chicago Theatre. It looks a little like the Malco. My mom bought popcorn. It was my reward for getting good marks in school."

I don't remember a separate entrance.

Jonas smiles. "Momma caught me reading *Alice in Wonderland.* Had me read it to her. She said her eyes were too tired from work. I'd always read to her." Jonas flexes his neck side to side. "Supposedly, they're letting us through the front doors of this place now. Didn't make a big announcement. Probably don't want the attention."

"We're going to the movies?"

"No."

He pulls off, eventually turning left on Vance Avenue and right on South Lauderdale Street. I commit the street names to memory. I make note of where and when Jonas turns.

Pay attention to street names, Sara. You never know if you gotta be the one to make your way home on your own.

Long-rowed, two-story, scarlet-bricked apartments pull into my view. Every entrance adorned with a small awning, two doors and a porch only big enough to fit one chair. Each building with an identical footprint as far back as my eyes can make out in the stingy evening light.

Jonas gets out of the car. I follow him. "This is where I grew up. Haven't been back since, well, since I left for Morehouse. Until now," he says, leaning back on the car next to me. "William H. Foote Homes." Turning around, he points across the street. "And there Robert Church used to live. He built a three-story house. Eighteen rooms. Beale Street wouldn't have been what it was without him. Hell, Memphis wouldn't have been the same. May not have been here at all. I mean yellow fever damn near destroyed the city, but he stayed, bought up land. Started the first black bank in Memphis. He was a millionaire. He was a legend."

"Then what happened to—"

"They burned it down almost ten years ago. His mansion. Boss Crump had it done as a final act of violence toward a legacy, to try and erase the possibility of another Robert Church. Wanted to destroy the belief that we're as good as white people. There was an 'exhibition' for new fire equipment, and they set Church's home on fire. Bastards." Jonas' voice lowers. "His home was a symbol. A lot of houses around here were owned by black people. Those were symbols too, but they were all destroyed. And the city built these."

"Used to think we had it better up North. Somehow we were better." I bitterly laugh. "You got Crump. We got Daley. White men who need the black vote, use black people. But we can't be great. Our power can't eclipse theirs." I lean back against the car next to Jonas. "It's the same thing.

191

The same damn thing. We have these too. Taller. Our own little dirty skyscrapers. They name the buildings after black people who'd have probably burned them down. You know we got a housing project named after Ida B. Wells? She spent her whole life fighting injustice, and they slapped her name on a building that keeps it going."

"White people build these places to keep us and them separate. Put the names of our people on them like they've done us a service. It's disgraceful," says Jonas.

"So you hate white people?"

"I don't hate anyone, Sara. Not white people. Not my momma's husband. Not my momma. Nobody. If I hate, I'm giving up one set of chains for another. Hating is a habit. Like loving is. And I make it a point to never take on bad habits if I can. What I know is that you can never destroy the possibility of another Robert Church or Ida B. Wells or anyone of the like. Our greatness is . . . inevitable."

"Joe Boy! Joe Boy! That you?"

A tall, muscled man jogs toward us, at least four inches taller than Jonas. He gives Jonas a big bear hug, lifting him off the ground.

"Ain't seen you since you left for college, boy!" He sets him down.

"Adam!"

"Stop with that Adam nonsense." He turns to me. "They call me Boochie. Nice meetin' you."

"Sara." I smile and shake his hand.

"You visitin'? You livin' up North now, right?"

"Naw man. Came back after college. Still livin' in Memphis. Teachin' up at Hyde Park Elementary. English."

Jonas' crisp diction and precise grammar falls away. His speech mirrors Boochie's. Easy, a heavier drawl honeys his words.

"Got a little nephew up there. Titus. He 'bout seven," says Boochie, looking up and down the street. "Anyways, I'ma go ahead 'bout my business. Nice seein' you Joe Boy. Don't be no stranger."

"You right, you right. See you 'round."

Boochie affectionally slaps Jonas on his back and strolls down the block. A light grimace pulls at Jonas' face though his eyes are still warm. He rotates his right shoulder, then opens the passenger-side door. I climb in and Jonas gets behind the wheel, driving past the streets of his youth. A life before I encountered him on a scorching schoolyard in an indigo suit.

He heads north. Turns left and left again, driving with confident ease, right hand on the wheel, left arm resting on the window frame. We find ourselves on Mulberry Street. A two-storied motel with fresh paint and seafoam-colored doors. A few feet away lies a pool. Crystal clear water shimmers and sparkles, lapping against the square concrete edges.

"A lot of musicians stay at the Lorraine Motel," says Jonas. "A bunch of them are from Stax Records from what I hear. Ethel Waters. Aretha Franklin. Lionel Hampton. Otis Redding." The sweet slow manner of his talk, the dropping of g's from the ends of his words I witnessed when he spoke to Boochie, disappears. The learned, sharp cadence of his speech returns.

All these singers. Talent. Drive. Hard work. Sweat. And they still must walk through back doors to sing on a stage. We can entertain white people, but that is it. Break your body for their distraction or amusement but don't ask, don't you dare ask, to be seen as a person. That's where the line is drawn.

"I love Nina Simone. I mean, well, I listen to her on the radio at The Scarlet when I'm cooking or baking. I like her voice. It's beautiful, deep, mournful in the right places, joyful in the right places."

"Her voice is haunting. So much depth. I don't have the right words to describe her, but sometimes I don't have words for you either." Jonas looks over at me and smiles and then returns his gaze back to the windshield. "Sam Cooke is my favorite singer."

"Has he ever stayed at this motel?"

"Think he did, actually. Refused to play at a segregated concert last year."

Jonas' hand tightens on the steering wheel.

"They asked a black man to play music where his people can't sit in the same seats as white people. Where there's sometimes a rope dividing a room or a balcony or whatever. I've always wanted to hear him sing, but I don't blame him one bit for what he did, why he did it. I'd have done that too."

"Still, being famous means you can call your own shots," I say.

"You know as well as I do fame doesn't cover skin color. Money either."

The Lorraine Motel beckons the weary among us. Something that is ours. Black bodies can sleep in warm beds; splash in the pools not separating black from white, but is this place safe from violence? Its grand existence swells my heart, but I'm hesitant in my happiness. Can we remain protected, untouched there? Our sanctuaries, the places where we find our joy and peace and humanity, never remain sacred. How long before something hateful kills what we hold dear?

Jonas stops his car in front of a squat brown brick building near East Butler Avenue. The Iris Club's name is hunkered in bold blue light above the door. Smoke floats from around the back, the enticing aroma of barbecue. My mouth waters. Taking my hand, Jonas leads me through a door, painted jade, with a small square window. I don't pull away.

"This is one of *the* best joints in the city," he brags.

Eight tables on black-and-white-checkered floors frame an open square where bodies sway and dance. Two booths anchor the left and right corners of the room. The hallway next to the right booth likely leads to the kitchen and the barbecue smoker in the back. A jukebox sits in the middle of the booths blaring a song. Husky and familiar.

"Try Me."

James Brown's raspy pleas saturate cigarette-heavy air. A long mahogany bar to my right hosts six stools, five of them occupied. Dim electric bulbs, haze and reckless laughter surround me. Three people enter behind us. I pull Jonas to the only empty table I see.

He frowns. "I wanted to make sure it wasn't occupied."

"That's nice, but while you were busy being polite, I was busy finding us somewhere to sit."

I smile. "Mr. Coulter, you've surely heard of this pressing legal precedent called 'dibs.' It's immensely popular in Chicago."

He laughs and looks around. "I don't think anyone was sitting here anyway."

"It means a lot for you to do the right thing."

"Doesn't it mean a lot to you?"

I shrug. "Right. Wrong. Justice. Oppression. It's all relative. We want these ideas to be concrete, but they're fluid. There's simply a gap. There's the world we want and the world we got."

"Mighty pessimistic of you, Ms. King."

"It's the difference between getting a seat and still waiting for one, Mr. Coulter."

Jonas digs into the inside pocket of his black pants and reveals a folded piece of paper. He slides it on the table. "For you."

"A check?"

"A poem."

"I'd prefer a check." I laugh and unfold the paper. My heart thumping against my chest. Jonas' hand covers mine.

"Wait until you get home."

"Jonas, I was joking. I want to read—"

"I got pretty thick skin, Sara. I know you were joking, but it's . . . well . . . I want you to read it without all this noise."

I place the paper in the shallow pocket of my dress. He gave me a gift, and I wonder what I could give him in return. Maybe tell him who I was before this, but that isn't a pretty story. It is ugly and we're having such a good time right now.

Jonas leans forward on the table. "You okay?"

"Fine. Thinking about home, I guess."

He reaches across the table for my hand. "Hmmm. I'd love to hear about your life in Chicago. Friends? Family?"

I pull my hand back from his and pretend to fix my hair. "Maybe some other time."

Jonas stands up. "I'm famished. Barbecue sandwiches? Iris Club has the best ones."

"Eh, Kansas City got the best barbecue. My momma took me there when I was younger. Just saying."

"I'm gonna change your life, Ms. King. You wait."

Jonas smiles wide and bright. He disappears in the crowd of sweating tangled limbs and smoldering electric glow. My bottom lip is chapped from biting it. He returns with two plates in one hand, sandwiches on each, and cradles two Coca-Colas in the other. Pork falls from the generously stuffed buns, sliding on the edges of the plate. A napkin dispenser sits in the middle of the table. I take five napkins, laying them on my lap, then grab a plate and a pop from Jonas. I remove the toothpick from the middle of the bun and take a bite.

I'm staying in Memphis for the rest of my life! Tang and sweetness. Vinegar and tomato. Brown sugar. Ketchup. Spices. Savory meat smoked with hickory melts in my mouth. Dainty. I want to eat dainty. How I imagine Cora would consume one of these sandwiches. I want to display good manners. Be delicate. I genuinely want to do that, but this isn't good manners food. This is lip smackin', lick your fingers until they're clean, leave not a morsel on the plate kind of food. So I eat. Ravenously. Without abandon. Without thought there are people around.

Guzzling pop, my ears finally register Jonas' chuckle. "Kansas City, huh?"

"I haven't eaten since this morning. And these are pulled pork sandwiches."

Jonas grabs a napkin from the dispenser. "Barbecue sandwiches. Saying pulled pork is redundant."

"No. That's what's on the bun," I say.

He takes a swig from his pop. "But it's barbecue. Would you say barbecue pulled pork sandwich?"

"No, but I said what I said."

"Alright Sara, but I know you ate that *pulled pork* sandwich pretty fast," says Jonas, a smug grin tugging at the edges of his mouth.

I stick my tongue out at him and finish my drink. He laughs harder. I look down at my dress. There is only a drop of sauce that escaped my body's ferocious hunger, and it landed on a napkin. I am unscathed. Wiping my hands, I glance around the dance floor. Jonas finishes the rest of his sandwich moments later.

Blues guitar boldly blares from the jukebox. A horn section right behind it. Music again envelops the joint. "Freddie King! 'Hideaway'! Love this song!" Jonas pulls me from my chair. We are surrounded by couples. Each with their own movement, rhythm and certainty.

Jonas has none of this.

His arms encircle my waist, he twirls us around

and steps on my left foot. He starts doing a . . . I don't know, a bow-legged dance. Flapping his arms at the same time. I stand there and watch, happy to know he's not good at everything. He's a worse dancer than Buster!

Bless his heart!

"You don't like this song?" he asks.

"I'm having a good enough time watching you enjoy it."

I would dance, but I don't want him to step on my feet again. I paid good money for these shoes. A minute later, the jukebox plays a brief guitar riff and nimble organ notes signal a slower song, a ballad. Bobby Bland, "I'll Take Care of You." He croons a vow to a phantom woman that he'll protect her, never let her down, never leave, and this is of course a promise no one can ever make to someone else. But impossible promises make for nice songs.

Behind us, a group of six people are crammed into the leftmost booth. Arms around shoulders. Easy smiles on faces. One of the girls feeds a french fry to her date. Perched above the group is a framed black-and-white photo of a woman on a stage in front of a microphone. An orchid in her hair. I focus on her.

Jonas' arms encircle my waist again, but he moves slower. Side to side. Jonas can do side to side. His embrace, the lack of space between our bodies, enflames a hotness in my stomach.

Jonas' hand remains in the middle of my back. He doesn't try to move it any lower. "Too close?"

"No."

Couples surround us, clinging to one another as if there'd never be another person that'd embrace them like this again. There is a ferocity to the intimacy, an unspoken knowledge that the permanence of love is a myth. It was for the people who came before us, on plantations, who'd be snatched away from one another at a moment's notice, most times never to reunite with the one they loved. Yet we'd still do this time and time again. Try to love. Find it. Possess it. No matter how impossible and dark the circumstance. In our very depths, there is a need for someone else and we chain this unyielding conviction to a small and helpless word like *love*.

I've run from this possibility as much as I can. Jonas runs headlong into it.

Breath hot on my ear, he starts singing the last words of the song. And I press my body closer to his, to hear him, to know if his voice is as intoxicating as his stubbornness and his heart.

The music stops. We still move. Side to side. In a smoky room. On a black-and-white-checkered floor. Raising my face, I kiss him. My lips on his take Jonas by surprise but he returns my kiss, this kiss, this intimate prayer of my mouth, with a fervor and tenderness. And I'm slowly undone by what I believed I knew about him, about myself, and to what loving myself and loving him, could be.

"You are . . . something else, Sara."

"Meaning . . ."

"I—I don't currently have the words right now."

I reach into my pocket and pull out the folded piece of paper Jonas handed me earlier at our table. "Maybe this has the words."

The jukebox plays another song. More people gather around us. Our table is now occupied by another couple.

Jonas' arms remain around me. We're the only ones still amid furious movement. Above the framed photo of the singing lady sits a clock. The short hand is on nine, the long hand close to the six.

Gently, I pull away from Jonas. "Take me back to The Scarlet."

He cocks his head with a sly smile on his face. "You Cinderella?"

"No. A mom. I'm not leaving Lebanon too long without me."

"Yeah, yeah. Little Man. Let's go. I don't want to make Ms. Lennie mad or have Mr. Vanellys searching these streets for me with a shotgun on his lap."

He laughs. I force a laugh too. I don't tell Jonas how close he came to some version of this happening. His hand in mine, we leave The Iris Club.

Streets curving and winding, ebony-etched roads spread before us. Jonas traces his thumb in small circles on my hand. This can be any night. I am anyone. I am content. There is no pressure, and things are presented open before me. Catching my reflection in the window. My face. Like Violet's. Her goofy little grin. The same one adorns my lips. And at this moment, I ache to talk to her. To share something precious I might've found in Memphis. My eyes water.

Jonas turns right at University Street. His face slightly puckers. "Someone 'cueing this late at night?"

It's not meat that's burning. Not like those delicious pulled pork sandwiches at The Iris Club. This is wood-on-wood fire. Faint plumes of smoke rise on the horizon. A horrid orange glow cowers beneath.

Leaning forward inches from the dashboard, my eyes scan, strain to see ahead. "That's not barbecue."

Jonas takes his hand from mine. He winds toward Hubert Avenue. Soot curls, hovering in the air. Embers softly land on the windshield. People clog the street. Some walk. Others jog.

Throwing open the door, I abandon Jonas. My legs move, pump, run. This can't be happening or can it? Happiness, or trying to grasp some frail measure of it, always costs me. Costs others. It is my punishment. And here lies the evidence of my sins. The atonement for my temporary happiness.

The Scarlet Poplar stands before me.

In flames.

TWELVE

Where is my son? Where is Lebanon?

Some people keep their distance from The Scarlet. Shielding my face with my hands, I charge forward. Heat licks at my skin. The fire is blinding. Spreading quickly in the living room, rushing back toward the kitchen. Smoke billows from the second floor. Jonas tries pulling me away, but I fight him. I need to get in there. If I die, so be it, but I have to do *something*.

People are in there. My people.

Chaos. Screams. Fire.

Lebanon. Will. Mama Sugar. Mr. Vanellys. Buster. Elvin.

Malone Blue and some of the other men on the street grab water hoses and buckets, whatever they can find to stem the tide of flame reaching farther up and out from The Scarlet. Malone fusses with one of the hoses as men run past him. "Can't get nothin' outta this one," he says. He squints. His stubby fingers clumsily searching for the problem.

I snatch the hose from his hand, quickly feeling my way down its length. My eyes stinging and watering. It's there! A knot near the middle of the line and pressure from the water trying to funnel its way through. I loosen and untie the knot. Water gushes from the hose. Malone nods his thanks and with some other men inch their way to the front of the house, trying to douse the front porch with splashes of water that steam and quickly disappear. Searing wind keeps them at bay. It is pointless but they're doing what they can. They'd want someone to do the same for them if it was their homes. There are only voices and shouting. No sirens. No fire trucks. Not yet.

"Sara! Sara!"

Mama Sugar stands across the street. She waves her hand, beckons me to her. Lebanon is asleep in her arms. Tears press against the backs of my eyes. I run to her with Jonas not far behind. I focus on Mama Sugar. I check everyone around her.

Mama Sugar. Lebanon. Buster. Elvin.

"Will? Mr. Vanellys?"

Mama Sugar gestures to the fire, her eyes terrified. "It happened so fast. We got separated. Will gave me the baby, pushed me out the front door and went to find Vanellys upstairs or near the kitchen. I—I don't know. I don't know." She covers her mouth, but a guttural sob escapes.

Jonas runs back toward The Scarlet. He stands in the middle of the street for a moment. He doesn't go toward Malone Blue and the other men near the porch. Jonas looks at me and then runs past the smoke to the side of the house, to the back-yard. I take Lebanon from Mama Sugar. His warm little body against mine. His breathing constant.

"Lord, what is he doin'?" shouts Mama Sugar. Buster looks at Elvin, who rubs his head. Mama Sugar clutches my free hand. Squeezing it so hard it begins to tingle.

Dancing. I was dancing. Laughing. Living. Hoping for once in my goddamn life. Now it's all on fire. Heat hotter than a hundred Chicago summers rolls from the house in waves, lightly singeing the homes on each side. Greedy tentacles of destruction curling themselves around the places near it.

My fingers sink into the soft skin of Mama Sugar's hand. "I should've been here."

"I'm holdin' on to you and Lebbie and I'm tryin' . . . I'm tryin' to hold on to hope for Vanellys and Will to come out that house. Keep yourself together. For me. I can't hold your guilt and mine right now. My arms and my heart gettin' ready to burst."

"Elvin! Elvin!" a voice shouts. Simone runs to him, hugging him. "Thought you were still in there." She lets go and looks at his face. "Then I thought that was you running back into that house."

"I ain't that brave, baby. I wish I was. For you," he says.

She grabs his hand. "There are a lot of things you ain't but you stay alive long enough, maybe, *maybe,* we can work on the rest."

There is something ungodly about the color of

fire when you see it consume, destroy. Hideous yellows. Abyssic blacks. Merciless, crimson-laced orange. The Scarlet Poplar stands as much as it can against the barbarous and timeless enemy of fire. The frame groans and creaks. This place where I bore my son. The rooms that have held countless bodies, kept their private stories. The porch where Will reads books. Where I learned Jonas wasn't who I thought he was. The stairs I walked down to meet Jonas for our first date a few hours ago. It is dying.

The smoke, now thicker, push Malone Blue and the rest of the men back. They retreat from the porch. Abandoning their hoses and buckets. Sirens blare, a commanding but distant sound, somewhere in the streets but not close enough. Not yet. The third floor is the latest victim. How does it spread so fast? Fingers of flame grasp at weakening roof rafters.

Hold on a little longer. Stay together a little longer.

Please. Please. Please.

Will. Jonas. Mr. Vanellys. I repeat their names like a prayer.

Like a tumbling deck of cards, the roof caves. Elvin puts his hand over his mouth. Mama Sugar collapses in Buster's arms. Her cries shaking both of their bodies. I bury my face in Lebanon's hair and I again listen to him breathe.

From the side of the burning Scarlet Poplar, a

swirling suffocating haze spreads itself across the street, thinning ever so slightly. Murky outlines appear.

Will. Mr. Vanellys. Jonas.

Jonas bears most of Mr. Vanellys' weight. All of them coughing, expelling whatever poison entered their lungs while in the house.

The sirens are deafening now. Rotating red lights bathe the street. People part as the fire truck, the number eight painted on the front and side, inches its way to the house. Men barrel out of the truck's door. A blur of skilled movement. White faces, but one of them is black. No, now it's two. But that's all. If we were in a different neighborhood, a white one, would they have been here sooner? Did they want The Scarlet to burn, like Robert Church's home? Could The Scarlet have been saved?

What if?

Mama Sugar holds Will's hand and witnesses the remains of her work vanish. Mr. Vanellys sits on the curb, and she clutches him with her other arm. "I'm alright, Lennie. I'm alright. You know I ain't gone leave you yet." He tries to laugh but coughs, his body shuddering as if his bones might collapse like the roof minutes earlier. Jonas leans against a light pole and takes deep breaths.

I poke him in the chest. "You're not invincible! What possessed you to run into a burning home?"

Smoke clings to his clothes. Jonas' face is

streaked with soot; his eyes reddened. "Wait, wait, wait . . . You almost ripped my head off when I pulled you back."

"That's . . . that's . . . What were you thinking? Why did you do that?"

"*You* were why. Anyway, I didn't do much. Went around the back and found them in the kitchen. But—" he lowers his voice "—there was a chair underneath the doorknob of the back door. Someone set that fire and didn't want *anyone* making it out." Jonas turns his head and coughs. Hard.

Placing my free hand on his back, I rub it in circles, willing, maybe even praying, whatever smoke still lingers in him leaves.

"I'm fine. I'm fine."

"Something's wrong with you, Jonas." Moving my hands slightly higher between his shoulders, working my way to the middle and repeating. Momma did this to me when I was scared or sick and I calmed down. It's the only thing I know to do. "You can't save everyone, but you keep trying. Don't know whether to kick you or kiss you."

"I'll take your *thank yous* any way I can get them, Sara. I'll take that kiss too."

A peck. A quick kiss on the cheek. That's all he gets from me. For now. "Stay here. Don't rush into any more burning buildings."

Jonas laughs then coughs again. "Nah, won't be doing it again. I promise."

Firemen wield gushing water hoses, training

them on the burning home, seeking to temper the destruction, but it's too late.

Will stands on the curb, staring across the street. "Mama Sugar told me what you did. How you got her and Lebanon out," I say. Will turns around and looks at me, then down at Lebanon. He lays his head on my shoulder. And we watch the flames.

The Scarlet Poplar as she once stood is gone.

Only small fires defiantly linger. Collapsed walls. Poisoned ash. Hubert Avenue isn't as full as it was hours ago. People lurk, solemnly grateful the burning home isn't theirs. A haze shades the rising sun a deep red. Mama Sugar holds a cup of tea that Ms. Mavis gave her. She stirs it with a small spoon and looks across the street. Lebanon yawns and lightly moves in my lap, waking up after a short nap.

Will draws his knees up to his chest. He encircles his arms and puts his head down. He mumbles something I can't make out.

"Lift your head Will and talk to me."

"I knew something was wrong," repeats Will. "The door open and closed. Thought it was Elvin coming back late. The door open and closed again. Looked outside my bedroom window, and Mr. Black was walking away real fast. Then I smelled smoke."

Will's eyes bore through mine. "He did this 'cause Dad owed him money, didn't he?"

"Where did you hear—Listen, it's—"

"Grown folks' business. Yeah, I figured."

Will now rests his head in his hands. "Granny isn't gonna want me after this. When she finds out I let this happen."

"You didn't let anything happen."

He narrows his eyes. "Sara, I'm—"

"Would you blame Lebanon for this happening?"

"No, what could he do?"

"Exactly. You're a child. I know you don't want to hear that. No one does when they're young. There's nothing you could've done. I wish someone told me when bad things happened it wasn't my fault. Look at me, Will." I squeeze his shoulder. "Sometimes I still blame myself for things. I'm grown and thought I could do something about The Scarlet burning. Like I'm a hero in one of the books you read. We always wanna give ourselves power in times we know we don't have any. It's natural."

Will then looks at the sky; errant embers float past firefighters with soot-streaked faces.

"Mama Sugar's got something up her sleeve. We'll be okay."

"No, we won't. Something bad always happens. After a few good times, there's something bad, and it's always big bad, awful bad. This bad," he says as his lanky arm gestures to the charred remains of the boardinghouse.

I know this, the "what can the world possibly do to me now" feeling. What can upend a despair so deep, you feel it easier to drown than to swim? But there are people who grab your hand and pull you to the surface. Violet and Naomi did it for me, so I will do it for Will. With my free arm, I crush him to me like he said his mom did. I hope he remembers love and comfort. I hope he remembers to breathe.

"We'll figure this out. All of us. I promise."

Mr. Vanellys coughs again. Dr. Morgan briskly walks toward us. Cora is half a step behind.

"This is awful," says Cora as she scans the remains of The Scarlet. She smiles at Lebanon and touches his arm. He reaches for her.

Cora hesitates but I put him in her arms. Her face lights up. She adores my son. I know that. Depriving him of people that love him is cruel. Even if the person who adores him annoys me to no end.

"I have some baby clothes back at the house I can give Lebbie. They were gifts but we . . . don't need them." She looks at Lebanon. "I think there are a few things we can find for you." He squeals in delight. "You can come and get cleaned up too when you're ready. We already have *everybody* at Clayborn Temple working on some kind of temporary housing. We take care of our own," says Cora.

"I see that."

"About time." She laughs. "Ah, such a tough nut to crack you are, but I get it. We can't be soft in this world. We can look like we're soft, but we can't be it."

Cora looks across the street. "This fire would break a lot of people, but not Mama Sugar, you or me. God, we've been through so much but we're here. Yes we are."

Lebanon babbles his secret little language. Cora hands him back to me.

"Whenever you're ready. We're in Orange Mound, near Hamilton Street and Douglass Avenue, not far from here. I can wait—"

"Jonas can take us over."

"Oh." Cora looks down the street at Jonas. "I see." She playfully shoulders me. "Well, that's nice. I'll look out for you *and* Jonas."

"Thank you."

"Oh, it's no bother—"

"No, Cora. Really. Thank you."

Cora wraps her arms around me, hugging me fiercely. Lebanon between us. And I'm still for a moment. These few days, weeks, months, have been the most affectionate. And the love and warmth and acceptance isn't transactional. It's unconditional.

In the smoke, in the aftermath of destruction, there is always some form of creation, rebirth, a resolved spirit against whoever and whatever was trying to destroy us in the first place. And for that, I'm grateful. Cora hugging me makes me grateful. So, I hug her back.

"Now breathe deep for me one more time," orders Lawrence, his head against Mr. Vanellys' chest. Mr. Vanellys inhales and rattles out his breath. A light frown crosses the doctor's face. He pats Mr. Vanellys' right shoulder.

"I'll take him to Collins to be safe. Need to be sure of the diagnosis. Can't do that here," he says. He turns to Mr. Vanellys. "It's smoke inhalation more than likely, but at your age, we should be cautious."

"My age! Every day I run circles 'round them boys at my garage. Feel as good as I did in my twenties."

Mama Sugar slides her eyes to the side at Mr. Vanellys and leans back ever so slightly. "Mmm-hmm. We goin' to Collins Chapel."

"Lennie Mae I said—"

"And *I* said," retorts Mama Sugar. She gives Ms. Mavis back the teacup, still full.

Lawrence gazes past Mama Sugar a few feet away. "Actually . . . Jonas! Come over here so I can check you out."

He rolls his eyes. "I'm fine, Larry. You should look at Mr. Vanellys. Make sure he's okay."

"Told y'all I don't need no gattdang checkup," objects Mr. Vanellys.

"Uh, why don't we go this way to my car? The Chevy runs great after you fixed the fuel pump," says Lawrence, his arm around Mr. Vanellys' shoulders ushering him down the street. "We'll be waiting for you, Ms. Lennie."

"Thank you kindly, Dr. Morgan. I'll be right along."

Jonas follows behind them. Mama Sugar turns to Will and me. "Vanellys think I won't lay him out in this street. He wrong. He know he need to get checked out. He bein' stubborn."

With a surge of energy and bravado, Will stands without preamble. "I'm sorry Granny."

"For what?"

"It was Mr. Black. He set the fire."

Mama Sugar swallows hard. "Oliver—I mean Lennox Black? He did this?"

"Yes ma'am. He was in the house before the fire started. Thought it was Elvin, but I saw him running across the street and . . . well, I didn't know what was going on at first. Didn't know if I should say anything 'cause I didn't want to upset you . . . since he's your son too and Daddy owes him money."

Mama Sugar looks at me for the quickest moment. "Where'd you hear that? Who told you that?"

"No one. The day he came to the house, Sara told me to go upstairs. Didn't go as quick as I should've."

Will keeps his head lowered. "I probably gotta go back to Dad, but I don't want to especially if

216

Mr. Black is after him. If you let me stay with you and Granddad, I can make it up to you. I'll be good, better."

Mama Sugar raises Will's chin with her finger to meet her eyes. "You already a good boy and you damn right you stayin' with me."

Will's mouth drops open. Mama Sugar rarely cursed or came close to it since I've known her. "There ain't nothing you can do to stop me from loving you or your daddy, even Oliver. My love don't break. Sometimes y'all might cause it to bend, but it don't ever break. Remember that," she says.

Will smiles but it falls slightly. "Is Granddad gonna be okay?"

"He'll be fine if he listen to Dr. Morgan and me. Besides, he ain't dyin' 'til I give him permission."

"What are we gonna do?" he asks.

Mama Sugar straightens her back, right hand on her hip. "Rebuild. Bigger and better. You get knocked off the horse. You walk up to that horse and knock it out right back."

I smile hard, but don't laugh. "That's not the saying."

"It's my sayin' so I'll say it any way I please and thank you. Startin' to sound a little like your man friend."

"Jonas? He's not—we're not—"

Mama Sugar says, "Yeah, yeah y'all been

217

circling 'round each other like the sun and the moon for the longest. Was happy he finally got the courage to ask you out 'cause you're not easy, Sara-girl. You worth it, but you ain't easy."

Mama Sugar stares across the street. Her bottom lip quivers for a moment, but she breathes deep and lifts her head. She turns to Will. "Come on. Let's go with Dr. Morgan and you can see for yourself how Granddad's gonna be fine and how much of a pain he's gonna be too."

They walk toward Lawrence's car, Jonas meeting them halfway. Mama Sugar hugs him and plants a kiss on his cheek. She whispers something in his ear. Jonas smiles and makes his way to me.

"What did she say?"

"You want me to take you to Larry and Cora's? They said you and Little Man could stay with them until things settle down."

"That's not what I asked."

Jonas looks at his feet, then down the street. "I know."

He turns to me. "This wasn't at all how I expected the night to turn out."

"Me neither."

"Yeah, see, the fire was supposed to come *after* the alien invasion."

Dropping my head, I smile grudgingly, annoyed his humor again has gotten the better of me. Annoyed I want to kiss him again. Annoyed even more I want him to hold me . . . to just hold me when so much is uncertain, and smoke still burns my eyes.

"What did Mama Sugar say to you?"

"That's mine, Sara," he answers, his voice low and polite and firm.

"I can get her to tell me."

"You can get the world to spin backward if you want it to."

Firefighters mill about. Wrapping up their hoses, loading equipment back onto their truck, off to lie in wait for the next disaster.

Lebanon's weight in my arms cause them to tingle. I've never held him this long. When I get tired of holding him, I put him back in Bonnie Lee's crib, but that's gone now. I sit back down on the curb. Jonas does too. "I told Will it was gonna be okay," I say.

"Do you believe that?"

"Didn't believe once I'd be able to stand your company for more than a few minutes, so I guess miracles happen." I playfully elbow Jonas in his side.

"You're so mean." He chuckles.

"Was it bad I lied to Will?"

"You didn't lie to him." Jonas stares at the burned shell of The Scarlet. "We all need to believe in something good when terrible things happen. Believe it enough for Will. I'll believe it enough for you and Little Man."

Lebanon's hand drops and grabs the lower part of my brand-new, now-ruined dress; there's a light crinkle of paper. I reach in my pocket and hand the piece of paper to Jonas.

"Read it."

"Sara, I—"

"Read it, Jonas. Please. For me."

A shaky breath escapes his lips. "Okay, for you.

*"In the vast onyx mists of the world, I
   search for you
On emerald pastures beset with golden
   flowers
The smell is sweeter than mythic
   Egyptian perfumes
There I wait by a coursing river
And a sky crimson with my blood
While orange warms my blue-black skin
Then underneath alabaster stars with a
   pearl moon
My weary eyes find you by the Old Bridge
Come to me"*

"Damn." My eyes shoot down, and Lebanon is thankfully dozing again. If his first word is a curse word, Mama Sugar will have my hide. Hell, my momma would probably come down from Heaven and whip me too.

Jonas clinches his jaw. "I didn't expect you'd want me to read it to you."

"You wrote it. You're the only one I'd want to read it. It's beautiful."

He lowers his head. "I wanted to be a great poet like Langston Hughes or Paul Lawrence Dunbar, but I don't have *that* talent. Though once in a great while something or someone—" he looks over at me "—gets me to put pen to paper."

"No matter why you did it, it's nice to have something beautiful with all the ugly."

Lebanon's doze was only a temporary reprieve, and he squirms. He reaches for Jonas, who looks at me.

"Go on."

Jonas takes Lebanon. Their faces, the way their smiles freely consume them, reveal an honest joy, a pure one. Yes, beautiful among the ugly. You find it in the small things when it seems there is something so big you feel it might break you. Beauty in the ugly. Beauty in the small moments. The grace in a cup of hot tea or a clean, warm blanket or a ride home.

I lay my head on Jonas' shoulder as he holds Lebanon. You can find salvation without a church or a Bible.

THIRTEEN

"Who taught you how to use a hammer, Sara-girl?" asks Mr. Vanellys. "I'ma keep you workin' right here with me. Mavis gonna have to do without you at the bakery."

"You see sweetie, it takes a woman less time to do 'man's work.' " Momma sands down the patch until it's no longer slightly domed, until it's as flat and smooth as the rest of the wall. Pale dust covers her fingers and forearm. Sunlight from the kitchen window makes her eyes golden. "Your daddy just gets mad sometimes." She blows away the rest of the dust. "He didn't mean to mess up the wall. But don't let him being mean make you mean. That's how he wins. You hear me, love?"

"My mom told me I should be able to do what a man does and better." I direct the weight of the hammer to the nail head a final time until it's flush with the wood. "Actually, she was better than I was with building things. Much better. She built me a bookshelf when I was a girl. Used to have a lot of books when I was little."

"That's nice, Sara-girl. Real nice." Mr. Vanellys nods. "Well, finish up and take the last of the wood over to Buster. Then go on home, get cleaned up."

222

I tighten the knot on my green scarf as it keeps my curls in their place. "It's not really home."

"Malone offering us his house makes it home enough, you think?"

Mr. Vanellys lightly grins, a grin beckoning a kind word from me. Like the kindness Malone Blue has shown us by giving us his home and staying in an apartment above his store.

"Yes. It is home enough. For now."

The footprint of The New Scarlet is almost the same as the old one. Living room and kitchen on the first floor. Four small rooms and a bathroom on the second floor. Three larger rooms and a bathroom on the third floor. One large room and a bathroom in the attic for Mama Sugar and Mr. Vanellys.

Stepping back, I admire my handiwork. A hard Saturday's labor. The third floor of The New Scarlet smells like a forest. I hear the steady screeches of saws against wood and the banging of hammers to nails. Elvin shouts orders to Mr. Vanellys, who shouts to the other six men on-site. Most of whom looked at me with amusement the first time I came here five months ago, until I put up walls in half their time. Now they nod and say good morning. One might ask if I'd like some coffee. But they are mostly quiet and they watch. And I work amid their curious eyes. My sturdy walls do my talking.

I gather the three excess pieces of wood and

lay them in the pile near Buster, who marks something down on his notepad. "You headin' out now?" His thick blue jean overalls and long-sleeved red flannel shirt are lightly dusted with lumber shavings.

"Got plans for the evening, and I've been here since sunup. You leaving soon?"

"Naw. Probably gonna stay 'til night. You know Malone got these new lamps. Halo-ben lamps. Or something like that."

"Halogen lamps," I correct him.

"Same difference," says Buster as he scratches something off the notepad. "Anyway, we can still get some more work done at night. Those lights are brighter than bright. Damn near another sunrise. We'll be done in two weeks like Lennie Pie want. Hell, she done told everybody in Memphis to come here June 16. We can't make a liar outta her."

Elvin drops pieces of wood carelessly on the floor next to my feet. He stretches. "Barely a year and we almost finished building this place. You can't tell me black people don't know how to get shit done."

"Careful Woodrow. Don't want your momma to hear you cussin'."

Elvin waves him off. "Don't no one care about that," he mumbles. "Where you off to Sara?"

"Probably with her new man," says Buster.

I roll my eyes. "Don't worry about where I'm

off to. Just make sure y'all do a halfway decent job now that I'm leaving."

"Well, tell Mr. Jonas we all said, 'Hi,' " taunts Elvin.

I punch Elvin in his arm. He slightly teeters back into the new wall leading to the third floor's bathroom, the wall I helped build *last* Saturday.

"Didn't hurt," he mutters while rubbing his shoulder, then rotating it.

"Sure it didn't," I say, and go downstairs, out the new oak front door. A black Impala gently rumbles across the street. Jonas steps out and smiles.

The sun hangs lower these past few hours as the sky sacrifices its clear blue to dusky pinks and purples. I roll down the window of Jonas' car, looking at the side-view mirror and fix the curls framing my face.

Jonas takes my hand, his thumb making small circles on my skin. "Since when have you feared an adventure, Sara? I picked you up a few hours ago helping rebuild a whole house."

Southern humidity is always ready to demolish any strand of coifed perfection, and I sat in a chair for *three hours* yesterday while Cora washed, dried, hot-combed and tamed this mane into something pretty. I take my hand from his and smooth my black stirrup pants. My button-down, rose-colored blouse remains unwrinkled. "And where were you?"

"It's June 2. My momma's birthday. Went to Mount Carmel."

The car hangs heavy with silence. I move to turn on the radio. "You sure clean up nice after all that labor," he ribs.

I move my hand back from the dial. "I'm not a fan of surprises."

"Trust me."

"Two small words with one big ask."

Jonas sighs. "Work with me, Sara. Instead of taking a walk in Gooch Park or dancing at The Iris Club, I want us to do something different. You get to see some more of Memphis. Get your mind off the rebuild."

Jonas stops the car on an empty road leading to the interstate and across from us a bridge. Long and broad. Steel trusses are angled for support atop thick hay-tinged brick limbs. And each truss after a long incline peaks at an angle, and then descends into a line until another steel-embedded peak. And another. A sloping hill sits a couple of feet from the car. Jonas grips my hand as we walk toward the incessant swish of the Mississippi River. Tall lush green grass tickles my calves, my black plain janes sink in the mud. Cars above us whiz by.

He hands me the camera. "I want you to take some pictures."

The camera is heavier than it looks. The silver top has a dial on the side with numbers and a small arm. Jonas normally flicks it back and forth and then hits a button. I mimic those steps.

Whir-click.

He chuckles. "That's probably the prettiest picture of grass I'll see."

"What's the name? Of the bridges?"

He points above us. "Memphis-Arkansas Bridge. Next to it the Harahan Bridge. They're building another one not too far from here, at least talking about it anyway."

Jonas stands behind me. Close. "You have a lot to work with. The bridges. The river. The sky." He touches my arm. "Find a piece of this world. Make it yours."

"That's why you like taking pictures?"

He nods. "Suppose so. Something to be said for finding all the perfect and imperfect in a single moment. A single moment that can never be repeated. It's captured forever."

Angling up, I focus on the brick legs of the bridge, how they rise and support steel manipulated by hands and heat.

I flick the lever. Press the button. *Whir-click.* "So, it's about power?"

"It's about preservation."

Drifting boats float atop the river, the color of coffee with too much cream. I turn the knob with the numbers. Too fuzzy.

"Did you need me to—"

"I got it," I say, turning the camera's dial until what I see is clearer. Not crisp. Just clear enough to see across the river to the other strip of land.

Jonas walks away. Stopping for a moment on the riverbank, his head tilts slightly to the side. His thoughts are his own. He grins with faraway eyes and stares across the water or wherever his mind takes him.

I'll preserve him. In the sunset luster of the oncoming night.

Whir-click.

In these past ten months, the streets of Orange Mound are more familiar. Malone Blue's home, though not nearly as big as The Scarlet, still feels like a palace compared to the apartment I shared with my father, Saul. But anyplace lacking shadows and secrets would feel much larger I suppose. People wave to me like I'm an old friend, and I wave back. I return their "Hellos" and "Good mornings." Damnedest thing is when I do this, I mean it. Maybe it was last Saturday's date with Jonas that has me in such a light mood.

Orange Mound is a different place from Hyde Park. The people here have a little more, which isn't much but enough for a slightly bigger home in a slightly nicer place, still not too close to white people. Jonas said the neighborhood is built on an old slave plantation. Once owned by a man named Deaderick. I didn't listen too closely. I didn't want to give thought to what happened on this land before, only what we built on it after, what prospers on it *after*. We live here freely, or more precisely, we live and fight for our freedoms inch by inch. When Jonas told me of Orange Mound's history, I thought of what could be; what I wish to perpetually abide on it; all the good the world has to give; actually, all the good the world owes my people, all the good the world owes me. To be near one another separated by small patches of grass. To hear the footfalls of children with no fear of what might come in the night or the day. To live without a lurking thought of safety or the horrors that can befall us.

Black families. Love. Prosperity.

That isn't just my inner plea for Orange Mound. It's for Hyde Park. Binghampton. Uptown. White Haven. All of Memphis. All of Harlem. All of Atlanta. Los Angeles. Chicago too. The nation.

Peace. I think with all the pretty words swirling in my head, it boils down to one idea—peace.

Warm air glides over my skin. Turning down Cella Street, I walk past the small shotgun homes and tall trees. Mama Sugar ambles down the stairs of Malone Blue's home, built of dirty brown bricks and a flat square roof. Her hair is pulled back in a tight bun, but errant strands frame her full cheeks.

I fiddle with the button of my flowered blue-and-white top. "He up yet?"

"Naw honey. Lebbie still sleepin'."

Will sits on the porch and reads. There are light shadows under his eyes. His satchel next to him, only a few things inside since summer break is barely a couple of weeks away. Giant clouds bully their way across the sky's borders.

"Enjoy your walk?" Mama Sugar leans her body against the ivory wooden banister of the stairs.

"I did. The people around here are always nice. So that's something."

Mama Sugar takes my left hand and squeezes it. "Well, one more week and we'll get almost everything we lost back. With Clayborn Temple donating money and the little I got from Tri-State Bank, we gonna be alright. Plus Vanellys been tellin' me how useful you are over there at The New Scarlet. Between workin' with Mavis at her bakery too. Whew chile, what I wouldn't give to be young again like that. Can do a hundred things at once and not miss a beat!"

"I miss sleep. I know I miss that."

Mr. Vanellys rushes out the door. He leans on the rail giving his left leg most of his weight then the right. "Come on, Grandson. We gotta stop by the garage, then I'ma drop you off at school."

Will leaps up. Quickly grabbing his bag, the book under his arm. He gives Mama Sugar a peck on the cheek. Then me; his head is now almost level with mine. Will and Mr. Vanellys pile into his black Ford F-100 pickup truck and drive down the street.

"He's having a good morning," I say.

Mama Sugar fans herself. "Seems to be. Didn't hear them floorboards creaking last night." She walks back into the house and starts to dust the cocktail table. She moves to the end tables and dusts them too. She then washes down the countertops in the kitchen. Starts the dishes.

Lebanon sleeps in the small bed Mr. Vanellys made for him the day after we came to Malone Blue's house. He painted Lebanon's name in red letters along the side. Battered and singed, my turquoise suitcase sits a few feet away. My clothes and Louisa doll still smell like smoke. Jonas' letters are hidden in the zipped pocket on the top. There are thirty-seven of them now.

It's a miracle anything made it," Mr. Vanellys says as he sifts through the rubble. A few pictures in his hands and a piece of Bonnie Lee's crib remains undesecrated from the fire.

Lebanon turns his head the other way. Eyes still closed. A soft breeze drifts through the open window. I stroke his forehead.

"Come on, son. The world is up. You gotta get up too."

He blinks but his eyes close again.

"Sorry, boy. It's time." Gently I lift his body.

231

Kiss him three times on his forehead. He whimpers. Short hiccupy cries leave his mouth.

"I know. I know. I don't wanna be up either."

His catching breath beats against my body. Bubblegum-pink bathroom tiles framed in black greet us as we enter. Turning on the water, my free hand checks the temperature. I plug the stopper in the drain, let it run and walk to the living room.

I hear the front door squeak and his voice. "Hello!"

"You missed 'em, son. Vanellys went ahead and took Will to school," Mama Sugar says, the light clatter of dishes accompanying her voice. Jonas looks at his watch, then at me and smiles.

"Nonas! Nonas!" Lebanon wriggles his limbs and I set him down. He runs crookedly, bow-legged to Jonas, who picks him up, spinning him around. Lebanon's cries forgotten, loud squealing giggles swell the space. "Well, Ms. King, I can give you a ride to the bakery."

"I still have to bathe Lebbie. Plus it's out of your way. I can—"

Jonas sighs. "Help. It's okay to ask for it, Sara."

"I can bathe him. Bring him over to Dr. Morgan and Cora's and then head over to The New Scarlet. See what the rest of them men are up to. Can't wait for that dedication. It's gonna be something else!" Mama Sugar's eyes shine with anticipation.

"It's just that—"

Mama Sugar puts her hand on her hips. "What? It's not a problem."

"No. It's just . . . it's our thing. I like starting the day with him."

"Are you pouting?" Jonas chuckles and puts Lebanon down. "I think Little Man will be fine with Ms. Lennie."

"Amen to that. You so stingy with him now." Mama Sugar sucks her teeth. "We'll see y'all at Dr. Morgan and Cora's tonight." She picks up Lebanon and takes him to the bathroom.

Jonas waits for Mama Sugar to leave and hands me a folded piece of paper.

I place it in the left pocket of my blue stirrup pants. "I'm not gonna have much more room for these."

"Just feeling inspired."

"Am I your muse?"

"Something mighty close to it."

I grab my purse from the couch. "Well then, Mr. Coulter, as your source of inspiration, a ride to the bakery would be appreciated."

Jonas opens the front door. "I'll pick you up from the bakery too. I do round trip service."

"Smart-ass," I whisper.

"Pot. Kettle."

My right arm rides the wind as Jonas takes Douglass Avenue. Mature trees line well-trod sidewalks. Small-framed houses and neat lawns shape each block and mile.

"Is Ms. Mavis bringing caramel cake to the dedication?"

"Yes. I'll probably be the one who makes it though. She leaves me in the kitchen and stays out front taking orders. It's nice, but I can't wait to get back to The Scarlet." I pull my arm back, fixing the top button of my blouse. "Ah, I sound ungrateful. She didn't have to give me a job."

"She didn't give it to you, Sara. Ms. Mavis was probably all too happy to steal you from Ms. Lennie for a while. Everyone knows you can bake. Maybe you should consider opening your own place."

Jonas focuses on the road. His lips in a line.

"You're serious?"

"Very. Have you noticed how it's *a lot* busier since you've been there?"

I fidget with the collar of my dress.

"You got a gift. Ms. Mavis is savvy with her business. Besides, you know Ms. Mavis or Ms. Lennie or any other woman wouldn't leave you in their kitchen if they couldn't trust you in it, so you're doing fine."

Jonas reaches for my hand, entwining his fingers in mine, his thumb moving in circular motions. My own bakery. A cute little place. Somewhere in Hyde Park. Close to The New Scarlet. Something bright and all my own. Something I can be proud of. Something I can pass on to Lebanon. My recipes and a map of our future in cakes and pies, in cups and tablespoons. Is it foolish of me to want this? Am I asking for too much?

"Sara?"

"Yes?"

"Will. I was asking how he is?"

"He's been sleeping better these past few weeks. Not as much pacing during the night. But he's still . . ."

"Scared?"

The scents of oil and rubber float under my nose. My skin again sticks to the leather of the seat. "It's like he's keeping watch. Afraid of another fire. Afraid Lucky will come back to Memphis and hurt us."

"He's long gone. Think he took Diane too. She hasn't been in school since last June, a little before the fire. Almost a year now."

"Probably up North somewhere."

"Could be anywhere. Not like the police are looking. No one white was harmed. No white person's property destroyed. They don't care." Jonas bites his lip for a moment. "What about Amos? Has he been checking on Will?"

I stare out the window. "No. He's got a job working as a driver. That's what Mama Sugar says, and that's all I care to know. Amos isn't my concern. Will's better off."

Jonas glances in my direction but says nothing. North Hollywood Street charges toward us, all the possibilities of black prosperity, black entrepreneurship painted on glass windows, brick-anchored signs hanging above open doors, welcoming in hurried bodies and potential purchases. Ms. Mavis waves to us. Her compact body standing in front of the bakery talking to Malone Blue. I let go of Jonas' hand as he parks.

"What, no goodbye kiss?"

"Boy, if you think I'm going to give these people a show, you're sorely mistaken. You best focus on those young minds waiting for you."

He chuckles. "See you tonight."

Cora and Lawrence's brown-and-gold sofa is my favorite piece of furniture in their living room. A cocktail table a few feet away boasts fresh flowers in a sunshine-colored vase. Tracing the pattern along the length of the cushion with my fingertips, I focus on the wood- and brass-encased television in front of me, sturdy legs supporting the rounded-square frame and speakers on the sides. Lawrence twists a silver knob, increasing the volume.

"We preach freedom around the world, and we mean it . . . but are we to say to the world, and, much more importantly to each other, that this is the land of the free except for the Negroes?"

Jonas folds his arms, taking a deep breath, his jaw clenching. Lawrence hunkers down on the matching couch with Cora's hand holding his.

President Kennedy's thick chestnut hair remains perfectly coiffed as he speaks on the injustices suffered by us, but what will become of eloquent words? What actions will be taken? What do these words mean for Lebanon and me and Jonas, for all of us? Will sits next to Mama Sugar. He glances at the clock above the television. Mama Sugar keeps Lebanon in front of her on the floor. He plays with another set of blocks she bought him last week. "He needs somethin' to keep his mind bright. He's creative. I can tell." Lebanon stacks the blocks, and they tumble, and he laughs.

"It's past his bedtime. I should put him down," I say.

"He should be here for this," says Mama Sugar, her eyes fixed to the flickering black-and-white television in front of her. "It's important."

"It's all important," says Jonas. "University of Alabama is integrating. They're integrating schools here too. Quiet as it's kept. The Memphis School Board would be fine to drag out integration for the next hundred years." Jonas turns to me. "They only had thirteen kids integrate around here. Thirteen!"

"It was a miracle to find those," says Cora. "Plenty of parents at the church didn't want to volunteer. Had Maxine Smith and the rest of the NAACP going out almost hat in hand begging for families to consider it."

Lawrence scratches his head. "Can't say I

blame them, sweetheart. They want to keep their children safe."

Cora stiffens her back, removing her hand from Lawrence's. "I know about wanting to keep children safe."

Kennedy continues, his bold northeastern accent punctuating the most important parts of his speech, acknowledging black people have a right to live a life the same as him or any other white person. That's something to commemorate. It shouldn't be. It should be common knowledge. It should be practice. The president of any country shouldn't have to talk about how people should treat one another. This should be obvious. It should be human.

"Who knows what's possible," says Jonas. "But I'm not putting my faith in the government. Especially a government full of mostly white men. That'd be foolish. We'll always have to do our part."

"And we'll be the ones who always have to shed blood," says Lawrence, his face calm. "I can't discount the dangers we face when we're fighting for what we believe in, but maybe Kennedy's speech will force others to look at themselves, take themselves to account for the parts they play in our oppression." He sighs as he rubs his stubbly chin. "We can only hope."

"Hope." My fingers again trace and retrace the pattern of the brown-and-gold couch. I stop, looking Lawrence in his eyes. "Now, that's where the real danger lies."

Lawrence breaks my gaze, returning it to the television.

"Where's the bathroom?" I ask.

"Just past the dining room. First door to the left," says Cora.

Framed pictures of faces, some grim, some smiling, haunt me as I open the door. This isn't the bathroom. Walls painted sky blue. A rocking chair. A white crib. A dangling mobile of the stars and moon. Dust and unopened boxes. The door closes abruptly behind Cora.

"First door on the left. Not the second," she says.

"I'm sorry. I didn't—"

"It's fine. It's fine," she says, waving her hand, her body still blocking me. "Come back when you're ready. I made some deviled eggs." Cora's voice falters ever so slightly. She clears her throat. Her eyes follow me as I retreat to the bathroom and close the door.

Will isn't the one pacing the floors right now. It's Mama Sugar. In the Saturday daylight she hums old gospels as we finish getting ready for the dedication.

I fasten the last button of Lebanon's shirt as he lightly twists side to side, ready to play and mess up his nice clothes.

"Okay, son, please promise me you won't get too dirty before we get to The New Scarlet. Be on your best behavior, you hear me?"

Lebanon giggles as if I've told him the best joke and wraps his small arms around my neck, and I return his hug. He's warm. He loves his momma.

Taking one last look in the mirror, I admire my blush, knee-length pencil dress. The color reminds me of Dorothy Dandridge in *Carmen Jones*. God, I loved that movie. I loved seeing a black woman on a big screen who wasn't a maid. She was her own in all her beauty and fierceness; she was complicated and unapologetic. I hated the way the movie ended.

Mama Sugar appears at the door. "Make sure you didn't leave nothin' behind. I wanna return this house back to Mr. Blue same way he handed it to us."

"Yes ma'am."

I check under the bed for any overlooked piece of clothing. A missing shoe. A small toy. The closet. The drawers. Empty. The bed. Made. Clean sheets. Crisp edges. Vacuumed carpet, though light indents of Lebanon's bedposts remain in the corner. The house is spotless. I dare a particle of dust to touch a desk, lamp or chair. There'd be no mercy from Mama Sugar.

She swirls around the living room one last time. Narrowed eyes gliding over every surface.

I touch her shoulder. "There's nothing else to do. We're gonna be late."

"I know, but I wanna make sure I do right by him the way he done right by me."

Light vanilla notes linger in the air. A pound cake with lemon icing in a glass stand sits on the dining room table. In front of the stand, a sheet of paper with shaky cursive in Mama Sugar's hand saying only "Thank you."

Lebanon grabs my finger and we leave this house, our temporary shelter. Mama Sugar closes the door and locks it, leaving the key under the welcome mat. And for the last time, we walk down the stairs of the brown house on Cella Street.

Cora already waits for us in the car but the moment she sees Lebanon, she exits. Lebanon runs around a small patch of grass in front. He hides himself behind a small tree, really a twig with branches, his pressed white shirt and navy blue shorts against the rough, sand-hued bark. Cora keeps up with him. Her cerulean short-sleeved sheath dress clings to her svelte frame. Her matching vinyl heels slightly sink into the grass.

"I gotcha!" Cora trots after Lebanon and he runs toward me, clasping my leg and giggling. I check his clothes for any dust or dirt. He's fine.

"Alright y'all, come on." Mama Sugar walks toward the wide-bodied blue Chevrolet.

"Jonas is picking us up, so we'll meet you there in a bit."

"Sara, I forgot to tell you." Cora playfully raps herself on the head. "Jonas asked me to take you-all."

"But he always—"

"It's nothing. He's going to meet us at The Scarlet. It's fine. I don't mind driving you."

Mama Sugar sits up front next to Cora. She readjusts the mirror. Avoids my eyes. I put Lebanon on my lap, and we drive. Cora's a horrible liar, and she's hiding something about Jonas from me. Just when I think something is good and I've found a family, there's something to show me I'm wrong, that I can't trust anyone.

"Larry went and picked up all the cakes from Ms. Mavis. And I know everybody's bringing a dish. There'll be enough to feed an army," says Cora as she drives.

"Hmmpf. All them church folk and folks from the neighborhood. That's 'bout ten armies," says Mama Sugar, who laughs.

Cora laughs too. But it's empty. She shifts her gaze again to the back seat. I avoid it and look out the window. Unfamiliar blocks become familiar as the car propels us back to Hubert Avenue. My chest tightens. What awaits us there? A new home, yes. But what else? Is Lucky gone or will he be back again in the night?

"You know they said it was supposed to rain

today," says Cora. She drones on about the weather. The food. Lawrence. She finally pulls up to a white wood frame house with crimson trim and an arched roof. Three large windows span each side of the home on the first floor and showcase the large living room. Each set of windows are separated by a large oak door. My eyes strain to see a glimpse of the kitchen. Above the door, a freshly painted sign reads, THE NEW SCARLET POPLAR.

Bodies gather on the front steps. At least a hundred people or more walk down the block, crowding around each other. With no room on the sidewalk, some stand in the street, necks craned skyward. Though many of us witnessed the horror of this home's destruction, we also get to witness the awe of its rebirth. This collective measure of joy and hope is almost as much of a wonder as seeing The Scarlet rebuilt. It pushes Jonas from my mind.

Railings with carved maple leaves are anchored by two sturdy square bannisters. Five wide wooden steps lead to an immense wraparound porch with a swing on the left side.

The New Scarlet is a testament, our testament. And we bear witness to a victory, the size of which doesn't matter, but what it represents, what it signifies, is nothing short of breathtaking.

Holding Lebanon tight, I stand in the crowd as Mama Sugar makes her way to the front porch where Mr. Vanellys and Will wait for her. Buster lingers a few feet away. Elvin is a few rows behind him, and Simone stands next to him, clutching his arm. Cora finds Lawrence in the crowd and whispers something to him. Then I see him, politely weaving his way to the front.

Jonas.

My heels pockmark the grass. People maneuver as best as they can to let me pass. Lebanon tries to free himself of my grasp. "Nonas!"

"Thought you were picking us up."

Jonas looks down at me and Lebanon, who reaches for him, but Jonas doesn't scoop him up in his arms like normal. "I had a last-minute thing, an errand. Couldn't be avoided."

"We could've gone with you."

"Figured you'd want to be here on time for this, and I wasn't sure if I was going to be late."

Jonas' shaky smile holds no comfort. He gazes ahead. "You're probably happy to be sleeping back here tonight."

"What's going on?"

He points to the steps. "Looks like Ms. Lennie's getting ready to speak."

Mama Sugar walks to the first stair. "I can't—" Mama Sugar dabs her eyes. "I can't begin to thank every one of y'all gathered here. I couldn't have imagined something so grand, so beautiful. There ain't one person here who didn't give of themselves to help me rebuild a dream I thought I'd lost." Mama Sugar looks behind her and then again at the crowd. "Every nail put to wood. Every lick of paint on a wall. Every prayer prayed. Every good and kind thought. I'm grateful. When people come together like this, to help one another, lift one another up despite all the evil going on in this world, you can't tell me Memphis ain't a good place. And I thank God I call this my home and y'all my family. Thank you. Thank you. Thank you."

Unhappy with the clapping, hooting, shouting, Lebanon puts his hands over his ears. Jonas' eyes remained locked on the stairs. Trickles of sweat roll down his neck.

"Okay now I know y'all came to help us celebrate the opening but y'all know we gone feed you so head on 'round back and then we gone say grace," says Mama Sugar.

"Jonas if you have something to say—" I look at him.

"Can you hold on a minute? I'll be right back."

People pilgrimage to the backyard. A tall, older man, the same one from the Clayborn Temple Revival, stands on the back porch, fanning himself with the same straw hat. Maybe he's the official prayer of prayers for large black gatherings. Heads collectively bow.

"Lord, we come to You . . ."

". . . humbly as we know how," I mumble to myself.

And I leave them to their prayer. It isn't long. The aroma of the chicken and barbecue, the allure of potato salad, and corn bread, pinto beans, and collard greens with ham hocks perfume the air. I imagine God wouldn't want to keep people in prayer too long for a feast like this. He'd probably want Mama Sugar to make him a plate too!

Jonas silently glides past as everyone prays. He looks at me and then away. I know what this is. I had thought him, believed him, to be a braver man. How can you pretend to care for me, for my child? How can you sit with me? Kiss me. Then turn your feelings off so easily. Unless he got tired of waiting for that ruse to pay off. Thought because I had a child I was easy, a "loose woman" is what Momma called it. But I'm not, and he probably figured I wasn't worth any more trouble.

That's what this is.

I knew I couldn't trust what I felt, but as smart as I am, I still fell prey to a fairy tale.

I should've known better.

"Sara-girl! Where you goin'?" Mama Sugar's hand catches my dress. "I'ma need you to help me serve this food."

"Can I . . . I need to go but I'll be back."

"Go where? For what? Why you in such a tizzy?"

Tears roll down my cheeks. Lebanon's fingers

clutch the collar of my dress. "Please, *please* . . . just let me go."

Mama Sugar's eyes widen. "Baby, what's wrong?"

Jonas walks toward the back porch where the preacher stands. Away from me. Fine. I'm okay without you. My son will be okay without you. I'll open my bakery and if you *ever* dare to show your face, Jonas, I'll make sure to give you a slice of cake I dropped on the floor or maybe put a hex on it. I think Momma was from New Orleans or did she say her daddy was from The Islands?

Either way, Jonas can leave. I don't need him. I don't love him.

"Excuse me. Excuse me ladies and gentlemen. Some of you don't know me and those who do, probably think I've been behaving a little strange today, but I got a lot on my mind. I got someone very special in fact on my mind. That someone special is Sara Michelle King. And, I want to ask her if she'd do me the great honor of becoming my wife."

The crowd goes quiet, and slowly, each head turns to me. An ocean of curious eyes search my face. Jonas waits on the porch for an answer about his life, my life, our lives. Together.

I was wrong. I was *so* wrong.

FOURTEEN

"There's no such thing as perfect so make peace with that now. Save yourself a lot of tears later." *Momma says this to me as we walk to Calvary Hope Christian Church one Easter Sunday. You couldn't have told me she wasn't perfect though or that I wasn't perfect either. We are beautiful. Our black skin soaking in the sunlight, braving a bold breeze. Momma glides and I try to glide, but I'm not as graceful as she is yet. Our shoes click upon the concrete. We are perfect. There's such a thing as perfect, Momma. But I don't open my mouth and say this. I hold it in my heart as I hold her hand. Inside myself I vow to be perfect for the both of us.*

The New Scarlet is better than a church for my wedding. It holds the people I cherish. It's the place of new beginnings. It's built on the land where I hold some of my most precious memories. It's the place where I'll make new ones without the residue of my past or my pain or secrets. I'll make The New Scarlet my sanctuary. My holy place. And why not join my life with another in my sanctuary?

Two bags and my turquoise suitcase sit in the corner near the door. My belongings and Lebanon's ready to go to Jonas' apartment. And

I have to learn again how to create a home for us. With another. Is this the right thing? Am I doing the right thing? Is it selfish for me to marry Jonas? Sometimes it still feels wrong for me to want to be happy.

"Hello, hellooo!" says Cora in her familiar singsongy voice. She knocks twice before entering my room, shielding her eyes. Her head bowed. Cora's evergreen full skirt dress stops at her knees, three white buttons fastened to the turned-down collar. A delicate gold necklace with an aquamarine stone is around her neck, not an emerald.

"Only the groom isn't supposed to see me before the wedding and that's a silly superstition anyway. Like when Mama Sugar says not to talk on the phone during a lightning storm."

"When she'd stand, my mom always stopped her chair if it rocked. Said it was bad luck. If you left the chair rocking, you'd rock somebody out of your life. Silly little things, superstitions." Cora takes a deep breath, lowering her hand from her face, raising her head.

"Oh wow, honey you look . . . stunning."

"Stunning is you putting a wedding together in a week," I compliment.

"Well, I wanted to work on something other than the church Revival or a church fundraiser or anything else church related. I like showing off my skills outside those confines when I can. Ego,

I suppose." Cora circles me, her eyes devouring my sleeveless ivory dress. She kneels and fluffs the bottom. "He won't remember his name when he sees you."

She stands up and smiles. "With the fire and all, I didn't know if you had anything old and it really isn't my business but if you needed something or . . . wanted something . . ." Cora unclasps the gold necklace. "This could be your something old, borrowed *and* blue."

"Three out of four. You're efficient."

"Got my moments." She turns me around to face the mirror and fastens the chain around my neck. "This was my mom's. She gave it to me before I left for Spelman. It was her mom's."

Cora fastens the clasp and walks in front of me. "We always got people watching over us. My people are your people, Sara. So, they'll watch over you too." She hugs me. "I know you don't do any of that mushy stuff. But of all the days, this is one where you need to feel as much love as possible."

We're interlocked, temporal and pulsating shadow on a freshly nailed pine floor. Cora lets go and wipes her eyes, taking my left hand and looking at the simple gold band with a small circular diamond. "Bundle of nerves I am. You'd think I'm getting married today. It's so beautiful. Love is beautiful. I mean no relationship is perfect. I mean Larry and I . . ." Cora bites her lip for a moment. "Well, what I want to say is I hope Jonas knows how blessed he is to have you. Love him fully and deeply and don't hold anything back." Cora shakes her head and laughs. "Don't know why I just said that to you. Lord knows you're never afraid to tell the truth—to him or anyone else!"

Cora circles me again. She lightly tugs at the swooped collar of my dress. Presses her hand to the back of my head making sure there are no errant strands among the flawless bun she molded earlier that morning.

"Come down when you hear the music. I made Lawrence practice that song over and over. Girl, he probably felt some kind of way about me but . . . ." Cora shrugs her shoulders.

"And you didn't—"

"Jonas won't know a thing about it until Lawrence starts playing." Cora pulls her hair behind her ear.

"Thank you."

She squeezes my hand. "I'll be right downstairs."

And now I'm alone in a lovely white dress. With a good man. And a beautiful son. Alabaster high heels carry me to the bathroom.

Lord knows you're never afraid to tell the truth—to him or anyone else . . .

I throw up.

The cold water feels good on my face. But

nothing washes away the me before Memphis. And if Jonas doesn't know about me, the truth of me, before I met him, how can he genuinely love me? How can I grasp at what love even means? How can I base my love for him on a lie? On my secrets? There's this void in me, this gnawing sense all I am before will rot me from the inside if I don't speak my truth. And the only way to be free, to know if Jonas' love is genuine and abiding, if my love for him is what it could be, is if I choose to trust him with my secrets.

Love should be a relief, shouldn't it?

Jonas, if you love me. You should know me.

All of me.

Maybe Jonas has already left his apartment and he's on his way to The New Scarlet and I missed him. Maybe I walked the three blocks to David Street and up three flights of stairs for nothing. I knock again on the thick red mahogany door. Maybe it's a sign to let this go. Let things be. Let my ghosts haunt only me and spare him. Muted footsteps on the other side of the threshold echo in the empty hallway.

Dammit.

"I just put on my best suit. Don't tell me you got cold feet now," Jonas jokes, a smile brightening his whole face, a face that is open and eyes that are kind and magical to me. My stomach lurches. I might vomit again. Sharp pain radiates across my temple. Beads of sweat roll down my neck, and there is a heat underneath my skin a violent breeze couldn't cool.

Grabbing his hand, I guide Jonas to a couch next to a small wooden table overrun with paperback novels. On the other side, there's a small end table with a clock set on top of three other books, his camera next to them. Framed above the couch, a picture of the Memphis-Arkansas Bridge spanning almost the length of the sofa.

"I love that picture of the Old Bridge," he says.

"It's nice."

Jonas smiles. "Like I said Ms. King, I'm a man of many talents."

He chuckles but slowly stops because I'm not laughing. Not chuckling. Not smiling.

"Sara, what's going on?"

"You love me, and I believe you when you say it."

His hand cups my face. This will be the last time he'll want to touch me in a gentle way. You can't love a person like me. Who's done ugly things. You can't love an ugly person. I'm as ugly as one gets. Tears gather behind my eyes.

I run my fingers over the smooth, overlapping square pattern of Jonas' dove gray suit. "I believe you when you say you love me, but you don't . . . know me, Jonas. Who I was before I came here. If you did, *if you knew,* you'd run."

"I don't care you have a child. I love Lebanon

253

like my own. I don't care if you weren't married to his daddy. I don't care about any of that. I love you, Sara. I want you. All of you. Every part I know and don't know. All the good. All the bad."

"Not this kind of bad. And once I tell you . . . what I tell you. I'll go. You can take off your nice suit. I'll tell Mama Sugar and everyone else it's my fault. It's okay to leave me, to not love me or even look in my direction."

"No matter what, Sara, I love you."

"We'll see," I reply. "We'll see."

Before I close my eyes, before I tell my story, I memorize the lines of Jonas' face, the gentle way he holds my hand. And I remember that though his love is something I cherish, it doesn't determine my worth. A man's love, a woman's love, anybody's love doesn't mean you surrender everything you are to it. Never let someone's love consume you. Let it make you better.

No matter what happens, at least I've freed a part of myself that's been caged.

"I'm gonna start this story off with something pretty. Even an ugly story needs a little pretty. My momma, Sophia, loved to write and she loved to read. She'd read to me every night. One of the books Will read, *Georges*, was her favorite. You're a lot like her in some ways."

"I'm sure she was a wonderful lady."

"I was young when she died. Cancer. After she died, it was like sometimes I was numb

254

and sometimes it came on suddenly. Rage and sadness and loneliness."

Momma's clothes hang in the closet in the morning. I come home after school and the closet is empty. Daddy sits at the table skinning an apple.

"Violet and Naomi were my friends, *are* my friends. I haven't talked to them lately, but they were the closest thing I had and calling them friends is kind of . . . well, it doesn't really say all they are to me, what they've meant to me."

"You never mentioned—"

My fingers press against his soft full lips. "This isn't a give-and-take right now, Jonas. I need to tell my story. I need you to listen."

He nods.

"Violet and Naomi told me everything, but I couldn't tell them everything about me. Not about what happened when I'd go home after we'd play or go to a movie. Or after we'd say goodbye at church. At night. My father. Those things I didn't tell them."

Jonas tightens his grip on my hand. "My father. He was the pastor of our church. Everybody loved him. Saul. His name was Saul and he . . . he was a bad man, Jonas. He lied and he stole and he . . . he . . ."

Forever and to the end. A jagged piece of glass baptized in blood. Naomi repeats, "What could I do?"

255

"Even though I didn't say it, Violet and Naomi knew what was happening to me. But we also knew no one would listen. No one would believe us. Even though I carried the evidence inside my body. I'm a woman, so they'd believe I did something to invite what I never asked for. And the color of my skin has no currency, no worth, in this country, in this world. So even if I went outside of Calvary, outside of my church, what good is my voice or my story?"

Breathe.

"Naomi said she could help; she had family down here, an aunt. She called Mama Sugar, asked her if I could come here, to Memphis. Violet and Naomi and I, we made a plan. After Revival at our church, I'd say I was sick, and I'd get on a bus and come down here. But I went back to get something Saul took from me. My doll. Louisa. He found me in his office at the church."

Darkness. I still surround myself in darkness. Keep my eyes closed. "We fought. He tried to kill me . . . I still feel his hands around my neck sometimes. And when he was doing it, I was ready to die. Almost happy to die. Least I thought I was but . . . Naomi stopped him. There was a piece of glass on the floor where we were fighting, and she . . . she saved me, and Saul died instead. Violet found me and Naomi. After. And we left Saul on the floor of his office. Covered him in a yellow blanket at first, but we threw it away and the glass. Congregation and police said it was a robbery. Money from his desk was missing. That money got me to Memphis, to Mama Sugar, to you."

I try to remember Jonas' face and how he looked at me before. Jonas' hand still holds mine. He traces his thumb in small circles. He's still here. With me.

"You are remarkable. Everything you've been through. How you can find a way to love again, love me or Will or Mama Sugar. You really are something else, something precious and brave." A tear escapes his eye. "I told you, *nothing* stops me loving you, Sara. Not a damn thing. Part of me wishes I could carry all of it for you, but we can carry this, all this ugly, together and we can make something beautiful."

We hold each other. Jonas and I. Everything before us. The people we were before we met; the things that happened to us in the past aren't liabilities, they're the tiny fires by which we're shaped and molded to love one another. Momma was right. There's no such thing as perfect. There are no perfect things or perfect people. But there *is* the person who makes us kinder and better versions of ourselves, living without fear of blame or judgment while you both walk life's journey. Together.

I breathe from my deepest parts. My eyes sting

from crying. Sad tears. Now happy tears. The throbbing in my head is easing, only a faint and infrequent thump remains. Love really is freedom. It is all we can be to each other and in this reflect the best parts of ourselves to the world.

Love isn't a cure of all the bad that's happened, but it is a balm.

Jonas looks down. "Well, I don't think I can wear this now."

Tears and traces of my lipstick stain the left lapel. "You know, I have the perfect suit for this occasion." He leaves the living room.

Jonas' photographs are fanned out in front of me on the table. The towers of Clayborn Temple. Abandoned storefronts on Beale Street. People I don't know. Some smiling. Others going about daily tasks. Lebanon and me at the Revival. The Scarlet Poplar burned. The Scarlet Poplar rebuilt. Will reading a book. Mama Sugar cooking. Me. There are pictures of me. At a distance. There is a picture of grass. A picture of Jonas standing on the banks of the Mississippi River. My pictures.

"The ones of you are my favorites," he says.

"I like the one I took of you."

Jonas offers his hand as I stand up. He's wearing the indigo suit. We are where we began but so far ahead of who we were when we met on that playground.

"You ready, Ms. King?"

"You ready, Mr. Coulter?"

● ● ●

Grasping the railing, with my other hand I clutch a bouquet of thirteen roses. Walking down the stairs, I count them. There are more steps than there used to be. Five stairs to one landing. Breathe deep. Look down. Only fifteen stairs left. Then seven. Then three. Zero.

Mr. Vanellys offers his arm; he grips the wide, dark-stained banister, lifting his right leg revealing his black sock, a pool of knitted, loose fabric around the silver of where his ankle would be. "Aww Sara-girl, I don't know I wanna let you go right now." His navy blue jacket and pants slightly bunch around his slender waist. He takes a step, but I don't move.

"Before we go in, I wanted to say you were right. About mercy. All of us need it."

"We surely do."

"Thank you for showing a little mercy to me . . . and my son."

In the foyer, Mr. Vanellys takes my hand from the crook of his arm and kisses it. He tries to hide his sniffles. "Lennie needs to come in here and dust or somethin'."

Click-click-click. Cora trots in from the hallway. "Are we ready?"

Squeezing Mr. Vanellys' arm, I nod. Cora stands in front of the living room's oak double pocket doors, each with beveled glass in the middle trimmed with gold inlay. She opens them.

It still smells like fresh paint. The walls are the color of honeybees. My shoes sink slightly into the carpet and my ankle buckles, but Mr. Vanellys steadies me.

Around me are the rest of my people. Mama Sugar holding Lebanon's hand. Will in a shirt and pants he'll likely outgrow in the next few months. Elvin fidgeting with the knot of his tie and Buster helping him to fix it. Lawrence at the piano. Malone Blue, his Bible open, wedding proclamations and vows ready. And Jonas in his indigo suit. With his smile. His heart that's all mine. And I am all his.

I can't say I imagined my wedding to be like this. Never thought about getting married. But I know I'm not traditional. My life isn't that. I can write my own story.

No wedding march. No bridesmaids. No groomsmen. No organ or grand entrance.

Jonas is less than eight feet from me, but those eight feet feel like eighty. I want Mr. Vanellys to move quickly. I want to move quickly. I want to feel Jonas' hands in mine. I want to hear him say words binding him to me forever. And I want to move so quickly because as real as I know this moment is, though I know I'm not dreaming, something this pure still feels like a dream and I am afraid of dreams because they don't last. Because good things are more of a mirage to me than the bad things, and it scares me how I hold on to the bad things and not the good things, like my son and Jonas and my family, the one I built when I came to this city.

I am only three feet from Jonas, and he reaches for me, and I give my roses to Cora and put my hand in his and squeeze it. I can learn how to hold on to the good things. And let go of the bad.

Lawrence turns around at the piano; he wields his elegant fingers delicately over the black and ivory keys.

"Wonderful World." *Sam Cooke.*

Lawrence slows down the song in a simple way. Flawless. And the lyrics are what I'd want to say to Jonas. I know how wonderful and brighter my world is, and his firm grip of my hand is a promise. This song is my declaration.

Jonas looks over his shoulder at Lawrence, then at me and smiles and kisses my left hand.

"Let me hurry up and find my verse before these two just go on ahead without me." Malone laughs and flips through the pages of his Bible. First stopping and then thumbing through the pages again. And finally settling on whatever he's looking for: *"Cause me to hear thy loving kindness in the morning; for in thee do I trust; cause me to know the way wherein I should walk; for I lift up my soul unto thee."*

I think Malone's reading from Psalms. It could be Proverbs. But the rest of his words don't reach me. It's like when I went swimming as a child and finally reached the surface, but my ears were still clogged with water. Sounds are far away.

Momma told me to count but if I tried right now, I can't say the numbers would be in the right order, that I can discern a minute from an hour. Everything now seems like an hour when I'm sure it's only a minute.

Jonas' arms encircle my waist and we kiss and there's clapping and cheering and Lebanon's fingers grasp at the end of my dress. I pick him up. And it's us three.

There are things I don't know. I don't know where I'll be from one moment to the next, what the next day will bring. But I know some things. I know the people in this room are my family.

The thing I know most in this moment is, I love you Jonas Coulter.

"Told you everyone wanted to come and wish you and Jonas well," says Mama Sugar.

I bend down and fix Lebanon's hair. "You told people you were cooking. That was enough."

"Well, I want to celebrate something good. Don't you?"

My headache returns not as potent, but a steady throb between my eyes. I turn the gold band on my finger with my thumb. Bodies spread onto adjoining properties. Five long wooden tables are draped in different-patterned tablecloths and arranged side by side. Ribs, ham, chicken, both fried and smothered; pinto beans with ham hocks, candied yams; potato salad, and other dishes, cold and hot, sweet and savory, are spread on top.

Checking for Cora's necklace, I then smooth the front of my dress. "A few people. You said a few people."

"This *is* a few people," says Mama Sugar.

"This is the whole neighborhood. And your church."

She rearranges the order of the cakes. Her pineapple upside down cake first. Ms. Mavis' caramel cake second. Chocolate cake third and so on.

"Yeah, a few. There wouldn't be room to move in this here backyard if I'd invited everybody."

Tables and chairs are set up near the garage on the left side. One small table holds a record player. Rich R&B ballads impart soulful that can be heard down the street.

Will walks from the east corner of the lot. "Elvin said he's gonna play 'The Twist' next."

"Oh! The Chubby Chester song!" says Mama Sugar.

"Chubby *Checker,* Granny," corrects Will, a small grin forming.

"Chester. Checker. Same difference."

"I love that song!" says Jonas behind me, his arms encircling my waist.

Booming and rhythmic, drums and saxophone hijack the air. Chubby Checker belts his confident rousing command to dance. Legs nimbly pivot in and out. Hips swing. On beat and on time.

Not Jonas.

Whatever he does is not what Chubby Checker asks. Will looks over; his eyes catch mine. He bows his head and snickers. Lebanon totters over, standing still in front of Jonas. And, then tries to move his little body in the same way. Offbeat and awkward and so cute. So damn cute.

"Come on, Sara." Will grabs my hand, moving his beanstalk limbs with easy energy.

A crowd gathers around Will and me. Smiling faces. Clapping in rhythm. We twirl. We shimmy. My feet in sync with Will. My body in sync. I move and I glide and I laugh.

Is this joy? Genuine, true joy?

Whatever this is, happiness or bliss or delirium, let it last. Let it last. Despite all the petty inconveniences life visits on us, despite the tragedy and trauma I've endured, let me hold on to this feeling. It makes me whole.

As the song ends, Will hugs me. "You can dance really good."

"You dance very well, Will," corrects Jonas.

"You dance very well, Sara," repeats Will.

"Thank you, Will."

He walks to Mama Sugar, who still watches

Brother Bernard as he removes the last of the barbecue from the smoker. Lebanon babbles something and points to the sky as Mr. Vanellys picks him up.

Jonas takes my hand as I catch my breath. "You do dance very well, Mrs. Coulter."

"Well, I am a woman of many talents, Mr. Coulter."

Elvin lifts the needle of the record player and switches the forty-five. As the sun starts to set, coral-shaded clouds and lavender-tinted skies take their measure of the horizon.

"I Only Have Eyes for You" floats through the dusk of day. The Flamingos serenade the neighborhood.

"Side to side, Jonas."

"What?"

"Dance. Just hold me and move side to side."

That smile. He smiles *that* smile. The one that makes me smile too. "Yes ma'am."

I cling to him. And he to me. In my mind I pray, I actually pray, to remember every bit of this moment. His scent. The feel of his hands on my back. The warmth of gold on my finger. The way my feet lightly ache in these shoes. I let go in a way I didn't at The Iris Club because now there's no fear. Only freedom. And gratitude. And this part of my present, and the rest of my future, is my victory.

Our love is a victory.

. . .

"I'm gonna start cleanin' up in a little bit so I can at least try and keep my eyes open during church tomorrow," says Mama Sugar.

Only a dozen or so people remain half an hour before midnight. Lifting Lebanon from my lap, I pass him to Cora. Mama Sugar touches my shoulder. "Chile, I'm not gonna let you or Jonas help me clean up after your wedding reception! I got many able bodies." Mama Sugar eyes the table. Buster, Elvin, Mr. Vanellys and Will all look off at some phantom in the stars.

"If y'all don't stop playin' with me—"

"Lawrence and I will be all too happy to assist you," volunteers Cora.

"My fingers are so sore. I mean, I had a surgery yesterday and playing the piano today and—"

Cora clears her throat and lightly elbows Lawrence in his ribs.

"Ms. Lennie, I'm completely at your service," he says.

"Hey Momma." Amos walks up from behind in a tailored black suit and a slightly crooked tie. His skin less sallow, eyes not so sunken. The pompadour he had is gone, replaced with a close cut and a small part on the right side of his head. Almost identical to Jonas. He struts around the table, kissing Mama Sugar on her cheek and looks at Will.

She pulls away. "Why're you here?"

266

"I, uh, came to see how y'all was doing—" he turns to Jonas and me "—and offer my congratulations to the new couple."

Amos walks toward Will. "Hey son. You got plenty big since I last seen you."

Will leaves the table. I stand. So does Mama Sugar. Whenever Amos is involved, Will runs.

"I'll get him," says Jonas.

Amos frowns. "He needs to show some respect."

Mr. Vanellys walks toward Amos. "We ain't seen you since before The Scarlet burned down. You didn't come and help rebuild. You ain't even talked to your son. So what respect is he supposed to give you? You ain't raisin' him. We doin' the raisin'. You come and go easy as a breeze."

Amos lifts his chin. "I still got that job over in Germantown. Driving for a nice white family. Got some money in my pocket and I'm aimin' to send for Will soon as I finished getting settled."

"I had enough. I've tried over and over and I . . . just leave Will to us," says Mama Sugar.

Amos looks at her for a moment, his gaze then drifting to Jonas and Will standing a few feet away next to the vegetable garden. Jonas' arm rests on Will's shoulder.

He buttons his jacket and straightens his tie. "I'ma be back for my son."

"You won't," Mama Sugar says. "You've said that before. Now, you mean what you say when it leaves your mouth, but somethin' else always grabs your attention. Will is the last thing you think about once you start drinkin' and gamblin'." Mama Sugar walks up to Amos and puts her hand on his heart. "You gotta love yourself 'fore you can even think about loving him, and you ain't never been able to do that. When you get yourself straight, and I mean straight, then we'll work with you. But until then, it's best if you stay gone."

Amos steps away from Mama Sugar, whose hand falls limply at her side. "You stealing my son from me, is that it? You think you'll do better the fourth time around?"

Amos glares at me. "Or the fifth?"

"You're gonna make me ruin my nice pretty dress. Get blood on my ring too. And I don't, I *really* don't want to whip your ass on my wedding day," I say, meeting Amos' flat brown eyes, "but I will."

Cora covers Lebanon's ears.

Buster whistles long and low. "My money's on Sara."

"Y'all ain't worth it." Amos stares again at the vegetable garden. "None of y'all worth it." He turns around, trudging off, the covetous mouth of evening swallowing him. The shrieking of rubber moments later announces his departure. Lebanon reaches for me and begins to whimper. I take him from Cora, place him on my lap, bouncing him up and down on my knee and he laughs.

Mama Sugar looks at the sky and then at the table. "Don't matter what happened just now. It was still a beautiful day." She turns to me. "And Sara-girl, I ain't seen no one look so pretty." She walks toward the back door of the house.

"I know that's right," says Buster.

"Indeed!" agrees Lawrence, who picks up his plate and a few others and heads to the house.

"Yeah, I guess you looked okay," says Elvin, a smirk on his face. He stands and stretches. "I should get on back to Simone."

"Simone can wait. You can help clean up," says Buster, picking up discarded cups and silverware. " 'Cause you not gettin' away from this hard work."

"Well Mr. Bellamy Fairbanks, you not the one who's givin' out orders."

Buster drops his plate to the ground. It's still in one piece. He checks to make sure Mama Sugar didn't see him and quickly picks it up. "How in the hell did you figure out—Who told you?"

"Bellamy Fairbanks! That's a movie star name, like Sidney Poitier," gushes Cora. "I love it!"

Buster grins. "Used to get hell for it when I was a kid. When Vanellys and I enlisted back in '42, he started calling me Buster. Name took."

Cora fiddles with the hem of her dress. "So that's when you-all met, in '42?"

"We always knew each other from 'round the neighborhood but when we enlisted. Well . . .

269

there are things that bind people I suppose," says Mr. Vanellys.

"I needed a job. I fought for my country, so you'd think we'd be in them parades and gettin' handshakes." Buster sniffles. "Didn't work that way for us. No gratitude. No respect. Still gotta go 'round the back. Get off the sidewalk if a white man is walkin' on the same block. Thousands of miles away fought like a man, bled like one, but couldn't get treated like one here. People was freed in their country, and we still not free in our own."

Lawrence puts his arm around Cora, who lays her head on his shoulder. She exhales long and slow. "My daddy too. He wasn't the same when he came back. I was young but I remember the air left the room if he was having a bad day."

"But we wasn't fighting for this country as it was then, as it is now, but what it could be for Will, Lebbie, all of y'all. So—" Mr. Vanellys rubs his right leg and clears his throat "—don't have no regrets about that 'cause I was doin' the right thing. We both was. Your daddy too, Cora. Can't help it if others wanna stay blind. Anyway, I ain't gonna let Buster keep lyin'." Mr. Vanellys sadly chuckles. "He kept showin' up 'round the house. Just couldn't get rid of him durin' combat . . . or after. Brought him back home. Like a stray puppy. 'Sides, Lennie Mae likes takin' care of lost things."

"Yeah, if it wasn't for this stray puppy, them garage doors wouldn't be open for as long as they've been. My fine arithmetic skills been keepin' cars flowin' in and outta there for the past fifteen years. I'm the brain in yo head."

"And the pain in my ass," retorts Mr. Vanellys.

Buster smacks his lips. "Anyhow, Ms. Cora, don't matter what I was called back then. I know what I call myself now." He looks at Mr. Vanellys. "And pain in the ass or not, everybody knows Buster. But Uncle Sam always go by your government name."

He turns to Elvin, right hand slapping his knee. "Henrietta! Yo momma told you my name."

Elvin crosses his arms. "I could've figured it out by myself."

Buster raises his left eyebrow. "Say I'm lyin'."

Elvin sheepishly smiles. "Yeah, yeah. Momma told me. She remembered since y'all went to Manassas High together."

Buster laughs. "Get on over here Woodrow and help with this mess."

"I told y'all before, Woodrow is a respectable name." Elvin turns around. "Hey Bellamy Fairbanks, what's 1,215 divided by 81?"

"I'm not an adding machine."

Elvin scoffs. "I knew you was tellin' tall tales. You can't—"

"It's fifteen. One thousand two hundred and fifteen divided by eighty-one is fifteen."

"Man, I can't tell if you lyin' anyway."

Elvin and Buster take a few plates, cups and forks from the table. Buster lightly pushes Elvin, who almost drops a plate.

Hands on her hips, Mama Sugar yells, "Y'all betta not drop a dish playin' around!"

"Well, this was quite an eventful evening," says Cora.

Unclasping the necklace, I place it in her hand, covering it with mine. You don't always need words. Sometimes they fall short so it's best to say nothing. She squeezes my hand, taking the necklace and putting it back on.

Thin arms hug me from behind. "Night Sara."

"Night Will."

He walks back to the house with Cora and Lawrence. He stops and turns for a moment staring at the street, then goes inside.

Jonas bends down, eyes level with mine. "Hell of a day."

"But a good day."

"A very good day." He looks at Lebanon and me. "Where are your things?"

"Upstairs in our room, well what used to be our room." I gaze at the middle window on the third floor.

He kisses me on the forehead. "I'll be back."

I place my naked feet on the grass. If I can feel the grass, then I'll know this isn't a dream. I know Jonas will come back and not disappear like a ghost. I won't wake up in a sweltering room, back where I started, with the injured heart I had, with the hope I lacked, with my joy depleted.

Lebanon nestles his little body close to mine and looks at me and smiles, and all I see in him is me. What I want to give him is the world. I'm not too broken to love. I'm not broken at all. I am not the things I told myself I was because of what was done to me. And he is not what I thought because of how he came to be. Lebanon doesn't deserve that burden. It is ugly and unfair. He is all of me. All that is good. And I'll help him see that. We can teach each other to see the good, and Lebanon must know something. He must always know this.

I love you. I love you, Lebanon.

Your mother loves you so very much.

FIFTEEN

Jonas' lips form a tight line. He crosses his arms, looks back at Lebanon playing on the couch and then returns his gaze to me. "I can't do it Sara. I won't."

Boxes of papers, journals and photo negatives line the back wall of the apartment. The end tables are free of overflowing books. Many of Jonas' pictures are framed, decorating the newly daisy-painted walls of the living room. The apartment is almost habitable, and it took me almost two months to get it this way.

"I've been at this since the day after our wedding. Your books and pictures kept you company. Now you have Lebbie and me. You have a whole family in a tiny space. Hard decisions must be made. Well, hard for you."

His eyes dart from left to right, then left again. "You're really making me do this."

The choice lies before him. One he can't escape, and I wish I could help my husband, but such things are for him alone to determine.

Three copies of Ralph Ellison's *Invisible Man* lay on the coffee table.

I slide my wedding band along my finger. "How does a grown man wind up with three copies of the same book?"

Jonas rubs the back of his neck. "When I couldn't find one copy, I bought another one. I wrote different notes in all of them. It's a classic piece of literature! Each one is special."

I fold my arms across my chest. "Well, find the most special one and part ways with the other two."

"We should start looking for a bigger place in Hyde Park. Something close to The New Scarlet."

"Uh-huh. Until then, you still have to make a decision."

Jonas' right hand hovers over the second copy, then the first, then the third and he repeats the pattern. He looks back at Lebanon. "Help me out Little Man." Lebanon looks at Jonas and laughs.

I thrust the first copy against his chest. I was wrong. I'll make this decision for him. I don't have the patience. Jonas takes the other two copies of *Invisible Man*, placing them in the leftmost box against the back wall.

He looks around. "You came in here like a tornado."

"And did the exact opposite of what tornadoes do. You can say thank you anytime you want."

He laughs then kisses me. "Thank you."

I set Lebanon on the floor to walk. "Let's go. We're gonna be late."

Jonas looks at his watch and groans. "Yeah, I'd normally arrive at the school earlier."

"Please tell me how the English teacher winds up with math classes in summer school?"

"As I've said, my love, I'm a man of—"

"Many talents. Yeah, so you keep repeating." I stifle a yawn.

Jonas takes Lebanon's other hand as I close the door. What I envied of Cora as she held Lebanon at the Revival; the way she looked with Lawrence, the way they looked together, I have that and it's not a thought or mirage or fantasy. It is fact and truth. We are a family.

Mature trees line University Street. Branches heavy with leaves sway against the ripening dawn sky. The Impala softly rumbles through the short blocks to The New Scarlet.

Inside, I find Mama Sugar sprinkling flour on the countertop. The dull smack of dough on the butcher block fills the kitchen. Billowy white tufts rise and disappear. She kneads the dough with a rolling pin into a wide sheet. "Feelin' in a decent mood. Makin' butter rolls today."

Lebanon runs over to Mama Sugar. She bends down, kissing his forehead.

"I can finish that."

"You ain't made butter rolls before, Sara-girl."

"Yes, I have. With Ms. Mavis at the bakery."

She folds her arms, a grudging smile spreading across her full lips. "Alright Ms. Know Everything. You go on and make them, but I'm here if you need me." She shakes her head as she takes off her apron. "You and Jonas two peas in a pod. I'ma tend to my baby. Where's Lebbie's blocks?"

Yawning again, I point to the bottom cabinet.

"Didn't get enough sleep?"

"I did actually. Can't shake feeling tired sometimes I guess."

Mama Sugar's eyes narrow. "Uh-huh. Maybe that's it."

Impatient footfall echoes in the back stairwell. "Today, I'm a man," announces Will. He puts his book on the pine table. *The Fire Next Time.* He places his schoolbag on the floor.

"Jonas has you reading James Baldwin? He's been talking about him and that book nonstop."

"Actually, *I* told him about it. See? A man."

"Boy if you a man, I'm the Queen of Sheeba," retorts Mama Sugar.

"Granny, I'll be in eighth grade next year. I'm gonna be thirteen in a few months. Taking summer classes. Getting ready to go to Douglass High. Granddad even said I could start working with him and Buster at the garage soon."

Mama Sugar watches Lebanon play with his blocks. "Keep up with your arithmetic, readin' and puttin' school first, and we can talk about the garage. Now hurry up. Jonas waitin' for you."

Will runs to the refrigerator on the right side of the kitchen instead of the left where it used to be. He grabs the lunch Mama Sugar packed for him.

I cut the butter rolls, making sure each is

evenly spaced apart before I pour in the sweet milk. "Excuse me? No 'hello'? No hug? A *man* remembers his manners."

Will smirks and kisses me on my cheek, his head officially above mine. "Morning, Sara." His voice is deeper, too. Slightly but it's a change. "Like your flowers?"

"Yes. I do."

Three blue-violet flowers bloom in a clear mason jar, a familiar branch of my past in a kitchen curated on a shelf by the rapidly growing young man in front of me. He picks up the book and his satchel, jogging out of the house, the door closing behind him. The light roar of Jonas' car echoes in the kitchen as they pull off.

"Before you ask me, he's sleepin' better. He might get up and roam around but not as much as when we was on Cella Street."

"The flowers are a good sign." I place the rolls in the oven, larger and newer than the one before it.

"If they find Oliver, maybe Will can be more at ease during the night." Mama Sugar leans closer to me and whispers, "Elvin said he heard Oliver was in Arkansas. Someone else said New Orleans."

"Amos come back around?"

Mama Sugar washes her hands in the kitchen sink. "Naw. He ain't seen Will either. Quit his job over in Germantown from what Carolyn told me.

She works for a family over there too. He'll be back 'round soon enough if he get desperate or hungry."

"You getting any rest?"

"Do we ever rest, Sara-girl?" Mama Sugar chuckles. "It ain't Oliver keepin' me up, the fear of him coming back to do harm. Sometimes I lie awake and think about my rights and wrongs. If one outweighs the other. And . . ."

"And?"

"I don't know. I don't know. Seems like a meaningless question. I'm torturing myself for no good reason."

Faint thumps above us grow closer, louder. The boarders are awake and will soon be ready for breakfast. Mama Sugar begins opening and closing the cabinets, craning her neck up and down the shelves. "I gotta get some more shortening and a few other things for dinner later. I'ma go to Sinclair's Grocery."

"Is he even gonna be open this early?"

"Paul will open up for me."

"I can go."

Mama Sugar takes Lebanon and puts him in a high chair, placing a few of his blocks on the small tray in front of him. "You stay here. Mind them boarders. Now Buster's back, he got all kinds of energy. We got three new people. One of 'em are coming the end of next week."

"Professor?"

"No, a lawyer, workin' for the S . . . C . . . L-something or other."

"The SCLC?"

"Mmm-hmm. That one. They doin' a lot of organizin' with Reverend King and all, so make him feel welcome. He goes back and tell his friends, we'll have more business than we know what to do with. I gotta justify takin' you back from Mavis somehow. She's still mad at me."

"Does that really bother you?"

An unrepentant grin crosses Mama Sugar's face. "Naw, 'cause you was with me first. I'm reclaiming what's mine."

I smile. "You sure you don't want me to go to the grocery store?"

"Chile, do what I ask."

There's no comforting creak as Mama Sugar returns through the back door; the new hinges are quiet. Four bags of groceries weigh down her arms. Buster takes them from her, placing them on the countertop. A relieving gust of wind flows through the stifling kitchen. Lebanon's face is covered with grits. He uses his hands as a spoon.

Buster stretches, letting out a long sigh. "Lennie, I saw perch in the bag."

"Yeah, we havin' perch, macaroni and cheese, and turnip greens for dinner."

Buster rubs his rotund stomach and walks to

the back door. "Thinkin' of that meal is gonna get me through this whole day."

"Sooner you get to work, the sooner you can get back and stuff your face."

Buster closes his notepad. "Let me go on ahead and save Vanellys from himself."

Mama Sugar laughs and looks over her shoulder. "Sara-girl after you finished eatin', wash them greens. Then put them on the stove and simmer and then season the flour for the perch. We don't gotta get started on the macaroni and cheese until later. I don't want the noodles gettin' all rubbery. I'll get started on tidying up these rooms."

I shake a generous amount of pepper on my eggs and eat faster, taking alternative bites of bacon and butter rolls.

"Slow down. I said when you finished! That food ain't gonna hop off your plate," says Mama Sugar as she closes the back door.

I slide a roll through the bacon grease. "Did you do something different with the dough? They're so good."

"I ain't changed my recipe and you cooked 'em."

I wipe my face with a napkin and then take a clean napkin and wipe Lebanon's face. After I lift him from his high chair, he puts his lips to my cheek and slobbers all over it. Leaning back, he admires his sloppy handiwork. His version of a kiss. This boy. I tickle his stomach and he giggles high, free. And that sound is wonderful to my ears now. His laugh.

Mama Sugar folds her arms. "Thought you didn't want us pickin' him up so much. Said he'd be spoiled."

"What I spoil, I can unspoil."

"So, you stole my line?"

I kiss Lebanon's forehead. "More like actively borrowing wisdom."

Mama Sugar walks up the back stairway. "You got a word for everything."

I set Lebanon on a gold knit blanket with white trim, and his favorite building blocks. He places them one on top of another. Knocks them down. Repeats. His favorite game.

It's relaxing to clean, rinsing off dirt and grime, whatever remains, clinging to the greens. I place them in a large silver pot, like the one we used to have, but this pot is larger and deeper.

There's a knock and the dull thud of paper hitting the floor. Lebanon still plays as I walk to the living room. I take the mail, separating each piece.

Matching white curtains cover three windows on each side of the door. Only a few of the same pictures survived the fire and sit on the mantel above the fireplace. Mama Sugar and Mr. Vanellys when they were young. The picture of Bonnie Lee in her dress. Mr. Vanellys and Mama Sugar and Amos as a child. The one of Lucky is gone. Maybe it burned in the fire. Maybe Mama Sugar burned that picture on her own.

The second to last envelope is thick, thicker than the rest. It's addressed to me. From Violet. It's been a while since her last letter. The one I destroyed. I should tear up this one too. It's part of my silence. Never a letter returned, or a call made. But Violet is equally as stubborn as I am, if such a thing is possible. Sisters don't give up on each other. They do for one another like no one else can or will. The clatter of wooden blocks hits the floor. There is a giggle. I open the letter.

Dear Sara,

I was in church Sunday. When everybody bowed their heads, I looked at the third row, on the right, where you and Naomi and I sat. I thought about us and the hopes we had for ourselves, for each other. And sometimes there's a heaviness I can't quite make sense of. Maybe it's the melancholy of a rainy day or maybe Thomas is getting on my nerves or maybe it's your absence.

Learning to get through the days in a different way is a challenge, but Jackson helps me fill the quiet hours. We named the baby Jackson Blaisdell Potter. Blaisdell is Thomas' daddy's name. I can't tell you how much I hate it, but Thomas loves his father and I love him, so I really didn't have a choice in the matter.

Naomi's wedding was beautiful! She was such a pretty bride. She danced at the reception if you can believe it! I'm certain Gialan realizes how lucky he is. I made sure he heard that from me. A lot. I told him for the both of us.

I know you have your reasons for not writing back or calling. Maybe forgetting about us is the best way for you to move on, but I'm selfish and I don't want to forget. Even the bad things I want to keep. I'll keep writing to you, but you don't have to read these words. I hope you're okay, that you're happy or finding your way to it.

Forever and to the end.
Violet

Tucked in the magnolia-scented paper are pictures. Of Violet. Her and Thomas. Jackson. All of them. Naomi at her wedding. Naomi and Gialan. Naomi dancing. Their lives captured in black and white, still moments, fleeting emotions. Enduring memories, merciful reminders of joy when the world is too much.

I'm not there in those pictures. I'm somewhere else. In another set of snapshots. Another life.

Violet and Naomi severed from it. By choice. My choice. Maybe I was wrong. Maybe there's a way to unite my two lives, who I was with who I am now.

Maybe it doesn't have to be a choice at all.

The phone in the living room sits on the end table next to the plastic-covered, pumpkin-orange couch. It's hard to fit my finger in the small circle of the rotary phone's printed numbers. I flex my fingers to stop the shaking. Deep breath. Dial the number, Sara. Do it.

Ring. Ring. Ring.

I pray Violet won't pick up, though I want to hear her voice.

Ring. Ring. Ring.

What do I say to her? I was lost. Then I found a new family. I found Jonas. I love my son.

Ring. Ring—

"Hello?"

Say something. Dammit. Say something!

"Hello? Is anyone there?"

I miss you, Violet. I miss Naomi. I want us to be friends again.

"Sara? Sara?"

I hang up. Write. I should write a letter instead. Writing is always better. With words on paper you can plan, take time to say all you want to say. I sit on the couch. A blank sheet of paper on the cocktail table. I flex my left hand before I pick up the pen.

Dear Violet,

It's been hard to write you. I could say I was busy getting settled, getting to know Memphis, but it wasn't that. After all this time, after you've been so patient in waiting to hear from me, you deserve the truth. And the truth is I'm not sure of a single reason why I didn't write or call. It was a lot of things: fear and pride and maybe grief because of what I believed I left behind with you and Naomi.

But after being in Memphis, in this city where I was so alone, I figured out I never really was. I never really lost you or Naomi. I think a lot about when we were younger. When we met. When you gave me my first pair of sunglasses. When I feel lost, sometimes thinking of you both keeps me anchored.

Mama Sugar and her husband, Mr. Vanellys, are kind to me and treat me like their daughter. Their grandson Will is, well, I love him like I love Lebanon. And I do love Lebanon.

And, this is going to surprise you, but I'm married. His name is Jonas Coulter. He's a teacher. He loves to take pictures like Thomas. He writes poetry and love letters. Violet, he's such a good man, one I convinced myself I didn't deserve, but I do. I deserve happiness and love and to be free from the past.

You were right. Don't get used to me saying that often.

I called you and hung up. I'm sorry. But I wrote this letter as a token, a symbol, of a new beginning for us. Like the spring, I'm hopeful everything again can be new.

Forever and to the end.
Sara

Everything is switched around, different at The New Scarlet. The kitchen isn't home yet. Things that used to be on the left are on the right and vice versa. This part of the house still needs to be tamed, dominated. Jonas sits across from me at the pine table, writing in the margins of a book, the one he and Will are reading together, *The Fire Next Time*. The scratching of his pen is almost unceasing.

I wipe down the countertop. "You writing your own novel?"

"So much good stuff here. It's like Baldwin reached into my head and pulled out all the things I feel but can't put to paper. Not like this. But—"

"But what?"

"Eh, when he's talking about racism, injustice, he focuses it pretty much on Harlem, but injustice lives everywhere, bleeds into everything."

"Yeah, but when you write what you know, where you know it, and how you know it, it rings truer. And James Baldwin doesn't have to speak for everybody, just himself. Seems doing that touched enough people. Touched you." I turn around and look at Jonas. "And *you* can write your own book. You sell yourself short."

"Oh, a compliment. Is that an early birthday gift?"

I roll my eyes and turn my attention back to cleaning the kitchen.

The scratching of Jonas' pen stops. "Speaking of birthdays, I was thinking about maybe having a birthday party here if Ms. Lennie would let me."

"A party?"

"It'll be a small party," says Jonas. "Well . . . smallish."

"I've seen the Memphis version of a *small* party."

Jonas walks over to the stove and lifts the top of the silver pot, the turnip greens now simmering in a chicken broth; the sharp, earthy scent briefly lingers in the kitchen. "Maybe we can even celebrate Little Man's birthday."

"Lebanon's birthday was in April. What's the point of a birthday party in August? It's four months late and he won't remember anyway." I slap his hand away from the pot. I stir the greens three times, placing the lid back on. "We already celebrated his birthday. I baked a cake. You bought him a new toy. We sang a song. Simple. I like simple, Jonas."

"It's about us doing it together. It'll be my first birthday with you, with Little Man. It's a milestone, you know."

"You wanna celebrate my birthday too?"

"Sara, I'm happy to celebrate every day I spend with you. I'll throw you a party whenever you want me to."

Jonas smiles that smile. That charming one and I feel my resolve fading. "We can wait until he's older. Have a nice, quiet dinner at home for your birthday this year. Why the need for people?"

"Because everybody should celebrate him, us, as a family. We'll look back on it and remember. Laugh at his face full of cake. I'll take pictures. And—" Jonas hugs me from behind "—I'll use those photos and show him how pretty his momma is."

"You know sweet talking doesn't sway me, so why do you do it?"

"It works a little." Jonas chuckles, kissing the nape of my neck. "And I'll try anything and everything I can."

He whispers in my ear, "At least consider it. It's good to create memories, look back on our lives one day and smile. Do it for me as a birthday gift."

"The party will be small?"

"Smallish," says Jonas.

I stop wiping the counter and turn on the faucet to run fresh dishwater. Artificial lemon from the dishwashing liquid stings my nose. "I give up. Invite who you want. It's your birthday." I yawn and look at Lebanon. "And apparently his birthday again too. I'm not gonna keep going back and forth with you."

He kisses me on the cheek. "Thank you, Sara."

I dry my hands and turn around. I caress his face. "Mr. Coulter, I have no clue what I'm gonna do with you."

Will walks into the kitchen. "I'm starving." He looks at the stove. "Perch, greens *and* mac 'n' cheese with corn bread. I'm sitting at this table until dinner's ready."

"No, you're going with me to the post office. I'm gonna drop off this letter. I want a little company."

"But—"

"Extra piece of corn bread in it for you."

"You didn't let me finish. I was going to say, 'But I would be all too happy to escort you to the post office.' "

Grabbing the letter, I walk toward the living room. "Come on Will. Get the lead out."

He jogs behind. The door rattles as he closes it. Will's stride is longer, his gait more confident. I haven't been in Memphis that long or have I? How is he growing so fast? Lebanon. He grows too. Changes. I carried him inside me. Then in my arms. Now he talks. Kinda. He walks. He laughs and is open and loves me. How do I commemorate the small moments, the ones rushing by disguising themselves as tedious flashes of time? A party. Jonas was right about that, I suppose. It'll be nice. I'll tell Lebanon stories of that day, even though it'll be some foggy dream on the borders of his memory.

"You're doing it again."

"Doing what?"

Will's right hand taps the tops of the fence posts of passing homes. "You're off somewhere else. Like your body is moving but your mind's on a trip."

"I do that a lot?"

Will nods. "It makes sense to me though. Sometimes I need the quiet to think."

"I like the quiet."

"Yeah, quiet's good."

Brash voices beckon on the corner across from us on Tunica Street. Four men hunch over on Eldridge Avenue. Wrinkled bills lay near each foot, a pair of dice faintly clack against the ground. Every man takes their turn, rolling, then snapping their fingers after they let go of the dice.

"Seven!" yells one of them. He snatches the money from the ground.

Will stares across the street, then quickens

his pace. I struggle to keep up. His longer legs now pump forward with power and anger. "Slow down!"

"Sorry," he mumbles.

"Hey!" A voice crashes into my ears. Will's eyes sharpen into slits, his jaw clenches. Amos' smell announces him before his body stands next to mine; sweat and liquor assaults my nose.

"Y'all took off quick as hell! Didn't you hear me callin' after you, boy? Wanted to talk. Had a good hand goin' too." Amos smiles as if waiting for a compliment on some supposed altruism while anyone with half a mind toward their kin would reason to stop gambling and speak to their son. It is the *least* a father can do.

Will grabs my wrist, pulling me along. "We need to be going. Got errands."

"Wai-wai-wait!" Amos reaches for Will, who pulls away before he can get a grip.

"I only wanna talk."

Will's eyes grow glassy. "I don't."

"I left them guys." Amos clutches crumpled dollar bills in his left hand, his teeth yellowed, hair matted. "Give me a little time. That's all I've needed."

"You've had my whole life. Nothing's gonna be different. You won't change." Will turns, still grasping my wrist. "I don't need you," he says, his voice cracking.

Amos' hand covers his mouth, bowing his head.

An errant tear falls down his cheek, but he wipes it and walks away.

I pry Will's hand from me. "Walk to the end of the block. I'll be right back."

"What're you doing?"

"What did I say?"

Will huffs and stalks down Tunica Street.

Amos stands at the opposite end of the block, clutching a wooden fence post. I touch his shoulder and he jumps. "Don't make me regret this, Amos."

"What?"

"There's gonna be a party at The New Scarlet. On August 25. You can come but you gotta do better than this." My hand gestures to his body. "You gotta give Will *something* to believe in."

Amos straightens his back. "I'll be there."

"You better because I won't go to bat for you again. I'm all too happy to have Will. So is Mama Sugar and Mr. Vanellys."

I turn around. Will stands half a block away. Waiting for me.

When I reach him, I say, "I invited him to Jonas' party."

"Why did you do that, Sara?"

"No one likes owning the harm they've done to others. It makes them hurt in a forever kind of way. Give him one more chance. I'm not feeling sorry for him, I'm just saying I understand him."

"You're not like that."

"Oh Will." I cradle his face in my hands. "I can be the worst of all, but . . ." I look past him as Amos unevenly totters away toward Eldridge Avenue. "I'm trying to be better. You help with that. Lebanon too."

A small grin tugs at Will's mouth. "And Jonas."

"Yes, and Jonas."

I put my arm around his shoulders. "You know that James Baldwin book you and Jonas are reading?"

"Yeah."

"You aren't the only two who read it. Jonas had another copy lying around. Probably has two more somewhere lost in our apartment."

Will snickers. The post office is a few feet away. A row of mailboxes sit in front of the small brick building. I drop Violet's letter in the slot of the first one. "When Baldwin wrote to his nephew, I saw your face. I saw Lebanon's and Jonas'. I saw mine and Mama Sugar's. And I thought it's sad he had to write that letter because no one should have to prepare you so soon for bad things. But we gotta be way more prepared than most in this city, in this country.

"Look at me, Will." He turns to me, the white of his eyes slightly tinted pink. "Really shitty things happened to you . . ."

Will's eyes grow saucer-wide.

"Don't tell Mama Sugar I cursed. Just listen. Really shitty things happened to you. And that

294

doesn't stop. But you, *you,* find a way through. Because if you can make it past all the hurt and anger and regret, you'll be so much stronger than you ever imagined."

"Strong like you."

"Stronger, Will. Much, much stronger than me."

"I'll take it . . . and that extra piece of corn bread."

I hug Will and chuckle. "Boy, you're too much."

Creaming together the butter and sugar by hand, my arm stiffens up, but I press on. Mama Sugar is right. Each act when you bake imparts whatever you're feeling. I add the rum last and pour finished batter into three cake pans. Making sure each pan is equally filled.

Mama Sugar sits down at the pine table and opens her mail, either smiling at a letter or lightly frowning at a bill. "Sara-girl, the party is five days away. Why you makin' the cake now?"

Placing the cakes in the oven, I check the dial, making sure it's on exactly 350 degrees. "Practice cake. Boarders can eat it tonight. One less thing for you to do."

I sit down. Again. Tired. Can't seem to shake it. "You alright?"

"Chasing after Lebanon. Getting up early. That's all."

Stifling another yawn, I rise, taking the bowls,

measuring cups and begin washing them. Mama Sugar shakes her head.

"What?"

"You eat more. Wanna sleep more and you still wonderin' what's goin' on?"

"Nothing's going on." Hot water cascades over the plastic bowls and spoons, washing away remnants of batter.

Mama Sugar sucks her teeth. "Chile, if you can't tell after all this time you expectin' another little one, I don't know what I'ma do with you."

Turning off the faucet, I face Mama Sugar. "No, no. I'm not—I can't be . . ."

I count backward. The last time I had my cycle, it was . . . June. I think it was early June.

"You can and you are."

I turn the faucet back on to finish the dishes. I count again. Then once more. She's right. Mama Sugar is right.

I'm going to have a baby.

The water still runs and the dish in my hand clatters into the sink. Placing my hands on the coolness of the butcher block counter, I brace myself.

"Women have children every day. No need to get so dramatic about it, Sara-girl."

It's more responsibility. It's more money. A lot of it. Most important it's taking a part of my heart, putting it into another living being and hoping to God I do right by them. Because I know, in the most desperate way, what happens when you fail a child, when you don't protect them. And I don't know if I can divide my heart into yet another portion. One for Lebanon. One for Jonas. One for this baby.

What would I have left of myself?

SIXTEEN

Marcus Lyons' fork hovers over his scrambled eggs. He needs to hurry up and eat them. Jonas' party starts in a few hours. It's been a week of planning for his birthday. A baby I haven't told him about yet. Five days of preparation and secrets. Five days of solitude.

Steam still rolls off the biscuits. A jar of honey sits in the middle of the table. "Never thought I'd live long enough to witness something like that, believe in something so deeply. Shoulder to shoulder in Dexter Avenue Baptist Church. Dr. King talked about Ghana, how they gained their independence. How we can gain ours. But it wasn't only his words. The imagery. The feeling. The belief we all held, we still hold, dear. It was rousing. It was hopeful. And I don't use that word lightly," says Marcus.

He looks down at his cooling food, and for a moment all I see is wavy hair, like a lake gently lapping at the shore. He pushes up his black horn-rimmed glasses. "Now, I'm here to do my part. Convince people to join us in this struggle. One of the best places are our local churches. Here. Alabama next. Florida after that. As many places as it takes. For as long as it takes."

Buster swallows the last of his biscuit. "You makin' any progress?"

"It's an uphill battle in a lot of respects. A church joins us, and there will likely be reprisals. The pastor. Congregation. But we got a lot of good people along with Dr. King. Mr. Rustin. Ms. Baker. Too many to name."

Grabbing the pitcher, I fill Marcus' glass of orange juice. "You."

Marcus looks up, his high-cheekboned smile shy but genuine. "Heh, doing what I can."

"What you think of that Malcolm X? He different from King?" asks Ben Carmichael, another new boarder. He chomps, openmouthed, on a piece of bacon. Wide and broad-chested, neck as thick as a tree trunk. His eyes drill into Marcus, who straightens his already straight tie.

"Well . . . we all have our ways of doing things. Our way isn't his. I'll just say that."

"Maybe it should be. All this marching and boycotting only getting us so far. I mean Kennedy makes a speech on television about how we all should be equal, but that didn't do nothing." Ben points his meaty finger at Marcus. "White people still burnin' crosses on our lawns. Y'all saw what they did to Medgar Evers, shot him down this past June. They put dogs on us. Beat us with batons. Killin' us and gettin' away with it. Why not fight back? I mean, ain't it about protecting ourselves too? Hell, all that hate is the reason I left Florida for New York. Had my momma not died, my ass would still be in Harlem. Anytime

I come down here, I hold my breath till I get back up North. I can manage a lot better up there than down here." Benjamin leans forward on the table. "Least Malcolm X speaks on a plan that don't involve us just laying down and taking a beating."

Marcus lightly massages his temples, his forehead deeply creased like lines of writing on a page. "It's not about us laying down and taking a beating, Mr. Carmichael. Seeing our sacrifices that way misses the point. Strength comes in many forms. Meeting violence with peace requires a strength greater than a billy club or a gun."

Ben grabs the last slice of bacon from the plate in the middle of the table. "Righteous sentiment, but a lot of our people are angry at this country, but bein' angry I guess means you thought this country was for you in the first place." Benjamin shrugs. "But where else we gonna go?"

"Our cause is just. Righteous. Doing my work here helps up North too." Marcus takes a sip of orange juice. "Lord knows there's problems for us no matter where we go in this country. We simply can't afford to fight fist with fist, an eye for an eye. We fight fire with fire, we'll all burn."

"There's something to be said for different perspectives," I say. "My husband, he's, well, he's more peaceful. Believes that people are ultimately, deep down, good."

Marcus smiles taking another bite of eggs.

I remove the plate, empty of the bacon Ben Carmichael eats like candy. "I on the other hand don't mind a fight. Never have."

Ben hits the table with his fist. "See, even the lady here agrees with me. She knows we men gotta be out here fightin' for our rights, protectin' our women. And—"

"No, no, no, Mr. Carmichael y'all don't get to play hero. Women have been organizing and marching right alongside you, taking the pain right alongside you. Protecting you! And doing it better. If anything, don't take all the credit. Say thank you."

I pour the last of the orange juice into Ben's empty cup and smile. He doesn't.

"Well, well this conversation's mighty enlightening," says Mama Sugar. She shoots me a look, placing the last of the bacon on the blue plate in my hands. I set it back down on the table. Ben grabs two more slices.

"Mr. Lyons, your stay here comfortable so far?" she asks.

"Absolutely. I'll head to Clayborn Temple tonight after a few stops." Marcus glances at his watch. He opens a biscuit and piles eggs on it and eats, trying to politely shovel food in his mouth.

Elijah Johnson, last night's arrival, yawns as he sits next to Marcus Lyons. He then finishes his last bite of eggs. He digs into a brown cloth bag, a muted clanging inside. "Do any of y'all know where The Iris Club is?"

Buster scribbles in his notepad. "You tryin' to sin this early in the day?"

Elijah snickers. Grabbing a handkerchief from his left pocket, he wipes his forehead, then resumes rifling through his bag. "Helping my cousin Eddie fix his smoker. He said it ain't heating up right, temperature's too low or something. Gotta finish that today, then heading back to my joint in Biloxi. Don't know how I'ma do it all. But we always make the impossible possible."

I place two pieces of bacon on my plate with eggs and two biscuits. "The Iris Club? East Butler Avenue near the Lorraine Motel. Brown brick building with a jade green door." I sit down, devouring the meal in front of me remembering those pulled pork sandwiches on my first date with Jonas. I could eat two of those sandwiches right now.

Everything is different with this baby. I'm not sick in the mornings. Or the evenings. Different children mean different things, I guess. Or maybe it's something deeper.

Elijah cleans his hands. "Thank you much."

"Must be heading off. Fighting the good fight and all," says Marcus. He stands and walks to the back door. Elijah and Benjamin rush out behind him.

"Well let me get on outta here so I can be back

in time for the party. We closin' up early today for it, but Vanellys need some extra hands. The carburetor on this '57 Nash Cosmopolitan is givin' him the blues. I wanna scrap the thing but that's why my behind is in that office most of the time and not with him fixin' them cars." Buster shakes his head. "Alright see y'all later."

Mama Sugar washes dishes by the sink. "So Jonas really took Lebbie?"

Again, I dump an ungodly amount of pepper on my eggs. "Yeah, he probably has something up his sleeve. He gets this look. I recognize it now. Same look he had before he proposed."

"You tell him yet? Been a week since I figured it out. Jonas can't be far behind me."

Opening my biscuit, I scoop on eggs and bacon and eat, chewing slowly.

"I'll take that as a no."

I shrug. "You can take it as I'm hungry. I'll tell him when I'm ready. Is that so bad?"

"Better to give him the good news now, all I'm sayin'."

"Is it? Good news I mean?"

"Children always good news. Even if you can't always keep 'em from harm or harmin' themselves. Sometimes there's equal delight and sorrow in a blessing. But I know you and Jonas will love that baby. That's the hope in it. That's where you find your happiness for now."

"You can't say for certain he's going to be

303

happy about it." I caress my stomach. "It's another mouth to feed. Jonas is a teacher. I work here. We have Lebanon. It's . . . it's . . . I don't know."

A thought creeps in. What if I didn't have the baby. Then I feel sorrow and guilt for the thought. But why should I feel these things? What is so bad for wanting control? It should be my choice. With Lebanon, there was none. There was the aftermath and the wreckage that ensued. Now there's some semblance of order. There's no desire to smash the world from the inside out. Those desires have quieted some, but they whisper. In the night with Jonas' arm draped over my waist, I stare at moving shadows on the wall and wait for something bad. And maybe that's what I'll always do because of what happened; it's who I am. But now there are good things, bright things. This baby is a bright thing.

It can be. He could be. She could be.

"Mama Sugar, all due respect, I'll tell Jonas when I'm ready."

"Keep a secret that's gonna show on your body in a couple of months?" Mama Sugar looks me up and down. "Hell, it's showin' now. Whatever this is that got your lips glued together for no good reason, you need to face it and fix it. We only got so much time on this earth and ain't no use wastin' it being scared."

"It's not about being scared. It's about what *I* want. People never really ask me what I want to do? When you were my age, did anyone ask what you wanted?"

Mama Sugar sighs, her hands slow in the dishwater. "Suppose not, but I made what choices I could when I could."

Heat slowly builds in the kitchen. I walk to the windows and open them. "I want my choice. That's all. I know what it's going to be, but we all deserve to have a choice."

"You right Sara-girl. I think about my children and I sometimes wonder . . ."

"What?"

Mama Sugar shakes her head; her hands move faster below the dishwater. "Don't matter what now 'cause everything's set but I see your point.

"So is this—" Mama Sugar's wet hand gestures to my stomach "—something you want?"

"Yes. This time it is. That's why it's precious. It's something out of love so yes, this is what I want."

"This time?"

"Yes. This time."

Mama Sugar stares at me, her eyes probing, gathering whatever questions dawdle in her head, but she won't ask out loud. My story might hurt her or cause her to visit a place she left far behind a long time ago.

"We should start settin' up for this party," she says.

"Yes ma'am. Let's do that."

. . .

I'll let the cakes sit twenty minutes before turning them upside down on each plate. People are already slowly gathering outside. Thirty so far by my count. Smallish. That means let's invite only half the city of Memphis instead of the whole city. Will jogs through the open back door.

"Granny asked if the cakes were ready yet?"

"They're cooling. You set up the tables and chairs?"

Will leans on the counter, glances up at the flowers, still firm and blooming. "Almost done." He looks around. "You think I could get a taste of—"

"No."

"Come on Sara just a little—"

"Nuh-uh." I glance out of the window. "You see your dad yet?"

Will folds his arms, looking outside. "He's not showing up. I'm not worried about it."

"People can surprise you. Sometimes good and sometimes bad. Either way, you'll learn from it."

"Well, can a poor orphan boy get a teeny, tiny slice of cake?"

"You're not an orphan."

Will rolls his eyes and I pinch his arm. "Ow! Okay, I'm not Oliver Twist, but have mercy on me."

"You are relentless." I open the refrigerator,

cutting a sliver of Ms. Mavis' caramel cake. "If Mama Sugar catches you with that, you don't know me."

Will grins triumphantly. "You like me don't you, Sara?"

I nudge Will out of the door. "Leave me be and finish setting up those chairs."

He eats the last of the cake, folding the napkin and putting it in the pocket of his blue jeans. Hints of smoked hickory waft in from the backyard. Mr. Vanellys stands next to a small barbecue grill. Buster unfolds a long table. Mama Sugar, like the conductor of a symphony, directs each person to their proper point. Her right hand fixed on her back above her waist, she leans over the grill, then smiles.

"Sara-girl!" she yells. "Bring out them hamburger and hot dog buns. Then finish up them cakes."

Did I say conductor? I meant four-star general.

Balmy gusts of air warm my skin. Grass tickles my feet as I walk to the table. A giggle and small arms wrap themselves around me. Lebanon. The force of him as he hugs my leg almost knocks me over. He's wearing a crimson shirt and dark blue shorts. So adorable. He really does look like me. Nose. Ears. Lips. Smile.

"You playing with me, son? You wanna knock your momma over, that it?"

He squeal-giggles in his way, hands flying up

to his mouth. He runs off. Will chases after him.

Whir-click.

I pull my hair behind my ear. "You're gonna use up all your film before the party starts."

Jonas' arms hug my waist, the bump of his camera wedging into my back. "Brought four rolls. I'm always prepared."

"Happy Birthday, Mr. Coulter."

Jonas takes off his camera, placing it on the table, and kisses my cheek. "Thank you."

The arms of his shirt are crimson. The same shade as Lebanon's. They have on the same outfit. Well, Jonas has dark blue pants. I don't know if I'd want him in shorts.

"That's why you were so insistent in taking him this morning."

He grins. "Tell me it's not cute though."

"It is. It is." I turn and face him. "You are a know-it-all. You are messy."

Jonas smooths his shirt and chuckles. "Well, if this is my birthday gift—"

"Wait for my compliment." I cup Jonas' face in my hands. "Jonas Coulter, you are sometimes the most infuriating person I've met. You challenge me and you love me. You love my son. And I don't know how I could've found a path to any of this, to being so happy, if you weren't here."

"Ah, you'd have figured it out."

"Probably, but you're the reason I figured things out much better, much sooner."

He lightly kisses my lips. "Glad to be of service."

"I love you, you know that."

"I love you too, Sara. You buttering me up or something?" He laughs. I do not.

Breathe. This is your choice. You love him. You have your family. You have him. I take Jonas' hand, gripping it.

He furrows his brow and looks into my eyes.

"I'm having a baby. *We're* having a baby."

Spinning. I'm spinning. In the air. Jonas' hands lifting me up. He's happy. Not upset. Not worried. Not angry. I don't have to fight him about what I want because he wants the same thing.

Mama Sugar, Buster and Will stare in our direction. Jonas puts me down, gathering me in his arms. "I'm gonna be a dad again."

Again.

He touches my stomach. "I hope it's a girl. I've always wanted a girl. Samantha after Sam Cooke. Or maybe Nina." He smiles, then shakes his head. "Nah, that's nice but . . . Oh! What about Gwendolyn, like the poet? Maybe Lorraine like Lorraine Hansberry."

"*A Raisin in the Sun*, Lorraine Hansberry?"

"Is there another?" He chuckles then, paces back and forth. "Yeah, she's from Chicago, right?"

"We have some time to figure this out. You don't need to be in such a rush."

Jonas stops and smiles. "We can name her after our moms. Sophia Lillian Coulter."

"I like that name. A lot. But how do you know it's even a girl? Besides, don't men normally want a son as their first child?"

Jonas looks over at Lebanon. "I have a son."

Lebanon zips across the backyard. Laughing. Crimson shirt. Dark blue shorts. Lebanon was mine and now he's Jonas' too. Lebanon was never different to Jonas, something to feel shame about, some burden to carry. Lebanon is a life, a world of potential to be protected and loved. And Jonas' love surrounds my son as it does me, this warm light. This messy, know-it-all teacher, poet, photographer will teach my son all it means to be kind and gentle, honorable and brave. Amid all that's standing against him, his skin, a city and a nation that will do everything it can to break him, Lebanon has Jonas and I to teach him how to become unbreakable.

All of us. Together.

Smallish. Jonas said smallish. This is a hundred people. Easy. Smoke from the grill billows high, vanishing, its scent embedded in my yellow skimmer dress with blue-green flowers. Strangers with food on plates or lemonade in cups roam, traversing from the front yard to the back of The New Scarlet. Lebanon plays with some of the children his age. He hit a child a few minutes ago, but the other kid took his hot dog. Don't mess with his food. But all is well now. They're playing like nothing happened. It's easier to forgive when you're younger. The world doesn't yet seem an unkind place, so the wrongs you suffered aren't so cruel or permanent.

"Such a nice gathering," says Malone Blue as he walks up to me and Jonas in the backyard. He pats his salt-and-pepper hair with a sapphire-trimmed handkerchief. "Almost same as the wedding. Y'all sure know a lot of people."

He glances at me and I squeeze Jonas' hand. "Well, my husband is certainly popular. It's nice so many people came out for his birthday."

"Your son's birthday too, isn't it?"

"Lebanon's birthday was a few months ago. But you know us, we never miss a reason to celebrate things. Big or small."

Malone Blue now presses the cloth to the bottom of his neck. "Ain't you right about it." He sniffs. "Mmm. Think Vanellys is done with them ribs. Gonna get me a taste 'fore they're all gone."

The ribs look delicious. Just the right amount of smoke and char. Tender. The sauce. Tangy, vinegar, sweet, tomato, spice.

Jonas turns to me. "Why don't I get you a plate?"

Playfully I poke his chest. "Yeah, you go do that. Penance for your *smallish* party."

"Mama Sugar did most of the inviting. You know how she is."

"You didn't object to any of this. Say you did."

Jonas flexes his neck side to side. "I'll get you some lemonade too."

He walks to the south part of the yard, where the trees are tall and thick with leaves. Lebanon is still smiling. Doesn't look like he's hit anyone else. The children play with a red ball, throwing it in the air and chasing where it lands. He's going to need the bath of baths tonight.

A throat clears behind me. Amos. He wears a clean white shirt that's loose around his lean frame. Gray pants a little too large, a black belt cinched around his waist. Hair combed. Clear eyed. I step closer. He smells of soap.

"Haven't had a drop in four days," he says.

"Am I supposed to clap?"

"Don't expect no pity from you Sara 'cause you obviously ain't giving none. Can you show me to Will, so he can see me? Please."

I point to the north edge of the yard where Will talks with Elvin. "Remember what I said. Do better."

Amos nods, heading in Will's direction. It takes everything I have to keep my feet planted here, to not run over and make sure Amos says and does everything right, because Will deserves it. And I know how uncertain the world is, how it's unforgiving one minute, then benevolent the next.

Jonas returns with my food. He hands me a plate and lemonade. "He'll be okay. You can't control everything."

"Please tell me all the other things I already know." I set my lemonade down on a small empty part of the table next to the herb garden. A group of people at another table play spades. Thin, worn cards slap down on wood.

Jonas shakes his head. "Sara, I'm only saying you have to let people figure out what's going to happen to them. I know you want the best for the ones you love but you can't fix everything. You can't control everything. That's why you get so angry."

Amos goes to hug Will, who steps back, standing apart. A patch of grass, an uncrossable ocean, a war-torn continent. I can't hear what they're saying.

"You think I'm angry?"

Jonas looks at the grass for a moment, then my eyes. "I think you want to go back and change things you can't, and yes, that makes you angry. It'd make me angry too."

I turn away from him and look north. Amos stands awkward for a minute. Will hesitantly raises his right arm. Amos takes it. He and Will shake hands. It's not a hug, not him falling into Amos' arms, but it's a gesture. A truce, a gray place where maybe they can build an understanding and from there, who knows.

Ripping a tender piece of meat from the ribs, I savor the melt of it on my tongue. I turn back to Jonas. "If I can't stop being angry, then what?"

"Only you can answer that. I'm not some wise man or fortune-teller, Sara." Jonas surveys the partygoers, not meeting my eyes. "I love you. Lebanon loves you. Will. Mama Sugar. Mr. Vanellys. You gotta try and make that enough to keep you afloat until you can let go of the past. As much as I adore you, I can't do that for you."

Jonas kisses my forehead. "If I could've, I'd have done it the day we met."

I smirk. "You didn't like me the day we met."

"And you didn't like me, but I knew enough about you by the end of that day that I'd have done whatever I could to bring you joy." He strokes my cheek. "You have that effect on people."

Cora and Lawrence make their way across the crowded lawn to Jonas and me. Cora holds a big green bag. "Just a little something for the birthday boy."

Jonas reaches for the bag, but Cora snatches it away. "This is for Lebbie."

Lawrence reaches inside his tan suit and gives Jonas a long slender box. "*This* is for you."

Jonas opens the box. A silver pen engraved with his name in ornate writing. Jonas gasps, covering his mouth.

"For all of those projects you got in that

watermelon head of yours," jokes Lawrence.

Jonas cocks his head and laughs. "Can we ever have a nice moment?"

"I leave that to Cora. She's the absolute queen of nice moments."

"I second that." I sip my lemonade.

Cora pulls her hair behind her right ear, looking around the yard. "If you'll excuse me." She walks to the group of children playing with the red ball. Lebanon runs to her and gives her the ball. Cora takes off her shoes and runs around the yard, the tribe of toddlers following her every move.

Lawrence stares at Cora for a minute, then quickly turns away. "Who's on the grill?" He looks toward the garage and grimaces as Mr. Vanellys leaves to speak with Mama Sugar. "Brother Bernard's there now. Oh well, I'm hungry enough."

I sit back down and take another sip of lemonade. Jonas sits too. I lean back against him as he takes the pen and carefully places it in the front pocket of his shirt. "Everything is what it's supposed to be."

"And is something wrong with that?" Jonas asks.

My heart thumps against my chest, rapid; heat flushes my cheeks. I shake my head. Slow my breathing. "Guess not." My fingertips lightly trace abstract patterns on Jonas' forearm. "Not always waiting for something bad to happen is a relief. Guess I should, *maybe,* thank you for showing me that."

Jonas kisses me on the cheek and grins. "Well, you've showed me plenty too. So, thank you."

"You're very welcome, Mr. Coulter."

In the backyard, there are two cakes placed on the table nearest the garage. One for Lebanon. One for Jonas. My son's greedy fingers reach for the caramel cake, unconcerned for the flames that sit atop the candles. Jonas aims his camera at me, at Lebanon, and the *whir-click* of his camera swallows the light, every detail: Lebanon bent over his cake. Cora's mouth wide, singing "Happy Birthday" off-key; Elvin talking to Simone; Mama Sugar's hand resting on Mr. Vanellys' shoulder as he sits in a chair, rubbing his right leg.

Whir-click.

"Come on, man, with the pictures," bellows Buster. "Blow out your candles so we can get some of this cake!"

"Okay, okay." Jonas places the camera on the table, bending over. "You ready, Little Man?"

Lebanon points his chubby little finger. "Nonas!" He tries to blow out his candles, but he only manages to slobber on himself more than blow.

Jonas chuckles. "Good start, son. Good start."

"Watch Momma." And I breathe softly, blowing out one candle. One more is left, and my son wrinkles his nose and tries to blow softly, like me. We try together. We extinguish the soft light from the candles. Only smoke and a light, waxy smell remain. Will sits on a bench with Amos. I measure Will's features, is he smiling? Is he frowning?

You want the best for the ones you love but you can't fix everything. You can't control everything.

Mama Sugar cuts cake and hands it out, Buster greedily taking a slice of the pineapple upside down cake. "Wooo, Sa-ra! You put both your feet, and about five elbows in this!"

Lebanon grabs my dress, his sticky hands staining the pretty yellow with crumbs and frosting. "Always making a mess aren't you, my son?" Dipping a napkin in water, I wipe his face. This is what we'll be, won't we? Clean your face. Patch your bruises. Protect you. It's my compact, a heart's contract.

"She's dead 'cause of you man! All of you! You couldn't give me the goddamn money!"

No. No. No.

Lucky stands in front of Amos, gun to his face. Will stands behind him.

"She was my only girl. Only thing I had. Smart just like her daddy."

Amos backs away from the gun, his right arm

trying to shield Will as though his withered bones could provide any protection. "I don't know what you're talking about."

Lucky advances. "My little girl. Diane. She's dead."

Mama Sugar clutches her chest. Mr. Vanellys holds her up. Barely.

"Man, I'm sorry about your loss. Truly—"

"Fuck that! I needed the money for her cancer medicine. She was gettin' skinny, losin' her hair. But y'all wouldn't know nothin' 'bout that. All sheltered up here. One big happy family."

"I ain't had it easy. I didn't have it to give and—"

"Excuses, all you got. Didn't have it to give, huh? Well you givin' somethin' up today."

Lucky's arm moves, pointing his gun toward Will's head. Amos reaches for the gun as Will runs toward us, a blur past me, Jonas runs toward him.

Boom. Boom. Boom.

Will crumples to the ground but Jonas covers him with his body. Elvin rushes over to Amos. Buster does too, his right hook catching Lucky by surprise and Lucky falls to the ground. Elvin holds him down. Lucky only screams, howls. "She was the only one. The only one I got!"

Over and over.

Will grabs his ankle, his hands shaking. Jonas pulls them away. "You're alright. You're okay,

Will. It's a scratch. It's only . . . a scratch," he says, breathless.

Lawrence shoulders his way through the crowd and crouches down in front of Will and Jonas. "Yeah, young man. You're fine. Maybe a stitch or two and you're good. No need to panic."

But Will's eyes grow wide. He shakes his head, pointing at Jonas. A small wet spot in his chest, small but getting bigger. Slowly. His crimson shirt. There's a scream. Not Mama Sugar. Not Cora.

Me.

I am screaming. Lebanon is crying. Mama Sugar lifts him from my arms. What is this? What is happening?

Breathe. Breathe. *Breathe!*

"The car! Get 'em to the car! Now!" orders Lawrence.

Buster and Mr. Vanellys grab Jonas, lifting him by the shoulders. The headlights of the Chevrolet brighten and then dim as Lawrence starts the car, and I climb in the back seat with Jonas.

God, if I ever believed in him, can't be this cruel. Mr. Vanellys said everyone needs a little mercy. So have mercy on me, God. On my Jonas. Have mercy on the idea of hope, the belief living can't be this constant nightmare, this infinite parade of hopeless memories. My life cannot be clutching my husband to me as his breathing slows, as the lids of his dark-rimmed eyes slowly flutter open and shut. This can't be my last moment with him; he struggles to breathe and yet his lips still somehow murmur to me, "It's okay, Sara. It'll be okay."

And Jonas' hands are sticky with his blood as he touches my stomach. "She'll make it okay," he whispers to me. The swerve of the Bel Air lurches my body closer to Jonas'. I press my hand harder to his chest, failing to stem the red tide of life leaving his body. I'm willing my palm and fingers to keep him with me, clasping them to his torn brown flesh and the bullet hole. I tally his breaths.

Focus on what you can count, gather in numbers, gives your mind somewhere else to go.

We approach a two-storied red brick building, Collins Chapel Hospital. Jonas' body is snatched from my arms, placed on a gurney and hurried down a white-tiled hall, past a set of creaky swinging doors. Lawrence runs by me. I struggle out of the car. Cora offers her hand, but I don't take it. Mine have blood on them.

"Lawrence is gonna do *everything* he can," says Cora. Mr. Vanellys and Mama Sugar follow. A rumbling car with Jonas' blood in the back seat idles behind me.

Cora leads us to a small room off the side of the nurses' station. "He's one of the best doctors in Memphis, in the state, the nation—" she takes a shuddering breath "—in the world."

But can he save Jonas when he couldn't save your own child? I remember a locked room painted blue with a white crib and dusty boxes. I keep these thoughts to myself.

One hour.

"See, this is good. The longer Lawrence is back there, the better," offers Cora. I look at the doors as I twist the ring on my finger. I look at the clock where a minute builds as if it's been a day. I've sat here forever. His smile. His laugh. Playing with Lebanon. Playing with our new baby. Making him fat off my cakes and pies. Yelling at him because he forgot to mow the lawn or put the toilet seat down or bought three versions of the same book because he keeps losing them.

I had that life this morning. I want that life back.

Two hours.

Mr. Vanellys doesn't say anything. I think he prays. He looks over every few minutes and tries to smile, to be calm, reassuring, but his smile falters and he can't hold my gaze long. Mama Sugar hums a song, an old gospel. I want none of God here with me right now, not in melody or air or hope. I want none of God. I want my husband. I want my Jonas.

Two hours. Twenty-seven minutes.

Hearing doors squeak open, I see Lawrence, his face, the tight drawn line of his mouth. He will utter the words that will destroy the person

321

I hoped to be, the person Jonas saw. And I can't hear those words, so I rise with Jonas' blood on my dress and wander outside the hospital and into the night. Mr. Vanellys was wrong. There is no mercy when people need it. There was none left for me.

Mama Sugar's wail rings in my ears.

SEVENTEEN

Momma pinches her cheeks to give them color. She cinches the belt of her robe. Tighter and tighter still. She ties her favorite sapphire-blue scarf around her head. She smiles in a mirror. "Too much," she says. She smiles again. "Too sad. My smile looks too sad." Again, she smiles. Then grimaces. She grips her stomach tight. Breathes and keeps breathing until the pain passes.

The door creaks open and she smiles the last smile. The Pastor comes in. "Lookin' mighty nice, Sister Sophia." She says God's been good. Momma told me not to lie so why is she lying on God, about him and his goodness? The Pastor reads Bible verses. Psalms about deliverance. Proverbs on wisdom. Corinthians speaks on love. The Pastor prays for healing. Momma shuts her eyes. I leave mine open. I'm quiet in my chair in the corner. I read my book. I read *Georges*. The Pastor passes me on his way out, but he doesn't say anything to me. He pats me on my head. Closes the door. Momma's skin is dry and ashen. The red in her cheeks faded and all but gone. Her jaw clenches again and she moans.

I get her water. And I ask, "Why did you smile

for The Pastor? Why didn't you tell him you hurt?"

"Don't show people your pain," she says. "Pain should be private. But I can show you, Sara. I trust you with my pain.

"Only you."

———————≈———————

Malone Blue fidgets with his Bible again. Turning the pages. From the front to the middle, then to the back. Over and over. Searching for whichever scripture is capable of soothing a crowd of mourners. The clumsy flutter of thin pages with meaningless words are the only sounds in this place. And I wish to be done with it. Staring at this hole. Sitting in this hard chair with Lebanon on my lap as he squirms and longs to play in the grass under an oak tree at Mount Carmel. Because to him a cemetery is the same as a playground. And he doesn't know Jonas is dead. And the only thing I see is a six-foot mouth of crumbling dirt and a mahogany casket in gold trim. I want Malone Blue to hurry up and find this fucking scripture so I can leave.

Malone Blue finally stops on a page. "I'm gonna read this little verse right here, 'cause I think it fits. Least, I hope it does." He looks over at me and then to the casket and then the sky, cloudless and blue.

The Lord is nigh unto them that are of a broken heart; and saveth such as be of a contrite spirit.

No, he's not. God isn't here. Lebanon moves again, trying to slide off my lap. I grab him, my hands tightening. "Sit still!" He starts to whine, then cry.

I can't. I can't do this. Not now.

"Here baby." Mama Sugar takes Lebanon from me. Mr. Vanellys takes Lebanon from her and he bounces Lebanon on his left knee. Lebanon quiets. Will sits next to Mr. Vanellys; every few minutes he looks behind him at the crepe myrtle tree.

"None of us want to be here today," says Malone Blue. "And it's hard to think, to fathom, yeah, that's the word. It's hard to fathom, why God called Jonas home so soon." Malone Blue looks down at his Bible. "There ain't a passage in here with the answer to that. I know. But I also know God gives us comfort when there aren't the words to fill a space, soothe a loss."

"Amen," Buster says from behind. Elvin adjusts his tie.

"Guess what I want to say to y'all, to you Sara especially, and even Lebbie, is I hope you take comfort in the times you had with Jonas, even though it wasn't as long as you'd have liked, as any one of us would've liked. He loved y'all. All of us could see that. When he'd talk about you and Lebbie, that boy's heart almost burst from his chest with pride." Malone Blue sadly chuckles. "And while nothing or no one can replace him, the love you returned to him in all the good and imperfect ways was enough for an eternity. One where, God willin', you'll see him again."

Malone Blue again holds my gaze. "Let us pray."

Boochie hugs me; his fierce grip is still soft and gentle. His black tie is slightly crooked. "Really ain't sure what I'm supposed to say 'cept when I saw Jonas with you, I knew you was perfect for him." He sniffs. "If you need anything, *anything,* you come find me. I live right around Foote Homes, where you first met me. You come find me. Them ain't just words."

"I know, Boochie. I know. Thank you."

He nods, trudging over to the tables filled with food in the living room with the pocket doors, where five feet away Lawrence played a Sam Cooke song on the shuttered piano. Jonas and I held hands and promised to love each other until death parted us. And Death decided to work a lot faster than I could've imagined, taking someone loving, someone that was *mine!* Death never seems to come for the bad people quick enough. I'm proof of that.

I'm still breathing. Jonas is dead.

I watch as black people in black dresses and suits slowly make their way down the line. Mama Sugar fills their plates and stomachs with food. She looks at me, then away. Her son killed my husband. She loved all three of us. Her only

326

means of atonement are a momentary glance and a plate of macaroni and cheese.

"Truly, it pains me to see him gone like that," says a man, short, rail-thin in a cheap midnight-colored suit. "But part of me is happy, y'know. He won't live to see what this world will become. Feel jealous if I'm being honest."

I want to slit his throat. He didn't know Jonas, not like I did. I can guarantee he'd want to be with me. Alive! These people, their clumsy, shallow grief is the deepest cut. They believe suffering is the best currency, better than crisp bills or polished coins. The thing I always noticed about the songs we sang in Calvary, the Zion praises as my momma called them, Death is always something to desire. Death means no more pain. Death means peace. But Jonas was that for me. My peace.

Whispers. People whisper after a funeral. I've noticed that too. People nod and they whisper. It was the same for my father, at his service. I don't remember much except the whispering and waiting for the police to haul me off to jail, but that never happened. Perhaps the lowered volume is some odd measure of respect, but it doesn't change anything.

I'd feel better if I screamed. That's what I want to do. Scream. I'm the reason Jonas is dead. When I came to Memphis, it doomed him. It doomed me. And this life I carry. And Lebanon, whom I now have nothing to offer. Because like the first Scarlet Poplar, I'm ash. I can't sift among my rubble and find a remnant of who I was even a week ago.

"Honey, take this. Eat." Cora hands me a plate with two slices of ham, collard greens, macaroni and cheese.

I drop the plate, bits of food and cheap, shattered porcelain cover the ground around me. Heads turn in my direction. At the shattering, the mess. And for a moment I'm lighter. I want to smash another plate, turn over the tables of food. Bang on the piano. Anything else to stop the whispers and sorrowful nods and this dingy offering of bereavement these people believe they're obligated to show on my behalf. As if that's what it means to mourn. As if it will make death understandable, palatable.

The only thing that can make this better, me better, is Jonas walking through the door. But I can't have that, so I'll break things.

Crush. Sever. Split. Damage!

Cora's eyes dart around the room. "Everything's fine. Shaky hands is all." She picks up the jagged pieces of the plate. Bent, curled, trying to fix and clean; make whole what is broken apart. I leave her to it.

Will sits on the porch with a book on his lap. Unopened. Sitting down in the chair next to Will, I kick off my shoes.

He hands me the book. *Native Son* by Richard Wright. "We was, I mean, *were* . . . Jonas would probably want me to say 'we were.' We *were* gonna talk about this one next.

"I was ready for him too." Will grins for a moment but it quickly fades. "All those tricky questions he'd ask. *Read beyond the words, Will,*" he mocks Jonas. "I wrote in little notes at the margins." Will sniffs and wipes his eyes. "It was gonna be a good talk. A real good talk."

"Yeah. I'm sure." I splay my feet and flex my toes. "I hate heels."

"I get it now, you know."

"You get what?"

"Grown folks' business." Will stands up and leans on the porch railing, his eyes boring into mine. "All the things I thought I wanted to know. I don't wanna know those things anymore. Lucky and Diane. My dad. Granny. I know enough. But now I can't unhear or unsee any of it."

"People believe if they don't say anything that means no one will know anything. But secrets have ways of telling themselves."

"I don't know what to do. Knowing what Lucky did, but he's . . . family. I didn't even know Diane like that. She was just this annoying girl at school, but she was my cousin, and Granny and Granddaddy knew it, but they didn't tell me and . . . and then Jonas." Will's eyes grow glassy, tears spilling over. "He died trying to save me."

I stare past the houses, the parked rows of cars in front of The New Scarlet, to the small part of Gooch Park I can see from the porch. "You live with it, Will. If you're asking me what to do. You live with it. Remember I told you shitty things are gonna happen to you, but you'll learn to live with it."

"But I mean—"

"I got nothing left, boy. Just leave me be."

Five boxes lie underneath the windows of the bedroom, covered in light dust. His body at Mount Carmel. His undriven car across the street. His life trapped in folded cardboard. Me alive without him. It is scary, this feeling or this lack of feeling. My haze in this anguish. The need to still function when so much of what was hopeful is in ruins. My memories of Jonas are this painful, aching collective of flashes, like his camera. Photos in my mind of him, of us, are still, unchanging. All his old notes to me are amassed on the table where I don't read them.

When it's dark like this, when I'm dark like this, I play a game. I pretend Jonas is in the next room of the apartment. He's reading or preparing for the next day's class, fussing with his camera, writing me a letter or a poem. If I take myself into the living room and he isn't there, I've just missed him. He's in the bedroom doing something else. He's just beyond me, somewhere close but I can't quite get to him in time.

It's a sad little game. But it's a game that keeps me from screaming. Playing this game, I can get out of my bed. I can eat a little food. I can feed Lebanon. I remember to breathe.

My hands run the expanse of my stomach, my skin stretching as *it* moves about, fluttering inside. She. The gold ring catches a thread from my green dress.

I've always wanted a girl. We can name her after our moms. Sophia Lillian Coulter.

Lebanon runs ahead of me as we roam the blocks to The New Scarlet, his shadow is long and distended in the brash yellow of morning. He races to the next block, the next one after that. Maybe he thinks Jonas will be around the corner, playing an extended game of hide-'n'-seek. Will walks toward us, his satchel on his left shoulder and a book in his right hand. He drops them as Lebanon rushes to him, and Will kneels to pick him up.

Spoiled. Lebanon is spoiled.

Will tickles Lebanon, his shrill giggle cracking the silence of the early morning. "Got some new boarders. Only two though."

"Okay. Put him down."

Will frowns, setting down Lebanon. "They, uh, finally got a new English teacher. He's not as good as . . . well, I think he's kinda boring."

"You said two new boarders?"

You're too harsh with him.

Well, you're not here to correct me, Mr. Coulter, and I'm running late.

Work with me, Sara.

Will's hand taps a fence post. "Yeah. Two. Can't remember their names right now." He picks up his satchel and his book. A new one, *Narrative of the Life of Frederick Douglass.*

I take Lebanon's hand. "Better get on to school. Dinner's at six o' clock."

"I . . . Forget it. Nothing." Will nods and readjusts his satchel, continuing down the block to school.

Lebanon runs through the front door of The New Scarlet as he normally does, free, happy, and straight to the kitchen. Four boarders sit at the table as Buster stands up and hands Mama Sugar his plate. He rubs Lebanon's curly hair. He places him in his high chair, next to the head of the table where Mr. Vanellys sits. He gives me a small smile as Buster leaves out the back door.

"Sara-girl, the sun's been up for almost an hour," says Mama Sugar, wiping sweat from her forehead.

"I saw Will. We talked. And I had to get that one and myself ready. Took a while."

"Got everything handled just the same. Take the time you need." She takes a fork, flipping the bacon in refined and nimble movements. "You can start the grits when you ready."

Mama Sugar's voice doesn't have an edge to it, no annoyance. She caters to me, my whims, to my changing body, my tardiness, my loss. She tiptoes around me now. They all do.

And why not; she by some extension is the cause of my pain. She raised the monster that murdered my heart. But even the people we love can become the cause of our anguish. Yet, we find some way to still love them despite what they did to cause us lasting harm. But there is a scar, a jagged tear of spiritual flesh never quite healing, the pain never fully fading.

"My wife still talking 'bout that Dr. King speech," says one of the boarders, his round barrel stomach pressing against the edge of the table.

Slowly, I boil milk and water on the stove in the silver pot. Three blue-violet flowers sit in the clear mason jar on the shelf in front of me. Slowly, I stir in the grits. Mama Sugar's eyes never drift in my direction.

"My son was there. In Washington," says the second boarder, his large eyes darting around the kitchen. "Said it was something. Thousands and thousands of people. I mean *everybody* worth somethin' was there. He said Mahalia Jackson sang. Love me some Mahalia! Also, said it was hot as hell that day though, so I don't know if I love Mahalia that much to be standin' in that heat." He chuckles. "My son, Renard, took some pictures of the whole thing. That boy loves takin' pictures."

Creamy. The grits look creamy. I dip a spoon into the silver pot and taste. Slightly gritty. A minute more or so and they'll be ready.

A sharp pain coils itself within my back. I stop stirring the grits, gripping the counter to my left, and breathe. Extending the air until my lungs have nothing left. My tasting spoon clatters to the floor.

"You okay, Sara-girl?"

"Fine. I'm . . . fine."

The sharp pain slightly fades. Pressing my hand harder and harder into my back, I massage until the knife slicing the muscles becomes a dull blade, until it becomes barely a throb.

Mama Sugar inches closer to me. "If you need to sit down—"

"I don't need to sit down!"

Mama Sugar's eyes grow wide. She picks up the spoon and drops it in the sink.

"I'm fine, like I said. Moving helps." I turn around. The boarders pay no mind to Mama Sugar and me as they shovel food into their mouths. "Would any of you like some grits?"

Their heads shoot up. I take the plates and scoop generous portions on each, returning them within a minute. The barrel-stomached boarder grabs for the sugar and butter set in the middle of the table.

The large-eyed boarder turns his nose up. "Man, you puttin' sugar in them grits?"

"How else you take 'em?"

"Not with sugar, that's for damn sure."

The barrel-stomached boarder chuckles as he scoops more sugar than necessary into his grits. "Then you ain't eatin' 'em right."

They laugh as they clean their plates. Good-natured fun, unavoidable ribbing. There are different traditions, distinct ways of being from one city to the next. Sweet grits versus savory. Baptist versus Episcopalian. Light skin versus dark skin. And all these differences, variances, both good-natured and destructive, bind themselves to us, inescapable as time and grief.

Mama Sugar now keeps a small blue bowl for Lebanon. I place some grits into his bowl and set it down in front of him with a spoon. He's a lot better with a spoon now. Most of the grits make it into his mouth. He brightly smiles at me.

"Finish your breakfast," I order, and return to the stove.

Mama Sugar turns on the hot water, steam rising, curling and disappearing. "You said you saw Will?"

"Yes."

"How'd he look?"

"Like Will, I guess."

"He went to see Amos this past Saturday at the garage. Once or twice a week Will goes over to see him. Help Vanellys. Well really Buster, up in that office. Amos been steady over there. After everything, guess he tryin' to do somethin' right by Will."

"Why are you telling me about Amos?"

Both boarders rise, plates in their hands. Lebanon awkwardly feeds himself the last of his grits.

"Oh, leave them dishes on the table, we'll tend to it," says Mama Sugar, a limp smile on her face. They nod and walk out of the front door.

"I'm only sayin' it's nice Will don't come away mad after he sees him now."

I shrug. "Nice to know your family is faring well."

"They shipped Lucky off somewhere outta state. Can't remember the name of the jail. Think he's in Arkansas. That's 'bout the last of my family and he gone. That make you feel better?"

"Him dead would make me feel better."

"Sara, you hurtin'. I know you are. But you gonna have to learn if you keep answerin' with anger, anger might damn well answer you back one of these days." Mama Sugar walks over to the pine table, taking the dishes and gently putting them in the soapy water. She takes a clean plate from the dish rack and three strips of bacon from the skillet, handing it to me. She looks at my stomach and then me. "Now, you need to eat somethin'."

I take the plate and set it on the table. Mama Sugar walks over to Lebanon, cleans his face and sets him down on the gold knit blanket. His blocks wait for him. He stacks them. Knocks them down. Giggles. Repeats.

Mama Sugar puts her hands in the scalding water. "You know there's a couple of rooms empty here. On the third floor."

"You need those for boarders."

Mama Sugar looks around the kitchen. "You hear how quiet it is? Been like that for a while.

"The rooms are here. 'Cause you need help, Sara-girl. You don't have much of a choice where help comes from sometimes."

"Nonas! Nonas!" Lebanon points to an empty corner in the room.

A flutter in my stomach. An ache in my heart.

"Nonas!" Louder.

"He does this with empty spaces sometimes." I look at Mama Sugar. "Calls Jonas. Empty corners. Empty rooms. Runs around and calls his name. Like he's there."

"Children can see—"

"Don't. I don't need old superstitious, home-spun wisdom about children and ghosts."

Mama Sugar stops washing dishes, wiping her hands on her apron. She picks up Lebanon and walks out of the kitchen but pauses. "I know bein' here is hard. I know I had a part to play in this. At the edges of your pain, your hurt. But

Sara-girl—" Mama Sugar exhales slowly "—you need to decide if you wanna be alone in this or share what you're carryin' because if you don't, it's gonna kill you from the inside out. Your children too."

I eat the bacon Mama Sugar put on my plate. In the kitchen. Alone.

"You're gonna have this little one any day now. Honestly, I'd recommend you stay here but most women like to rest at home before the birth. I don't think that's a bad thing at all," says Lawrence in a white-tiled room. I hear the hollow scratch of his pen on his clipboard as he writes something I can't see. "Everything is as it should be."

"No, it's not."

"Sara, I didn't mean—"

"Oh God, please don't look at me like that."

"Like what?"

"Like everyone looks at me now. Not really meeting my eyes. Whispering with their gaze instead of saying things out loud with their mouths. Like 'Poor thing. Her husband died.' 'She must have awful luck.' 'She ain't no good, but I hear she makes a mean pineapple upside down cake.'"

"I'm sure that's not what people are saying, Sara."

"You a mind reader too, Larry?"

Lawrence scoffs and leans back on the counter, two jars stuffed with cotton balls to his right and a container of tongue depressors on his left. "Apparently there's only one of us."

"Jonas one time asked me if I have to make everything difficult."

"And?"

I touch my stomach and somehow a smile or the beginning of one crosses my lips. Thinking about that day when he asked me out. Our first date. "Maybe that's the only way I know how to be."

Lawrence lays down his clipboard and rubs his eyes. "Sara, I know—"

"You don't know."

"Dammit! You're not the only one allowed to mourn! He was my friend. And I tried . . . I tried so hard, but I couldn't . . . ." Tears linger behind Lawrence's eyes. He looks up at the ceiling and exhales. "When it's time, call me. No one will tend to you but me and the two nurses I trust most."

Lawrence opens the door to the white-tiled room. "Now go home and, if you can manage, try to rest."

Buster and Elvin talk on the front porch. Elvin lights a cigarette, casually exhaling the remnants in the air. I wonder if he can blow a smoke ring. They both nod at me as I walk through the front door.

A sharp pain surges down my back. I grip the wooden railing and stop on the third step.

Elvin tokes on his cigarette again, blowing smoke out the side of his mouth. "You okay?"

Exhaling slowly, I answer, "Fine. I'm fine."

I follow the sound of Lebanon's clumpy stride as it echoes from the kitchen. Mama Sugar picks up Lebanon and sets him in his high chair. I wash my hands in the sink.

"What Dr. Morgan say?"

Hot water cascades over my skin. I flex my fingers. "That everything is as it should be."

"That's nice."

My red apron hangs on the hook and I fasten it around, managing a small knot. Mr. Vanellys comes through the back door. "Sara-girl you really helpin' with dinner? Maybe it's best you rest up. I can bring you some food in a bit."

"No need. I've missed enough work as it is."

Mama Sugar unties my apron. "Nuh-uh. Go upstairs. I ain't a fool. You probably gotta go right back to Collins Chapel."

"I'm fine." Sharp as a knife and just as merciless, a fresh stab of pain from my back to my stomach drives me to my knees. Mr. Vanellys barely grabs me in time before I crash to the floor.

"Get the car! Get the car!" yells Mama Sugar. "That baby's coming. We ain't got time."

EIGHTEEN

"The baby doesn't want to come out," says a nurse, her curled hair now drooping to her eyes. She's taken off her cap. Small smears of blood on her uniform. "We might have to cut, Dr. Morgan."

Concern etched on his face. Brow deeply creased. "We're not there yet. This one is stubborn like the momma." Lawrence looks at me, his eyes smiling. This gown sticks to my skin. My hair is matted to the back of my neck. The room smells of bleach and chemicals. I swear there's an ache from my back to my thighs. And it pulses stronger, then weaker, almost bearable. Then it returns. Ruthless. This pain is personal and even though I know I've done bad things, does anyone deserve a pain like this? I want it to be over. The sun was setting when I came here. Now each of the three windows in the room boast the deepest shades of black. Lawrence stands in front of me.

A white room. Lawrence's voice. Pain. Pushing. Exhaustion. Somehow I still expect to see Jonas when I turn my head. Isn't that strange? But it's not him. It's the second nurse, her cap still on, holding my hand and I squeeze it. A collective of voices urge me, beseech me, beg me. Bring forth life. Do it amid death and rage and sadness.

Lawrence twists his shoulders from right to left. He pulls something, someone from me and places it on the table behind him. And there's silence. I look up and over. He takes his finger and digs around in its mouth, rubs the heel of his hand gently on its chest. Seconds expand again. Like when I waited for him to tell me about Jonas. Can he save my child? But then cries. Loud. So loud. Lawrence breathes deep and laughs or maybe sobs. I can't tell the difference. My focus becomes blurry. The first nurse walks over with Lawrence. They whisper and clean the baby.

"You have a girl, honey," says the first nurse. She places her on my chest.

I don't hold her. "I'm tired," I say. "When can I sleep?"

Her face falls. "Soon honey, you can sleep soon." She takes the girl back. Somewhere. I don't know.

Focus on what you can count. Collect the numbers of things. It gives your mind somewhere else to go.

I lay back and look at the ceiling tiles. I count them.

One. Two. Three . . . Seventeen. Eighteen . . .

Momma showed me a picture of a painting once. There was a man on the ground, or it looked like a mountaintop and next to him was a small plant. And in the sky was a misshapen pink hand or it looked like a hand, and it was reaching out to him. To help him. Maybe it was receding back into the sky. Abandoning him. There were circles overlapping one another and a rainbow with no color on the other side. Wavy lines at the top where the hand was. Momma said the painter was famous. And black. A man named Aaron Douglas.

Momma runs her hands over the picture in Ebony *magazine. "It's called* The Creation. *Isn't it beautiful? Isn't what our people make beautiful?"*

Rain pelts the windows. In dull thumps. Rivulets of water trickle down, turning the trees outside into a swirly moss green mass. She is a pretty little thing. She. Jonas was right. And there is nothing behind the acknowledgment of her newborn beauty. Only that she is here. Jonas is not in the chair on the other side beaming at me. Holding her. Lebanon isn't running across the room, peeking at his little sister either happy or downright upset that he's no longer alone. And I want to reach into this space, this imaginary world like the ones Buster makes up and grip a sensation other than numbness. But there's only detachment, an awareness something is here, but I don't have the energy to peel back the flesh and reach down and dig it out.

Jonas told me she'd make it okay. And I watch her sleep in the bassinet with Jonas' nose and my lips. I wait for the rain to stop. For the sun to shine. For the baby to open her eyes so I can see who they belong to. She's swaddled in a white blanket, dark hair tufted around her ears, those I'm not sure if they're mine or his.

"How's the happy momma?" A nurse barges into the room. The one who placed the girl upon my chest. And I didn't hold the baby. Her spotless white uniform and nurse's cap brimming as brightly as her smile, the one she expects me to have, the one she's waiting for, the one I do not give and so, hers fades too.

"You need some time Momma, and you'll be so in love with this little one." She looks down at the baby in the bassinet. "Aren't you precious. Such a good baby." The nurse looks at me. "Name's Jainey Mae, and who's this little one?"

Does almost every woman in Memphis have Mae as a middle name?

I shrug. I have energy to do little else. Jonas thought of names. Samantha after his favorite singer. Gwendolyn after the poet. Lorraine after the playwright. Sophia Lillian after our mothers. His ideas for her name and our life together washed away in blood. To watch her grow, to witness her likely become more like Jonas in manner and look and sound and heart, it's mourning him without end. The girl will be the living, unending reminder of what's to never be in my heart, in all my wonder and pain. Can I bear that?

"Why don't I let you get some more rest. I'll

be back in another hour for the feeding. We're supposed to keep a special eye on you. Dr. Morgan's orders."

She leaves the room, softly shutting the door. I close my eyes waiting for darkness and something hopefully deeper and more permanent.

"I had a feeling you'd like roses," says Cora. She sets down the flowers tied with twine and wrapped in patterned paper, along with an empty azure-colored vase on the table next to my bed. "We'll get this room a tad more cheerful."

"Won't be here long enough for some flowers to matter."

She takes off her plum-dyed trench coat and matching purse, laying them gently on the pea green plastic chair in the corner.

"You left the apple," she says, pointing to the mostly empty food tray at the foot of my bed.

"I hate apples. I'd have eaten a peach or an orange."

The baby coos. Cora's face holds this strange mixture of excitement and sadness. Her arms already outstretched, she still asks, "May I?"

"Sure. Go ahead. Already fed her." I sit up in the bed, careful not to move too suddenly or else there's a twisting, burning feeling that will make my eyes water.

Cora gazes into the bassinet, turns her head and smiles. She carefully picks up the girl and cradles her, smelling the top of the baby's head. "Mmmm."

These are things I should do or want to do. I let Cora do them instead. The girl deserves to be held. To be loved. And I love her, somewhere deep, but I can't reach it yet. Like Lebanon. All I know myself to be: a reluctant mother; conflicted murderer; grieving widow. I don't know how to dive past these identities, compressed together in brown flesh and ever-evolving regrets.

"Lebbie misses you. He goes, *'Where's momma?'* We tell him he'll see you soon."

"Okay."

Cora strokes the girl's hair. "What's her name?"

I twist the ring on my finger. "Don't know yet."

Cora frowns and shakes her head, placing the baby back in the bassinet. "I'm not doing this."

"What—"

"Mama Sugar wants us to be gentle with you for a little longer. That's what she said. Lawrence agreed with her but my husband, he knows bodies, he doesn't always know hearts."

"What are you babbling on about?"

"*This!* You!" She takes a deep breath. "Sara . . . Sara I know you're hurt. I understand but—"

"Why do people keep saying they understand? You don't understand—"

"You *know* I understand loss, that deep kind, hovering over like those clouds outside. I damn well know *that* hurt, *that* sadness. And not even

346

you, Sara Coulter, gets to tell my story in your foggy little head. You don't get my power."

Damn!

Violet. She reminds me of Violet. She's not willing to take my shit. This calling to the carpet was the part, *is* the part, I hated-loved about Violet the most. Now Cora, she has that same spirit and I'd have never guessed it, never saw it in her, but then again, I never tried to because I thought I knew who Cora was. Like people who think they know who I am. I love doing to others the very thing I hate them doing to me.

"You saw the room. The one I keep closed." Cora walks to the window and opens it a crack; a few drops cling to the window, slowly dripping onto the ledge, then the floor. "I was in the room next door a few years ago. No baby in the bassinet."

"I'm not looking to dredge up old tragedies."

Cora grabs the vase and walks into the bathroom. "Aren't you though?" The splatter of water follows her question.

She walks out, setting the vase on the table, and unties the twine on the paper. Roses spill out. "Bad things that happened to you. I don't know them all, like you don't know all of my heartbreaks. But I know you use your grief, your secrets, as a shield to beat back everything else. Good and bad. Probably feel you're safer like that."

"You got a head shrink degree at Spelman?"

"No. A bachelor's in history and a master's in English. Psychology was my minor."

A hard grin moves across Cora's face. "I'm not trying to tell you about yourself to belittle you. I'm telling you so you can figure it out, all of the chaos, before it eats you alive, like it almost did me."

"You? Ms. Perky? Ms. Perfect? Always got a big smile on your face."

Cora digs in her purple bag, bringing out a moderate-sized pair of scissors. "Smiles hide so many things. You know this."

She picks off every other leaf on the first rose stem. "I was angry and sad and alone when we lost Jacob. One day he was safe, and I was gonna be a mom. And then . . . I was here." She cuts a stem at an angle at the bottom and places it in the water. "No one talked to me, not really. They only asked if I was okay. I wasn't but no one wanted to hear that. They asked me to eat, and I ate, but nothing had taste. Then came the platitudes. The 'you can try agains,' the 'God never puts more on us than we can bears,' the 'it was God's plans' . . . That one made me the angriest, but I smiled. I smiled and thanked people for making my anguish that much worse."

She clips the end of another rose stem, placing it in the water.

"For a while that's all I did. Smile. Slept and

smiled. I smiled when I left the hospital. Smiled at church. At the grocery store. At the dinner table with Lawrence. And when I was alone, which was so damn much, I'd finally stop smiling and then I'd drink. Cognac."

"I prefer whiskey."

She cuts another rose stem.

"Lawrence knew I drank, had at least an inkling of it though he never said anything. The empty bottles should've told him all he needed to know, but maybe he didn't have the energy. Maybe he didn't have the will. I guess he battled his own grief and left me to my own wars. With Lawrence, I suppose he does what a lot of doctors do, try to find every remedy they can. If they can't cure an ill, they push it down and away. That's what Lawrence did with the memory of our son. It's down and away somewhere. Maybe with every person he saves, it helps him forget he couldn't save Jacob. And with every person he can't save, it brings back that pain so much worse."

"So, what did you do? Pray?"

"Don't sound so scornful. Yes, I prayed. Mostly I thought about Jacob, how he'd want me to be, that if I was ever blessed to become a mom again, I couldn't be what I was becoming. One day, and there wasn't anything really special about that day, I simply made a choice, one I now make every day, to figure out how I want to live my life, to be rid of all the bitterness, the feeling the world owes me something because I read a Bible or go to a church. I do good things to do them. I'm trying to be grateful for every good thing God puts in my life. Even if it's for such an unfairly short time."

"Is that door in your house still closed while you're busy being grateful for all God has done to you? Oh, I'm sorry, I meant *for* you?"

Cora swallows hard and plucks two leaves from a stem. She inspects it for thorns and sets it in the blue vase.

"Did you come to lecture me about how you found your way through, or is this talk supposed to stop making you-all feel bad. So you don't have to think about your dead son and Mama Sugar won't have to think about her drunk one and her jailed one?"

"My God Sara, you can be a hateful little thing, can't you?"

"It's what I do best."

Clip. In goes a rose. "And while you're busy reveling in your hate, like a pig in slop, you're going to push everyone away. And only someone who cares about you, even when you're so eagerly cruel, will try to help you out of this."

"Mmm-hmm."

"I never said I was done missing my Jacob. I never will be. You won't stop missing Jonas. Or your mom. Or anyone else you've lost. Grief has its peaks and valleys. But like I said Sara, you don't get to walk my journey for me. I don't walk yours for you, but if I found some small light for my path, the kindest thing, the most *human* thing I can think of, is to share that light with you."

"How so very selfless of you."

She plucks two leaves, cuts the stem, puts a rose in the water. The room is silent for a while.

"You don't think I want to be rid of this? I don't know how else to be. That's my problem. Maybe that means Jonas was wrong about me. Most important, I was wrong about myself. Maybe I'm not the good person I hoped to be. And what happens when you don't know . . . *yourself?*"

"The same thing that happens to all of us. You figure *you* the hell out! It won't be the last time you or me or anyone else will have to do it. Everything we go through reshapes us, makes us new. Be a new you, a better one, for Lebbie and your daughter."

Cora arranges the last of the flowers, fluffing them, slightly tweaking the placement. "Don't look at me like that," she says.

"Like what?"

"Your eyes are all bugged out."

She walks to the right side of my bed. "We all love you. Jonas wasn't the only one. You must know that."

"I know I'm tired, Cora. And I don't want to go back and forth anymore. Thank you for the flowers."

"Fine Sara. I can only tell you what I know. You either listen or shut down, but I beg you to keep your heart open until the next good thing, no matter how small the good thing is. That's how you keep moving, find some hope."

"I told Larry this once, in your house as a matter of fact. Jonas dying only proved me right. Hope is a dangerous thing."

I turn away from Cora, closing my eyes. Hollow footsteps and a gently closed door declare her departure. I don't need a blue vase of roses. I don't need lectures or sermons. I don't need friends.

I don't need to be saved.

"We thought it'd be best if you rested here until you feelin' a bit stronger, more like yourself," says Mr. Vanellys. He sets my burned, battered turquoise suitcase in the corner of the room in The New Scarlet. I know this room. I got ready here. Put on an ivory dress. Cora let me borrow her gold necklace.

A small crib, freshly built and painted mint green, sits across from my bed, farthest from the two windows on the opposite side of the room. A dresser is next to the door.

Mr. Vanellys points to a blue-green RCA radio on a desk in the corner. "Lennie said you might want some music, so that's yours. She also got the one downstairs if you wanna listen to music when you workin' in the kitchen. That one's white, like the old one."

He then hobbles over to the dresser. "We also brought you some things from back at the apartment. Make it feel a little more like home. Lennie Mae is downstairs cookin'. Swatted my hand 'fore I could get a good look."

"Blackened catfish. Okra. Mac 'n' cheese. And . . . mashed potatoes."

"Oh Sara-girl, that nose of yours. Lennie made me peel the potatoes before I left for work. Buster ducked out 'fore she could get to him. I reckon he'll make it back somehow just in time for dinner."

Mr. Vanellys chuckles as he runs his hand over the crib. He walks over to the bed with an empty oak nightstand on each side and smooths over the already smoothed sheets. "Ms. Mavis still talks about how you were a big help to her. Says you can come over to the bakery anytime you want. You know, if you wanna take a break from here." He looks over his shoulder. "I'll talk to Lennie so she don't give you a hard time about it."

I take off my ring and put it next to the papers and pictures. Mr. Vanellys took a few of the photos and put them in old, chipped frames. Jonas standing under a bridge on the banks of the Mississippi. Lebanon on my lap at Revival. A picture of grass. All these fixed pieces of my history meant to bring comfort, and all I see is loss.

Mr. Vanellys picks up a picture, then gently places it back on the dresser. "Wasn't tryin' to go too deep into your personal things, but I figured some of these keepsakes might make the room a little less bare. Got all that paper on the living room table. Brought it here in case it was something important like bills."

I pick up a piece of paper. Jonas' loopy handwriting catches my eyes.

> *. . . underneath alabaster stars with a*
>   *pearl moon*
> *My weary eyes find you by the Old Bridge*
> *Come to me*

"Nothing important here. You didn't need to bring these."

Mr. Vanellys looks down in the baby's crib. "Hey there girl. You lookin' 'round at this world, huh? Like what you seein' so far?"

I sit on the bed. It gives way. Soft. I'm still tired. So damn tired. "Can you please hand me the suitcase?"

"Ooop! Oh! Look at that! Sara-girl I promise you this chile looked directly at me. Like she knew what I was sayin'. Yeah, this here one is smart as a whip. Can already tell."

"Mr. Vanellys?"

He looks up from the crib.

"Suitcase. Can you hand me my suitcase? Please."

"Sorry. My ears ain't what they once was." He lifts the turquoise luggage with ease and sets it on the clean sheets.

"I need to feed her. Would you please—"

"Say no more. I'ma go see where Lennie is on that food. Bring you up some. We'll keep Lebanon with us 'til you get settled some more."

He looks back down at the crib. "Hey girl, you and me gonna have some good talks, huh?" He smiles wide. "But you gonna listen to what I say. Ain't gonna be no back talk."

The girl starts to whimper the tiniest bit.

"Okay, okay. I didn't mean it. Didn't mean it. I was playin'. I was playin'."

He's already smitten. Like with Lebanon. Will too. Mr. Vanellys is a softie. He's only going to see your best self until you show him your worst.

I open the suitcase as Mr. Vanellys closes the door. Louisa looks at me. Black button eyes. Stitched-on smile. Only a light scent of smoke lingers as I lay Louisa on the bed. My chocolate-colored dress with pearl-sized white polka dots tightens around my stomach as I rise, carefully. A muted rattle from my left pocket reminds me of Lawrence's gift. A bottle of pills, the same color as the ones Mama Sugar gave Amos when he broke his leg, same as the one I took in the hallway when Amos was an asshole to Will. It made the ceiling shrink and the dust sparkle.

Percodan. For discomfort Sara. The birth was difficult so you can take one every six hours if you need it. These can be powerful so no more than four a day. You understand?

I understand simple math, but what Lawrence failed to mention was which type of "discomfort" the pills are supposed to alleviate. He didn't explain exactly what constitutes discomfort either. The painful throb of my muscle or if I want to forget; if tentacles of memory continue to wrap themselves around my nightmares, the ones of Jonas' blood on my hands and dress; the one where I reach for him in a deep forest, and he disappears into a grove of twisted trees. I follow him and fall but I get up and still run after him. And I never, *ever* find him. Would this medicine cure those things? An argument could be made for either—relief of the flesh or mind.

Two wide windows, opened only a crack, invite a miserly breeze. I carefully open each one as high as it'll go. Mr. Vanellys is right about the girl. Her eyes dart around the room, taking in the whole of her view before her large brown eyes find mine.

She's so pretty isn't she, Sara?
The girl looks like you.
What are you going to name her?

I cradle her in my arms, unbutton the top of

356

my dress and let her feed. She's not greedy like Lebanon so I don't have to switch to my other breast. She takes what she needs and no more. She's a good baby.

Her eyes drift open and closed and then she sleeps. She doesn't fight it. I've decided she has Jonas' eyes, big and clear, like she can see the beautiful things in you that you can't see in yourself. Maybe I'm being like Mr. Vanellys, finding the best in her until she's proven other-wise. Has my heart grown enough, to keep both her and Lebanon loved? I don't think it has. I don't believe I'll have enough room for all of us, for me to love all of us. At least not yet. Sometimes your desire to love someone doesn't manifest into love itself.

She's dry. I swaddle her in a blanket, white with soft pink trim, and lay her down in the crib. I take three pills, lie down and hold Louisa in my arms. Sam Cooke plays in my head. Our wedding song. The last part of about the world being wonder-ful with the person you loved in it. Just this part. Such a pretty song. I know . . . I know why Jonas . . . Nice song . . . pretty, pretty, pretty . . .

He shakes me hard. Will.

"Sara, Sara! Hey, dinner. Wake up!"

It was nice and black, my dream. Or if there's nothing in your dream, can you still call it that? "I'm not hungry. Go away."

Will balances a book underneath the tray of food. He puts the book on the bed and the tray on the left nightstand. "You gotta eat something. Granny won't let me take this plate back full."

Blackened catfish. Okra. Mac 'n' cheese. Mashed potatoes. I knew it.

"Then you eat it. I told you I'm not hungry. Leave me be."

He grabs the book from the bed and sits on the edge. "I'll finish reading and you can start eating."

"I'm not hungry!"

Will keeps his head down. "I really like this part, Sara." He reads aloud from the Frederick Douglass book, the one he carried last week. Some part about being loosed from moorings and being free but being in chains. All the words are jumbled. I want silence. Peace, whatever that sounds like. No one bothering me, nagging me, lecturing me. Praying. Hovering. And I push the food off the nightstand onto the floor.

Will jumps up. "Sara, why'd you do that?"

"I told you I wasn't fucking hungry! But if you wanna be stubborn, then I'll find another way to get my point across. Now get out!"

Will comes toward me. Arms outstretched, then wrapping them around me. "It's okay. Calm down. It's me. You love me. Come on, Sara. Remember what you said? Find a way through when you're hurt and angry because if you do, you'll be a lot stronger than you were before."

"Get out! Get out! Leave! Get the hell out of here! Now!"

The baby whimpers. Then cries. The same hiccupy rhythm as her older brother. Dammit! I don't want love. My words thrown back at me. Will still clings to me, hoping, wishing, a hug can repair what's been damaged. That his love can overcome what I've been through, what's been taken. Not just in Memphis but before I came here. And it can't, because I won't let it. I don't want it. My heart can't take opening up, not again.

It will kill me.

He's so strong. I didn't realize how strong he's gotten. I pry Will's arms from around me. All my strength, all my anger. He falls back, crashing to the floor.

The girl cries. Louder.

"I didn't mean . . . I said to let go of me! Why don't you ever listen?"

"What in God's name is going on? I heard y'all all the way downstairs," says Mama Sugar. Will quickly scrambles to his feet.

"Sara, I know you didn't push my grandchild!"

"I tripped," says Will. He wipes his face and hurries out of the room.

Mama Sugar's eyes follow him. "That boy's a terrible liar like Vanellys." Her gaze turns back, and she walks up to me, face to face. "I don't care what you goin' through, you don't put your hands on Will like that."

"It was an accident. He's fine and—"

"Nuh-uh. Bad things happen to people, but you don't visit it on someone else. You don't drown in your misery. Reach out to your people so they can pull you to shore. Like it or not, we your people."

"*My people* killed the man I loved. I don't need people like you."

Mama Sugar walks to the crib and gets the girl, who quiets down. "I'ma take her with me for a while. She don't need to be around you like this. It's poison."

She closes the door. In a dark room I stand alone. A ruined bounty of catfish, okra, mashed potatoes and mac 'n' cheese lay to waste on the floor. That was gonna be a good meal. I'm dumb as hell for doing that. The dinner plate is shattered into five or six pieces. One of Mama Sugar's good plates for special company.

Steady hands. I command them to stop shaking as I pick up shards of porcelain. My hands don't listen to me. Using the dirty silverware, I scoop the smashed food onto the tray, some of it clings to the floor. I've done what I can. I need a broom and mop for the rest. I'll go downstairs and get them when I don't hear Mama Sugar in the kitchen.

Gusts of wind rustle the papers on the dresser. I have nothing to put on top of them to keep them from flying, to keep them still, so I hold on to them. Jonas used words deliberately and delicately. Spun them into silken sentences, sturdy assurances of adoration; he stitched poems and stanzas that wove themselves around me and the fabric of our love in such a way I thought us invincible. Now all I have is paper. His words in smudged ink.

Why torture myself with these souvenirs? With a ring? With letters and pictures? Jonas remains so real to me. I still hear his laugh, that knowing deep chuckle and the smile following it. Or maybe I am perfecting him in my mind. Isn't that what we do with the dead? Make them legends in our memories?

Wind whips up again. I gather the framed and unframed pictures, balancing them against my chest with my ring. The papers flutter in my clenched right hand. The ring slips and rolls under the bed. Doesn't matter. I walk down the back staircase. The kitchen is empty. Mama Sugar and Mr. Vanellys are in the living room. Their voices carry in hushed tones. They should be in the second drawer on the left of the stove. Mama Sugar keeps them in case of an emergency. I place the photos down for a moment, opening the drawer. I take what I need and walk out the back door. The middle of the backyard is good a place as any to leave him behind. There's no ceremony. No scriptures. No songs. No tears.

Only fire.

I let the letters drop. Pictures too. I strike a match. The biting scent of sulfur wafts above me as I marry the flame to all of it. I don't look. I let it go. Let it all go.

"Oh my God! What the hell? What you doin'?" Mr. Vanellys shoves past me, a water hose in his hands. Errant embers float around me, black snow, charred paper, abandoned memories. If things don't exist, you don't have to remember. You don't have a word or an image ripping you apart.

Mr. Vanellys tosses the water hose aside and inspects the damage to my mementos and the lawn. "You want this place to go up again? You wanna kill us?"

"No. Not you."

Mama Sugar looks on from the top of the back stairs. Water still runs in tiny rivers from the snaked hose laying on the grass. Singed. Most of the papers and pictures are destroyed but only in small parts. Maybe water will do the rest for me. Bubble the photos, distort them, make the ink runny, shrivel the paper. Her thick fingers grip her housecoat. Yellow with blue flowers. "Sara-girl?"

What other words can she use to follow my name? I return to my room, its windows facing

362

the front street. There's only the setting sun. Children on bikes. Arched rooftops of homes. Oak tree branches heavy with leaves cover patches of lingering August daylight.

I hear the rustle in my left pocket. The calming click-click-click of a plastic bottle with temporary salvation in tiny chalky capsules. Salvation. I had that until William woke me up. True, I lose Jonas in nightmares. But nightmares or dreams he's still with me. That's enough. What are three more? I need to see him. And he me. I'll come back when it's easier. Not a lot easier. Bearable. I'll sleep until things are bearable.

Because now. Because this. Because me.

No.

Things creak. A door. I think it's the door.

Why does he shake me? Who's crying? Yelling? Why do I float?

Away.

NINETEEN

Fingers pinch and press on my flesh, the veins of my wrist. Blotchy shapes hover above. A figure with undefined angles. Light musky cologne. Low, hazy lights. Bleach. Fresh roses. Faintly they echo, the cries of babies. Am I still here? Was it a dream? When did I have the girl? Where's the bassinet?

Larry's voice comes to me in layers, like I'm below ground and he's speaking to me from far above. I'm in a casket and he's outside it.

I sit up. Or I try to. Everything is unsteady. My stomach lurches. I throw up on Lawrence's shoes. His nice wing-tipped, caramel-dyed shoes.

"How many did I tell you to take in a day, Sara? I said no more than four!"

I wipe my mouth. I feel better. A little bit anyways. "I know what you said. I was in pain. I was tired. I did what I did to stop being both."

Lawrence grimaces as he walks to the door and opens it. "Nurse, please call someone in here. The patient had an accident."

He grabs one of my pillows, removes the cover and wipes down his shoes. "Will found you. On the floor. Thought you were dead."

I see more clearly, the roses held in a green vase. "Cora got these?"

Lawrence grabs a plastic, dusty blue pitcher. He pours water into a white cup and hands it to me. "Did you hear what I said? They barely got you here in time!"

"I told you I needed to rest." I swallow hard, washing the sour taste from my mouth. "I wasn't trying to do anything. Or maybe I was. Maybe I'm mad I woke up. But about Will . . . I'm sorry about that. Truly. I'd never want that."

"Tell him you're sorry. Tell everybody. You're not the only one who misses Jonas. You're not the only one who's ever lost somebody in this world."

I drink the last of my water and place it on the table next to my bed. "Stop talking *at* me. You and Cora. Y'all belong together. You two plan out your lectures before you give them?"

Lawrence folds the rancid pillow cover and throws it in the hamper. "You're a grown-ass woman. I'm not lecturing you. You can be happy. You gotta want to be though. You bake, right?"

"I know what I can be. I know what I am."

Lawrence pulls up a chair. "It's just—I want more for you, Sara."

"You know that whole not talking at me thing, you're failing."

He drags his hand over his face, the whites of his eyes a muted pink. "I'm saying you can find your way back doing something you love to do. Plus you have us. We'll help you with the kids. Cora and I."

"You want kids of your own."

"Sara don't. Don't say something you're gonna regret."

I take one of the roses from the vase. "I'm not trying to be mean. I'm saying. You want kids of your own. You'll get tired of trying to help me with mine."

"We can't."

"You sound naive, Larry."

Lawrence clenches his jaw, his voice almost a whisper. "With Cora and I, there's no—it's not possible for us. Not after . . . Jacob."

Loss no matter how it's experienced takes something from us. Opens something aching and jagged. And why is this sensation, this mournful dance, something I almost welcome? Because it's expected. I know pain and hurt. We are comfortable enemies. And I think maybe Momma always told me to watch where I was, take note of my position, because knowing where I am and who I am no matter how ugly, is better than wondering who I could've been.

I hold Larry's hand. "Life isn't fucking fair to us."

"No contract anywhere says it has to be. That's why we even the odds in our own ways, whatever little bit we can."

He stands up, looking me in the eyes. "Let Lebbie and the baby stay with us. When you get yourself together, come by and get them."

I prick my thumb on a thorn. Cora left some of them on the flowers.

Lawrence lets go of my hand and toys with his stethoscope. "Being alone in the house with Cora, that door always closed, it's heavy. That's the only way I can describe it. All the things I didn't do. All the things Cora needs me to be and the despair I feel because I can't be that for her. I'm trying to be strong. Maybe I'm not as strong as she is. No, I know I'm not as strong as she is. Quiet as it's kept, men never are strong as women. That's a fact of life they don't cover in medicine journals." Lawrence pinches the bridge of his nose, blinking a few times. "Geez, I'm tired and babbling. The kids will be a welcome distraction. Trust me. Please."

"People tell me things even when I don't want to know. Must have one of those faces."

"Is that a 'Yes Larry' or a 'Go to Hell Larry'?"

I nod. Rather my brain makes the decision to move my head up and down but my heart screams this is somehow a trap. It must be. In his way, Jonas was a trap without meaning to be. I was a fool to fall for it, for him. Everything in me aches. Bones, muscles, things they don't have names for, are weary and worn. I'm always sleepy. Even talking takes effort. My tongue is heavy. Words are jumbled. But somehow, I can move my head up and down.

It'll be good. Stay here for a day or two. Go

back and get my children. I have to clean the apartment. Put things away in boxes. Dust. Mop. Figure out where I'm going to fit the girl. I can't keep staying at The New Scarlet. Working in the kitchen looking out at the backyard where I lost him. Straighten yourself up, girl. Do what you need. Move on.

"I'll be back in a day or two."

"Okay, Sara."

"I mean it."

"It's not a trick. Not a scheme. We know you'll be back for Lebbie and . . ." Lawrence tilts his head. "Have you thought of a name for her yet?"

We can name her—

I know what you want to name her.

What? You don't wanna admit I'm right, my love? It's a pretty name. You always had a problem saying I was right.

You did that enough for the both of us, Mr. Know-it-all.

Pot. Kettle. That's why we're so good together.

We were together. Not anymore.

Ah, there are many ways of being together. You think death will stop me?

Death stops everything.

Not me. Not our love. Not ever!

"Sara?"

"Hmmm."

"Not ever what?"

I place the rose back in the green vase. "Sophia Lillian Coulter. That's her name."

After our mothers.

"After our moms."

Lawrence smiles. "Pretty name for a pretty little girl." He walks to the door. "I'll have the birth certificate taken care of by the time you leave."

"Tell Cora I said thank you for the flowers."

"You tell her when you see us in a few days."

Jonas didn't stand here. I've spent the past two hours out of the hospital trying to figure exactly where he stood in the picture I took. It wasn't in front of the Harahan Bridge where the trains travel on iron tracks. I walk farther. He was closer to the Memphis-Arkansas Bridge where cars screech or rumble above me. He was here. And I snapped the picture when he smiled, and I still don't know why he smiled in that moment.

It's foolish for me to think the world would somehow stop. I know that doesn't happen. We all at the time of our loss assume it's singular, deeper than someone else's. But my loss isn't special. People still laugh and love and eat. Children still play. The day Jonas died is the day someone else was born. Life is just as relentless as loss. This hurts almost more than losing him.

I'm never lost to you.

My feet sink deeper in the grass. Muddy water

rushes past. The impatient rush, murky waves crest and fall. Boats briskly make their way down the river. People walk. I roam aimlessly. I don't pay attention to street signs.

Somehow, I'm here. The Iris Club. The squat brick building with the jade green door. Maybe something else guided me more than my feet did.

"Ooooh, I know you hungry. Can hear your stomach all the way over here," says a tall balding man a few feet away, next to a smoker. The width and girth of his body seems something out of a fairy tale. More giant than cook. Who knew John Henry barbecues on East Butler Avenue? Traded in his hammer for basting brushes and tongs?

The man opens both hatches of the smoker, removing brisket, spraying it with water on the table and then putting it back in next to some ribs. He grabs four hickory logs, gingerly placing them in the firebox. "Yeah, now you actin' right, mama. Thought I was gonna have to call Elijah back up to help you out." He takes a towel from his back pocket and wipes his face. "Brisket and ribs ain't gonna be done for another hour or so, you can come back 'round then."

I smooth the front of my dress. "I'm not coming back."

"Damn girl! Everyone come 'round for Eddie P.'s cookin'."

"I just meant—I'm going back home in a little while." I shrug.

"Oh. Alright you 'bout stopped my heart." He laughs, then closes both doors to the smoker. "Actually, that pulled pork 'bout done. Can fix you a sandwich 'fore you head on back."

He uncovers the pork on the table in front of him and stuffs two buns full of the savory meat. Pickles and that sauce.

First date, remember? You kissed me.

"How much?"

Eddie shakes his head and hands me the two sandwiches. "Don't worry 'bout it. Looks like you need a little kindness is all. Hell, most of us do. Just do a little kindness in your own way if you come across someone else who needs it."

"Thank you."

The New Scarlet is dark from the back. A sliver of light makes its way to me but not enough to illuminate the kitchen. It's there. The third lower cabinet left of the stove. The long skinny bottle neck, the comforting swish. I keep myself hidden, but can see Mama Sugar as she cleans.

"You heard from Sara-girl?" Mama Sugar sweeps in the front room.

"Nah," says Mr. Vanellys. "Me and Buster can go out lookin' if you want."

"If she don't wanna be found, then it won't do much good. Maybe she'll come through those doors any minute. Probably worryin' about nothin'." Her voice cracks on the last part. I should tell her I'm here. Walk up to the living room and give her a hug. Give her comfort that she hasn't lost another child. But . . . she has. Lying to her isn't the answer. It isn't kind. Eddie P. said to do a kindness for someone. The bottle is cold in my hands. And it's three-quarters full. Buster could probably tell me how many shots I can get out of a bottle of rum that's three-quarters full.

The new stairs don't creak or betray me as I walk up. The bedroom is clean and smells of fresh linen. Low blue light caresses the pine floors. I sit on them. I eat pulled pork sandwiches. I drink rum.

Do you remember the first song we danced to?

His voice is constant. In my head. Always. Our moments. How he looked in his indigo suit. How he held me. His smile. His face. How he protected. How he died. Is this the way I grieve now? I never heard Saul's voice, though there are so many things I think of, I remember, and I don't want to.

I want to drown out Jonas' voice, this incessant ache, this open wound of love. Make it disappear. If not forever, then for a little while. Relief from his love for a little while.

Drink. More. *More!* There's a warm sensation. In my stomach. It spreads, travels to my back. Now my head. And I sit in the blue light. And I wait for his voice.

Nothing.

Blessed silence. Memories, not as crisp as pictures from a black-and-silver camera. Sounds and colors bleed into each other.

Drink.

Half the bottle is left now. Push it down and away like Cora said. Lebanon and Sophia need me to push it all down and away. And I need more . . . I need . . .

Drink.

Then sleep. Let me put the bottle under my bed first. I have a quarter left. I'll save the rest. For the morning. Or tomorrow night. After they're asleep. I'll drink alone. No matter what. That's the rule. My rule. They won't see me. Not the kids. Mama Sugar. Will. Mr. Vanellys. Buster. I won't allow it.

We're sliding together. Me and the blue light. The indigo light. And I know the night always keeps its secrets. I always keep mine. It's a contract.

It's a small gift.

Sunlight makes its unwelcome presence known through the billowy white curtains. I am not on the floor. I managed to get myself in the bed at least. A blanket is tucked around me. A cooling plate of grits and sausage and two biscuits. Not biscuits. Butter rolls. Light, doughy, sweet. I chew as I grasp for the bottle under my bed. I reach slowly, carefully, letting go of my breath when my fingers clasp the neck of the rum bottle. Still a quarter left. Good. I'll save it for tonight when everyone is asleep except for me and the blue light. I put it back. The squeak of floorboards and the urgent clamor of voices from below beckon me from the room, but I can't get the edges of my vision to sharpen as quickly as I'd like. Who am I today? What am I doing today?

Remember.

Lebanon. Sophia. Cora and Lawrence.

The hallways are empty. I brace my hand on the wall. The bathroom is two doors away at the end of the hall. Feels like a thousand miles away. Standing. Lifting my head. It all takes effort. The dust doesn't sparkle like it did with the pill but the voice, Jonas' voice, isn't as clear. And that's good. The less of him, the better for me. Good things don't last. You torture yourself when you remember them.

The bathroom shields me from the sunlight and prying eyes. I wash the dry, rancid taste out of my mouth though it lingers.

Wash your face. Smile. No, that hurts. Not smiling hurts too, but less. Find a dress. One that's loose. Brush your hair. It's there. My wedding ring. When it fell out of my hands, I didn't look for it but it's somehow back on the dresser. Go downstairs. Help before you leave.

Maybe Mama Sugar needs you to peel potatoes. I need to see her face so she can see I'm sorry for last night, the night before too. I'm thankful she tucked me in. Somehow, I'm still so mad at her because of Lucky, and though I know in my head it's not her fault, I still need someone else to blame. Someone else to hate.

Sometimes that's her. Sometimes that's me.

Seventeen stairs to the kitchen. Two new boarders. One young. One old. Mama Sugar stands over the stove. Her right hand fixed to her back as she stirs her customary pot of grits. Only three butter rolls sit in the middle of the pine table. Will grabs one. Two rolls left.

Buster looks up and smiles. "Yeah, Lennie Pie, I'ma need plenty of sustenance. Elvin got me helping him move back in with Simone. Why she forgave him I don't know, but now my knees gotta pay the price. Can I get some more bacon? What you makin' tonight?"

"I'm thinkin' salmon patties and coleslaw. Peach cobbler for dessert."

Mr. Vanellys clears his throat as I stand perched atop the last three steps. Mama Sugar minds the bacon, expertly flipping it. The old boarder grabs another butter roll. One left.

Walking to the pine table, I sit down next to Mr. Vanellys. "I can pick up groceries if you need it."

Mama Sugar shakes her head. "I'll do it. Thank you, Sara."

Will smiles, a shaky thing, and looks out at the window, then at Mr. Vanellys. "Don't we need to leave soon? You said you were gonna show me around the garage." He takes his dishes and places them in the sink. A paperback is curved in his back pocket. I can't make out the title. He leaves out of the door without looking at me. Mr. Vanellys pats my right arm, stands up, kisses Mama Sugar and follows behind Will.

"I don't know when I'ma be in after helping Elvin, but Lennie Pie, make sure I get some of them salmon patties, please."

"Ain't gonna let you starve."

Buster looks over at the boarders. "If y'all still need a ride, there's room in Vanellys' truck."

The old boarder wipes his mouth and stands. "Many thanks to you. Let's go Grandson."

The young boarder shovels bacon into his mouth and takes the last butter roll from the pan, nods to us and leaves with his grandfather.

"I'll bring my dishes downstairs," I say.

Mama Sugar drains the grease in the cast-iron skillet into an old coffee can. "Mmm-hmm."

"You're not talking to me now?"

"I'm tryin' to think about what to say to you. Don't got the right words yet."

I grab the remaining dishes on the table and bring them to the sink. I turn on the water. "Never stopped you before."

"Guurrlll . . ." Mama Sugar bangs the cast-iron

376

skillet back on the stove. "Have you lost your damn mind? Tryin' to set the backyard on fire. Takin' too many of them pills—"

"You didn't mind giving them pills to Amos."

"Listen, after all I done for you, you ain't gettin' ready to throw nothin' back in my face!"

"So, you, a God-fearin' woman, gets to keep score of all your good deeds? I forgot where that's in the Bible."

"Blasphemin'. Throwin' God back in my face. What else you got? What else your wrath, your anger, get you to say to try and make me hate you? That's what you want, isn't it? For me to hate you 'cause you hate me now? 'Cause of Lucky?"

Mama Sugar takes a step toward me and puts her hands on my face. "Go on then, chile. Hate me. Put it all on me. 'Cause I'm gonna take it. I'm gonna take your hate and your regret and your sadness and I'ma return you only love. I ain't gonna stop loving you. Or feedin' you. Or lettin' you stay here. No matter what you do. I love you. You hear me, Sara-girl? Nothin' you say or do stops that."

From my throat this scream, this strangled cry, escapes me. It is frightening. It is everything without words. It is colors. It is the mahogany and gold of Jonas' casket; the silver of the bus that carried me to Memphis; the blues of night from my rum bottle; it is the purples of the bruises on

Momma's arms; the green of Lebanon's eyes and the brown of Sophia's; it's the gray of my path.

But Mama Sugar holds me as I sink to the ground with her. She lets me cry. She doesn't shush me. Tell me things will be okay. Give me some rank idea of hope. She lets me be in all of my ugly and jagged edges.

And somehow there is this brief respite of not having to hold myself together for the sake of others. It is precious to let yourself be broken for a while. That doesn't mean you're weak. It means you trust yourself enough to let go. And maybe this means I'll be okay. Shedding all of this makes me lighter.

"We all need a good cry, Sara-girl."

I nod, I look at the mess I made of her yellow dress. It's one of her favorites.

"Fix your face. Get some fresh air. Take some time to yourself 'fore the babies come back in a few days." Mama Sugar softly chuckles. "Then you won't have time to yourself."

I clutch her dress. "I—I'm s-sorr—"

"Nun-uh. We family and sometimes what family need to say to one another ain't always pretty, but it needs to be said. Now go for a walk, you hear me?"

"Yes ma'am. That's what I need."

Lebanon is so bad at playing hide-'n'-seek. Larry pretends to not see him behind the tree. His laugh consumes the street. You don't make noise when you hide, son. You stay quiet. You don't know who's coming for you.

"Where is Lebanon? I can't find him," says Larry. He smiles. It's wide. Cora holds Sophia, sitting on the top step of their home in a sleeveless brown blouse and matching ivory-and-brown pencil skirt. She rocks back and forth. Looking down every few moments. "Where's Lebanon? We can't find him," she says as Larry creeps closer to the tree. Lebanon's laugh grows louder. He runs for Cora, but Larry grabs him from behind and he squeals, kicks his little legs, then holds Larry around his neck. Larry's smile fades but he holds Lebanon. Tighter.

This was my life. It was almost my life. If only.

We are all playing a game. The "What If Game." What if Jonas was alive? What if Jacob would've lived? What if I was a person who deserved happiness? What if good things happened to good people like Cora and Larry?

What if the world was just?

I hate the "What If Game." I can never answer the questions.

I step from behind the shrub hiding me. Unlike my son, I'm good at hide-'n'-seek. I turn right at Hamilton Street and cross to Douglass Avenue. Lebanon's laugh still rings in my ears.

"Gosh! I didn't know you were coming to get them today," says Cora, who plasters a smile on her face. "Let me get their things together. Shouldn't be more than a few minutes."

Larry, still holding Lebanon, offers Cora his free hand, which she takes, effortlessly rising with Sophia in her left arm.

She glides through the living room. "Sorry about the mess," says Cora.

There's no mess. Only Lebanon's toppled blocks sit next to the clean rug and perfectly patterned matching sofas; the one against the wall where I sat next to Jonas as we all watched President Kennedy, a white man, talk about equality from his seat of undeniable power.

Larry finally sets Lebanon down. He runs to me. I pat him on the head. "Go play with your blocks."

He plays. He stacks blocks. Topples them. The hollow wooden clack as they fall is muted on the carpet. On the other side of the table, Larry sits on the couch, the soft cushions highlighting his already stilt-like legs.

"I'm not here to get them right now."

Cora lets out a long breath. She smiles, genuinely. "Oh. Well, like we said, we're happy to have them as long as you need."

"I know you are."

"Sara, I only meant—"

"Don't. It's okay to want them here. To be sad when they leave."

Cora sits down on the sofa. She brushes Sophia's hair from her eyes.

I sit down next to her. "But . . . what if one of them didn't have to leave?"

Lawrence moves to the edge of the couch, his knees knocking against the table, shaking it slightly.

Cora tilts her head. "Excuse me?"

"You're smart. You know what I'm saying. What if, what if you kept Sophia with you? What if I didn't come back?"

TWENTY

Cora stands, walking to the second door to the left. She opens it. The room is still blue. The dust is gone. She lays Sophia in the crib meant for their son. A fresh vase of daisies sits on the dresser to the right. "You want us to take Lebanon and Sophia?" she says, turning to look at me in the hall.

"No. Only Sophia."

"How's this supposed to work? We'd see each other all the time. Lebanon and Sophia look so much alike. They look like you. We can't keep a secret like that. It's not fair to them."

I take Cora's hand and squeeze it. "You're horrible at keeping secrets. And I'm not talking about things being fair."

I tug at the high collar of my orange-and-white sheath dress as we sit back down on the couch in the living room. "I wouldn't be here. Lebanon either. I'm going back to Chicago."

Lebanon topples his blocks again. He laughs.

Larry stands. "You're still upset about everything. It's understandable. Why don't you—"

"Do me a favor and promise me you won't tell Sophia what she's feeling? I do know enough about my daughter to know that'll make her angry something fierce." I look over at Cora. "And if she's anything like me, her anger isn't something you'll want to deal with."

My white flats lightly sink into their gold rug, a bone-white looping pattern vertically etched from one end to the other. "I can't stay here. Work at the place where Jonas died—"

"Then don't work at The New Scarlet," says Cora. "Ms. Lennie would understand."

"It's not that simple. Not for me. I can't stay in the place, in the city, where I lost him. Maybe you both stay in this house 'cause it makes you feel closer to Jacob. But I can't be that close to what I lost. It doesn't bring me comfort. And if I gotta be devoid of peace, I can at least go back to a place where I'm used to feeling torn apart. I don't want to taint this place or you-all with my anger or my hatred. Jonas loved this city so much—" I swallow the lump in my throat. Hold my head back so my tears won't fall.

"Wait. Wait. This is all moving too fast. You just walk in and announce you're giving us Sophia? What about Lebbie? He needs to know about his sister. Jonas. Us. Memphis," says Cora.

"And it'll be my story to tell. *If* I want to tell him. It's up to you if you want to tell Sophia everything. But do you want to do that to her? All of the pain. All of the things I feel right now. Do you want her to feel *that?*"

Larry walks to the kitchen. He comes back with

a crystal tumbler filled with dark brown liquor. Cora looks at the glass, then away.

"If we even agreed to this, Sophia is going to need to know how this came to be. Why she's with us and not you."

I stand up, grabbing his glass and drinking it in one gulp. "She won't need to know anything."

Larry scowls. "We can trust her with the truth when she's older and maybe—"

"Don't talk about lives in maybes. You don't have that luxury with children," I say.

"This can blow up in our faces. Most likely will. There are always consequences with things like this. Things we can't know," he warns.

The liquor still burns as it settles in my stomach. "And who among us can tell the future?"

This can't be what you want to do.

She'll be safe. You want your daughter safe, don't you?

From you?

Yes, from me. I can't trust myself with her. Not like this.

I go to the kitchen and open the top cabinets. Dishes. Glasses. Bottom cabinet. No cognac. Whiskey.

I pour. I drink.

Please Sara. I love—

I pour again. I drink again. I wash the glass. Dry it off. Place it back in the cabinet with the other matching crystal tumblers.

Cora and Larry whisper to themselves in the living room. They stop when I appear.

"It's okay to want this, you know. Doesn't make you bad people. I think God can forgive us for keeping secrets. He probably has plenty."

The warm sensation is back. The one starting in my back. "I know *you* know it won't replace Jacob. Nothing will. But imagine life with Sophia. What if you raise her? What if you paint the room pink or yellow instead of blue? What if your family was made whole in some small way?"

What if I could make myself feel better by having a part in that?

Cora drums her fingers on the edge of the table. Her manicured nails falling in perfect time on the dark wooden trim. "This isn't something I want to hold on to. I do want . . . I mean I think about our lives with a child." She looks at Larry. "But to raise Sophia as ours only to have her possibly hate us for keeping you from her. And you want us to forget about Lebbie?"

"First of all, you're not keeping her from me. It's my choice to let her go. And Lebanon, well, I'm raising him. That's my burden to bear."

"He's not a burden, Sara."

"You don't know what he is to me, Lawrence."

He leans forward in his chair. "I know he's a child and if you'd want us to take Sophia, then shouldn't she and Lebbie be raised together. I mean he's innocent—"

"No!"

I didn't mean to shout. But they don't know him. And they don't want him. Not really. They hold a dream in their heads and imagine who he could be. But the boy who stacks his blocks and knocks them down over and over, the origins of him, are only something I understand, because I am half of him, because I brought him into this world knowing how he came to be. It's the kind of darkness Cora and Larry couldn't hope to tame. Sophia, she's unburdened from my love, its patchiness and impatience. She can't grow to hate me if she doesn't know me.

And Lebanon, well, we're tethered by something with only feeling and no name. I can't be alone in this world without him; without someone who shares a secret, one that runs through his blood, but a secret I hope never again to share. I don't want to be alone without the memory. That night in Memphis, when I told my son I loved him. When there was hope for me in this world. I don't want to forget that moment, the person I was because maybe I can be that person again. Away from here. I want to hold again what hope felt like to me. He's the memento I've chosen.

I won't let him go.

"You want to do this. If you didn't, we wouldn't be talking in circles. The sooner you both come to yourselves, the sooner I can tell you how we'll get this done. And, Cora, you're going to keep this secret. You want to know why?"

She stops drumming her fingers on the table's edge, meeting my eyes. "Why Sara?"

"What if you tell Sophia she's not yours? What if she leaves you to find me? Do you want to risk losing another child?"

Cora looks down the hallway. At the door she left open. The door that was once closed and furnished with dusty boxes. She smooths her unwrinkled skirt. "What do you want us to do?"

Larry's jaw clenches. "Honey, we have to think—"

Cora holds up her finger. "I sat on that step. I sat on that step watching you and Lebanon playing, holding Sophia. Half of a dream is better than no dream at all. We owe ourselves. This is what I want." She takes a breath. "You owe *me*, Lawrence."

He sits back in his chair. His hands forming a temple over his mouth.

Cora turns to me, her eyes calm, narrowed. Her voice low, even. "I ask again, Sara. What do you want us to do?"

Standing at her grave is better than going back to a place where Momma isn't there. I visit the one place he won't come. The one place where my pain and my peace find some way to exist

387

together. It's frightening and wondrous. He left me nothing of her or from her. Her pearls. Her pictures. Her books. I hid one away. I came home after school and he'd packed her up like old Christmas decorations. Discarded the boxes in the alley. But her memory hovers. It haunts Daddy. And when he looks at me, he sees Momma. I am her ghost in flesh.

I fidget with the blue-green RCA radio in my bedroom. The large silver knob is stiff as I move it from station to station. I miss the old white RCA.

Static and then music. It's a simple melody on the piano before Nina sings poetry about kisses of fire and lost love. And a golden ring. "Black Swan." Nimble fingers pluck guitar strings. The piano slowly builds, its urgency matching Nina's voice, riding her pain, until the last notes fade, until everything fades.

I'm left wiping tears. Again. Don't stop moving. Louisa doll sits on my bed. I pull the suitcase from the corner. I put her inside. Three dresses. Three pairs of shoes. My large red purse and in it $200 I've saved for a rainy day. And these last few months of my life have invited the downpour of downpours.

Nina keeps playing in my head. Kiss of fire. Golden ring. Lost love.

I open the bottom drawer and pack clothes for Lebanon. Cora and Larry will buy Sophia everything she needs and wants, and a ton of shit she probably won't ever use. I'm doing the right thing. Knowing me will kill her. Knowing me killed her father. She'll have a chance. A better one without me. I'll keep saying this until I believe it. For now, this is my new prayer.

Amen. Amen. Amen.

Keep moving. Finish packing before Mama Sugar comes back from the grocery store. But I hear a door open and shut. An uneven shuffle from the front of the house to the back. I tuck my turquoise suitcase in the corner. Put my purse under the bed. Below me echoes the light banging of skillets, pots and pans, their clanging melody reverberate through the hallways. I join Mama Sugar in the kitchen and find her washing bell peppers and peaches in the sink.

"Sara-girl, there you are! Crush up them crackers. Don't want 'em ground to dust, but break 'em up good."

With a small paring knife, Mama Sugar skins each peach, cutting out the pit and slicing them. Every movement of her worn hands is efficient and learned. She hums another gospel I do not know. Moments in this kitchen. In the one before it, I took for granted. Once we're comfortable, we think things will always be as they are, even though the very experience of humanity continues to show us otherwise. I stand and watch Mama

389

Sugar. This will be our last time together in a kitchen. And I try to remember each detail. Take the pictures in my head like Jonas' camera and store the negatives away.

"Sara-girl, you done with them crackers. Cut up them bell peppers nice and fine, then start pickin' these bones out of the salmon. Can you make them patties? I'll make the coleslaw and finish up them string beans. Those gonna take a while anyway."

I know this. I know how to do all of this. How to make salmon patties, picking out the bones. Every step. But even her bossiness I'll miss. Mr. Vanellys warned me, *My wife is a difficult woman to deal with but master of this humble domain. And you must do whatever you can to help her maintain order over her realm.*

She places the peaches in the pot with sugar and salt and stirs. In a bowl, I mix the salmon, crackers, egg and green peppers. All around us is a sweet, smoky, earthy, Southern fragrance. Mama Sugar and I use our hands, our bodies, to form and fashion food for empty bellies. Add spice and seasonings. Fry patties in oil. Toss cabbage in mustard and mayonnaise and vinegar and sugar and salt. We work by instinct, invisible measurements, pinches and handfuls. In this kitchen, I'll make magic for the last time.

"This is gonna be a fine meal, Sara-girl."

"Yes ma'am. It will be."

• • •

In the garage, I hide my turquoise suitcase behind fresh-cut wood and rusting car parts. If I tell Mama Sugar or Will or Mr. Vanellys what I'm thinking, what I will do, they will beg me to stay. And I'll say yes. And I'll stay and hate them. I need to remember how they loved me and how I loved them.

It's the only way I'll survive. The only way I'll remember some part of who I was, who I could've been.

A light from the back room flickers on, then off. I hunker in darkness, but no light from the house returns. No bodies in the kitchen. No noise from the living room. Maybe I imagined the light.

You can stop this.

In the shadows, I grope around for the bottom cabinet and open it. No new bottle with a long neck.

Stay here. With me. With Lebbie. With Sophia. It's not too late.

It's done. I have to go. I have to let you go.

It doesn't work like that, Sara. You don't let go of the people you love.

It's not about what I want. What you want. If it was, you'd be here, right?

I . . . Yes more than anything I'd want to be here with you.

It's unfair you ask me to stay tethered to the

place that brought you to me, then took you from me.

But I'm not the only one who loves you! What can I say to convince you to stay here . . . with us?

Nothing! Stop haunting me. The very thread of my life is tied to yours. Let me go.

The windows are closed. A breeze cools my skin. It's probably a good thing I didn't find a bottle. I need a clear head for the morning.

I put clean sheets on the bed. Edges are tightly and neatly tucked at perfect angles. I take the empty old bottle from underneath the bed and hide it in my red purse. I'll throw it away later. I open the windows the tiniest bit for some fresh air and put my wedding ring in the pocket of my red-and-white dress.

Will sits on the living room couch. His head in his hand. On the table is a book. I don't take the last step yet, standing on, watching Will, his lips pursed, brow furrowed.

"What's wrong with you this morning?"

He still stares out the window. "Shouldn't have picked this book to read. That's all."

"What book?"

"*The Street*. Ann Petry."

I walk over to Will sitting next to him. "Homework?"

Will shakes his head. "Nah. I was reading on my own."

"Was it bad?"

"No! It was beautiful! I think I love Ann Petry. I wanna write just like that when I grow up. She might be my new favorite writer."

"I'm not hearing a problem, Will."

"The book has a sad ending." Will turns to me. "See, Lutie, that's the mom, she had to leave her son, Bub, at the end of the story. She wanted a better life for her and Bub, but it got all messed up and she killed this guy and had to get on a train and left Bub behind." Will's eyes bore into mine, as if to unearth my secrets, ones he has no idea I'm holding on to. The secret where I'm Lutie and he's Bub.

Will sighs. "Should've read something with a happy ending. Jonas was better at picking stories. He knew when I needed something happy."

I clear my throat, looking down at the book. Heat rushes to my face. "You want to write when you get older?"

"Yeah. Dad said there isn't any money in it. There's not a lot of money working for Grand-dad either, but he does that now. We'll see for how long." Will reverently touches the book. "Besides, being a writer is my dream. I'm doing it. It's not up to him, right?"

"No. It's not up to him at all." I pick up the book. "You know you can read these stories to Sophia when she's old enough. You'll do that, right?"

"Yeah. Her and Lebbie. They'll get sick of me,

393

but I'll make them like reading. Besides, I'll be grown by then. I can figure out which stories they need and when they need 'em."

From the living room, brash voices invade our quiet space. Shouts. Laughter. Hard, rushed footfall. I ruffle Will's head with my free hand. My fingers tangle in his curls for a moment.

"Come on, Sara." He laughs, pulls a brush from his back pocket and fixes his hair.

"Get on to school. Future big-time writers gotta graduate *at least* eighth grade."

Will hops up, grabs his bag and runs to the door.

"Wait!"

He turns around. "What's wrong?"

"Your book. Don't forget your book, Will."

He grins as I hold it up and he takes it. I crush Will to me, needing to remember how he smells. Like soap. Fresh ink. Cinnamon from the butter rolls Mama Sugar made this morning. And flowers. "I—I . . . Be good, okay?"

Will smiles. "Of course, but you know, I'd be even better if you and Granny make another peach cobbler like yesterday. Oh! Or a pineapple upside down cake."

"Boy, get out of here. Leave me be."

"You like me don't you, Sara?"

Will laughs and closes the door. I sink to the couch as my knees lose their strength. Breathe. Don't cry. Breathe.

At the kitchen table, I find Buster calculating in his notebook. Mama Sugar turns on the sink to run dishwater. The scratching of pencil and lazy slosh of water are the only sounds in the room. Buster picks up a sausage patty, eats it in two bites, wipes his hands, then picks up a receipt. He squints. "Lennie Pie, Vanellys ought to give me a raise. How does this man hand me invoices out of order with no clue what goes with what? It's like some terrible talent." He shakes his head.

"I know. I know. I'm the one with the mind for business but he got you to help him," says Mama Sugar as she gently cleans her cast-iron skillet, patting it dry and placing it in the dish rack. She turns around. "And I got Sara-girl to help me."

Buster chuckles. "Yeah, I know that's right. They both fall apart without us, right Sara?"

I put my red purse on the table next to me and sit across from Buster. "What's 878 times 22?"

"Oh Lord, not you too! You hangin' 'round Elvin?"

"For me. I won't doubt your answer."

Buster looks at Mama Sugar, who shrugs and returns to her dishes.

"Please," I say.

"I ain't never heard you say *Please*." He rubs his chin. "Eight hundred and seventy-eight times twenty-two is nineteen thousand three hundred and sixteen."

"Thank you . . . Bellamy."

"Gattdang it, Sara."

I reach for Buster, squeezing his hand. "Bellamy is a good name."

"I'ma let you have that one, but I better be getting some pancakes tomorrow."

Buster gathers his notebook and pencil. "Alright, see y'all this evening. Or the next day if these books don't balance right." He chuckles again and walks out the back door.

My eyes sting. My throat is dry. I take Buster's dishes and place them in the sink. Mama Sugar wears a housecoat, white with pink and green flowers. On the shelf above her are three stems of blue false indigo. I turn the silver knob of the white radio.

Solomon Burke blasts through the small speakers with soulful begging. "Cry to Me." I turn it up.

"Ooooh! I know who this is! Solomon Burt. Yeah, I heard some of the young people playin' it a little bit ago and asked 'em who it was. That Solomon Burt is a good singer."

"His name's not—never mind. It's nice you like this song."

"Sara-girl, old people always talkin' 'bout how this is the devil's music when we know full doggone well we listened to the same kinda thing. I know how to appreciate some of this new sound. Not all of it. Most of it really is too much for me. But yeah, some of this music I like. It sound like he singin' gospel, but most of these singers comin' from the church now anyway."

"Probably 'cause the money's better at Motown and Stax."

Mama Sugar swats me with her dish towel, laughing. "Hush with all that blasphemin'."

Maybe I should stay. Maybe it can always be like this. Smiling and laughing. Cooking and music. Likable strangers and their stories. Mama Sugar shuffles to the back wall. Opening the windows.

"Gotta get some fresh air in here. It's gettin' stuffy," she says.

The backyard. Green grass. Jonas' blood leaking onto my dress. Lebanon crying.

"Mr. Vanellys left already?"

"Mmm-hmm. He was restless all night. Left earlier than usual. Means he'll probably get home faster. Especially now Amos actually showin' up and workin'."

I wanted to say goodbye in my own way to Mr. Vanellys. But I never get what I want, do I? I open the upper cabinet doors. "Looks like we need some more grits."

"We not that low on them yet. We could wait—"

"Might as well get some now. One less bell to answer. One less egg to fry. Literally."

I force a laugh from my mouth. I'm giving myself away. Mama Sugar will know. She'll see right through me.

"You right, Sara-girl. Get some grits. Get me

my King Cotton bacon and sausage too. Three new boarders coming tomorrow."

"I'll head out now. Then pick up Lebanon and Sophia on my way back."

Mama Sugar smiles wide. "Finally! Please bring my babies back home. Been aching to see my Lebbie and hold the little one."

I will burn for this. I will burn in Hell. But I'll learn to live with this like I've lived with everything else. No one can question what I do to survive.

No one.

Wrapping my arms around Mama Sugar, I hold her. She returns my embrace and tightens her grip. "All you needed was time to figure it out. Now it'll be okay."

Her housecoat is soft, smells lightly of vanilla. I keep hugging her when she's relaxed and ready for me to let her go.

Just a little longer.

Mama Sugar laughs. Soft vibrations from her chest ferrying themselves to my body. "I ain't gonna be able to get dinner ready if you don't stop huggin' me."

"Yeah. Got a little carried away is all," I say, grabbing the red purse.

"Alright. Alright. I'm gonna fix up these rooms. I'll see you in a little bit."

"Yes ma'am." I bite my bottom lip. Mama Sugar goes upstairs slowly.

There were seventeen steps that led to my room. The home I made with Jonas was four blocks away. I had two children. Soon I'll have one. There are twenty-one steps to the front door. I open it and leave.

In the garage, uneven spots of dried motor oil etch a narrow path to my suitcase. It remains hidden behind wooden slats and engine parts. The suitcase zipper is loosened, exposing part of a green dress. I close it again, glancing at the back door of The New Scarlet. No movement in the kitchen windows. The backyard is littered in blazing crimson and gold leaves. They crunch under my feet as I walk down Hunter Avenue, turning at University Street. To my right is a garbage can. Taking the empty rum bottle from my purse, I throw it away.

The Bel Air idles at the north edge of Gooch Park. Lawrence sits behind the wheel wearing a white cotton shirt and tan pants. He rubs his eyes, his head darts left and right before he catches my reflection in his side mirror. He gets out and places my suitcase in the trunk. The car is spotless. No traces on the outside of dust or dirt. On the inside, no traces of blood.

"Ready to get going?"

I clutch my purse. "Yes."

The weather is kind today. The windows are down. Soft winds cool and caress my skin, but sweat still dots my forehead. It's hard to breathe. My fingers tingle. Jonas' last words were in this car, the car driving me to Lebanon. My heart pounds, like it might burst from my body. I grip the handle. Harder. *Harder!* I try to busy my mind and look out the window. I count the houses. How many have shutters. How many don't. How many have chimneys. How many lack them. The women walking the street with grocery bags. The men on the corner shooting craps. The churches embedded on blocks. How many barbecue sandwiches will Eddie P. sell by tonight?

The Bel Air crawls to a stop in front of Cora and Lawrence's home.

"You don't need to yank on the handle like that, Sara. I'm unlocking the door."

I pull on it until I'm free. Dropping my purse, trying to catch my breath. There's not enough air!

Lawrence takes my left arm, turning my palm upward. His two fingers linger on my wrist. "Let's go in and sit down."

I snatch my arm away. "Give me a minute. Stop hovering."

He backs up two feet, looking at the house every few seconds.

"I said stop hovering, goddammit!"

Lawrence walks to the door, unlocking it. Leaving it open. I hear Cora's voice. It's faint. I don't have the energy to make out what she says. All I do is breathe. Try to clear my head and breathe. My red purse lies on the ground. I pick it up and lean on the car for a few minutes. And then I walk, trying to steady my pace with each step as I enter the house. Lebanon naps on the couch. On the living room table, there's a glass of water on a coaster. I drink it. Slowly.

"Lawrence went to run a small errand. He'll be back shortly," says Cora near the second door in the hallway. She cradles Sophia. And there's a sharp ache. Familiar. Like when I lost Jonas.

"Let me hold her."

Cora swallows hard. She walks toward me, her steps measured. "Of course."

"Don't worry. I just need to—"

"To say goodbye. I know. But my heart can't take it if you change your mind and come back. If there's some part of you that's always going to yearn for her, if that's the case, stay. Because I won't be able to compete with you . . . and I don't want to."

"I'm giving you Sophia for a reason. For you to raise her. So she turns out strong and smart, proud of who she is. Make her unapologetic for wanting her place in this world. And don't let any man, not even Larry, try to keep her from it."

Cora looks down at Sophia, then at me. "I promise." She hugs me firmly but gently enough so the baby is not wakened.

I put my purse down and Cora gives me

Sophia. Her body nestled against mine. I walk to the second bedroom. There is a yellow wall behind the crib. Two cans of paint sit on the floor. I ease into the rocking chair next to a vase of daisies.

You won't grow up to hate me because you won't know me. Your heart won't be hardened. Not like mine. There are so many things I want you to have, but the one thing you're always going to need to be is strong. That you're getting from me. You don't know what strong is yet, but it's that voice deep in your soul telling you what you can do, even though your brain and other people may say you can't. You'll hear the word No *a lot, but follow your heart my lovely Sophia. Be more like your dad than me. And one more thing, don't think because I never came to find you, I never wanted you. I did. I do. But I have faith you're with the right people. Knowing you'll be here with Cora and Lawrence to love and guide you. Mama Sugar to feed you and show you how to never give up. Will to read to you. Buster to teach you numbers and tell you wild stories. Mr. Vanellys to show you how to fix a tire and spoil you when no one else will. I'm leaving you with the few people I trust. And I pray you know that means I loved you more than I think I've ever loved anyone. Know I love you so much, I'm letting you go.*

There's a knock on the door. "You ready, Sara?" asks Lawrence.

I look at Sophia. She still sleeps. I place her back in her crib next to the vase of daisies. In her nursery with one wall painted yellow. In her new home. With her new parents.

"It doesn't matter if I'm ready or not. It's time to go."

TWENTY-ONE

"Thought you might like this better," says Lawrence. He looks at me through the rearview mirror of Jonas' Impala. Lebanon dozes on my lap.

"Mmm-hmm."

"He gave me an extra set of keys. For emergencies. Lost his twice."

Three copies of *Invisible Man* lay on the table. Jonas can't decide which one he wants to keep. *"When I couldn't find one copy, I bought another one. I wrote different notes in all of them. It's a classic piece of literature! Each one is special."*

"Ms. Lennie is gonna be furious when she realizes you're gone." Larry adjusts the rearview mirror again. "With Lebbie."

"She'll make peace with it, with what I did. All of you will."

He clears his throat. "Hope you're right."

My left hand stiffens. I open and close it a few times before the muscles relax. "We need to make a stop."

"Where?"

"To see him."

Lawrence cruises from Dunn Avenue to Elliston Road until the ornate iron gates of Mount Carmel

404

overtakes my view. This time I'm not searching for a boy under a crepe myrtle tree.

"Stay here. Watch Lebanon," I order.

Larry looks at his watch. "It leaves in an hour. The bus."

"Won't take long here. Watch him."

I walk past crooked stone rows, looking for an oak tree with a knot in the middle. Near that tree lies Jonas' grave.

There's nothing conscious about my short journey. It's a pull to him. Some ethereal tether. It's a simple headstone. Dove gray, the same color of the suit he wore our wedding day before he changed into the indigo one. He blew smoke rings on the porch to impress me. He was a horrible dancer unless we moved together, side to side. He was a passionate teacher. He took pretty pictures. He wrote beautiful poems. He saved people from fires. He loved Sam Cooke. He could be so damn siddity. And messy. His laugh made me laugh. He believed the best about people. He loved my son. He would've loved our daughter. He's gone.

They don't make gravestones big enough for all the things Jonas was to me, to others. How can we fit all we are onto something so small?

Jonas Alexander Coulter
1938–1963
Teacher. Husband. Father.

I place my ring on top of the headstone. And

I leave him behind. His voice. His smile. My hopes. Our love. This dream of who I was here in Memphis.

All of it.

The Impala rumbles at the cemetery's exit. Lebanon yawns in the back seat. I buckle us in. Larry follows Elliston Road. We wind our way past Effie Road, then Hernando Road, and others until Union Avenue bursts forth in all its gritty glory. Some storefronts are occupied. Others abandoned. Beale Street, its legend and shimmer, dulled in the daylight; dulled by time. I know the stories of this place, of what it once was. Blinding lights against sable-saturated skies. Music. Shopping. Drinking. Dancing. Gambling. Political quid pro quo. Corruption. People looking for their fortune, making it or doomed to lose it. Blackness in its sexiest and savviest and surliest natures. I wonder how magnificent it was. I wonder what Memphis was before I came. What will it become when I leave?

Across the street, a bright yellow brick building encompasses the block. The Greyhound name fixed to the side. Silver buses brim with bodies. Chatter. Kissing. Hugging. Laughing. Crying. Promises to return soon. The low hiss of brakes. Gasoline fumes. Oil stains.

Larry drags my suitcase from the trunk of the car. In his left hand a brown paper bag. Small grease spots in the middle and the bottom.

"Cora said it'd be a long trip. She didn't want Lebbie or you to be hungry. Fried Chicken. Ham sandwiches. Some pound cake. Ummm, and peaches. She said you liked peaches. Hated apples."

"This is enough for seven people."

"You know Cora."

"Organized. Prepared. She'll be good with Sophia." I take the paper bag from Lawrence, rearranging the purse so it can hold the food. "You will too."

Lawrence avoids my gaze for a moment, looking down at Lebanon. I grab the suitcase, but he doesn't loosen his grip. I tug again. Harder. Lawrence's grip tightens.

"I knew you were gonna do this. Can't be happy with what you have. You always want more."

"Yes! I want more for him!" says Lawrence, his voice booming. A couple of strangers look in our direction.

"First you don't want Sophia. Now you want her *and* Lebanon?"

"I always wanted a child. I want Sophia. I already love her. And I know I'll have to tell her about you. Jonas too. What happened here. I know it will be hard for her to hear, but she'll have a good life. But what about Lebbie? He deserves that too. A good life."

"He'll have that. With me!"

Lawrence's hand still grips the suitcase handle.

"I'm not leaving my son. I've given up enough. Him I keep."

"Are you mad because I'm asking or are you mad because I'm right? Because you know somewhere deep down, whatever binds you to Lebanon is going to destroy you both. Why you want him has nothing to do with love, Sara. It's something else. Something I don't need to know about. But if you let him stay with me, with Cora, there'll be part of you that can be free, knowing you did the right thing by them, by yourself. You know it's true. I saw you. The other day. How you were looking at us when we were in front of the house. You saw the happiness they could have. Wouldn't a mother want that, the best for her children? The *both* of them? I'm begging you. Let him stay!"

"Tell Cora thank you for the food." I snatch the suitcase from Lawrence and take Lebanon's hand. He awkwardly turns around, ambling unevenly to match my stride.

"Wait!" Lawrence kneels. He hugs Lebanon. "You be a good boy for your momma." Lebanon vacantly smiles.

"I forgot something else," he says. He jogs back to Jonas' car, retrieving another bag. Smaller with funny angles stretching past the borders.

"Cora made me promise to give these to you."

In the bag are wooden blocks. His favorite toy. I take the bag and Lebanon's hand again. Trying to balance all I have in my left hand while I hold his small hand with my right. Walking into the station, I sit us both on a bench to gather myself. The zipper sticks for a moment as I open the suitcase and put Lebanon's blocks inside. On top of the clothes sits a tin, covered in roses and inside the tin are pictures, letters, poems. Singed or burned in spots but saved. Jonas' face. Will with a book. Mr. Vanellys leaning against a car. Mama Sugar cooking in the kitchen. They didn't burn. None of it really did. Not badly. Who knew I was shit at setting fires? There's a piece of paper on top. New. Bright white.

Sara-girl,
Saw you look at this one day at Malone Blue's store. Wanted to give it to you for your birthday but I didn't know when it was. I know you feel like you got to go. And I won't hold you here. But you can always come home. Vanellys.

Again I fight the tears, always threatening to fall, the unceasing sensation of being torn apart; the guilt for pushing everything down and away; being proud of myself for doing this because isn't that what strength is? I'm only sharing my pain with my son. Momma said I was the one she showed hers to.

It's our secret to keep now. His and mine.

I grab my ticket from a man behind a desk,

boredom etched on his face. The bus waits for passengers on the west end of the terminal. CHICAGO on the top right of the front window. Lebanon runs to the back of the bus, then the middle before he stops and laughs. He's so fast. A woman in a mint green dress and hat smiles at him. He smiles back. An empty row of seats beckons to my right and I sit down with him on my lap, placing my purse on the floor in front of us. The only empty space available. The bus jerks forward ever so slightly. An old man makes his way to us and sits. He exhales long, exaggerated. "Thought I wasn't gon' make it." He grins, but I don't return it.

On the bus, the city blurs by in different shades of blue and brown and green. Memphis. People. Homes. Storefronts. Cemeteries. What if I got up right now and told the driver to stop the bus? What if I stayed in Memphis? What if . . . What if . . .

A highway leads back to what I hoped to forget. To the people I'm bound to by fate or circumstances of my own making. No matter how far I run. No matter if I try to become a good person. Nothing changes in the end. Whatever small peace or happiness I manage to unearth, something in this world rejects, refuses my joy. Buries it. Buries me.

Lebanon squirms on my lap. He starts to whimper. Then cry. Eyes cut my way.

"Ssshhhh. Quiet."

Now he wails. God no! I open my purse, then the paper bag. I offer him a piece of cake. No. Sandwich. No. He's dry. His blocks are locked at the bottom with the luggage. Dammit!

"Want me to tell you a story? Is that it? Okay, okay. Once upon a time, there was . . . a princess and she had a son, a prince. They lived alone in a castle."

Lebanon begins to quiet. He puts his hand on the window and looks outside. "And they were happy for a while. The villagers were kind and funny. Sometimes they were irritating, but they always meant well. And eventually the villagers became her family. One day the princess and her son met someone in the kingdom. A knight. He was funny and sweet and made them very happy. But he . . . had to travel far away . . ."

On my lap, Lebanon begins to doze. Stories. The ones we tell ourselves. Fairy tales we use to calm our hearts, so we don't lose our minds. I tell myself a story.

Once upon a time, Jonas comes home. And you run to him. Begging to go outside so you can play. He smiles. Sophia's at the table reading a book. I'm baking a pineapple upside down cake. It's his birthday. Jonas kisses Sophia on her forehead, and she smiles. He puts his arm around my waist, trying to steal a cherry. I shoo him away. He laughs and kisses me. You make a face.

411

Sophia giggles. And in our home, we are happy. In our home, there is laughter. In our home we are all together. The end.

"Nice story you told your son. Little sad for my tastes though," says the old man next to me.

"Well, him being asleep is what matters."

"Oh, didn't mean no harm, miss."

"It's fine."

The old man looks down the aisle, then again at me. "You goin' home?"

My throat tightens as I look at the stranger, then at Lebanon. "I was just there, but I can't go back."

TWENTY-TWO

Has Chicago always been this loud? This unfailingly bright? Crowded bodies. Chaos masked as ambition and energy. Clenching Lebanon's hand harder, I maneuver between rushing throngs of people as we make our way from the bus terminal at Clark and Randolph to Union Station.

Framed, barrel-shaped windows guide pillars of light into the cavernous hall. Two statues, one looking at the ground, one to the sky, hover above.

A bank of pay phones is to my left; almost all are occupied except one. I pull Lebanon, jogging to it before someone beats me there. Fishing for any change in my purse, I find a dime, put it in, but hang up. The dime clinks to the bottom slot. My mouth waters. I'm not hungry. I'm thirsty.

Breathe. I put the dime in the slot again. Dial. Ring. Ring. Ring. Ring. Ri—

"Hello?"

It's crowded here. So many bodies.

"Hello?"

You're gonna lose your dime. You're gonna lose your chance. Speak!

"V-Violet?"

"Sara? Sara! Oh my goodness! I was just reading your letter again. How're you doing?"

More people filter into the hall. Then out. Whistling and hailing taxis. Hugging. Kissing. Laughing. Crying. "Can you come get me . . . and the baby?"

"In Memphis? I—I—yes. Let me talk to Thomas and—"

"No, I'm here. Union Station. I'll be on South Canal Street."

There's silence on the other end of the phone and the roar of activity in the hall surrounds me, pushes in on me. And my heart thumps again, like on the front lawn of Cora and Larry's home.

"Give me half an hour. I'll be there," says Violet.

Hanging up the phone, I pull Lebanon toward the exit. Across the street stands a small grocery store. The tinkling bell from people walking in and out lightly echoes above the cars and trucks and buses driving past. Sour-faced, the owner glosses over me as I walk to the counter.

"Jim Beam. Behind you." I grab a small silver flask from a shelf to my right, putting it in front of him.

He looks down at me, then glances at Lebanon. "That's gonna be a lot of money."

Digging into my purse, I take out thirty dollars from an envelope. "Didn't ask you about that. And give me my *exact* change."

The grocer snatches the money from my hand. Setting down the whiskey. He puts my $5.02 on the counter. I take my change, the bottle and flask, put them in my purse, and head toward the door with the tinkling bell.

Lebanon looks at me and points behind him. "Yeah, he was a jackass," I say.

Swallowed by concrete and glass and steel, the horizon is strangled by progress, by skyscrapers and car exhaust. We sit on an empty bench. Dibs! I open my purse. The paper bag still has two ham sandwiches. Both peaches are gone. Giving Lebanon a small piece of pound cake, I eat some too. It's not dry. Not like Ms. Dorothy Ann's.

Unzipping my suitcase and taking out Lebanon's blocks, I place them and him on a small patch of grass in front of me. The blocks tumble sooner on the uneven ground. He still builds. Still laughs.

I pour a small amount of the whiskey into the flask and take a sip. The bottle and flask I place next to the rose tin and struggle to zip the suitcase. I take them back out and instead put the whiskey and flask at the bottom of my purse and the food on top.

A light green Ford Fairlane slowly inches to the curb and stops. Thomas, Violet's Thomas, waves, then pushes up his brown horn-rimmed glasses. Violet steps around the car, in stirrup pants, the color of mature cognac, and a sleeveless ivory top. Jackson is in her arms.

"He looks a lot like you. Handsome little boy."

Violet laughs. "Just because you been away doesn't mean I forgot what you look like when you're lying." She shrugs. "I know Jackson looks like Thomas. Made my peace with that."

Thomas walks up, grabbing my suitcase. "Hey Sara. Staying long?"

Violet cuts her eyes at him, the smile never leaving her face. "I'm gonna put this in the trunk. I'll let y'all catch up," he says and walks to the car with my suitcase.

"You like Thomas 'cause he's a good man, but you love Thomas 'cause he'll do what you say."

Violet puts Jackson down. "Go and play with your friend. He's got some blocks."

Jackson teeters over to Lebanon. I hold my breath. Lebanon hands Jackson a block. And they play. Peacefully.

"You gonna ask?"

"You would've told me why you're back. You didn't. I'm not pressing the matter. Your business is yours. I wanted you to be happy. That's all," says Violet, shielding her eyes to check on Lebanon and Jackson. "They're doing good together. Told you our boys would be friends."

"Talk to Naomi?"

"Told her you were back. That's all I knew so that's all I said." Violet tugs her ear. "She wants to see you."

"Alright."

"Are you gonna tell me why you're back?" she asks.

"Thought my business was my own, that you weren't pressing the matter?"

Violet pulls at the collar of her blouse. "Wasn't pressing. I was asking."

Lebanon and Jackson laugh. Playing a game with the blocks and only they know the rules. Mama Sugar and Will and Buster know I'm gone by now. Did Mr. Vanellys tell them? Did Lawrence or Cora tell them? Does it matter anymore?

"The man I told you about, my husband, Jonas—"

Violet clenches her fists. Her eyes widen. "He left you? That sonfabitch—"

"He died, Violet. He died."

She grabs me, her hug suffocating. "I'm so sorry."

I escape her embrace. "It's over. I don't— Thanks. I'll be alright. World doesn't give us a choice to be anything but."

Violet looks away for a moment at Thomas in the car. He sits smiling at Violet. She smiles at him, but it fades as she reaches in her pocket. Violet turns to me, handing me a set of keys. "The apartment. Kept them after that night. No one's been there since your . . . since Saul died. The church still pays rent on it for whatever reason. You and Lebanon can stay there as long as you want."

I'm holding stones in my hands. Memories. Darkness. But what are my choices? The keys make a hollow jingle as I place them in my pocket. I gather Lebanon and the rest of our things. "Let's go."

Violet sits Jackson on her lap. I sit Lebanon on mine. "We're going back to Sara's old house," she tells Thomas.

The car is warm. Lake Shore Drive winds past the museum and the planetarium. Whitecapped waves crash against concrete barriers. Thomas propels us to the South Side of the city. Greystone apartments, raised ranches and brick bungalows inhabit each neighborhood. Children freely run up and down the street.

Thomas turns on the radio. Sam Cooke's voice fills the silence. "Bring It On Home to Me." Violin and cello strings elevate the piano and drums. The light gravel and plead in Sam's voice slowly cracks something open. I bite my lip. I breathe. Tears still fall. I wipe them away quickly.

"Sweetheart, turn off the radio, please," Violet says.

Thomas turns the knob to the left and the music blessedly stops. He glances back at us. "Should be there in another five minutes or so."

The last tears dry on my cheeks. "Drop me off at Calvary. We'll make it home from there."

"Sure."

Violet reaches out, taking my hand. I take hers.
"Forever and to the end," she says.
"Forever and to the end."
And we drive.

ACKNOWLEDGMENTS

It took five years to write *Saving Ruby King*. It took five months to write the first draft of *The Two Lives of Sara*. Deadlines are unforgiving, but I knew this was a story I wanted to tell. I don't know why, but I knew Sara wasn't done with me.

Second books are a special and beautiful kind of torture. You get to see what you're made of creatively. And I don't think I've needed to lean on people more. Not even with the wonderful, muddled mess that was my first draft of *SRK*. I think I believed the first book was a fluke. I believed myself to be a one-hit wonder as I, for a second time, gathered my words in a certain order and curated scenes that eventually turned into a story. But in proving something to myself, to those ruthless demons of imposter syndrome and self-doubt, I learned I'm not "Me" without the wonderful and generous people who helped guide me on this journey.

Thank you to my family. Thanks Mom. You fielded endless calls about this book. You listened to my ideas, my fears, my triumphs and my failures. You made me laugh. You made me realize that I'm worthy; that I am not crazy to dream big; that it is my duty and my right to do so. Thanks Bruh. I needed those philosophical talks. I needed your belief that our stories need to be told without permission, with passion, with pride. You're my go-to when I'm not sure about anything art-related. You're one of the few people whose creative crazy matches mine, not just because we're siblings, we're something far more connected and dearer than that. We are hovering over the bounds of infinite, we are. Thanks Pops. Believe it or not, you really did help me see that I just need to write. I don't need to worry about what someone before me has done because the way I tell my story will always be unique and needed.

I don't believe I'll ever be able to express enough gratitude to my wonderful agent Beth Marshea. You took a chance on someone who had crazy ideas about what I wanted to do with stories, and you didn't bat an eye. You cheer me on. You tell me what I need to do to make my book better. You are unapologetic in how hard you go for not just me but all your clients. I appreciate how much you always check on me to make sure I'm not stressing out or overworking myself. I can't ask for a better person to navigate the scary and uneven terrain that is publishing.

Laura Brown of Park Row Books, what can I say except that I'll always freak out during developmental edits, and I appreciate you letting me do this while knowing all the while I'll figure it out. But I always know you have my best interests and the story's best interests at heart. I know whatever I give you will come back a million times better. When you tell me this is a collaborative process, you don't say those words to say them. You follow through and are a person of your word and that is rare not just in publishing, but in life.

Taj McCoy, Lane Clarke and Andrea Williams, you ladies are true ride or die. Thank you for always having a listening ear, fantastic ideas, unending support and laughter. So much laughter. I wouldn't have gotten through this book without our talks. I'm so blessed to know you all and humbled to call you my friends.

The Two Lives of Sara takes place in the phenomenal city of Memphis, Tennessee, a place I knew would be the perfect setting for my story about found family, love and loss. Though I was unable to visit because of the pandemic, I was put in touch with some wonderful people who let me interview them about their lives there. My everlasting gratitude to Trudina Fraser, Era Hart, Tomeka Hart-Wigginton and others. Thank you for trusting me and opening up to me. It was a treasured experience.

To my aunts, uncles and cousins, you all are so encouraging. The way you cheer me on and support me brings me close to tears *every single time* I think about it. Y'all really love me and I really love you!

Lastly, thank you to every writer, singer, artist and civil rights leader I mentioned in this book. Black art, Black culture and Black history are beautiful and should be celebrated. This discussion shouldn't be censored so we don't have to come to terms with the complicated and ugly history of this nation. If anything, let the benefits of our heritage guide you to a better understanding of who Black people are, how we've contributed to the birth and the sustained greatness of America, and our undeniable magnificence!